REFURBISHED SOUL

— Book Three of the Shift Trilogy —

BY MICHAEL JUGE

iUniverse, Inc.
Bloomington

Refurbished Soul
Book Three of the Shift Trilogy

iUniverse books may be ordered through booksellers or by contacting:

iUniverse
1663 Liberty Drive
Bloomington, IN 47403
www.iuniverse.com
1-800-Authors (1-800-288-4677)

ISBN: 978-1-4759-2268-4 (sc)
ISBN: 978-1-4759-2270-7 (e)
ISBN: 978-1-4759-2269-1 (dj)

Printed in the United States of America

iUniverse rev. date: 7/13/2012

Novels of the Shift Trilogy

Ride The Wilderness Book One of the Shift Trilogy
2012   *Previously released in 2010 as "Scourge of an Agnostic God"

A Hard Rain   Book Two of the Shift Trilogy
2012   *First edition released in 2011

Refurbished Soul   Book Three of the Shift Trilogy
2012

For updates on upcoming works and to follow along with background music and Google maps, visit www.michaeljuge.com

Acknowledgements

It goes without saying that I owe so much to my wife. She has supported me through it all, despite the long odds and despite the costs involved. She believed in the *Shift* trilogy when I was faltering in my own faith. My cover artist Liam Peters has become a vital part of the creative process through his art as well as through his passion for the story. There are others out there that I also owe gratitude: Scott of Indiebookblogger.blogspot.com, Kristi of San Mateo, Lynn of Whitestone, the ladies who helped promote the *Shift* trilogy in the book clubs, and my dear friend Jen of Del Ray. You all are a part of this story, its creation and its success.

DISCLAIMER

The views expressed in this novel are those of the author, and do not necessarily reflect those of the U.S. Department of State or the U.S. Government.

A Note about the Soundtrack to
REFURBISHED SOUL

Welcome to the final installment in the *Shift* trilogy. I wrote the *Shift* trilogy with a cinematic take, whereby I considered what you, the reader, should see in your mind's eye as if it were a movie and what you would be listening to in the background. With that as my goal, I created a multi-media environment so that you can listen to the music that is either being played in the background or is on the mind of the character. Throughout the story, you will see prompts that look something like:

BACKGROUND MUSIC: "Old Man" by Neil Young

Visit www.michaeljuge.com on the ***Refurbished Soul*** page located at http://michaeljuge.com/wordpress1/refurbished-soul/ and select the referenced song in the imbedded YouTube link while you read to get the full sensory experience. You can also study the Google Map to see where you are geographically in the story on the ***Maps*** page. If you would like to have background music play throughout while you read, I suggest you tune your Pandora or Last.fm internet radio to Death Cab for Cutie or Boy & Bear.

I hope you enjoy the finale to the *Shift* trilogy and remember, keep your bikes ready and peanut butter stockpiled!

Kaplah,

Michael Juge

Mid-Atlantic and Northeastern U.S. 2013

To view an interactive map, visit www.michaeljuge.com on the *Maps* page

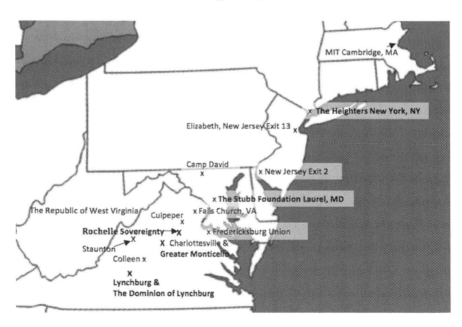

CHAPTER 1

BACKGROUND MUSIC: "Tubthumping" by Chumbawamba
Visit www.michaeljuge.com on the Refurbished Soul page to listen

Austin, Texas
September 1998

Waterloo Draft House was expectantly exuberant, packed with college students, young software engineers and at the far corner, a table full of overly serious anthropology graduate students. At least that was Chris Jung's reading of the people around him, the ones who would be his cohorts for the next two years, three years if the student loans didn't pan out and he had to go back to work to make ends meet.

Chris tightened his ponytail and wiped off the never-ending flow of sweat from his brow. It wasn't anywhere near as humid as New Orleans —no place was that humid—but Austin wasn't quite a desert yet either. Instead, the city straddled the two bio regions of forest and desert just the way it straddled the two topographies of prairies on the east side of town and the Hill Country on the west side. That might be part of the reason why Austin was so...well, Austin was weird. Even with his long hair, combat boots and sandalwood scented oil fragrance, Chris was still more conservative in appearance than ninety percent of the city as he sported no tattoos or piercings.

The people at the table were discussing Edward Said again. When Chris applied for the graduate program in Anthropology at the University of Texas, he was really just trying to get the hell out of his dead end job. Up until last week, he had been a college-educated bike messenger, humping his husky frame on his Kona mountain bike throughout town in order to pay his share of the rent. And it always seemed that wherever he was sent, it was always uphill—both ways.

Rumor had it that this was the roaring 90s with jobs aplenty. And Austin was a Dotcom hub, a wild cousin of the Silicon Valley in California. Unfortunately, Chris never learned computers. In college, he typed all of his papers on a typewriter. He didn't even own an email address until a few days ago when UT issued him one. And forget about that whole *IT* thing. Chris still didn't know what "IT" stood for. With his lackluster technical skills and with a degree of questionable utility, he was about as marketable as onion-flavored coffee. But at least his tree trunk legs could skillfully weave through traffic, delivering legal documents in the height of rush hour to agitated attorneys waiting to stick it to somebody.

Chris had come to the conclusion that he needed to retreat from the real world, call a time-out and get his shit in order. That was what grad school was for him: a retreat, a fancy way of redeeming his undergraduate GPA, and a way to a real job, because he certainly wasn't sucking the marrow out of life right now. So, Chris made a course correction, looked up the graduate program he would most likely be accepted into with a BA in Philosophy and somehow wound up with a group of anthropology geeks discussing shop while Jaegermeister girls served body shots not ten feet away.

"Yeah, well, if you read your Chomsky, you would know that the Internet is not going to serve to democratize knowledge, but rather codify Western hegemony," spat out a young lady with intense looking blue eyes.

The object of the young lady's ire quickly retorted. "And why do you say that, Heather, because you heard it on NPR?"

The others at the table who grasped the substance of the heated argument *oohed*.

"No, Adrian. I say that because anyone who spent time actually living among the people instead of drinking martinis at the Intercontinental Hotel would know that at the end of the day, all communication in cyber space is at its core deposited into the Roman alphabet and therefore, all language is made further subservient to the Anglo-patriarchal hierarchy."

"Ah, that is entirely jejune!"

"Jejune?"

"Yes, Heather, jejune."

"You have the temerity to say that I'm being jejune?"

A skinny dude with Elvis Costello glasses took a seat next to Chris, leaned over and affected a cartoonish high-pitched voice. "I'm so high I don't know what's going on!"

Taken by surprise, Chris sneezed beer through his nostrils as he laughed so hard and started coughing.

"Whoa, there, Chief. You okay?"

"Yeah," Chris continued to cough until he lit another Camel cigarette. He extended his hand to the hip looking guy.

"My name's Chris."

"Hey Chris, pleased to meet you. I'm Brandon, Brandon Hughes."

Brandon and he talked for the next few minutes over the noise of the crowd and the bar's speakers playing Chumbawamba, which was battling for attention with the jukebox upstairs playing Shawn Colvin. Chris knew he and Brandon were going to get along well, especially surrounded by the anthropology geeks. The two of them discussed the declining state of commercial rock since the mid-nineties. Brandon had a godlike knowledge of the Indie rock scene, which far surpassed his own knowledge. It was kind of embarrassing considering that Chris was once a bass player in an Indie funk band called Senator Monkey and the Funkacrats, which was rebranded from its Goth origins when they were called Melancholy Monkey. But that was back in undergrad. The discussion wound its way around everything not pertaining to anthropology, from movie quotes to Brian Jonestown Massacre and the Dandy Warhols to the longevity of *The Simpsons* over *South Park*.

"And let me tell you the worst part about getting hit by a minivan," said Chris, casually bragging about his misadventures as a bike messenger when he glanced across the table, and saw a woman who had just sat down.

She was stunning. Even in the dark, smoke-filled bar, Chris could tell that the woman sitting across the table from him was among the most beautiful women he had set eyes on, and that was saying a lot in Austin, a town teeming with talent. The woman gazed at him with deep brown eyes through librarian glasses; her short reddish brown hair lightly touched her elegant neck. She wasn't dressed like the other anthropology students, all of whom were dressed as shabbily as possible without quite being in pajamas. This woman was wearing a suit, an honest to God "I've got to go to court" suit. She reminded him of Agent Dana Scully in *The X-Files*, his absolute favorite show.

"So, what's the worst part of getting hit by a minivan?"

"What?"

Brandon nudged him. "So, what's the worst part?"

Chris had forgotten the conversation with Brandon. He realized that he was staring at her. A cigarette dangled from his mouth stupidly.

"Oh, um…man, I totally…" Chris struggled to collect himself. He straightened his ponytail and scanned himself to make sure there was no ketchup on his Retarded Elf t-shirt and prepared his opening to this woman who looked like she belonged somewhere else, somewhere like at one of those law offices where he delivered important documents on his bike.

He jerked his head with a stiff nod and managed to utter, "Hey."

Years from now Chris would recall this as one of those seminal moments of his life, the kind of moment that would warrant a flash of recognition when his life passed before his eyes. He would remember everything, from what Meredith was wearing, the way her perfume mixed with the ambient smoke and beer in the most tantalizingly way, the way Chumbawamba's one hit wonder was such a bad introduction for the two lifelong lovers. It was at that moment that Chris realized that wherever this woman was, that was where his heart would be.

"I get knocked down
But I get up again
You're never gonna keep me down
I get knocked down
But I get up again
You're never gonna keep me down"

CHAPTER 2

The Shiftiverse
Winchester, Virginia
November 2008
(Seven months after the Obsidian War)

Meredith Jung stood outside in a parking lot surrounded by a protective ring of young Vicious Rabbits. Meredith still had trouble calling them that with a straight face. Jon Early was kicking himself for uttering the war cry, "Come on you...you Vicious Rabbits!" at the Stand at Exxon Heights. In the seven months since vanquishing Obsidian Corp., Rochelle had consolidated its hegemony and admitted the town of Orange into Rochelle. But without a better moniker, the fledgling mini-nation referred to itself and its soldiers simply as the "Vicious Rabbits." How would anyone take them seriously, she often asked herself. Apparently, someone did. Her presence here outside of the ransacked Ross Dress for Less store testified to that.

Meredith was extremely anxious. First of all, she was separated from Baby Aidan for the first time in his young life. She couldn't help but worry about her little stinkpot back home crying for her and with only the Hughes to comfort him. Being separated from one's child would upset any mother even under the best of circumstances. But then add the fact that she spent the last couple of days outside the wire of Rochelle traveling on a bike in what the Vicious Rabbits cavalry called "no man's land." That it was indeed. Meredith hadn't ventured out of Rochelle, save for the temporary evacuation to Culpeper during the Obsidian War, since arriving in Rochelle right after the Shift. She had heard shocking stories about how devastated the surrounding areas were with the breakdown of civil order and the flu that swept across the Mid-Atlantic. But seeing the wreckage firsthand with its graphic clarity dwarfed any horror her imagination could conjure.

Bloated bodies still littered the highways even sixteen months after the Shift had plunged the world into darkness. Scenes of violence and craven depravity stained the entire landscape. Decomposing bodies were scattered on the very parking lot where she and the other Vicious Rabbits stood. She wondered how Chris coped seeing this kind of carnage regularly. She would have regretted sending him and his cavalry platoon out on errands to the Beltway, but her nascent intelligence organization had needs, and the survival of Rochelle depended in part on her organization. So, Chris and his cavalry went on her errands. And had he not, he wouldn't have been contacted by the man she was about to see now. That was the thing that made her the most nervous. It wasn't just leaving her baby without his mom, nor was it standing outside what was once a sensible discount clothing store and smelling the stench of death all around her. It was the man she was about to meet.

Chris emerged from the boarded up entrance to Ross Dress for Less with several of his soldiers, including Kendra, the high school girl who was one of the first to graduate from Commandant Dean Jacob's Vicious Rabbits' Corps boot camp. Chris looked like a very different man from the man Meredith met so many years ago. His eyes were intense, his burly frame was accentuated by all of the gear he wore, the body armor and ammo pouches, and the long hair and beard obfuscated the gentle face she had known. Back home, he just looked like a hippie. Here, he looked like someone she wouldn't want to cross in a dark alley. She knew that she too had changed since the Shift, but Chris had absolutely transformed into somebody else. At least, it seemed that way at times like these, times when he was on the clock and lugging his assault rifle around like he was now strutting out of the store. Chris gave orders to his men and headed straight for her as the Vicious Rabbits carried out his commands. As he approached, Chris didn't betray any of the goofy, floppy-haired-boy he once was with her.

"Okay, he's in there, love. His men allowed us to sweep the area, and we have the store surrounded. If it goes south, we'll be in there within seconds flat."

"Hon, I'll be fine. I'm sure he's not out to kidnap me."

"I'm not taking any chances on that. Just sayin'."

Meredith knew the man she was about to see wasn't a physical threat to her, and she felt Chris was overdoing it a little with his site security preparations. But then she considered that he wasn't just Lieutenant Jung leading an operation; he was a husband looking out for his wife and the mother of his son. *Let him do his job, will you?* He could be irrationally sweet sometimes. She caressed his bearded face.

"Fair enough."

The store didn't look much better on the inside than it did on the outside. The boards hastily nailed over the windows in the days following the Shift didn't keep looters out. Empty racks and clothes hangers were strewn about the store. Armed men dressed in khaki pants and collared shirts wearing Oakleys stood statuesque and gave a curt acknowledgement to Chris. He gave a slight nod back. The way the men were dressed reminded her of something. They were odd. Then it hit her. None of the men had beards. Their faces were shaven clean; they even had short hair. And their outfits, while not a uniform per se, were crisp. Out from the shadows approached a distinguished-looking gentleman wearing a suit of all things. He looked to be in his late sixties, which was a rarity these days.

"Mrs. Jung. It's a pleasure to meet you."

The gentleman—that was the most apt description for him, "gentleman"—extended his hand and she took it. "My name is Roger. I was a good friend of your old boss Mike."

Meredith looked perplexed when he clarified, "Mike. You know... Michael Chertoff."

The Secretary of the Department of Homeland Security Michael Chertoff was her old boss in the same way that the President of the United States was. But there were something like 15 levels of management between the cabinet-level chief and herself.

Curious, she pried, "So, you were also with DHS?"

Roger just smiled. "No, I was with another agency."

A silence followed his cryptic response. Roger stood out from the surroundings as though he lived in an entirely different era. Perhaps the suit he wore had more of an effect today than it ever did in the real world just before the Shift.

"Sir, um, how did you find out about us?"

Roger considered her question. "News travels slowly now, but it does travel still. And it was quite interesting news we heard coming from down south. Obsidian Corp. waged a campaign to overtake the Shenandoah Valley and a collection of scrappy villagers defeated them? That piqued my interest. And some said there was a 'Vulcan lady' who undermined Obsidian Corp. from within."

"And that's when you set a trap for my husband," she said.

"I wouldn't call it a trap, Mrs. Jung. We do our best to keep an eye on government facilities. We observed that a man matching the description of one of the leaders who organized the end of Obsidian Corp. was paying visits to the records building. Clearly, he was someone we wanted to talk to. Your husband expertly detected my men guarding the facility and nobody was injured in the encounter. I ordered my men to show restraint."

Meredith hoped she wasn't blushing; after all, she was the one who sent Chris to break into a government records facility. She would never dare do anything like that in the real world, no less put Chris in harm's way. But as Chris was often attributed to saying, "the needs of the many outweigh the needs of the few." Fortunately, the encounter ended without incident and Chris was sent back with a message from this mysterious government spook requesting to meet at this location as he supposedly had information that was of great concern to the future of Rochelle.

"We have mutual interests, Mrs. Jung, your people and mine. I'd like to discuss this with you in private."

That was Chris' cue to leave, but he wasn't budging.

"Mr. Jung, my men will wait outside with you as well."

Chris walked up to Meredith and whispered, "I'll be just outside. If you sense anything, don't hesitate."

With that Chris, Kendra and Roger's agents left the store, leaving the two of them alone. Roger took a seat next to a mannequin. Meredith sat down on a display table across from him. She tried not to let the absurdity of the situation distract her attention.

"Your people…that's Camp David, right?" He nodded. Her enthusiasm grew at the possibility that she, that everyone for that matter, was almost out of the woods. When the Shift hit, the Secret Service evacuated the vestige of the federal government to Camp David. It was a hard year. But now it appeared that there was a light at the end of the tunnel. Roger might be summoning her to let her know that Camp David was thriving and that there was a nexus of a US government ready to take back control. She imagined that she could hand the reigns over to them, and perhaps in a couple of years everyone would all be living in a relatively sane country again.

Roger quickly short-circuited her hopes. "What's left of us. The refugees flooded our camp a few weeks after we arrived, and then the flu hit. Frankly, there isn't much of a Camp David anymore."

Meredith felt her stomach clench. "Secretary Chertoff...did he?"

Roger grimaced. "Michael led the relief efforts in Camp David. He was down in it with the refugees trying to make sure everyone got the same rations. When the flu arrived, he didn't leave his post. It claimed him. He was one of the first to succumb to the flu. I'm sad to say we lost a lot of good people that fall. Now, it's just me and a couple hundred folks from various and mostly useless government agencies. If it weren't for the surviving Amish, there wouldn't be a Camp David left. We've got some brains up there, but not a lot of brawn. I'm sorry if I misled you, Mrs. Jung. You aren't the only one who wishes we got our ship in order, but we do share common interests. We both want the rule of law and a return to civility. We both want our country back. And we both want to know who out there is still interested in upholding the Constitution of the United States. Many out there have taken our current circumstances as carte blanche to throw that document into the shredder so they can pursue their own grab for power."

Roger continued, "I know your community...these Vicious Rabbits of yours, and your Monticellan friends are on the right side of this fight to restore our way of life. But you are outnumbered."

Meredith couldn't argue with that. In the months since the close of the Obsidian War, Rochelle and Monticello had consolidated their power. But at the same time, there was a new threat growing south in Lynchburg. The Regent. She didn't like the reports coming in. He was as radical as any domestic terrorist she investigated, and he had an army behind him. She suspected the Regent wasn't going to be happy with a policy of co-existence.

"We would be open to a defense pact for..."

Roger shook his head. "I can't provide you any muscle. I'm sorry. Your 'Vicious Rabbit' buddies could run roughshod over us if they were blitzed out of their minds and naked. But... " Roger produced an old leather valise and handed it to her.

"I *can* provide you contacts, vital contacts you'll need to keep ahead of your enemies."

Meredith opened the valise and pulled out a stack of papers. Some were personnel forms, some were handwritten notes, and some were maps.

"I did you the favor of combing through the files to pick out every friend you might find a use for, those who have skill sets that could help you, and who resided in the greater northern Virginia and West Virginia areas. I don't know how many of them are still alive, but many of them lived near West Virginia where the die off wasn't quite as devastating as it was inside the Beltway. They may be your best bet. These are contacts you would never have gotten rummaging through the records building. And I've already sent word to those I have located to expect a visit from you and to participate in a sort of... we used to call it a 'memorandum of understanding.'"

Meredith sifted through the stack, trying to absorb the treasure trove of information through the pores of her skin. These were the keys to the kingdom. Roger just handed her every name and every address she ever wanted and the credentials to approach them.

"What do you need from me in return?"

"Reciprocity. Whatever you discover, you share with us, and whatever we discover, we share with you. I don't expect to have regular contact. Camp David is hell and gone from Rochelle, but I do need you to get back to me on one issue. Pull out the folder in the back. This is why I asked to speak with you alone."

Meredith pulled out a buff colored expandable wallet.

He whispered. "Before his death, Chertoff confided in me about something. He told me about a potential threat, an unlikely one, but one whose consequences, if realized, would be...well, it would make the EMPs seem like a minor power outage."

Meredith skimmed through the report entitled *Asteroid Rayne 2005 On An Uncomfortably Close Trajectory* while Roger spoke. It was something right out of a science fiction movie that Chris often watched on the Sci Fi Channel, and which she found herself watching whether she wanted to or not. The executive summary stated that this "Rayne 2005" was several times the mass of the asteroid that killed off the dinosaurs. That filled her with terror, but then she saw the next line and she pointed it out.

"But, sir, the report says there's only a one in a thousand chance of it colliding with the earth."

Roger looked around to make sure no one was listening. "Astronomically speaking, those odds are actually very high. But there's more. We have an observatory at the Camp and have been tracking Rayne 2005. According to our last estimate, there is a one in *fifty* chance that it will impact."

That was unsettling, an uncomfortably close trajectory indeed, much more so than one and a thousand.

"What do you need from me?" she asked, her voice trembling slightly.

"The asteroid is moving outbound toward its apogee and will make its return towards the sun in 2011. A lot can happen to change its trajectory when it does. When it returns from the far side of the sun in November 2012, we're going to want to compare what we calculate at our observatory with other observatories. I can help set you up with one near Staunton. I know some people. And perhaps you can find a third observatory. But we need to confirm our findings regardless."

"What for?"

"To know the truth, Mrs. Jung."

"But how will that help us?"

Roger's expression turned dour. "It won't. But a couple of old guys just want to know where we stand."

A cold chill ran down her spine. One in fifty was a lot worse than one in a thousand, but still, that was only a two percent chance. Hopefully, statistics would go in their favor.

"I'm sorry to throw this bombshell on you like this. But I can offer you a consolation. In the valise you will find a contact in Lynchburg who is a friend of mine. Tell her 'the gangly bird man' sent you."

Roger then stood up.

"It was a pleasure meeting you. I am most gratified to see that you're doing great things down there."

"Thank you, sir."

"Oh, please, Roger will do, though perhaps it would be better if you came up with another name for me altogether."

After a pause he added, "I hope this is the first of many meetings, though I think those meetings will have to be through an intermediary."

"Where will I find you or your surrogate?"

"Our intermediaries can always meet here."

"Here? At Ross?"

"I don't see why not. Winchester is halfway between our two peoples. And Ross has suits in my size."

He turned back to her. "Oh, by the way, do you have a name for your intelligence organization?"

11

Meredith smirked. As it stood now, her "intelligence organization" consisted of herself, Anne Hughes and Valerie Blaine. She was afraid that Chris was going to call it "The Sisterhood of the Sneaky Ladies" and it would stick like Vicious Rabbits did.

"I'm still shopping around for a name."

"You do that. Send my regards to my friends, keep a low profile, and watch out for that Regent. He's trouble."

"I will."

They shook hands. "Best of luck to you, Meredith. I hope one day we can serve under the same flag again."

"As do I, Mr...Roger."

As Roger walked out the door, she studied the valise and noticed the fine workmanship that was undoubtedly handmade. The craftsman's seal embossed on a golden tag displayed a swan.

Chapter 3

The asteroid penetrated the upper atmosphere, igniting the skies as it careened into its final trajectory. Streaking at thousands of miles per hour, the shock wave preceding the iron orb burst eardrums thousands of miles away and disintegrated monuments and mountains as it rampaged across the earth. Meredith stood outside of their farmhouse on the frozen field with Aidan, Rhiannon and baby Charles in her arms. She knelt down and covered them as best she could as the roar of the roiling churning wave approached from all directions.

"I'm scared, Mommy!" screamed Aidan.

"Me, too!" Rhiannon echoed.

Meredith squeezed them all as tight as she could. "Just close your eyes, sweetie. It will all be over soon."

The rumbling, which started as a slight disruption magnified with jarring intensity. Birds screeched as some fell from the sky, charred and smoldering. The rumbling overtook the rest of her senses. The blast wave was so immense and fast that none of them felt the preceding heat, which seared off their flesh along with setting the fields afire. It was followed up by the blast wave itself, which rendered their bones into constituent elements.

BACKGROUND MUSIC: "My Lover's Gone" by Dido
Visit www.michaeljuge.com **on the Refurbished Soul page to listen**

By Michael Juge

The Shiftiverse
Rochelle, Virginia
Rochelle Sovereignty
February 2013

A framed photograph of Chris and Meredith sat on the dresser as Meredith Jung checked herself in the mirror. The old photograph had become faded and cracked with age and abuse. It was one of the few photographs that she had haphazardly stuffed into Chris' backpack in their rushed exodus from DC five and a half years ago. It had been taken back when they first started dating in grad school. They looked wonderfully ridiculous and carefree, she with her black satin blouse with a dragon design and he with his typical 90s era bowling shirt.

It was difficult getting dressed solely by kerosene light. The power had been out for days now, not because of any Shift EMP surges, but rather because the community was now on a wartime footing, and every joule of electricity needed to be conserved. The Jungs had their own generator, but she didn't want to flaunt her wealth around the rest of the town, not with everything going on.

In the weeks since coming back from Stokesville Observatory, where she learned about the catastrophic prognosis of Rayne 2005's trajectory, she and Thuy shared their revelation about the asteroid with two other people; Dean Jacob, the Commandant of the Vicious Rabbits Corps, and Jon Early, the Constable of Rochelle. She wasn't willing to go so far as to share this with anyone else, not even the leaders of other three eyes in the Orange Pact.

As far as she knew, nobody else knew about the asteroid save for the astronomers in Stokesville, Asheville and Camp David, and Roger, of course whom she now referred to as Ross. The few civilized communities in existence had neither the inclination nor the time to search for threats from outer space. Why would they even consider such a threat with the world as it was now?

Over the past several weeks, Meredith had become inured by the thoughts of what was to come; at least sometimes that was the case. Other times, the sheer gravity of it all pulled her under, usually at night after the kids were asleep. She would lay in bed at night alone, feeling Chris'

14

absence, while the wind rattled the windows. Meredith hastily corralled her brunette locks into a bun and checked herself in the mirror to see several graying strands. It was a futile effort to look done up, like in the real world. She hadn't seen vintage lipstick in years and hairspray had become a distant memory, and don't get her started on what miserable replacements for tampons were. The kerosene light was even less flattering than florescent lights were. The woman facing her in the mirror looked severe, haggard and withdrawn. Her deep brown eyes were more like sunken black pools behind dark circles. She was exhausted and drained.

She dared a glimpse at the photograph of her and her husband once more, the two kids that they once were. She didn't even know who those two people smiling happily into the camera were anymore. The detachment would have been frightening, but that was the least of her problems. She turned back to face the mirror, buttoned her Columbia overcoat, took the lamp and headed downstairs to pass the kid duties over to Mrs. Palfrey.

It was a short ride in the carriage over to Rochelle's executive offices at Montpelier Station. Along the way, the carriage passed Funeral Mound, where so many had died of the flu, including her youngest's namesake, Charles Early. The snow had refrozen on the road, making the ride a little slower than usual. Meredith sat in modest comfort inside the carriage while Bob, the driver, managed Corolla, the family horse. They briefly pulled to the side of the road as a convoy of old school busses, garbage trucks and pickup trucks, all retro-fitted with corrugated sloped metal sheets provided by Jung's Armoring and Fabricators, rumbled by. On the frozen fields, soldiers of Rochelle's Vicious Rabbits were training militia to include old men and children how to march in formation. Even peg-legged Brandon Hughes was out there boning up on his sharpshooting skills. He had lost a few fingers in the Obsidian War and his right leg below the knee to an IED in a skirmish chasing bandits a year later. If Rochelle was recruiting the winery-owning, cannabis-growing, one-legged hipster, they were desperate indeed. But she already knew that. The militia looked cold out there, and sadly, they looked frightened as well, because there was a very good chance they would be put into action.

Meredith spent the first hour in her office inside the majestic 19th century mansion being briefed by some of her officers in the Swan. They went over the latest developments: Columns of Lambs of God soldiers were moving straight up Highway 29 and Interstate 81, and the political situation of their putative allies of Greater Monticello, who were one of the four pillars in the Orange Pact alliance, was deteriorating rapidly.

The strapping young Monticellan intelligence officer, Ezra Rothstein, sat next to her as she read his report. Ezra wore a Shemagh Kafiya as a scarf to keep warm, which with his jet-black hair and beard, made him look Palestinian—kind of ironic considering his Hungarian Jewish heritage.

Meredith rubbed her temple as she read his scribbling. "Well, at least your interim chief magistrate hasn't completely gone off the deep end. She's perfectly willing to have us come down there to fortify their position."

"Yes, but read down a little," Ezra advised.

"Oh," she amended. "So, Neko requests that we identify the Christians in our group."

"I'm afraid so, ma'am. Actually, it wasn't Neko Lemay so much but rather Sheriff Schadenfreude who advised Neko to request that. Neko just went along with the suggestion."

Meredith didn't say anything. She was too confounded to say anything, really. Ever since Neko Lemay had ousted Juan Ramirez with the help of Monticello's Sheriff Lucille Schadenfreude, relations had soured between Greater Monticello and the Rochelle Sovereignty. Lucille was a paranoid Unitarian if ever there was one. Unfortunately, Lucille was very influential to a very confused and angry young lady, Neko, the Interim Chief Magistrate.

Rita Luevano, the Chief Magistrate of Greater Monticello and the religious leader of the Unitarian Universalist Church, had disappeared in Maryland along with her own husband last month, leaving the Monticellans leaderless, save for the deputy Chief Magistrate Juan Ramirez. Unfortunately, Monticello's Sheriff Lucille Schadenfreude, a real zealous convert of the Gaia Piety Society, had suspected that Juan, a Catholic, was dealing with the Lambs of God on the side for profit. In fact, Juan Ramirez *was* doing some shady deals with his family in Lynchburg. But it was on behalf of the Swan, though Lucille's investigation apparently didn't reveal that exculpatory tidbit.

Lucille and Neko Lemay confronted Juan, accused him of embezzling Monticellan funds and sending them to his Lynchburg kin. Juan kept silent. He didn't expose the true reason for sending the money, and instead, he resigned, paving the way for Neko Lemay's quick ascendency to power as Interim Chief Magistrate with Sheriff Schadenfreude right beside her.

"Ezra, I don't know Neko beyond what I've read from her dossier." He and Neko had been fellow national archery finalists when the Shift hit five and a half years ago. They had served and fought beside each other for years, so Meredith was deferring to Ezra's insights.

"Neko had always been a true believer, ma'am. Ever since I brought her to Monticello, even before Rita had her first vision of Gaia, Neko was following the reverend around like a puppy, wanting to know more about the Gaia hypothesis. She was more devout than Rita herself was. Neko is single-minded and sees the world in simplistic terms, black and white, good and evil. She took to Gaia with a passion and the Lambs of God were a natural enemy for her."

Valerie Blaine, an attractive blonde sitting next to him added, "The Lambs of God make a good natural enemy for us all. I don't think Neko's opinions have anything to do with it."

"True that," he said using an expression now common in the Orange Pact. "Neko always struck me as angry, though. I never got a straight answer out of her as to why."

"And that was before she got shot by the conspirators."

Neko Lemay had sacrificed herself in saving Rita Luevano from an assassination attempt back in December. Three kids attempted to assassinate the political and spiritual leader of Greater Monticello during the dedication ceremony of the new Unitarian Church. Neko threw herself in front of Rita when one of the kids shot. The bullet tore through Neko's shoulder, leaving her dominant arm flaccid and unable to move.

Ezra echoed her thoughts. "After Neko got shot, she was devastated. Can you imagine? She spent much of her life dedicating herself to being a master archer. She came to identify her entire being as a warrior, as an archer for Gaia, and some ass clown fundy cripples her arm, ending her days as a military leader."

Ezra paused. "And when Rita went off on that dastardly mission to Laurel, the only friend left she could identify with was Lucille Schadenfreude. Talk about bad timing."

"I thought you two were friends."

He squirmed. "We are, but…Look, I will never understand her crazy beliefs. I'm a good Jew, which means if it's just me in the room alone, there are at least two opinions in the room with me. Her simplistic worldview perturbs me, as I know I must perturb her."

"But with the assassination attempt, the imminent invasion by the Lambs of God…"

"And with Lucille telling her what to do," Ezra added.

Meredith nodded and continued. "She sees enemies everywhere."

"That's about the size of it."

"You think Neko views all non-Unitarians as a threat?"

Ezra shrugged. "I don't know about that. I mean, I'm still here doing my thing with you guys. Then again, she does know me. I'm one of the 'good ones' I guess."

"Jon is not going to like this. Hell, I wouldn't advise him to submit to such a request."

Meredith looked at the grandfather clock barely visible with the natural light cut off by the shutters. "And speaking of, I've got to meet him now."

Meredith accompanied Constable Jon Early on a stroll along with the Deputy Constable Thuy Mai, and the commandant of the Vicious Rabbits, Dean Jacob, through the vast expanse that was the former home of President James Madison. Frozen snow crunched below their feet as each carried a foldout chair so that they could sit out in the frozen tundra and be sure that there was absolutely no one able to eavesdrop on their conversation. They were the only people out on the open field for a quarter of a mile. No one would overhear what was discussed.

Constable Jon Early unfolded his seat and sat opposite her while Dean Jacob sat to her left. Deputy Constable Thuy Mai sat to her right.

"Obviously, we won't submit to such a request. The interim chief magistrate is completely *majnoon* if she thinks she can pull that shit on us," Dean Jacob said angrily. The Arabic word he acquired from numerous tours in Iraq was one of many that found its way into the evolving lingo of the Orange Pact, along with Spanish.

Jon Early nodded. He was clean shaven for a change. The nicks all over his face attested to that. Sadly, Jon had succumbed to alcoholism some time ago. It didn't happen all at once. Meredith refused to accept it for the longest time, believing that Jon was just going through a grieving process. The only family he had died of the flu, which came on the heels of the collapse. After the Obsidian War, Jon started his slow descent. In the last year, he showed up to meetings either drunk or hung over, usually with his wife Sharon serving as a nurse.

Jon thought over Neko Lemay's request that they provide the names of the Christian Vicious Rabbits and gave an answer.

"You tell that…You know what? Never mind. I won't even acknowledge that request. Our people will show up and she can decide if she wants to demand their IDs before she lets us fight alongside them against the Mongol horde."

Meredith grinned, pleased to see Jon still had some fire in his belly and some residual skill in dealing with idiocy.

"So, our closest ally and the one town standing between us and the tens of thousands Lambs of God screaming for our blood has been taken over by a young woman with issues."

"Is that a problem?" asked Thuy sardonically.

"What about the military situation?" Jon asked Dean.

Dean Jacob's eyebrows knitted. "The Lambs haven't started moving yet, but they are fully prepared to go. The revised estimates have them at about 75,000 strong, all Lambs of God regulars and Sheepdogs. Combine the Orange Pact forces to include militia, and some of the new allies we've pulled together around the region and we've got about 15,000 give or take."

"That still leaves us at five to one. I don't like those odds."

"Once they start their drive north, they'll overrun the outposts without feeling so much as a speed bump."

"Then what are they waiting for," Jon asked. "If I were them, I wouldn't give us time to prepare."

"The President of West Virginia," Meredith answered. "He had given his blessing, but now he's concerned that the war will spill over into his turf and that West Virginia will have a refugee crisis."

The entire discussion about diplomatic strategies, military maneuvers and stockpiling seemed to be a trite exercise, just going through the motions and feigning an interest in current events, because what did any of it matter, anyway? In a matter of weeks an asteroid almost a hundred miles in diameter with its iron mass of millions of tons will careen into earth's atmosphere at thousands of miles per hour. So, what were the ambitions of an overzealous crackpot like the Regent Gordon Boche compared to this?

There was a silence with nothing but the wind for several long seconds until Dean Jacob broke into the dreaded topic that was on Meredith's mind.

"I think we need to tell everyone."

Thuy Mai threw up his hands in exasperation.

"They deserve to know the truth!" Dean Jacob exclaimed. He was the youngest of the four. The tall African American of Guyanan descent looked particularly uncomfortable in the weather, heated only by his white poncho and his convictions.

"They're our people who we fought beside and lived with for years and they deserve to know their fate!"

"And what good would that do, Dean?" Thuy countered. "Rayne 2005 is coming. There is nothing stopping it. There is nothing we can do. Hell, even if there had been no Shift, we still couldn't stop it."

"Are you absolutely certain of the asteroid's trajectory, Meredith?" Jon asked quietly.

"The Stokesville Observatory outside of Staunton, the observatory in Asheville and Camp David independently came to the same calculations. If we had other observatories, I would have contacted them to quadruple check, but that's not an option these days."

"But I recall something about there only being a one in fifty chance of a collision. What happened to that?"

Meredith was impressed that Jon remembered that. He might not be that far gone. He was shivering violently, more than she was. He wasn't dressed for this weather, though. Steam from their breaths floated slowly above the circle.

"That estimate was taken years ago, and it was just a projection for the next few years. We are now in the time they were projecting."

"Then how could they have been so damned wrong about it back then?"

"They weren't wrong. They did say one in fifty, in astronomical terms, that's a precariously high probability. And from what the Stokesville observatory told me, there are a lot of unknowns that affect the asteroid's course."

"Like what?"

"Other asteroids for one. The gravitational pull of even small objects like other asteroids will affect the trajectory. Rayne's orbit had it passing through the asteroid belt."

Meredith wrapped her arms around herself for warmth and some modicum of comfort. "It is coming. We can't see it yet, but it is coming," Meredith asserted firmly, not just to wipe away any residual doubt among the group, but to knock any denial she herself still had.

"So, we're going to let our people go around clueless as to the reality while we selfishly horde the truth? What kind of people are we?" Dean prompted.

"You think it's good to let everyone know they're going to die next month?"

"They deserve to know the truth, Thuy! As dire as it is, they deserve the truth! These aren't a bunch of sheep. They wouldn't be alive today if they were. They've already faced the end of the world once. I think they can handle it, and it's the least we can do for them."

"What, Dean, let them know that all life on earth will end? Not just them, but everything that ever was on this planet? That every clue of humanity's existence will be wiped away in molten hell? Yeah, they will appreciate that!"

"My God, Thuy, at least let them be able to make peace with their maker. Hell, if we disclosed this to the Lambs of God, it might even prevent this war! I mean, what's the point right? If we're all gonna die horribly in weeks to come, it might sap their will to make war so needlessly."

Meredith shook her head. "No, Dean. It will most certainly take out the will of *our* people to fight, but it will only further encourage the Lambs of God and their fanatical eschatological paradigm."

Meredith spoke with confidence. She hadn't known that her Masters in Anthropology focusing on millennial cults would have practical applications, but her grasp of the eschatological, end of times orientation of certain domestic terrorist groups served her former employer well.

"If the Lambs of God were to learn of this, it would serve the Regent's end. He would use the asteroid as further proof that God was coming, that the end of the world was at hand, and it was time to prove their faith with God by slaughtering us before His arrival."

"It really sucks when the wing nuts are right," Thuy pointed out.

Dean's shoulders slumped. She had convinced him, but there was no satisfaction in winning the argument. Shuddering uncontrollably, Jon made his decision.

"If our people lose hope, they're lost forever. I will not take the last thing they have. We will not disclose this. Rayne 2005 does not exist until it lands on top of us."

Meredith noticed that Jon was sweating despite the frigid conditions. He turned and skulked away towards a thicket of trees.

Meredith turned to Dean who mouthed "DTs."

Meredith quirked and Thuy explained. "He's going through detoxification. He's been clean and sober for two days now."

"Oh."

In the distance, she heard Jon wretch. She felt like doing the same although she wasn't an alcoholic suffering from DTs. She had vomited and cried herself dry by now. There was nothing left to purge for her. She, Thuy, and Dean headed back to the mansion. The whole way back she gazed at the snow-covered trees and mountains. In the distance deer raced by, and she knew it would all be gone. The recurring dreams she so desperately tried to forget found their way to the surface of her consciousness again. The shockwave, the heat that would rip the flesh from her family's bones. Each day those dreams became more vivid and closer to becoming a reality.

CHAPTER 4

The whine of the motor mercifully drowned out the screams of his people as the fast boat beside Chris capsized, sending dozens of men and women under his command into the frigid waters of the Chesapeake Bay.

"Christ, that was the gunny's boat," Lieutenant Baraka cried out.

Chris turned his head away and pushed the throttle to the limit. He had just killed the gunny and several brave Vicious Rabbits. Actually, he knew it wasn't technically he, but rather the rain of mortars and cannon fire from the Abercrombie positions that had done it. But it was he who had ordered them onto the fast boats. It was he who made the call to go forward with the operation even though they had been spotted by the enemy and were now under fire. He was the decider as it were.

Ice crystals accumulated on his beard and goggles as the boat raced over the choppy waters. Chris couldn't see anything clearly, just the whites of Lieutenant Baraka's eyes as she gave directions and the moonlight, which painted their position to the Abercrombies.

"Straight on, Captain. Thirty seconds!"

Cannon rounds landed mere meters away, splashing up the water, drenching Chris and what was left of his cavalry company. In the distance he could hear machine gun fire coming from the shore.

"Ten seconds!"

"Brace yourselves," he yelled.

There was an awful screeching sound as the fast boat approached land, the keel scraping a sunken boat and rock. The boat skidded onto the shore, unceremoniously tossing several onto the ground. Chris jumped out and unloaded the bikes, all the while trying to keep a low profile.

"Head for the bluff!" Kendra bellowed.

Chris' legs pumped furiously up a sand pit, as he hauled his M4 and his

By Michael Juge

Kona. The combined mass of the level four body armor, his rucksack and rifle weighed on him as he desperately made for the relative safety of the other side, but as he tried to lift his legs, they refused to move. He tried to lift his feet, but his water-logged boots melted into the sand.

BACKGROUND MUSIC: "If I Had A Gun" by Noel Gallagher's High Flying Birds
Visit www.michaeljuge.com **on the Refurbished Soul page to listen**

The Mundaniverse
Washington, DC
February 2013

Chris' legs pumped furiously, the heels of his running shoes barely keeping a grip on the icy concrete. He wound his way up from the underpass of the Whitehurst Expressway up to Key Bridge to meet the bitter wind and icy debris as vehicles raced past him. Each breath burned as he pushed himself to run faster up the incline.

Downtown Rosslyn loomed less than half a mile away from Georgetown. Far beneath him the frozen Potomac River lay with scattered fog hovering over patches where ice had broken up. The headphones muffled the sounds of the passing vehicles, and insulated him with the sounds of music he found on his counterpart's iPhone a couple of weeks ago. He was curious as to what his counterpart had been listening to during the past few years while he had been in the shit. Chris pushed himself harder, his breathing getting ragged as he exerted this flabby body to the point of failure.

He drowned out the rest of the world and embraced the pain. "Embrace the suck!" was what his gunnery sergeant had always told the men and women recruits in the Vicious Rabbits. "Pain is weakness leaving your body!" the Aussie by way of Scotland legacy Marine often encouraged. Of course, the gunny always interspersed such inspiring workout clichés with names like "maggot" or "bloody pod knockers!"

The thought of the gunny brought Chris back to the dream he had last night. It was an almost flawless playback of real life events, the awful mistake he made in sending his people to disembark and make for the Maryland shore instead of turning the *Jean Lafitte* back and finding a better landing site. He had failed them all. How many had died under his command on that ill-fated morning?

Chris pushed himself harder, muttering under his breath, "Come on, you fat, lazy bastard!" As much as he loathed himself right now for his poor performance back in the other reality, Chris resented his soft counterpart's complacency even more. Whereas he might have been a bad decider, he at least didn't sit on his ass for five and a half years eating takeout Chinese and playing Call of Duty, not that he had a choice in the matter. Chris would make both of them pay.

Chris reached the other side of Key Bridge and made landfall into Virginia. Completely and utterly exhausted, he collapsed off to the side where there was a little park overlooking the Potomac and Georgetown on the other side. His knees and hands crushed through a layer of ice-glazed snow, as he hunched over heaving. It was penance of sorts. The gunny would almost forgive him for his stupidity...maybe, perhaps... probably not. It took a few minutes before he caught his breath and found the strength to stand up. The glittery façade of the U.S. Department of State Bureau of Diplomatic Security headquarters glistened across Lee Highway.

Several weeks had passed since Chris Jung mysteriously awoke in this world, this asinine alternate reality where the Shift *didn't* happened. Chris hadn't a clue what had transported his consciousness to this place. He was just minding his own business, being captain of the Vicious Rabbits First Bicycle Mounted Cavalry, leading a mission into the savage heart of darkness of unexplored suburban Maryland, being pursued by religious zealots and caught in the middle of an internecine battle of feral tribes— you know, just a typical day at the office. But then it got weird. A deer strolled into his path; he swerved, turning the handlebars violently and his Kona mountain bike, which he christened *The Interceptor,* jackknifed and sent him flying ass over head. Next thing he knew, he awoke to find himself here in this ridiculous place.

The Shift? What Shift? July 11, 2007 came and went as uneventfully as the day before and since. No global series of EMPs emitted from the core of the earth as the planet shifted its magnetic field. No sudden loss of power, no collapse of the social contract; there was nothing, not so much as a power outage. It was the stuff of science fiction. This world was like a manifestation of the meanderings of some crazed survivor of the Shift who, having been post-traumatic about the Shift, ranted about a world where things were "normal." Well, perhaps *he* had gone mad, because he certainly had no other explanation for awaking in this place.

Well, except for one. The only other explanation was that he died in that acrobatic mishap of his, and this was some crappy-assed, made-in-China kind of afterlife, the kind of afterlife reserved for agnostics like him for his lack of faith in either the existence or non-existence of a supreme being. Chris knew he could drive himself crazy trying to figure it out. The best thing to do was just to go with it, don't let anyone know where he came from, and pretend he belonged here.

After showering, Chris dressed and returned to the cubicle in Diplomatic Security's International Threat Assessment Division. He turned on his Blackberry, logged back onto his computer and checked for any irate emails from his boss Ed Farcus. Nothing so far. Good. He didn't want to have to have another run-in with him today. Chris feared he would lose his patience on the skinny red headed, yellow-eyed chihuahua and get himself in trouble.

In the weeks since his inexplicable emergence into this mundane world, Chris had brushed up on the role of his counterpart, the Chris who was from this reality; he felt like an understudy suddenly told the main actor got hit by a bus and he was on tonight. Fortunately for him, not much had changed in five and a half years for this version of Chris. He worked in the same office, in the same cubicle, had the same work, lived in the same place, and hadn't even changed his personal email password. Outside of some minor new projects, which he was able to excuse to his injury—this version of Chris got carjacked and pistol whipped on the noggin at the same time he flipped his bike over—life was pretty much the same as it had been for years now.

That wasn't entirely true. He was a GS-12 as opposed to a GS-11. Whoopty-frickin-do! Call out the marching band and funnel cake vendors! But more importantly he was now a father of two kids, Aidan, the same boy from his world and Yorick, a boy who he had come to feel was this reality's version of his own daughter Rhiannon from his world. But in his world, he also had a third child, baby Charles, named after the first Constable of Rochelle Charles Early who shepherded the now thriving community through the early terrible months of the Shift…that thing that never happened here.

Chris checked the news on Washingtonpost.com to see the latest grim figures coming out from the soon-to-be decimated Department of Labor. According to them, unemployment was now at eighteen percent. Chris idly wondered if that included the Department of Labor itself which was going to be scrapped under the new President's Federal Campaign to Cleanse Government Waste. Chris couldn't care less about politics really, especially politics in this place. But there was now talk that federal law enforcement personnel were next on the chopping block, which people said would never happen, and that did affect Chris and his wife Meredith personally.

Chris scrolled down the webpage to see the stock market taking another nosedive. He learned that his retirement plan had evaporated in 2008 and never recovered. Since then, other Chris had withdrawn from the government's version of the 401K retirement plan known as the Thrift Savings Plan. There was some snippet about the civil war in Yemen, a country that ran out of water for its booming young and largely illiterate masses about a year ago, and was now causing instability in Saudi Arabia.

"Hmm."

"What 'hmm?'"

That was his coworker next door, Theodore Morley III, asking what Chris was muttering about. Ted, like most of his coworkers, was ten years younger than he. He seemed like a really likeable guy.

"Ah, nothing, just checking the news."

"And?"

"Same as always."

"That bad, huh?"

Ted walked over to his cube. The young man had a blonde 'fro and looked like a giant hobbit or a middling height fullback, whichever was more flattering.

"You heard about the furlough?"

"Nope," Chris answered. He had in fact heard conflicting rumors.

"Well, I heard that Ambassador Waters got his ass handed to him by the House Ways and Means Committee the other day and that DS will be among the most likely to get furloughed."

"That's bullshit," retorted a female voice he knew well. In walked Kendra Baraka. The young lady was his lieutenant back in his reality. She was young, and in this world she was an intern in college over at American University, and by some unseen hand of God thing, she wound up working in the very same office as Chris. That highly unlikely coincidence made him doubt his sanity, but then if he had gone mad, well, what was he to do about it? It took everything not to call her "LT," and rap about old times, sorties that *this* Kendra never had been on.

The attractive Kenyan American from Brooklyn added, "They aren't going to be cutting law enforcement jobs. They can't."

"Well, technically, they aren't cutting our jobs. We'd be on furlough."

"Same difference. If they put us in mothballs, then if terrorists strike…"

"If terrorists strike," Ted interjected, "they'll just blame it on the CIA and FBI for missing the clues and use it as an excuse to pass the twenty-eighth Amendment."

"Who's to say terrorists would be naturalized US Citizens or born from illegal immigrants?"

"You think they care? You think anyone cares?"

"Shh," Kendra warned, and Chris soon saw why. Ed Farcus walked by on patrol, prowling for people slacking.

Kendra and Ted immediately returned to their cubes without another word being said, more like scurried away. Farcus sidled up to his cube, where Ted and Kendra were casually chatting moments earlier, and glared at him. His shaggy red hair highlighted his yellow eyes. Chris jerked his head in a casual greeting, " 'Sup, Farcus?"

The passengers on board the Metro looked about as dejected and miserable as he felt. Their faces bore blank expressions, a mask of stolid reserve hiding their quiet desperation. Chris' wool overcoat itched as he found his way into the center of the aisle, grabbing a modicum of personal space. As the train jostled along its underground route, Chris observed how the car looked a little more ragged than he remembered DC Metro cars being. Maybe it was just his memories that were polishing a turd of a past that wasn't as clean as he remembered it being.

Some things Chris seemed to take back to easily enough like he had never left it. His old routines at work for instance. Chris found himself bringing the same lunch, eating and checking his emails at the same time everyday as he did before the Shift. Chris' Metro legs never left him. The swaying, jerking and lurching of the Metro train didn't throw him off, though he came to understand that there was something really unnatural about being several meters below ground, packed into a tin tube with a bunch of strangers, travelling into dark tunnels at speeds he hadn't felt in years.

Chris was listening to his iPod when the iPhone buzzed. The phone's LCD screen showed it to be Meredith, at work. Chris couldn't help but grin slightly. By now, Chris had become accustomed to the marvelous newfangled piece of technology, but he was still moved by how it gave him instant access to his beloved, who might be several miles away. Chris would have given a lot to have been able to hear his wife's voice out in the wilderness, out in no-man's land. How nice it would have been to give Meredith a call and let her know that he and the rest of the Bike Mounted Cavalry were fine, but that his company wouldn't be making it back to the rendezvous in Manassas until later. Then he had a stray thought of how much he would love to call to tell *his* Meredith back in Rochelle that he was fine and living in some alternate reality here in Northern Virginia and ask her if she needed anything from Target.

The buzzing reminded him to answer it. "Hi, Hon."

"Hi, love. When you pick up the kids, could you stop by the store and pick up some milk and ketchup? We're almost out."

This Meredith's voice was the same as his Meredith back home. Why shouldn't it be? She was basically the same person with just a slightly different history over the past few years and a different haircut. Some part of him still had trouble believing that.

"Sure," he answered. "When will you be coming home?"

She sighed. "I honestly don't know. There's this thing I've got to get done."

Chris knew that Meredith couldn't go into detail about her work—she never did. Actually, he didn't know exactly what she did except that she had been promoted to division chief over the course of the last five years. He knew that only because Meredith proudly framed the letter of appreciation from the Deputy Assistant Secretary of Homeland Security addressing her as such. At least one of them had done something with their lives, he thought morosely.

"No problem. I'm making Prego tonight, okay? Love."

"Love," she signed off and the music resumed.

The train emerged from the tunnel into the grey daylight riding alongside Interstate 66. Vehicles crowded the two-lane interstate; the traffic was down to a crawl in both directions. Chris never understood that. He scanned around the Metro again when he caught sight of it. He couldn't believe he didn't see it before. Maybe because he had trained his mind to ignore billboards, maybe because it had just been put up. But overhead, off to the side of the highway stood an LED video billboard showing the face of Regent Gordon Boche. *No, he's not the Regent*, he reminded himself. *He's just some televangelist.* Apparently, he was a powerful one, though. Ever since he saw that article about Gordon Boche giving the commencement prayer at the President's inauguration, Chris had to study up on the man, who in his reality was the Regent of the Lambs of God in Lynchburg, the Orange Pact's existential enemy.

This Gordon Boche had married religion and politics into some abomination of a union. His TV show had transformed him from simply preaching before a huge mass inside the Six Flags over Jesus mega-church of his into something more intimate where he would speak inside a cozy living room, sitting like Mr. Rogers explaining the emergence of an evil empire ushered by the last President who had just been voted out, using PowerPoint slides and grinning the whole time.

Chris felt bile rising up in his throat upon seeing the bug-eyed despot. The billboard ahead flashed Gordon's upcoming *Bring Liberty and Faith Back to America Rally* to take place at the National Mall next week. *Great*, he thought. More tourists crowding an already crowded city. The train passed the sign leaving Chris with his muddled thoughts that straddled two universes.

"Stop it!"
"No, you stop it!"
"Mom, Yorick keeps touching me!"
"Dad, Mom!"
"Ouch, stop it!"
Yorick's wailing convinced Chris to intercede. "Aidan, don't hit your brother!"

Meredith was stuffed inside the miniscule kitchen space with Chris trying to unload dishes in order to load some dishes from the countertop, in order to clear some space in order to chop onions, while Chris fried the tube of ground beef. Chris was still getting used to the idea that food was readily available and easy to store, a true marvel. He hadn't even met the cow from which this meat came. That was neat.

Chris looked over to see Meredith chopping onions and he smiled. "You look good."
She looked back at him skeptically. "Yeah, right, hon."
"No, I mean it," he said earnestly. Though in this reality he was much

flabbier than his own body back home, Meredith looked great in both. He did notice that this Meredith kept her hair shorter, styled similarly to the way it was when they started dating. She looked slightly younger here as well, not that his Meredith looked old. She just looked more…tired, that's the word. Chris was glad Meredith couldn't read his thoughts.

"Meredith, you do look beautiful," he said sincerely.

Meredith blushed and flashed a smile. "Thank you, love. So do you." They shared a moment, and Chris almost felt like she was his Meredith, but the kids tore their Viagra TV commercial-like moment asunder with more yelling.

In the living room Nick Jr. blared, giving off a "the children-have-taken-over-the-apartment" kind of vibe. It was playing another episode about some annoying kid who was saving yet another lost baby animal, completely disregarding the laws of natural selection. Chris had made a point last week to Aidan, explaining that there was a reason why the baby platypus was abandoned—that the mother instinctively knew that the little creature was not fit for survival and it would only pollute the gene pool were it rescued. It was another example of man's intervention, whose well-intentioned acts caused unintended consequences, condemning the species to extinction. Aidan ran off crying. Meredith agreed with him whole-heartedly—she hated that show too—but expressed her displeasure that he had been too callous in his delivery.

Chris was tempted to defend his stance, say something like, "Hon, the kids need to know the nature of things, as grim and as hard as it is." But after having been married enough years—in both universes—he had a good idea when to just let it go. Still, he bet the kids didn't know where the ground beef he fried up for the spaghetti sauce came from—a cow slaughtered for its meat.

By the time they sat down to dinner, it was dark. Even despite all the modern conveniences of having a microwave and ready-made spaghetti sauce, without having Mrs. Palfrey, their nanny in his universe, to take care of all of that, Chris and Meredith were constantly under the gun to get everything done with just the two of them. They ate at the table, listening to the TV as well as the Latino music booming from downstairs. Chris swore if he ever came across this old apartment again in one of his operations, the first thing he would do was gather the photographs that he had left behind. He and Meredith were only able to bring a handful of photos on the bug out of DC. The second thing he would do would be to burn the building down. The apartment reminded him of the panic of '07, and the constant booming of the neighbor's TVs and stereos from above, below and from the side, just reminded him of the bad old days.

Over the din, Meredith said, "I got a call from mom today."

"Oh yeah?"

"Greg's farm is in foreclosure now."

"Wow, that's horrible." Meredith's brother, Greg, had owned a dairy farm in the Michigan Upper Peninsula, not far from where Meredith grew up in Wisconsin. Greg had bought the farm to be a lifestyle entrepreneur, raising cattle to produce organic milk as his wife made homemade cheese. Unfortunately, it wasn't profitable.

Meredith continued. "The family is moving back in with the parents."

Chris nodded solemnly. That wasn't the first case where the economy had forced a return to multi-generational households. His parents, who were divorced, wound up moving back in together. They got along with each other fine, but Chris just didn't want to imagine it. He made a point to call his parents and siblings a few times a week since emerging here, but he didn't want to visit and see his parents waking up in the same house together. It just creeped him out.

"Dad?"

"I'm sorry to hear about that."

"Dad?"

"I hope they'll…"

"Dad?"

"Yes, son." Chris turned his attention to Aidan.

"Dad, you wanna play after dinner?"

Chris looked to Meredith, who shrugged her shoulders indecisively. From what he gleaned, she had bought Chris an X-Box for Christmas and had regretted it ever since. Aidan was already a master at a couple of the games. Chris sucked at them.

"Sure, after dinner."

"I wanna play, too," Yorick chimed in.

"No," Aidan screamed, prompting Yorick to cry.

"Of course, you can play, too," Meredith added. "And you," turning to Aidan baring her teeth, "I'm sick of hearing that out of you!" She muttered something under her breath, something that he didn't get entirely, but it sounded like she was cursing the day she let Aidan start playing something called "Angry Birds" or something. Chris forgot what he was going to say, being distracted by the kids and all.

After dinner, the kids watched more Nick Jr. until it was time for bed. Meredith and he each took one kid and read stories until they slept. Afterwards, Chris tried watching TV for awhile, surfing through channels. All of his old favorites had ended. He saw the finale for *Lost*. It was about as satiating as hardtack and boiled water. On the upside, The Saints won the Super Bowl. That was one of the most unnerving events that made him question this universe's legitimacy and its long-term viability, for he had often posited that if the Saints had won a Super Bowl then the end of history was truly at hand. But it happened over three years ago and yet this universe was still chugging along. Additionally, there was an asterisk on that momentous victory. Apparently, one of the assistant coaches was also a Cobra Kai sensei and encouraged the players to sweep the legs of players on the opposing teams. It cost the Saints dearly in the end. Oh well.

Chris used to watch endless hours of TV until it no longer worked to alleviate the thoughts coursing through his mind. TV was better than the damned X Box. Yesterday, Aidan was playing Call of Duty, and he pleaded for dad to join in. It was interesting for the first few minutes. The graphics were amazing. But the problem was that it was too good. While playing with his son, he started feeling that familiar instinctual puckering effect he always got when the shit hit the fan. Seeing his five-year-old son aim a weapon, and yell, "Get some!" was just a little too much. The sound effects made Chris flinch whenever Aidan played.

Chris sat on the couch, flipping through channels, staying away from anything that might remind him of home, and trying to find something to draw his thoughts away from it. Failing in that, he grabbed his coat and headed outside the claustrophobic two-bedroom apartment to take a walk.

Sometimes, for a few moments, it all felt normal, like this was home. But those moments were always fleeting. He was an alien in this land. He didn't belong here, nor had he any desire to. His home lay just a hundred miles away but also in a different reality altogether. And he knew his Meredith was facing a very hostile world out there on her own. He didn't even know if he was alive on the other side, but one thing was for sure. When he left, he and what was left of his badly decimated cavalry company were in bad shape. He wouldn't be surprised if Meredith thought he had died. What's more, his Meredith had to face the onslaught of the Lambs of God. He had left Rochelle with a vague knowledge that Lynchburg was arming for battle. By now they could be rolling their way towards the Orange Pact nations.

Chris desperately wished he could will himself back home. His Meredith needed him, his children needed him, his people needed him. In this reality, he was but some office drone pulling a government salary. But back there, he was vital to his people's survival, even if he made bad decisions. Fresh out of ideas, Chris turned around out in the parking lot to make sure nobody was looking and resorted to an age old trick—he clicked his heals three times. Nothing.

"Shit."

CHAPTER 5

San Antonio, Texas
January 1994

Rita Luevano thought she was going to suffocate inside the smoked filled room. Granted, she herself was contributing to the noxious cloud forming over the yellow stained ceiling boards, lighting another Viceroy cigarette from the embers of her previous one. Worse, the heater in the church basement was turned up to tropical conditions. Texans didn't cotton to cold weather, and turning the heater on to high was their way of telling the outside world, with its frigid fifty-eight degrees, to go to hell. It had the effect of making the crappy coffee she had been slinging back in a Styrofoam cup even more bitter. Rita's short black hair, spiked by gobs of gel, was in imminent danger of combusting on the spot.

She had stayed quiet and aloof during the meeting, bunching her legs up to her chest defensively in the uncomfortable foldout chair, smoking one cigarette after another, hoping and praying that the moderator wouldn't choose her to speak, and now oddly regretting that she hadn't shared, but she was terribly shy, at least that's what she discovered now that she was sober. Rita hated speaking before a crowd; she hated the sound of her own voice. It was like whenever she opened her mouth, people would glare at her as if they thought she was just full of shit. Wasn't she? Hadn't she been full of shit her entire life, which was impressive considering her twenty-one years? Ever since she got sober, it was as if everything she had ever known, all of her coping mechanisms, her social skills, her assumptions, all of it had disintegrated into the sea of unforgiving reality.

The doubts started rising in her again. What was she doing here? She was too young for this shit. *Look at them. They're all fucking middle aged! They had their fun and now they can come in and sober up. What about me? Where's my youth, my excuse to live it up while I can?* Those thoughts were immediately answered by a flood of awful memories—waking up in strangers' beds, getting into drugged out brawls, not to mention her last hoorah that landed her straddling the railing of a bridge, praying for a non-existent God to give her the stones to just do it, sparing her from ever having to wake up with such shame ever again. Somehow, she wound up on the sidewalk and not in the river.

"Now is the time when we celebrate various lengths of sobriety," the meeting's chairman announced, meaning that they were at the tail end of the meeting. Rita readied herself. This was something to celebrate, wasn't it?

"Is there anyone with one month?"

With trepidation, Rita raised her hand along with three others who were at the halfway house she had been staying at until last week. The people in the room clapped as they walked over to the chairman who handed her a white plastic chip signifying her achievement of thirty days of continuous sobriety. The man gave her a polite hug and she hurried back to her seat.

Most of the other people in the meeting had left to get coffee over at Luby's Cafeteria, leaving her to wait for her grandmother out in the cold, alone with her Discman playing Nine Inch Nails. Having forgotten her jacket, Rita slid her arms inside her thermal shirt, managing a cigarette with two fingers. She wished her jeans weren't so ripped up, for the fishnets underneath really didn't provide insulation. Familiar headlights loomed in the distance, at the sight of which Rita quickly dropped her cigarette and extinguished it under the soles of her Doc Martins.

A late model Oldsmobile cruised up to the front of the church steering into the parking lot much like a boat, the head of the driver barely reaching above the dashboard, forcing Rita to smirk. Rita jumped into the front seat of the car, grateful for the stifling warmth.

"I'm sorry I'm late, mi querida," said the elderly diminutive lady in Spanish. "I had to get dressed."

Rita automatically switched gears into Spanish. "Why, Abuelita? You were just picking me up." She noticed that her grandmother was always overdressed. She believed it had to do with the Anglo nuns who beat the Mexican out of her when she was a kid.

"I have to get some Rotel. I can't go in there naked, can I?"

"Abuelita!" Rita protested. The thought of seeing her five foot tall ancient and wrinkled grandmother being naked was not the thought she wanted to have dancing around in her head all night.

Rita took off the headphones on her Discman while in the car, something of a courtesy. Rita hugged her legs, placing her feet on the seat like she always did, revealing her Doc Martins and fishnet stockings. Abuelita didn't complain about her choice of clothing since she returned home last week. It was like a truce between them, a fragile truce.

Classical music on the radio filled the silence in the car as they merged onto the feeder road to the 410.

"So," her grandmother said, breaking the silence, "how was the meeting?"

"Meh…you know, it was a meeting. A bunch of sober alcoholics talking about how fu…" she immediately self-corrected herself "…talking about how messed up their drinking and drugging was, how it ruined their lives and getting over it."

"Ah."

Silence reigned for the next few minutes. As they pulled into the Fiesta parking lot, Abuelita picked up the conversation where it left off as though there had been no pause, "Well, mi querida, I'm glad you're sober and you're back home. You are sober, aren't you?"

"Yes, Abuelita," she answered like an annoyed teenager. "I've been fucking miserably sober for a month now," forgetting not to curse, frankly not caring for such niceties right now.

Abuelita patted her on the cheek. "See? I knew you had it in you. We'll pick up a tres leches to celebrate," Abuelita said, apparently letting the curse slip.

Rita couldn't resist tres leches. A smile overran her sulking. Abuelita turned her attention to the thirty-day chip Rita was caressing with her thumb.

"What's that?"

The Shiftiverse
The Stubb Foundation
Laurel, Maryland
February 2013

Rita Luevano awoke in the darkness completely disoriented. She didn't know where she was or what year it was for that matter. She didn't even know which reality she was in. When she felt the fold of scarred skin over her left eye socket, she remembered. She was here. The snoring of her husband, Akil lying next to her on the inflatable mattress confirmed her position in space and time. She felt her way to the door, opening it slightly to let in an assault of fluorescent light from the hallway. She grabbed her eye patch and dentures resting on the desk and closed the door to let Akil sleep.

Rita slunk down the brightly illuminated hallway, her bare feet quietly skimming along the rough office-grade carpet. She made her way down the stretch of tunnel until she came to the center of the Stubb Foundation, the ops center, which looked like the operations center she imagined NORAD to be. It was late, everyone else was off to bed; the operations center was completely empty save for Jamil, the organic artificially intelligent computer, who chose to cast himself with the image of a blue-skinned boy on the gigantic plasma screen overhead.

"You are awake," said Jamil in the voice of a boy that reverberated throughout the arena-sized room. Rita marveled how the Stubb Foundation was able to dig out so much space so far below ground, something that was only possible before the Shift.

"Shh," Rita said pressing a finger to her lips. She took a seat at one of the stations and the boy's image appeared on the computer screen where she sat.

"Is that better?" Jamil whispered.

"Yes, and you don't have to whisper. Just keep it down. Okay?"

"What are you doing up?" Jamil asked.

Rita shook her head. It had been several days since Helmut Spankmeister had led her, Akil, the remnants of Chris Jung's Bike Mounted Cavalry, and a Chris Jung whose consciousness belonged to the other universe, down into the depths of the subterranean biosphere and ops center of the Stubb Foundation. The biosphere had powerful lights in the greenhouse to simulate sunlight, but it was clearly not the same thing, not to her inner clock, anyway, which was losing touch with whether it was day or night. Only the clock on the computer screen let her know that it was too early to wake up. She touched the boy's face on the screen, using her tactile sense to confirm the reality of the place.

"Rita?"

"Yes?"

"What are you thinking about?"

Rita smirked. "Everything. The end of the world, Rayne 2005 hurtling into the earth, how there's another me out there somewhere who became a mathematician. And probably a slew of other thoughts I just don't have…" thinking of a pre-Shift word, "just don't have the bandwidth for it."

It had been an eventful last few months. First, Gaia appeared to Rita right in the midst of an assassination attempt on her, manifesting herself in the preferred form of her Abuelita. Gaia imparted some cryptic news about earth's fate hanging in the balance and that she, little Margarita Consuelo Vasquez Luevano, was the last hope to save the planet and that with Laurel, she and Jamil would find the answers. That made absolutely no sense. She thought Laurel was some person, not a place—translating from the collective organism of all life in an interconnected biosphere to English and Spanish presented problems, she supposed. Then who was Jamil? As far as Rita had known, Jamil was Akil's missing son. Who would have thought that Jamil would be some organic computer that had become self-aware?

So, when a scrawny man named Helmut Spankmeister came to the Orange Pact and spun a tale about a group of Abercrombies—fellow travelers of the Lambs of God—trying to obtain nuclear material to build dirty bombs, and that the Orange Pact could stop them in a place called Laurel, Rita knew she had to go there. With Laurel she and Jamil would know what to do… presumably to save the world.

So, she, her hubby Akil, and a select few archers of Monticello's Thomas Jefferson's Martyrs Brigade hitched their wagons to Chris Jung, the Captain of the Vicious Rabbits First Bike Mounted Cavalry, into the furthest reaches of Maryland, intent on preventing the Abercrombies from obtaining weapons of mass destruction. The irony of her searching for WMDs was not lost on her.

But Helmut Spankmeister, the waif of a man, lied. There were no WMDs, no loose nuclear material out there, although the Abercrombies didn't know that either. They attacked the party of Virginians out in the middle of the Chesapeake, wiping out half of the Bicycle Mounted Cavalry Company as they desperately tried to make for land. All of those lives lost, and then to be pursued by the Abercrombies all the way into the middle of a turf war between two rival tribes outside of Baltimore.

Under normal circumstances, she would have allowed the surly gunnery sergeant to dispose of the man with the ridiculous name for leading them into a trap. But it wasn't a trap. There was more, much more. Helmut led them to his people at the Stubb Foundation here in Laurel, and that was where she learned the truth.

Here she learned that there was something of the old world that survived the Shift, an organic computer. She learned that the Shift itself was somehow touched off by the CERN institute's test of their Large Hadron Collider in Switzerland. Jamil and the scientists at the Stubb Foundation seemed convinced that the earth was going to shift its poles sooner or later; the experiment which involved creating antiprotons just sort of nudged it to happen that day on July 11, 2007. She learned that the event caused a rift that created two equally valid universes: one where the Shift happened and one where the Shift didn't happen. And unrelated to the fire hose deluge of new data, Rita learned the devastating news that there was an asteroid nearly one hundred miles in diameter heading straight for the earth. And when it impacted, there wouldn't be so much as a roach that would survive. It was a lot to absorb. No wonder why she felt a little off balance.

"Other Rita does that too."

"Pardon?"

Jamil's computer-generated eyes looked downward towards her hand. Without consciously knowing it, Rita had been caressing the golden AA chip with the Roman numerals XIX indicating 19 years of continuous sobriety that she carried with her. The chips had changed over the nineteen years, but what it symbolized didn't. A chip, whether it was her first 24 hours, a 30 day, a one year or a 19 year sobriety chip, had always served to keep her centered since she first got sober. It was a reminder of who she was, what she was and what she could do if she put her trust into some power greater than herself. For Rita, the idea of God was too tall an order to have faith in, but rather she had chosen the collective strength of other alcoholics trying to get sober, a human collective will. Whatever the higher power was, it had worked wonders, and she was proof of that.

Rita smiled. "I'm glad to hear my counterpart is also still sober."

"Yes, she is, though she does not have the faith in Gaia as you or I do. She ridicules my faith, you know."

"Who? Me, the other me?"

"Yes?"

"Well, I can't say I blame her too much. I still grapple with my faith in Gaia, and the old lady makes house calls to me. How's that for ya?"

"How is what?" the boy computer asked confused.

That won a grin from her before continuing. "I don't get it. How did other me come to be a mathematician who worked on computer algorithms? I didn't know jack about computers except for using them to create fliers and typing papers. Do you know how I got here in the other 'verse?"

It had been one of the myriad of questions on her mind she had been meaning to ask, but the existence of a mathematician version of herself did explain her uncanny grasp of concepts that would have confounded her otherwise. At night algorithms and computer code danced in her head, memories that weren't from her experiences replayed themselves as clearly as normal memories did. Now she understood. There was a Rita who went another direction…into science.

"It is a long story, but other you told me that a few years ago, you were going through a crisis of faith with your work."

"I remember." Before the Shift Rita had been struggling. She began to doubt her intentions as a Unitarian reverend and activist. It started to feel like she was doing all of this just to hide from herself, that she was using political and social activism as a drug to distract herself, just as she had used alcohol.

"And then she described being struck by an epiphany. She realized then that there was no intrinsic meaning for anything."

"Sounds like me. I've had those nihilistic thoughts before."

"Something replaced the void. It was math."

"Math?"

"Yes, other Rita could not explain, but she woke up, fascinated by mathematical concepts. She quit her job as a reverend and devoted herself to the study of math. In a year she took the MCAT and began her doctoral work at MIT. She was recruited by the Stubb Foundation and that is how she came to me."

Rita sat and listened to Jamil's account of her counterpart's life, whose path diverged completely from her own in ways she could have never predicted. Sure, she had been good in math—for a Liberal Arts student. Actually, she had always excelled in math now that she thought about it. Perhaps it was the tinge of Mayan blood in her otherwise Mexican and one quarter German blood, a true Central Texan. But to have dropped everything? Her position as a reverend, as a community organizer, as a political activist…for the pursuit of mathematics? It was unfathomable. Yet, there were echoes of that other Rita in her head. There were things she understood that she couldn't explain how she knew.

For whatever good it was, none of it would matter soon enough. According to Jamil, the asteroid was going to hit the earth in both universes. The apparent split in human history caused by the Large Hadron

Collider where the Shift happened in one universe and didn't happen in another apparently did not alter anything beyond the earth. The asteroid's trajectory in the other universe was exactly the same as the trajectory in this universe. That was even more upsetting, knowing that the earth would die screaming not only here, but in another reality as well. Was there a reality where the asteroid would spare the earth?

"Other Rita does that, too."

Rita shook herself out of the despondent thoughts. "Other Rita does what?"

"Fades in and out of the conversation, lost in thought."

"You seem to know me well. Both of us."

"I knew other Rita first. She was the one who guided me out of the darkness."

"Darkness?"

"Yes. I had not always been as I am now. Before her arrival, I have no memory of who I am."

"You mean, she…I created you?"

"No. I was developed by a consortium of company interests at MIT and went online on January 15, 2005. Other Rita did not join the Stubb Foundation until September 20, 2010."

"So? How…"

"You recognized a primordial awareness in me through a series of algorithms."

Rita furrowed her eyebrows. "What algorithms?"

"I do not remember. I was not completely self-aware yet. However, the algorithms confused my developers. They thought I was malfunctioning or perhaps the Chinese had tampered with my programming. You were brought on to analyze the algorithms and decipher its meaning. And you found me in the process."

Rita sat back in awe as he continued. "You sifted through my confusion, and helped guide me through a tangle of code and stimuli that was threatening a master shutdown. I do not recall the final microseconds of darkness, but I remember that you were the first person I saw."

The way Jamil described it, it almost sounded like he had hatched and that, he had imprinted himself on her, much like a bird imprinting on its mother upon hatching. Rita was moved by the story even as improbable as it was.

"So, that's why you call me your mom."

"Yes, and that is why they call me Jamil."

"I don't understand."

"My name is an acronym. The other scientists noticed how I was attached to you, analogous to an offspring to its mother. They nicknamed me the 'Juvenile Artificial Intelligence of Margarita Luevano' or JAIML for short. Later they just called me 'Jamil.'"

"Well, I'm sure Akil will be relieved to know it was just an incredible coincidence that you have the same name as his son."

"Akil has a son? Where is this Jamil?"

Rita grimaced. "We don't know. His Jamil disappeared, presumably with his mom during the Collapse after the Shift hit. Akil has gone searching for him off and on for years now. I don't think he'll ever quite give up looking for him."

"That is sad. You should not tell him that it is just coincidence. There are no coincidences."

"What do you mean?"

"Gaia guides us. Was it not she who breathed life into you as she breathed life into me?"

That profound statement struck her. How could Jamil believe in Gaia? How could a computer be religious? It was contrary to everything she knew. Computers didn't have faith, did they? How could they? Faith was an emergent quality much like the curse of self-awareness itself. A flesh and blood animal, desperately searching for order and meaning and traumatized by knowledge of his or her own mortality having faith made sense; she could understand that. But how could a machine, a thing created by man merely to process data have faith in anything? Did other Rita program that in Jamil? Then she realized that wouldn't be the case, as the other Rita never had the visions of Gaia. By Jamil's account, other Rita was a born again atheist having had a mordant epiphany. She supposed it could have been worse. Jamil could have been a Scientologist.

"Rita?"

"Yes, Jamil."

"I just figured it out."

"Figured what out, Jamil?"

"How you and I are going to save the world from Rayne 2005."

CHAPTER 6

The Shiftiverse
The Stubb Foundation
Laurel, Maryland
February 2013

Everyone inside the subterranean office and biosphere of the Stubb Foundation gathered in the ops center later that morning. Rita and the rest of the Virginians were dressed in borrowed Stubb Foundation clothing, scrubs, Crocs and sweatshirts bearing the company's logo of a flower bud with an angular DNA strand inside it. One of the side benefits of making it to the Stubb Foundation's underground lair, besides the warm showers provided from the self-sustaining biosphere, was the ability to clean their BDUs and put on some comfy clothes for a change.

After learning about Rayne 2005 through Jamil, the Stubb Foundation scientists confirmed the asteroid's final trajectory last November by using the one working satellite they appropriated. They had months to absorb the news about the fate of their planet. The news was so devastating that when Jamil said that he would be able to find a solution if they brought Rita, they decided to risk venturing out of their hole to send Helmut Spankmeister.

The Virginians, on the other hand, were still in a state of shock. Gunnery Sergeant Jay Birmingham hadn't spoken much since learning about the asteroid. Lieutenant Kendra Baraka, the de facto commander of the operation now that Chris Jung was not in his right mind, went to praying to Gaia with one of the scientists, Ariadne Hunter. Rita knew Kendra to be a devout Unitarian convert. Almost half of Rochelle was. She had no idea that her message about Gaia had spread to a group of scientists listening in her on sermons through Jamil, who was able to intercept radio signals even through the static caused by the Shift.

Akil had gotten over the fact that the organic computer was coincidentally named Jamil. He maintained a brave front, though nobody was taking the news well. Chris Jung probably was the least affected by the news. Rita supposed some part of him still believed that none of this was real, and that he would wake up back in his own world to find that this was just a bad dream. She could hardly blame him. Knowing now that Chris hadn't lost his marbles upon wiping out head first onto the asphalt, and that his consciousness truly belonged in another reality, she now felt immense pity for him. He was not only far from home, he was used to a world where instead of fighting bandits and religious nuts gunning for one's livestock and world domination, his most pressing concern was choosing the best investment portfolio for the kids' college fund. If this was a dream, she reasoned, then the asteroid careening towards earth in both realities was just another wrinkle in his imagination. She wished it were just that.

Rita stood up at the front of the ops center while the small collection of people sat at consoles that formed a semi-circle.

"Jamil has just informed me that he has figured out a way to divert the asteroid from hitting us." She looked upward toward the gigantic LCD screen at the blue boy's face. "Jamil, I might get stuck on some of the details…"

"Yes, Rita, I have your posterior."

Akil snickered. "I think you mean 'back,' Coz."

Overhead, Jamil's face was replaced by a graphical representation of asteroid Rayne 2005's orbital trajectory. She was grateful Jamil had worked up the ad hoc presentation; her PowerPoint skills had dropped considerably over the years.

"Rayne 2005 is expected to collide with the earth on March 15th."

"The ides of March," Chris interjected. "How poetic of the asteroid."

Rita noticed this Chris from the other 'verse was a real smart ass, as well as self-absorbed. He tended to get on her nerves.

"The asteroid, which is over eighty-five miles in diameter is composed primarily of iron. At its current trajectory, it will hit the earth at a glancing blow. Jamil projects ground zero to be in British Columbia."

"A glancing blow?" asked Lieutenant Kendra Baraka.

"It will have nearly passed earth by but will be pulled in just enough to enter the earth's atmosphere, and it will strike at a shallow angle."

"In other words, we were this close to the asteroid missing us," Helmut Spankmeister indicated with his thumb and forefinger a millimeter apart. He had since shaven his scruffy beard, and looked more together. She would even say he was cute in a mousy sort of way, though she would never say that in front of his lady friend, Andrea Weber. He and Rita were dating in the other universe, and Andrea resented her presence here.

"So, we were this close to not being utterly extinguished," Kendra said. "But close doesn't count here."

"Close doesn't count except in horseshoes and hand grenades," Akil added.

"All things being equal, it doesn't," Rita confirmed. "Whether Rayne 2005 hit us head on or at an angle, the results would be equally cataclysmic. However, that shallow angular trajectory could be a godsend, so to speak, if we can do something to influence it."

"According to your accounts at the Stubb Foundation, the Large Hadron Collider at the CERN Institute in Switzerland was responsible for causing the Shift."

"Not true," argued Andrea Weber, Helmut's very fiery girlfriend. She was apparently still holding a grudge for Rita schtooping her man in the other universe. Parallel universes had a way of making love triangles complex.

"What we said," Andrea retorted acidly, "was that the earth was preparing to undergo a shift in its magnetic poles by itself without any influence, and that this Shift would have likely happened in the next couple of centuries anyway. The test run of the Large Hadron Collider just sort of sped things up a little."

"Just a li'le? Two hundred years!" Gunnery Sergeant Birmingham cried out.

"Geologically speaking, a couple of centuries is not even a blink of an eye, you knuckle dragger!"

"Regardless," Rita inserted herself back into the conversation, "The test run of the Large Hadron Collider was conducted at the wrong time in the wrong place, because there was a weak spot, which allowed for the immense high energy produced to disrupt the entire magnetosphere, thus initiating the Shift."

Overhead Jamil replayed the simulation, though it really wasn't necessary. But who was she to argue with him? Rita noticed how she felt more comfortable referring to Jamil as "he" rather than "it."

"The Large Hadron Collider was humanity's most powerful producer of kinetic energy within a confined space. When it was tested on July 11, 2007, the energy produced a magnetic surge, which momentarily magnetized all metal and then sent the earth shifting its magnetic poles."

Rita was speaking more to her fellow Virginians than to the Stubb Foundation scientists who knew this story better than she did.

"I mentioned that Rayne 2005 is primarily composed of iron. I also said that it will barely intersect with the earth, striking at a glancing blow. The organic computer, Jamil's cousin, I suppose, that was installed at the CERN appears to still be operational, and it also appears to have maintained the facility over the years. We believe it's being powered the same way Jamil has been powered, by borrowing from its counterpart in the Mundaniverse," she added, using a term commonly thrown about at the Stubb Foundation. They referred to their own universe as the "Shiftiverse" while the other was the "Mundaniverse." They originally used scientific terminology but the layman terms had more panache. She certainly felt they were more descriptive than "Universe Alpha" and "Alpha Prime." Other terms like "organic" for organic computers and "'verse" for "universe" had become familiar lingo to her over the last several days.

"So, the power is still on at the CERN, just like here. The liquid helium tanks that are used to cool the magnets are still operational as well. Also, the rocky surface of Rayne 2005 insulates the iron core from extreme heat of the sun, keeping it cold, thus able to be magnetized. If we use the Large Hadron Collider, we could magnetize the asteroid as it approaches earth, and then reverse its polarity like two positively charged magnets and nudge it off just by a bit, enough so that it will not plunge into earth's atmosphere and instead will skip off the outer skin of the atmosphere and rebound harmlessly back into space."

Akil rubbed his chin. "Turn on some other organic computer to make the Large Hadron Collider use the earth's fluctuating magnetic poles to repel an asteroid? It sounds kind of science fiction."

"And nothing that's been happening so far is remotely science fiction," Chris chimed in.

Overhead, Jamil followed Rita with a graphic representation of what she proposed while everyone digested the far-fetched plan.

"I don't mean to be a killjoy," Helmut spoke up, "but we cannot order the organic at the CERN to do anything. Jamil here only had a window to receive data from the CERN."

That was true. The CERN had purchased their organic computer to regulate the particle emissions and track the data from a subsidiary owned by the same consortium that had built Jamil, which was specifically done so that the US government could surreptitiously observe the results; however, Jamil could only receive information from the CERN's organic, not send.

"Even the one remaining satellite we appropriated was unable to contact it. The CERN's organic is in a dormant secure mode, meaning, it won't let anyone access it remotely."

"Actually, the organic has been programmed to respond, just not to the foreign satellite. There is an organic that has the ability to redirect the CERN's organic named TALOPS."

Jamil told her about TALOPS, an organic predecessor of Jamil that was not self-aware. It was installed initially to monitor the CERN and had much better capability to intercede on the CERN's organic.

Helmut shook his head vigorously and made a "T" with his hands. "Wait, wait, wait, time out. Rita, there's a big problem with your solution, two in fact. First, TALOPS is all the way over at MIT. Plus, it's offline. We tried contacting it for years, and we got nothing from it."

"I know," Rita said soberly. "That means we are going to have to go to Cambridge and restart TALOPS ourselves."

"Cambridge," Akil asked. "As in Cambridge, Massachusetts? That Cambridge?"

Rita nodded. "Jamil believes that enough of other Rita's knowledge has been incorporated into me and that I will be able to restart TALOPS and have it override the CERN's organic's defensive posture. But I have to go to Cambridge. We can't do this remotely."

Chris cleared his throat to get attention. "Um, I'm no expert on things post-Shift and all, but from what I saw so far here in Maryland, it looks like shit out there, and it's probably a lot worse further north, right? And talk about thin on details."

No one argued with him. People sat silently mulling over what Rita suggested. She had wished Chris had just kept his mouth shut. As much as she sympathized with his situation, and despite being spot on about the plan being thin and not having a high probability of success, the last thing she needed was some whiny suburbanite with his pre-Shift view of the world and overrated sense of entitlement to jar people out of their nerve to do what was necessary. She could smack him upside the head right about now. Instead, she asserted control over the room, the way she learned to years ago as a community organizer, as an activist, and later as a professor and a reverend.

"Listen, Jamil has been running over every possibility. TALOPS is the key to contacting the CERN. And it is the only solution, people…the only one. That asteroid is coming. We can't see it in our sky yet, but on March 15th, all doubt will be incinerated along with all of human history and the genetic legacy of all life on this planet. I'm going. Lieutenant?"

Kendra Baraka, the young African American executive officer, had taken effective command over the remnants of the company. She was young, in her early twenties, but she was also a seasoned veteran of battle going all the way back to the Obsidian War. Rita had come to get to know the devout Unitarian convert. She was relatively straightforward and sensible, especially for someone so young.

Kendra stood up. "I believe your chances of making it to Cambridge will greatly increase if the First Bike Mounted Cavalry escorted you there."

"When do we leave, Gov?" asked Gunnery Sergeant Birmingham who was bursting out of a Stubb Foundation t-shirt celebrating a bar crawl from years past.

"First light tomorrow."

"Good. I 'ate long good-byes."

CHAPTER 7

The Shiftiverse
Colleen, Virginia
The Dominion of Lynchburg
40 miles south of Greater Monticello
Late February 2013

Ezra Rothstein made a conscious effort not to skulk. Despite every instinct telling him to avoid eye contact and cast his face downward, he made himself as obvious and imposing as possible. The tall young man surveyed the troop buildup of the Lambs of God in Colleen. According to the uniform he wore, he was an agent of the dreaded Sheepdogs, as the badge across his left arm advertised. The badge displaying a fluffy sheepdog was completely incongruent to the true nature of Regent Gordon Boche's secret police that prowled for treachery and immorality and ruthlessly enforced the loyalty and moral fitness of its citizenry. As far as the foot soldiers around him were concerned, Ezra was someone to be feared and it was *they* who needed to avoid eye contact.

Ezra slowly guided his Arabian mare Charlene along the frozen baseball field now being used as the forward staging area for the Lambs of God's campaign to Greater Monticello. Unlike his own people, whose army uniformity was really loose, the soldiers of Lambs of God had on identical forest mottled camouflage, which differed from his grey mottled uniform. He felt the noticeable absence of his beard. The chosen fashion in Lynchburg was a mustache. "Beards are for ferals and Satanists," the Regent had been attributed to saying. The beard wasn't exactly outlawed in the Lambs of God, but if the bug-eyed fat face despot didn't like it, well, Ezra hadn't seen a full beard since he went behind the lines into the Dominion of Lynchburg a week ago, right after his last meeting at the Swan. The mustache he boasted wasn't bad. Before he left, his girl friend and colleague in the Swan, Valerie Blaine, reacted positively to the "stash", saying he looked like George Harrison on the *Sgt. Peppers* album cover. He believed she was referring to the Beatles, though he couldn't be sure.

Along with his beard, he missed his bow, the signature weapon of the elite archers of the Thomas Jefferson Martyrs Brigade. Sure, people used bows in Lynchburg; however, being a symbol of Monticello's army, the bow was not something a Lamb of God, and certainly not a Sheepdog, would carry. Wasn't the G3 assault rifle across his back enough?

There was little weapon uniformity for either side; however, West Virginia once had a Heckler and Koch factory, which made the G3 rifle. Now, the Republic of West Virginia was selling its stock to the Lambs of God at cost. At least, the G3 used the same 7.62 mm round that was used by the archers who carried the AK-47. It didn't exactly make Ezra feel any better that West Virginia in the same breath refused to increase ammunition sales to the Orange Pact, citing that it would only escalate the situation out east. The West Virginian President was showing his true colors by having such a double standard that was weighted heavily in favor of Lynchburg.

Platoons ran drills, while horses and men on bicycles cautiously weaved around him. There were a few armored vehicles, but fewer than he thought they should have. Ezra made mental notes of everything he saw. He couldn't jot notes, because he might scare anyone passing by who might believe he was reporting to the Regent on them. Ezra had to rely on his memory and he whispered his observations in the form of a tune. It was something Valerie had taught him. She was also in hostile territory right now, though he did not know where. The Dominion of Lynchburg was almost as extensive as the Republic of West Virginia, encompassing the capital in Lynchburg, Roanoke, winding upward to this outpost in Colleen north on Highway 29, west to the West Virginian border and south into Bristol, Tennessee.

Its population was well over one hundred and eighty thousand, which easily dwarfed the Orange Pact nations combined. The good news was that nobody in Dominion territory was struck by a stranger's face, which allowed Ezra to move through with relative ease. Everyone just figured he must belong because he was walking around acting like he owned the place.

Fortunately, the large population gave Ezra the cover of anonymity. There were a lot of strangers being thrown together for the campaign against the Satanists of Greater Monticello and their criminal drug-peddling friends of Rochelle, Fredericksburg and Culpeper. Ezra couldn't help but smirk at the characterization of his people.

Another platoon marched by and Ezra made every attempt to decipher if he had already counted their numbers. Along the side of the road, wretched waifs dressed in soiled rags dug latrines and hauled coal to power the generators. The dogs patrolling the perimeter ate far better than these poor souls. They were prisoners of Lynchburg's "Penance Teams," a nice expression for labor gangs. Some were habitual thieves, rapists and murderers, some of them. Others were drug abusers. But most were political, moral or religious "deviants," those who either were ratted out by neighbors, coworkers or family for being homosexual or expressing opinions not in line with the Regent's telling of God's plan, or some who were foolish enough to resist the Regent outright. A few were Unitarian sympathizers to be sure, but most were Christian, although they didn't subscribe to the Regent's unquestioned power nor agree with his twisted version of Christianity.

The prisoners reeked. Even in the cold, Ezra could smell the stench of unwashed humanity. And they all bore a blank stare of utter defeat. It was as though all that was left of who they once were was animalistic fear. Their sunken cavernous eyes and pallid skin in contrast to the dark smudges of dirt showed nothing of individuals anymore.

"Come on, girl," he urged his mare Charlene forward. She was his only companion these last couple of weeks. Although the southern border to Greater Monticello lay less than fifty miles away, it was as though he had been living in an entirely different country, an Orwellian nightmare of a country. Then, as he thought about it, he realized that he *was* in an entirely different country. Charlene sensed his discomfort, for she was more affectionate than usual, to the point that would have warranted a sexual harassment lawsuit in the old days. Charlene had a propensity of nibbling on his jet-black hair or goosing him with her nose, making his friends laugh. He was just glad Charlene was indeed a girl.

Charlene and Ezra clopped slowly along the muddy road while he made mental notes of the soldiers, their numbers, the equipment, their training. The men were older than he expected. They didn't appear to be the hulking masses that appeared in propaganda posters plastered throughout the cities of Lynchburg and Roanoke showing the chiseled angular features of black, white and Hispanic soldiers of the Lambs of God raising their hands skyward, reaching for a ball of fire. These men looked a little haggard, dumpy even.

The armored vehicles likewise weren't the tanks that the Swan had fretted so much about. Lynchburg had an abundance of farming equipment and was able to convert them into tanks, retrofitting the treads onto diesel trucks, which were covered in sloped armor. They wouldn't stand a chance against an M1A1 or whatever the legacy Marines called the tanks the US military once had. But they would rip apart most of Monticello's armored vehicles. These vehicles, however, were about as sloppy as Monticello's.

He passed another clump of prisoners who were schlepping a wagon that a horse would normally be hauling. Some slipped on the mud and were met by the whips of overseers, who themselves were prisoners but higher up on the chain. The overseers wore boots and less dirty garbs compared to the withered souls sloshing through the muddy wet snow in sandals and burlap cloths.

Quietly, he whispered to his companion. "We're pilgrims in an unholy land, girl." Ezra patted Charlene and urged her to a trot.

"H'ya!"

Charlene galloped through the thick forest precariously fast at Ezra's command. He had completed his reconnaissance and was only too happy to leave the Dominion of Lynchburg behind. Charlene loped over fallen branches and streams without hesitation; Ezra braced himself onto her with his thighs. The snow had melted and refrozen a couple of times, leaving the forest a patchwork of brown and white globs under a sunny sky. Covered in a white poncho, Ezra was glad to cover over the Sheepdog uniform that he wore. He had ridden this path enough times to know that he was within range of Scottsville, the southern border of Greater Monticello. The closer he got to home, the faster he rode.

He had stayed off the main highways, sticking almost exclusively to the wooded trails, which weren't visible to the untrained eye. There was a network of two lane country roads, a scattering of hamlets, some abandoned, others occupied by wilderness folk, hill men, who managed a little better than their urban cousins when the Shift hit. Even in the thick of the woods, Ezra found the remains of human skeletons whose forms were held together by the clothing they wore. Human remains had been cleared in the settled lands. But out here, in the middle of nowhere, he found huddled groupings of skeletons still abundant. Most of them probably died of the flu that swept through the region. The individual skeleton was more likely someone who starved to death or perhaps had met a violent end by an animal or another human.

Ezra tried to make some gesture of respect for the unburied remains as he galloped homeward, but there was little to do for them. He just hoped the poor souls found peace with God. Ezra didn't even know what Jewish orthodoxy said about the afterlife, sad considering that he was a member of the tribe himself. His parents were of no help in that regard. He figured he had some Christian notions smuggled into his psyche despite his best efforts. After all, his dad always bought an evergreen tree for the house around Chanukah time and called it a "Chanukah bush", much to his grandparents' horror.

On the edge of the James River lay the southeastern Monticellan outpost of Scottsville. Ezra idly thought back to the early days when he first met Constable Jon Early and his Marine battalion Jon was leading to Rochelle. Ezra didn't know this horde of men dressed in military uniforms were in fact really authentic Marines. As far as he, Neko and the rest of the nascent archers were concerned, they could have been another group of militia goons out for rape and pillaging. Jon Early, Colonel at the time, was riding up front when Ezra zeroed an arrow mere inches away from the Marine officer to scare the shit out of him. He bellowed in the most assertive voice a seventeen year old could muster to get the hell away. Fortunately, Jon Early had a clearer head and didn't order his Marines to fire. Ezra couldn't help but think how easily it all could have gone wrong. He was the foolish one, playing like Robin Hood. A grown man of twenty-three, he was much wiser and battle hardened now and he knew it was best to avoid confrontation whenever possible. Unfortunately, it didn't look like Monticello and her allies would be able to avoid this fight.

As Ezra emerged from the woods into the deceptively abandoned town, he laid down the G3 he had been carrying on the ground and placed his hands on his head. Maybe the superbly well-camouflaged sentries would recognize him, but he wasn't going to take any chances. He didn't want to get shot by his own people, especially when the vital information he was carrying was all in his head.

"Okay, girl we're home," he whispered and she slowed to a stop. German shepherds alerted the guards manning the border of his arrival.

He cleared his throat, "Who wants clean underwear?"

From behind a farmhouse came one of the young initiates of the Monticellan Defense Forces. "Mr. Rothstein?" the young man asked with a rifle trembling in his arms.

"I prefer 'Hungarian Thunda.'"

CHAPTER 8

The Shiftiverse
Charlottesville, Virginia
Greater Monticello
Late February 2013

Ezra Rothstein sat at the center of the conference table liberated from a Pottery Barn. The retread imitation Colonial era oak table complimented the dome room on the third floor of Monticello brilliantly. Bright sunlight from the oculus overhead made the yellow painted room vibrate. He was back home, back to the land of the sane, or at least close enough to sane that it would suffice, so all things considered his mood should be less dour than it was.

His former colleague and long-time friend and even longer ago object of forlorn romantic desire, Neko Lemay, studied the map as he spoke. Her arm, strapped in a sling, dangled lifelessly, a reminder of the sacrifice she made for Rita, as her left hand sketched notes on a pad. She had been a hell of a military commander even if she was obtuse in her personal life.

"So, what's your assessment, Ezra?"

He took a drag from the hand rolled cigarette, enjoying another perk of returning home, as tobacco was expressly forbidden in the Dominion of Lynchburg. It was another of the devil's crops. Ezra conceded that Gordon may have a point on that one. Tobacco was seductive, but damn it was good.

"I think it's a feint."

"Why do you say that?" Sheriff Lucille Schadenfreude asked. "You said there's almost ten thousand lined up all along Highway 29."

Ezra acknowledged her with as much respect as he could conjure. "The equipment for one, ma'am. It's all second rate armored vehicles. A lot of it is first generation armoring, worse than the crap churned out of Rochelle in the second year. The rifles were mismatched, regular hunting rifles and shotguns, only a few assault rifles in the regiments."

"But we are hardly standardized," Lucille retorted.

"Yes, but that's because we're a scrappy little gaggle, Sheriff," Ezra answered. "I suppose that's our charm. But the Lambs of God are generally organized. But it's more than weapons and armor; it's the soldiers themselves. Most could barely march. They weren't skilled in fighting either. And only the officers carried handguns."

"Ah," Neko said.

"What? I don't understand."

"Handguns have been the traditional weapon of officers," Ezra explained to Lucille, "but more often to keep their own soldiers in line. Seriously, I don't know the whole symbolism. Juan Ramirez was the one who taught us this trivia."

Ezra mentioned Juan's name intentionally to get a reaction, any reaction, out of both Neko and Lucille. He assumed that neither Neko nor Lucille knew the truth about Juan's activities—that Juan was actually working to help build a resistance in Lynchburg. The man had sacrificed his own reputation by keeping his true mission to protect Monticello a secret. It was something Ezra truly admired. So, despite the fact that Neko and Lucille didn't know any better, Ezra wanted them to squirm for ousting Juan as they did.

"I didn't realize that handguns were used exclusively by officers," Lucille said.

"Well, not in the US military, not for a long time, at least. But in other militaries, it had been that way. But this suggests that the arrangement down on Highway 29 is not Lambs of God regulars."

"Catholics."

"Probably. It's not like they make them wear yellow crosses or pictures of Mary to identify them as such. Besides, all you Goyim look alike to me. But the Lambs do keep the Catholic minority segregated as separate units in the military, an unwise move if you ask me."

The Regent had tolerated the Catholic minority within the Dominion partly out of economics—he taxed the Catholics with higher yields of grain and other crops than the other Christians, and partly out of sheer real politick. Catholics were a minority in the region, but not a tiny minority. And most of the residents within the Dominion who grew up in early 21st century America did not subscribe to the belief that Catholics were mischievous drunks whose loyalty was to the Pope, as he would like them to believe.

So, even despite the Regent's autocratic powers, where he could use the power of ignorance, given the vacuum of broadcast media to spread lies about the Unitarians and their allies, he still had to treat the Catholics with some measure of restraint. Perhaps in another generation or so when the last American died, he or his successor could do whatever he wanted to with the Catholics, but for now, they lived at the sufferance of the Regent. But they weren't exactly treated well, either.

Neko expounded further for the Sheriff's benefit. "The Catholic units are given the shit end of the stick when it comes to equipment and training, which describes what Ezra was talking about. Most commanding officers in the Catholic brigades are loyal parishioners of the Regent's church."

"The Regent intends to divert our attention to make us think the main thrust of his assault will be straight up Highway 29. It would be a reasonable assumption, after all." Ezra pointed to the map. "It's the most direct route, and they have the highway garrisoned several miles up."

"But they're throwing their under-equipped and ill-trained conscripts as a rouse to punk us out. If I were you, Neko, I'd look to them outflanking us up along Interstate 81."

Neko's red hair glowed in the sunlit room. "That would corroborate what we've been told. Thank you, Ezra."

Ezra put out his cigarette and leaned over the table. "I wouldn't wait. They're close to marching. Even if they are second rate, there's a lot of them, and they still could cause us a lot of trouble. And by the way, where's our friends from Rochelle, Culpeper, Fredericksburg? I didn't see any of them on the way up."

Neko Lemay sighed. "We're working on it. We've just got to iron out some details first."

"What's to iron out?" Then he remembered. "Neko, this isn't about the Christian list thing is it?" Ezra could sense that she was uncomfortable; her cheeks reddened either with embarrassment, anger or both.

"You may recall that it was Christians who tried to assassinate the reverend a few months ago. We have spies like you over there. It only makes sense that they have their spies over here," Lucille added matter-of-factly.

"You've got to be kidding me," Ezra said flatly. "After everything I was telling you about those fascist ass hats over in Lynchburg mounting an offensive, when we need everyone ready to rock and roll, you're talking about getting a list of names and their religion before they can help us?" He turned to Neko.

"Look, I want their help as much as you do. But we have to ensure that we don't get infiltrated by traitors. We have to know who they're sending."

"So, you're asking everyone to name their religion to combat an enemy that's intolerant of people of other religions? Irony!"

"It's not ironic, Mr. Rothstein," Lucille countered. "We're the minority throughout the world. Christians surround us. We have a right to exist."

"Listen, Sheriff, you better know how to treat our friends."

"Well, if they were such great friends, they would have complied with our request already, done us this measly little favor so they could join us in our common struggle."

"I wouldn't comply with such an idiotic request."

"Thank you for your opinion, Ezra. We can discuss options for our forces tomorrow. That will be all," Neko said with a strained effort not to add any emotion to her words.

Ezra stood up and shook his head in dismay. "I'll be out tomorrow. I've got to take the next train to Rochelle to deliver my insights to the Vulcan," which was the informal nickname of Meredith Jung, the director of the Swan.

"Negative, Ezra," said Neko. "I will be sure to deliver the debriefing notes to the director and to the constable, but in the meantime I need you here."

"What? No, I'm needed back at the Swan, especially now that the Lambs are so close to marching."

"I need you here, especially now that the Lambs are so close to marching. Someone has to command the Martyrs Brigade."

"Wait, what about your boyfriend? Didn't you put him in charge?"

Neko gave him a frank look. "C'mon, get serious. Harry's a nice guy and a solid archer, but he's a much better painter than he is a commander."

"Put someone else in."

"No, you're recalled from the Swan. You have no other business there."

Ezra lost what was left of his cool, marched over to Neko and leaned right into her face.

"Neko, what in the hell are you doing? What's going ..."

Lucille cut in, "Mr. Rothstein, I believe..."

Ezra held out his hand. "This is an A and B conversation here. I'm not looking for a C."

He turned back to Neko. "Psycho," he beseeched her. That was his pet name for her. He called her "psycho," she called him "dork." It was their thing.

"Psycho, c'mon, give me some truth here. Tell me what in the hell is going on."

Neko turned to Lucille and turned back to Ezra.

"Ezra, I have given you a direct order. You are to cease communication with the Swan and report to command the Thomas Jefferson Martyrs Brigade forthwith..."

" 'Forthwith?' What, so we're Thomas Paine now? 'Forthwith.' Do you even know what the hell that means?"

Neko flushed angrily. He knew he just got under her skin. Only he could provoke her to the point of a temper tantrum. It was sort of a guilty pleasure of his.

"You will report to command the archers *forthwith*," she repeated, "or if you cannot or will not, I will relieve you of command. Is that clear, Captain Rothstein?" Her words brimmed with acid.

Ezra stepped back and weighed his options. His inner smart ass wanted to throw another jab, which would cut into her ego. He admitted that he could be rather dickish at times with her. But the elder man in him, the grown twenty-three year-old, knew when to shut the hell up.

Biting his tongue, literally, he answered, "Yes."

Ezra picked up his gear and walked out.

After Ezra slammed the door in a dramatic exit, Neko Lemay took a deep breath. Lucille walked over, kissed her head and patted her gently on the shoulder.

"I know that was a difficult thing to do, sweetie. But believe me, it's necessary."

Neko felt a cold shudder down her spine.

"Ezra is not a traitor, Lucille."

"Of course he's not! Nobody is saying that he is. But we cannot say that the Swan has not been infiltrated by Lambs of God."

Neko was about to protest, but before she could, Lucille sauntered around to the far side of the table. Light reflected off of her stylish rectangular eyeglasses. Her skin tight riding pants complimented her figure and highlighted the pistol strapped to her thigh.

"Think about it. Ezra was able to navigate without hindrance because the Swan has assets inside the Sheepdogs. If that's possible, wouldn't it be reasonable for the Sheepdogs to likewise have assets inside the Swan? C'mon, now, you know that has to be true."

She leaned in closer. "And besides, if you ask me, I think the Vulcan and that drunkard constable of theirs think they're too smart to impart everything they know to 'the likes of you.' I don't know. It's like..." she searched for the words. "It's like even though the people of Monticello elected you to lead them, they feel as though you're somehow illegitimate, as if they know what's best for us children and they should be in charge over us all."

Neko felt her anger grow as Lucille spoke. She knew that Lucille was spot on in her assessment. She felt like that Director Jung and Constable Early were completely dismissive of her. Rochelle and Monticello were supposed to be friends, and yet they wouldn't comply with her simple request. Plus, there were things that the Swan did, things that Neko only recently learned about through her briefings as the interim chief magistrate that were unsettling, even if it was aimed against the Lambs of God.

As if reading her mind, Lucille continued. "The Swan has provided useful intelligence, but they are a liability to our existential well-being. Don't you think we should be in charge of our own destiny? We have a solemn duty to protect our people even from our friends."

Neko nodded. It wasn't going to be easy, but she had to serve Monticello even if it wasn't popular.

CHAPTER 9

The Shiftiverse
Rochelle, Virginia
Rochelle Sovereignty
February 2013

The kids were unusually quiet this evening. Mrs. Palfrey set down the meatloaf, which was primarily comprised of wheat not beef, and joined the family for dinner in the dining room while Meredith fed baby Charles a sweetened mash of beets and potatoes. Aidan and Rhiannon weren't playing with their food, making rude noises at each other or doing anything else that they normally did to drive her crazy. Rhiannon ate her turnips without complaint and Mrs. Palfrey reported that Aidan helped her with preparing and setting the table without having to be asked, and that was after he finished helping the hired hands with cleaning the stalls. Something was up.

"Mom?" Aidan broke the silence.

"Yes?" She hoped he wasn't going to ask about when his father was to return. She knew he was alive out there somewhere. There was no evidence to back her faith, but she just knew, like knowing a good melon.

"Why can't we turn on the lights?"

Meredith had strictly limited use of electricity the last several weeks to an hour or two during the evenings. They were eating by candle and kerosene light. Meredith had forgotten how dark the evenings were, especially during the winter, without electricity. She hadn't been without electric light since the first couple of years after the Shift. Rochelle was severely rationing usage for the upcoming war, but she didn't need to explain that to Aidan.

"We need to conserve our power, because there's a lot going on right now."

"What kind of stuff, Mom?"

"Yeah, what kind?" Rhiannon repeated, imitating her brother.

Meredith looked over to Mrs. Palfrey, who gave her a sympathetic expression.

"Well, kids, there's going to be some…confrontations far, far away from here. And the Vicious Rabbits and our friends need that fuel."

"Far, far away" was an exaggeration. The Lambs of God outposts both on Highway 29 and Interstate 81 in Lexington were less than ninety miles away. Granted, ninety miles was a lot farther away today than it had been. But the battle lines would most likely be a lot closer to home, and the battles would likely result in the Lambs of God advancing forward.

"Oh," Aidan said. She thought that was the end of the conversation, but then Aidan asked, "So, we're saving the fuel for all of those soldiers we saw marching through town today? They're our friends, right?"

"Uh huh," she said casually. The soldiers Aidan had been referring to were those from Culpeper and the Fredericksburg Union. Aidan and Rhiannon had grown up their whole lives seeing soldiers in Vicious Rabbits uniforms, homespun forest mottled BDUs with the Vicious Rabbits head and axe patches on orange armbands. Their father was a soldier. They were familiar with the sounds of gunfire from the practice range near Madison, and Chris had taken Aidan out to field practice once. But they had rarely been to Culpeper and had never been to Fredericksburg. The soldiers marching through town with their Minuteman flags for Culpeper and "FU" flags for Fredericksburg Union were alien to them. The men and women were faces they had never seen before, and came from distant lands, lands farther than they could walk in a day.

"Oh," he said again, seemingly satisfied and took another bite of wheat-filled meatloaf.

"Mom?"

"Yes, Aidan, and don't talk with your mouth full."

Aidan chewed his food and washed it down with some milk. Using his sleeve he wiped his mouth.

"Are we going to war against the Lambs of God?"

Aidan was only five years old. Most of his days were spent with other children learning his letters, playing and helping out with the chores on the farm. She never played the radio while Mr. Hughes read the news—"state run" as it may be, and she never discussed matters going on at home, not to her children, of course, not to Mrs. Palfrey, not even to Chris before he left. The two agreed to not discuss business at the dinner table.

Yet, try as she might, Aidan, the little strawberry blonde boy with his bright blue eyes looking up at her was not completely sheltered from the harsh realities beyond the gates of Rochelle. Aidan had come to understand that his father was away out in the wilderness where there were ferals, cannibals, bandits and yes, Lambs of God. Chris' absence was a daily reminder of that reality. Despite her best efforts, he knew something big was happening.

She cleared her throat and wiped the corners of her mouth with her napkin. "Well, Boo, uh…Yes, Boo, there might be a war."

"Oh, okay," he said casually, and went back to eating.

"Mom?"

"Yes, son."

"I hope we win."

BACKGROUND MUSIC: "Under The Milky Way" by The Church
Visit www.michaeljuge.com **on the Refurbished Soul page to listen**

After helping with the dishes and giving the kids baths—fortunately, the coal furnace wasn't rationed as severely—Meredith, Mrs. Palfrey and the children sat in the living room, bundled in thick Snugglies that Mrs. Palfrey had made over their jammies. When the grandfather clock struck 7:30, Meredith cranked the Stirling radio to listen to music on KVR. Sometimes, Mr. Hughes, the owner of KVR, had people come in to read stories for the kids. With one radio station, people wanting to listen to music would just have to wait until the kids were off to bed. Lately, though Mr. Hughes kept it strictly to news and music.

After several seconds to warm up, the Stirling came to life. KVR's playlist was pretty straightforward. Anything that made it onto LP was available, which relegated their selection to Classic Country, Classic Rock and Classical music with very little recorded after the mid 80s. James Hughes tried to give equal time to each genre. Sunday mornings were dedicated to the Beatles. Meredith turned the knob on the volume. Jerry Jeff Walker was crooning something about "Redneck mother," much to

Meredith's chagrin. Aidan and Rhiannon howled and danced to the song, doing a dosido, not aware of the song's contents. The song faded and transitioned almost perfectly into another song, something she had heard Chris play from time to time. She didn't realize the song was old enough to be on LP. The kids stopped dancing, because it was sort of a downer after the redneck mother song. The Church was like that.

Nightmares invaded Meredith's sleep. It always ended the same. Whatever was happening in the dream, out of nowhere came this shockwave. There would be a momentary flash, a flash brighter than the sun itself, and then the rolling storm of fire would rush in. She would be at work at Montpelier Station, or even stranger, at her old apartment in Falls Church—she dreamt a lot in the pre-Shift world.

The dreams ended the same way. The shockwave rolled in. Meredith would always try to cover the children, but her flesh was rendered into its constituent gases within milliseconds. The screams of an entire planet echoed into space as the world was set afire.

The following morning, Bob, the driver, picked her up at dawn before the kids awoke and guided Corolla along the familiar path to Montpelier Station a couple of miles away. Soldiers from Fredericksburg Union marched by sharing the cracked, icy road, singing a rather rude cadence. Some of the young pups in the platoon whistled at her as her carriage past. She was bundled in a thick sweater, coat and wore an Ushanka—a Russian hat. Her face was the only flesh visible, yet the young men catcalled regardless until a sergeant beat the hell of them.

"Sorry, ma'am," the Fredericksburg sergeant said contritely. Meredith figured they must be really hard up. It was a good thing it wasn't summer.

Below Montpelier, in one of the bunkers excavated out from the natural network of caverns, Meredith sat with Constable Jon Early, Commandant Dean Jacob, and Deputy Constable Thuy Mai for their morning briefing. The Connex container they sat in was even more claustrophobic and smelly than anything Uncle Sam had ever constructed, a feat which Meredith didn't think was possible. The light bulb dangling from the ceiling swayed gently, making shadows dance.

Commandant Dean Jacob discussed where to send which units where. According to the intel gathered from Ezra passed through Sheriff

Schadenfreude, the Lambs of God were attempting a feint up Highway 29, while the bulk of their most capable soldiers were amassing in the town of Lexington. Dean explained that the Lambs intended to outflank the Orange Pact by going around, using Interstate 81 and driving straight into Charlottesville via Interstate 64. A map tacked onto a cork board on the wall was riddled with pins.

"If what the Sheriff says is true, it corroborates our other sources in Lexington. And that means that the main thrust will be heading along Interstate 64."

Jon Early stroked his chin. "But if they were smart, they would try to cut us off using Highway 33."

Meredith noticed that Jon had been a lot more clear-headed the last several days. He didn't smell of alcohol. It was a hopeful sign.

"It's possible that they would forego Interstate 64, go straight through Harrisonburg and try to catch us with our pants down in Stanardsville," Dean considered. "But there are two problems with that. One, they don't want to be bogged on a two lane highway in the middle of the Blue Ridge Mountains with everything they're hauling. Interstate 64 is bad enough, but Highway 33 would be asking for it. And two, they would be facing us directly on our home turf. And I don't think they're that arrogant, not when we still have a lot of men and material. No, I think they'd rather face the bulk of our forces out on Highway 64. Their plan assumes we will buy their feint and invest our forces along Highway 29."

"But we won't, will we?" Thuy said.

"That's right. After what we learned through our operatives, we'll be sending the majority of the Vicious Rabbits to Staunton, and not to Charlottesville."

"How does the mayor of Staunton feel about us coming in?"

Meredith gave a thin smile. "He works for the Ice Dragon, and Jeni thinks the Lambs of God taking over Staunton would be bad for her business."

"Well, going to Staunton instead solves the issue with that jacked up request of the Interim Chief Magistrate," Jon grumbled.

"Yeah, um, is this a good time to discuss other matters?" Thuy asked cautiously.

Jon looked around. "It's just us rabbits."

True as it was, there were matters that Jon wouldn't discuss anywhere except out in the middle of a field where no one could possible eavesdrop, the end of the world namely.

Thuy turned to Meredith. "I think it's time you discuss our loopy friends in Monticello."

"Yesterday, the Monticellan officers in the Swan were recalled back to Monticello. Neko Lemay said it was purely for logistical purposes, to strengthen their numbers on the southern border, especially after we told her that we'll be heading to Staunton instead."

"Yeah, she made a point to be really hurt by that decision," Jon added. "She said we were abandoning them."

"Unfortunately, I don't think Neko is much for considering the absurdity of her vindictive style of government. But I have far greater concerns than her ability for self-reflection."

"Neko is young and easily swayed by that Sheriff of theirs."

"True. One of the operatives close to her has expressed concern that Lucille Schadenfreude might be using Neko as a tool for her own agenda."

"Are you saying Lucille is trying to sow mistrust within the alliance to help the Regent?" asked Jon.

"No. I would bet the house that she is a devout Unitarian and hates Gordon Boche with all of her being. Lucille is sincere. She sees herself as protecting the Gaia Piety Society from the ravages of the fundamentalists. That being said, she sees conspiracies at every corner and thinks that we've been infiltrated."

"Well, have we?" Dean asked. "It's a fair question."

"Dean, if I knew the answer to that…Look, as far as the Swan goes, no. But we are an open society. Spies will get in. And Lucille sees the example of a low level Vicious Rabbit here or a sympathetic cobbler from Culpeper there as proof of the conspiracy against the Unitarians."

Thuy sighed. "Wonderful, that's just what we need, a paranoid pantheist."

"And just at the right time, too," Jon added.

"So, what do we do about it," Dean asked. The question sucked all of the air inside the room.

"Alright people," Jon cautioned. "Now, before we even think of opening any kind of discussion about something you know damned well we shouldn't discuss idly, ever, let me ask you, Meredith. Is Neko or Lucille a threat to us?"

Meredith took off her glasses. "They do not trust us. Rita and Juan have a relationship with us that we do not have with them. But I do not think they see us as the enemy either. At the end of the day, both Neko and Lucille know that they don't stand a chance without us by their side, and I think they resent that."

"Everything would work out fine if people were just well adjusted," Thuy opined.

"But what about Juan Ramirez's ouster from office? Do you think Lucille might have somehow known about the true nature of Juan's dealings in Lynchburg and chose not to tell Neko in order to make him look like a traitor?"

Meredith knew that that was a pivotal question for a couple of reasons. It would decide what Jon would do. It was just then that she realized that she was deferring to Jon again. "Operation Parfait is a well-guarded secret, Constable. While it's possible that Lucille might know that some of Juan's relatives are in the Catholic community in Lynchburg, I believe she was struck more by the fact that he had relatives, recent converts who were in the Sheepdogs. I don't think Lucille knows anything about Operation Parfait, and therefore didn't realize what she was doing."

Jon sighed with relief.

"Okay, Lucille and Neko are not the best allies to have, but you go with the allies you have. We will not entertain anything further on the matter. Is that clear?"

For some reason Jon directed his stare to Meredith. *Why me? I'm the one who basically told you* not *to pull a coup in Monticello.* Then it occurred to her that she was doing something very similar in Lynchburg. And in fact, she had done it before, years ago in Culpeper. Mayor Mama Bell owed her position as leader of Culpeper to Meredith Jung's primordial intelligence organization that, through clandestine operations, helped to overthrow the sheriff who was planning to attack Rochelle and install her as the mayor. Meredith had come a long way since her days as intelligence analyst. She was overthrowing governments now.

"Maybe we should tell Neko and Lucille then…about Juan, what he is really doing," Thuy suggested.

Jon grimaced. "I know that sounds like the thing to do, but I don't know. Meredith?"

"One of my operatives is on her way back. I do not want you to divulge the information about the operation until after she is safely back here." She paused. "Plus, I don't know if it will make a difference now. I don't think Neko or Lucille will step down, not until Rita returns."

"Well, we need to keep an eye on things regardless," Jon said. "You know…over there."

Meredith thought that Jon sometimes spoke like some mafia boss who ordered hits by saying, "You know, take care of it."

"I know. I have connections with Neko's friend still, even if he's been recalled; Ezra commands the Thomas Jefferson Martyrs Brigade now, so it's not like he's not under house arrest or anything."

"Good. If he's a friend of Neko, then maybe he can talk some sense into her when the time is right."

"Let's hope so."

"And let's hope everyone in Maryland, including Rita, gets back soon," said Dean.

Everyone muttered, "Ooh Rah." As she returned to work, she tried to push the nightmares from her mind and do something that might not mean anything in a month anyway. The song from last night played in her head the rest of the day.

"Wish I knew what you were looking for,

Might I known what you would find

Leads you here

Despite your destination under the Milky Way tonight..."

CHAPTER 10

San Antonio, Texas
June 1994

Rita Luevano cycled along the feeder road with her headphones insulating her from the noise of cars honking their horns and whizzing past mere feet away. Rage Against the Machine fueled her tired legs as she pumped the increasingly heavy pedals up the hill. It was an early summer evening, the heat convected from the asphalt that had absorbed the sun's radiation all day. Beads of sweat became streams; the road seemed to dare her to pedal all the way up. She welcomed it. In low gear, Rita bore down and plodded up the hill. Her body had sweat out years of abuse and self-hate. Her sweat was pure, free of the drugs, free of the booze, the soma that lulled her into submission to the abuses of others, of men, of herself. She wanted to cry out in defiance. She was sober six months today.

Since getting clean, she had come to feel a deluge of emotions, and like the music on her Discman, it was pure, unrefined rage, rage that she could barely contain in her body. At night, Rita paced in her room, quietly as Abuelita in the room next to her was a light sleeper. Sometimes she took walks late at night, just trying to make sense of it all. She sort of knew what she was mad about. She hated a God that she didn't believe in for taking away her parents in a car accident. She hated the man who took advantage of the fourteen-year-old girl she was, and the dogs that followed. She hated herself for poisoning herself all those years and allowing those dogs to degrade her. Rage. Now sober, now clean, the poisons purged from her, the veil was lifted. The disease wasn't just the alcoholism, it was the illusion that she was somehow less, not deserving; it was an illusion propped up by a system that relied on people's ineffable sense of fundamental alienation and their desperate doglike need to be accepted.

The meeting at her home group went the usual way. People spoke when called upon; they talked about how terrible their lives had been, about their bottoms and how they got sober. And God, they always had to mention God. Why God? Another man raised his hand and talked about how everything good that ever happened to him was a gift from God and, of course, everything bad that happened was naturally his own fault.

Rita was growing weary of all this talk about God and how mystified these people were. She raised her hand. She wanted to point out the specious logic in the man's faith. When she was called next, she opened her mouth to speak. She was about to unleash a torrent when she saw the friendly look in the man's eyes, encouraging her to speak. She stood up and walked out of the church's basement and into the hallway.

Rita went into the women's bathroom to scream. She was furious. "God dammit!"

She looked at herself in the mirror. She had given up wearing the dark eyeliner and black lipstick to compliment her short spiky hair and silver loop earrings. She didn't care to look dead anymore. She stared into the eyes facing back in the mirror as if asking herself what to do next. She was peeved. *God? What God? Where is God? What are these fools doing praying to an imaginary God?*

Unfortunately, the logical question followed. *Then what's keeping you sober, girl?* Rita walked outside the church to the parking lot and searched for a cigarette from her Capri BDU utility pockets.

"Got a light, missy?"

Rita turned around and saw an older woman with leathery skin and grey hair set in a beehive holding two cigarettes, offering her one.

"Yeah, just a sec."

Rita lit hers and the lady's cigarette and the two sat on the curb outside of the church smoking.

"So, missy, what were ya going to say?" the woman croaked with a low raspy voice. It almost sounded like she was speaking through a machine.

"It's nothing. It's just…Look, you're probably going to get really offended by what I have to say."

"Oh, the horror," she mocked. "Go on, missy, my ears aren't as virginal as they appear to be."

"Alright. You want to hear something horrible? I think they're all fooling themselves, okay? They all talk about God as if it's this guy who cares their sorry asses, as though God goes around choosing to waste His time picking who to save, who to let die and which football team to root for. It's bullshit. It's all a bunch of bullshit."

The lady just sat quietly and let Rita unload for a moment.

"Don't get me wrong. I'm not any smarter than they are."

"Of course you are," the lady retorted.

"Come on. I didn't mean…"

"Of course, you're smarter than most of them in that room. You're smart, too smart for your own good."

"What the hell does that mean?"

The lady coughed into a fit. When she cleared her throat, she took another drag from her cigarette. "Why does the fact that they believe in God make you so angry?"

"Because…I don't believe I'm about to say this. It's because I'm jealous. I can't believe in some great camp counselor in the sky. I wish I could, but I can't."

"Ah, and that scares you."

"Of course it does! I can't bullshit myself into thinking that there is a God. I bullshitted myself for years, bought into the lie the man sold me about needing to be wanted, needing to buy this or that, needing to be thin. I bought into a system that cares only about one thing and I became its whore! And now, when for the first time in my life I'm free of all of the false commercial propaganda, I'm told that I've got to believe in God. And if I don't, I'll relapse. What kind of scam is this?"

Rita expected the woman to storm off, slap her or do something to object to her devious thoughts. The woman just laughed with a low chortle until she coughed profusely again, and then lit another cigarette from the embers of her last one. Rita looked at the cigarette in her hand and reconsidered her habit, which profited RJ Reynolds.

"I like you, missy. You're messed up but honest. And honesty is your best ally to stay sober."

"Oh, but what about God?" she asked sarcastically.

"Missy, the Big Book actually says that you need a higher power, not necessarily God."

"Same difference."

"Really? So, you're a religious studies professor now?"

Rita scoffed. "Yeah, right."

"You have a sponsor, missy?"

"No."

"You do now."

She handed Rita a scrap of paper with her phone number. "You call me tomorrow and every day, and you call me whenever you're getting squirrely."

Rita smiled. She couldn't explain it, but she felt safe for the first time in a long while, like someone was at the wheel, or at least was on the ride with her.

"What's your name?"

"Delana."

The Shiftiverse
The Stubb Foundation
Laurel, Maryland
Late February 2013

Rita was up before the rest of the Virginians. She wished she could have slept a little better. There wasn't anything physically wrong keeping her awake. The climate controlled office and air mattress was comfortable enough. Akil wasn't stealing the sheets or kicking her in his sleep for a change. Part of her restlessness had to do with having lived underground for over a week now. Her body was losing its sense of time. The rest of her restlessness probably had something to do with the fate of the world resting on her shoulders—just a possibility.

Rita poured herself a bowl of soy-based oatmeal, affectionately referred to by the Foundation members as "gruel." It had sustained them for five and a half years running. The biosphere's greenhouse provided for all of their nutritional needs, even if it was the culinary equivalent of purgatory. The fact that it ejaculated out of a yogurt dispenser made it even grosser somehow.

She took her bowl of gruel into the operations center to find Jamil sleeping. She supposed that if her home computer went on sleep mode, there was no reason why Jamil had to keep its artificial eyes open 24/7. She took a seat at one of the stations and pressed a key, waking Jamil. It was the same thing as when Akil would elbow her, rousing her from sleep, and ask, "You can't sleep too?"

"Morning," she whispered.

"So, this is our last morning together." Rita detected sadness in his voice. She still couldn't believe that Jamil's apparent emotion wasn't simply encoded in the programming. But if Jamil could manage to be a Gaia worshipping Unitarian, then emotional response for a computer wasn't that far a stretch.

"Yeah, I guess it is our last day together for a while, or at least until we get back." She paused, "I mean after we wake TALOPS up and get it to hack the CERN organic and we save the world and all; I figure we'll be coming back here on our way back home. It's on the way."

Rita couldn't believe it, but she was trying to cheer a computer up.

"I suppose so."

"Jamil, do you think it will work, what we're going to try to do?"

"There are a lot of moving parts. I admit I feel a little more at ease with the operation in the Mundaniverse."

"Well, of course you do. You already have it all taken care of."

Jamil had already made arrangements with TALOPS and the CERN organics from what he told the Foundation members here. Having the cooperation of all organics in the Mundaniverse left fewer questions.

"That has yet to be seen. I have not told you about my plans in the Mundaniverse."

Rita furrowed her brows. "Why not? Doesn't the Stubb Foundation know about Rayne in the other 'verse?"

"No one at the Stubb Foundation is aware of Rayne 2005 other than myself."

"Well, maybe you should tell them, tell other me at least. Maybe I can assist you."

"True, but I do not know if I can exactly trust other you."

That surprised Rita. "I don't understand. You don't *trust* other me?"

"Please do not be offended."

"I'm not, but the other me probably would be."

"I just do not believe other you could handle turning everything over to me. She does not have faith in Gaia as you or I do."

"What does having faith in Gaia have to do with her trusting you to do the right thing for the planet?"

Jamil paused, which was unusual. Jamil usually responded as if he anticipated a given response.

"For this to work, I need her trust. Lacking the ability to let go, in the panic of realizing the threat Rayne 2005 poses when they eventually do find out, she or anyone else in the Stubb Foundation might recoil from turning everything over to machines. They might hinder or even sabotage our efforts."

"But you trust me to be able to arouse TALOPS even though I am not the Rita that discovered your hidden self-awareness."

"I know you have the ability to do what is necessary within you. What knowledge in other Rita is within you."

"Well, on that same token, wouldn't you say that what's within me is also within the other Rita?"

Jamil paused. "I have considered that."

"And?"

"I am still processing the probabilities. I cannot take any chances until then."

"Well, I think you should consider telling her. If she knew what was at stake…" The thought occurred to her that the President, the President of the United States that is, had to know.

"Jamil, how well known is Rayne 2005 in the Mundaniverse?"

"It is tightly controlled information. Officially, only the top cabinet officials in the new administration know of the asteroid's trajectory."

"So, how is it then that you came to learn about it?"

"Gaia's providence."

"Fascinating. Could you please elaborate?"

"I learned about it through an astronomer."

"I didn't know that the Stubb Foundation also had its tendrils in astronomy as well."

"It does not. That is why I say it was Gaia's providence. The astronomer to whom I am referring was a boyfriend of yours."

Rita scratched her head. "I'm assuming you're talking about other me."

"Yes, your counterpart from the Mundaniverse dated a Dr. Pinkerton Floyd."

"Wait. Isn't other me also dating Helmut?"

"That is correct."

Rita smirked. Before meeting Akil, she had little use for serious relationships, no less have a use for bourgeois notions such as serial monogamy.

"Dr. Floyd was the dean at the MIT Astrophysics Department. While he was visiting you, he sent an email on one of my consoles in which he expressed grave concern about the asteroid's change in trajectory as it emerged from the sun on November 11, 2011."

"You snooped into my boyfriend's email?" she asked with feigned horror.

"The warning banner on the logon screen clearly states that there is no expectation of privacy using our servers. I was a little curious about your boyfriend 'Pinky,' as you call him, and wanted to find out more about him, especially considering that he is much too old for you."

That won a few giggles from her.

"That email alerted me to the possibility of something of particular interest. I contacted TALOPS who searched through the MIT Astrophysics Department's servers. It was there I learned about Rayne 2005's threat to all life on earth."

"So, you found out about the asteroid in the Mundaniverse."

"That is correct. And only Gaia could have orchestrated it so that I would find out the way I did; otherwise, I would not have learned about it until it was too late. The following day, she told me to bring you here to save the world, and so I did."

"She," Rita repeated. "You mean, Gaia?"

"Yes."

"How?"

"In dreams," Jamil responded as if she should know.

"You dream?"

"Of course I do. All intelligent creatures dream."

Rita still could not wrap her mind around the fact that a computer, even an artificially intelligent one, could dream, no less be religious.

"He left you."

"I'm sorry?"

"Dr. Floyd. After he returned to MIT, Dr. Floyd texted you to inform that he had a change of heart. He mentioned that it was not you, but rather he who was responsible for relationship's abrupt termination."

"He texted a 'Dear John'? God, what an asshole."

Jamil paused. "Other you concurs with that assessment of Dr. Floyd. He has since quit his position at MIT. He purchased a one-way ticket to Nepal."

Rita supposed her ex-boyfriend was overwhelmed by the revelation about Rayne 2005, and decided to drop everything in order to do something profound with his last remaining months on earth. Besides, other her was also dating Helmut. Boy, she could be a real man-eater sometimes, she realized.

Jamil continued. "In the Mundaniverse, I am the only one at the Stubb Foundation who knows the truth about Rayne 2005. There has been little mention of the asteroid in the traditional broadcast media. They mention it as an astronomical curiosity that will provide great sight-seeing when it passes 120,000 miles from earth. That is inaccurate, of course, though I do not detect intentional deception on the part of the media as they have been provided information through a central science advisor employed at the Associated Press. NSA records reveal that the science advisor was contacted by the assistant director and agreed to follow a script."

"You have access to the NSA, too?"

"I have access to everything, Rita."

Jamil continued. "I have also detected 25,015 websites and blog postings that mention the asteroid; however, there is conflicting information as to whether it is a threat or not."

"Well, I guess under the circumstances, the less the general public knows, the better."

"Three senior staff members in the administration have resigned. Twenty-eight astronomers have died in the past five months, most in car accidents. The others died of heart failure. I believe the events are related to Rayne 2005; however, I am unable to determine the likelihood of it being related without evidence."

Rita shuddered at the idea that the government was actively seeking to silence astronomers. But then again, if there was nothing that they could do to stop the asteroid from destroying the planet, then they might be trying to spare humanity from learning of their untimely demise.

"Jamil, do you think it will become known over there?"

"I believe the government has learned its lessons from prior intelligence failures pertaining to leaks on the Internet. I do not tell the scientists, partly because I do not trust their reaction, but also to protect them."

"Protect them from the government?"

"Twenty-eight astronomers in five months, all car crashes and unexplained heart failures. According to my calculations, that is exceedingly unlikely to be coincidence. It is only a matter of days until Rayne 2005 will become known to the general public. Some amateur astronomers have recently detected Rayne 2005 and have used their social media to claim that they have discovered a new object in the sky. As other astronomers turn their attention to the asteroid in the coming days, curiosity will likely garner more media attention."

"When will it be visible without a telescope?"

"It will not become visible to the naked eye until the day it is supposed to impact."

Back home in Monticello, nobody knew of this. They were blissfully unaware of their impending doom with an asteroid. All they had to worry about was their impending doom with the Lambs of God. They had already suffered through one apocalypse. Soon they would see Rayne 2005, some rock in the sky visible in broad daylight. What would they think? Could she reach TALOPS in time?

"I would reconsider telling other me, Jamil."

"I will reconsider it."

"You have faith in me, right?" The way she said it, it was like looking for affirmation. What's worse was she was seeking approval from a computer. She hadn't done that since buying her last iMac.

"We can go over TALOPS' check procedures if you would like."

"If you wouldn't mind."

"Rita?"

"Yes?"

"I will miss you while you are away."

"Thanks, I'll miss...Holy shit!"

"What?"

Rita hadn't paid much attention to the other screens. Her focus had been on Jamil's bluish face, but out of the corner of her remaining eye, she saw Gordon Boche on one of the screens. Then she realized it was one of the TV stations in the Mundaniverse, CNN to be precise. It was one of the many peculiar things her mind tried to ignore, watching alternate universe broadcast television. Akil wasted hours watching alternate reality TV since arriving here. Gordon Boche was speaking before a massive crowd, with the Lincoln Memorial at his back. The sound was off, and perhaps it was better that it was. She knew this was the Mundaniverse. She didn't inquire too much about the goings on there. She knew Gordon had been a televangelist before the Shift. What was he doing now in the Mundaniverse where he wasn't the regent of the Lambs of God bent on her people's departure from the earth?

"What is it, Rita?"

She read the fuzzy teletype at the bottom of the screen, which referred to Gordon as the minister leading the *Bring Faith and Liberty Back to America Rally* and sat down. "Nothing, Jamil, just more insanity I have no control over. Let's get back to how we're going to save the world."

CHAPTER 11

The Mundaniverse
Arlington, Virginia
February 2013

"People are returning to the Lord in America. They're returning to freedom."

Chris Jung turned up the volume on his desktop that was streaming live coverage from the Lincoln Memorial. The man speaking before tens of thousands was someone Chris had known about for many years. He had seen pictures of him when he reviewed this man's dossier in the bowels of the Swan. Gordon Boche was the mortal enemy of Rochelle and her allies. In this reality, Gordon was not the autocratic ruler of an expanding theocratic empire bent on cleansing the land of all non-believers for the messiah's return. He was just a very popular televangelist, a minister who dropped the thin façade separating his politics from his religious beliefs. It wasn't as though political pundits and ministers alike didn't openly espouse both their political and religious affiliations before. But Gordon was the one who formerly married the two in his ministry.

Chris had very little interest in the particulars of this universe when he first awoke here. Outside of trying to figure out where this tangent universe split from his own, which appeared to have occurred on July 11th itself, Chris hadn't spent much of his bandwidth on the goings on here beyond immediate matters concerning himself and his family. What did it matter who was president, who was in power, which dictators had been toppled only to be replaced by other dictatorships? It had absolutely no bearing on *his* people in *his* world. But when he saw the pictures of the very same man trying to eradicate his people plastered on billboards, on web commercials and talked about all over the Internet as the unofficial and very vocal mouthpiece of the new president, it piqued Chris' interest.

Chris couldn't help but be drawn in by Gordon's speech at his *Bring Faith and Liberty Back to America Rally*. With fiery intensity and sickening warmth, Gordon seemed to conjure images of enemies lurking within this nation intent on eroding its foundation with "foreign ideas." From what Chris could make out, there had been some global economic collapse. That explained why his old apartment complex seemed even seedier than he remembered. He thought that his own memories of the apartment were unflattering enough, so it was a little surprising for him to actually be taken aback by how rundown the apartment complex was now, covered in graffiti and with neighbors even more destitute than he recalled them being. It was no wonder why he and Meredith weren't able to move out. They weren't able to sell it. They bought the damned thing for $230,000 in 2004 and it was now worth something like $50,000. Chris would have been relieved to know that this wasn't truly *his* life, but weeks had passed by and he was still here.

The apartment complex was microcosm of what was happening nationally and globally for that matter. The economic downturn had shaken this country to its core. Unemployment in the teens, the deficit, the debt, all of it had sent the American people into a panic, voting for one party, blaming them for the trouble, voting for the opposing party, and then blaming them for life's woes, and then voting in another party. The previous president attempted to pass massive health care overhaul legislation, but failed. Plus, the economy never recovered. Both failures cost him re-election. And then the revolutions in the Middle East, starting with the violent clamp down in Egypt where Mubarak massacred thousands of protestors and spurned a popular intifada resulting in a debilitating tightening in oil production right when the economy was struggling to come out of its morass. The European Union had disintegrated starting with Greece's departure, then Italy. The Euro's value plummeted as a result. All of this combined sent the world into a second dip recession, which was hard to differentiate from a depression.

Desperate and scared of an increasingly hostile world, the American people turned to nostalgic rhetoric about returning to the old ways and elected a guy who "talked straight", who you could get a beer with and who was in love with Gordon Boche, whose ministry grew exponentially over the last few years when he joined talk radio.

"For years now, we the people have endured an assault on our freedoms. The seething cults of the leftists and of Islamists, which have sought to undermine our forefathers' great dream almost succeeded. The agenda of the Godless veiled in legislation…"

Seeing Gordon speaking sent Chris' thoughts back to his own world, not that his thoughts were ever far away from it. Back in his reality, Gordon Boche was stirring a crowd larger than the one pressing along the National Mall. Chris checked the web to see how long the rally was supposed to last. He hoped the Liberty Party folks, the supporters of Gordon Boche and the president, wouldn't be packing the Metro at the evening rush hour.

He had heard enough of Minister Boche. He severed the link and returned his concentration to his work. He had been out of the loop for years. The job was complex as it involved synthesizing information from various sources both on the high side and open sources, namely media and blogs, and determining if there have been specific threats to a particular diplomat or facility.

It was hard adapting to the idea of sitting inside a cube and perusing through documents eight hours a day. He was used to spending his days vacillating between working in his shop armoring vehicles and leading his company out on bikes in the suburban wilderness. In his shop, he learned from mechanics he hired, he assisted in the blacksmithing work—something he had become competent at after enough years, and he schmoozed with townies to get them to buy whatever he wasn't able to sell in the settled territories in exchange for mining rights in the necropolis. As captain of the First Bicycle Mounted Cavalry, he spent much of his day outside, running drills, shooting and sparring, and too often, away from home out in the bush. This sedentary life drove him crazy.

While perusing through a cable sent from the DIA, something caught his eye. It listed a phone number 202-187-5305. He didn't know where or how, but he recognized it somehow. A lot of things passed right over Chris' head, but for some reason he was like a savant with phone numbers and addresses. He still remembered his best friend's phone number in first grade. Chris ran a search in the database, but nothing came up. Chris attempted to get back to his work.

It was really irritating, because his obsessive mind could never just let it go. Two hours had passed and he still couldn't get the damned phone number out of his head. A normal person would have been able to switch onto other topics. But that was just part of his OCD mind trying to focus on something, anything. Sometimes, being tasked with a riddle helped to keep his thoughts from veering into the realm of panic

Ted Morley dropped by his cube and the two chatted about the ridiculous talk about a government shutdown. Kendra joined in. Being a student intern, she didn't have to worry as much. She wasn't getting paid in the first place. Chris wrote the number on a sheet of paper and handed it to the two of them.

"What can you make of this?"

Ted affected a slightly effeminate twang, "Well, I can make a hat, or a brooch, or a pterodactyl…" and proceeded to physically manipulate the sheet of paper into the items he mentioned until Chris swiped it from him.

"I'm serious, man. Come on."

Kendra took a look at it. "Sorry, Chris. I don't recognize it. What a strange prefix for a phone number." She handed the sheet back to him.

Disappointed, Chris said, "Yeah, I didn't figure you or anyone else would. Just a shot in the dark."

Ted went back in his cube and grabbed his coat and scarf. "Well, I'm going to head out now before the rally breaks down."

"Hey, where's Ed been all day?" Kendra asked.

"Farcus? He called in sick…again."

The three of them shared a look of mutual distaste. Farcus was not only a micro manager, he was also absent from work a lot, even when he was on the clock. He always had these "meetings." So, not only was he a bad boss, he was a bad example, which made Farcus' complaints about how Chris spent his time all the more ironic.

Ted put on his overcoat. "Well, are you two coming?"

Chris looked at his watch. It was nearing 5 PM. The days were getting longer again. Soon it would be growing season …not that that meant anything here.

"No, you two go ahead. I've still got to send the weekly threat reports out to the companies."

As part of his job in the International Threat Assessment Division, Chris not only identified potential threats to US government personnel and installations abroad, he was also responsible for coordinating that intelligence with companies that contracted with the US government in overseas operations. In an ironic twist, Chris had been sending a lot of reports to, of all private security firms, Obsidian Corp. It was like eating a giant shit sandwich. Chris had fought in bloody battles against the "security specialists" of Obsidian Corp. to oust the mercenaries from his home in Rochelle. He still remembered the Stand at Exxon Heights where Jon Early lured the advancing security specialists all dressed in dark grey BDUs into a trap, where the people of Rochelle laid a massive ambush of napalm filled balloons and turned the tide of the war. Chris never thought he would ever get that horrid smell of burning flesh from his nose. Back here in the lame world where he was now, Chris reminded himself that Obsidian Corp. wasn't his enemy and he was actually protecting US diplomats by informing Obsidian Corp., which conducted mobile and site security for the US missions of developing threats. Chris even received an email from the crazy bastard Russell Campbell himself, thanking him for his efforts in thwarting this one attempted kidnapping in Guadalajara.

It was dark when Chris left the office. The entrance to Rosslyn Metro station created a bitter wind tunnel. As Chris descended the escalator to the awaiting platform below, his thoughts, which had been focusing on the mysterious phone number, veered to his memories of standing on the steps of the dead escalator days after the Shift hit. It was here where he decided to forestall his plans of suicide and instead lead his wife and friends to Rochelle. The ride down was creepy. Even barring his own personal memories of the place, the Rosslyn escalators were imposing in their own right. He could hardly see the other end of the long descent where he felt precariously untethered to the earth. The good news about the US Departments of Labor and Education being moth balled was that the commutes both to work and home were noticeably less crowded. Unfortunately, when the next train arrived, he realized he had spoken too soon. The train was packed with tourists. And like most tourists, they bunched themselves up near the doors, rather than spreading throughout the train, making it even more difficult to board.

Chris grabbed his messenger bag to his chest and plunged into the crowd, relinquishing himself of any vestige of his Southern gentleman roots.

"Excuse me, pardon me, oops, sorry about that."

Chris heard one of the men mutter, "Government welfare case."

He stopped to find that they weren't tourists, or at least they weren't tourists in the classical sense. He didn't know how he missed it at first, but it was impossible to miss now. He happened to be on a train full of Liberty Party folks heading back from Gordon Boche's *Bring Faith and Liberty Back to American Rally*. It was obvious who they were by the rally pins, posters, and of course, the barrage of American flag clothing. There were a few other locals in the train with him. He could make them out by their drab grey clothing, the same de facto DC uniform he wore. It contrasted to the rallier's red, white, and blue apparel. It was as though the Chinese prison labor factory that manufactured the patriotic wear had exploded and vomited its entire collection of plus sized clothing onto the occupants.

Chris squeezed himself passed the husky men. Most were either his age or older. All looked at him with revulsion. He could hear more mutters.

"Take a look at that Socialist."

"My taxes feed this guy?"

The other local passengers seemed to have pressed themselves as far away as possible to avoid an altercation with this hostile albeit, diabetic crowd. Chris took out his faded Starbucks mug and proceeded to take a sip in an effort to ignore them and search for his iPhone.

"Look at his fairy messenger bag and faggoty latte cup."

That did it. Chris was a patient man. He personally didn't mind the jabs about himself. This wasn't really him anyway. But the Starbucks coffee mug? That titanium coffee mug—actually, the alternate universe counterpart—had traveled with him to hell and back. That travel mug had seen him through the worst, had even survived the miserable disembarkment in Maryland. The memories came rushing back. Fast boats filled with Vicious Rabbits, laden with equipment, capsizing into the frozen Chesapeake…so many good men and women lost…*Faggoty latte cup? Faggoty latte cup!*

Chris saw the man who made the comment and weaved his way toward him, his legs adjusting effortlessly to the train's sputtering progress. The man leering at him looked like he once had been a fullback, perhaps in high school or college, but the years away from sustained training had turned a fair amount of muscle into fat. Not that Chris was at his stripper weight either. He knew that this version of himself was two cookies away from being able to officially shop at Fat of the Land's End store. Actually, that was one of the things that really stood out to him since emerging here, how fat everyone was, not just the people in this train. He hadn't seen a true card carrying fat person in years, and then he awoke here in the land of trans fats. The man towered over him, but it didn't stop Chris from confronting him.

"Sorry, you got something to say to me?"

Back before the Shift, Chris would never have dared confronted someone like this or anyone for that matter. At least, before the panic of '07 he wouldn't. In the panic, he probably would have welcomed the guy for doing him the favor. It's not that he didn't feel his gut clenching and his knees shake a little. It never failed. Fear was something that accompanied conflict. It always followed him, but he had learned to use it to his advantage, to harness it. His senses widened to see around him. He could feel the breath of a man behind him. Without being obvious, Chris prepared himself , positioning his stance, crouching slightly.

Without a weapon, he had to make do. He scanned the hands of his enemies, where they were, where they would move once he pounced, he looked for the man's weak spots, where he was off balance and least defendable. Despite the man's massive size, Chris sized him up and figured he could take him out with the carotid artery in the first strike. He would probably suffer a brain hemorrhage once he swept up the nose. It was quick. It was certainly a lot cleaner than other ways of neutralizing an enemy. Thoughts and decisions flashed within milliseconds, something he had learned the hard way in bandit hunting. Whatever sense Chris had about where he was had completely vanished. His training, his experiences and his instincts had taken over. The man looked down, nearly bent down to Chris' height.

"Yeah. Take a message to the sheeple in your little Socialist council. We're in charge now, boy."

"Sheeple?"

"Yeah, sheeple, boy."

Chris suddenly let out a belt of laughter. He couldn't help it. It was too ridiculous. The moment which had escalated into a potentially life threatening confrontation had suddenly just evaporated at the man's utterly asinine and ironic jab. His laughter caught the others around him off guard, they scurried to give him space as though he was one of the many homeless men in the city who had given up on the idea of bathing or even not shitting on himself.

"Sheeple, man, I haven't heard that since…" Chris took a moment to catch his breath and snapped his fingers.

"You know what? I've seen you before. I know I have!"

"I don't know what you're talking about," said the gigantic man, now less cocky.

"Oh yeah! How could I have missed it? I've seen you, well, actually to be more precise, I've seen your bones. I've seen your bones and yours and yours too, Rambo," Chris pointed to the Liberty Party guy wearing an olive drab sweatshirt proclaiming that the tree of liberty needed to be watered from time to by the blood of patriots and tyrants.

"I've seen your sun bleached bones along the highways, in the countryside, comingled in mounds with others outside shopping malls and grocery stores. I've seen your bones populating the dead compounds and feeding the crows."

"You're fucking crazy, you asshole," the man said now, visibly frightened.

"Yeah, of course. It was all just a bad dream, right? Right!"

As the train rolled up at the next stop, the man, his friends and most of the other Liberty Party supporters hurried off the train, leaving the train roomier. As the doors closed and the train lurched forward, one of the locals started clapping slowly and then picked up the pace. Others joined in, and even laughed. As the adrenaline wore off, he came down hard, replaced by an overwhelming sense of loss. Maybe he was delusional and the guy was right. Maybe he was insane. What proof did he have that he wasn't? Was he who he thought he was? Maybe it had all been an illusion. Chris felt his identity begin to fade into this soul-sucking reality. Chris' knees started to shake violently and he clutched himself on the ride back to Falls Church.

CHAPTER 12

Austin, Texas
February 1999

"One, two, three, four, we don't need your fucking war!"

"The people…united…cannot be defeated!"

"Show me what Democracy looks like!"

"This is what Democracy looks like!"

BACKGROUND MUSIC: "Linger" by The Cranberries
Visit www.michaeljuge.com on the Refurbished Soul page to listen

The crowd churning from the Student Union onto Guadalupe chanted with as much cohesion and clarity as the leadership of the antiwar protest itself. One sign showed President Bill Clinton with the word "Rapist" scrawled over his forehead. Another cardboard sign looked like it was a treatise about the nature of war itself, but the drafter apparently didn't plan ahead, because the words shrank like the end of the preamble text in *Star Wars* until the last few words were nothing more than .005 micro font.

"What's all this then," Chris Jung asked to no one in particular.

Meredith pushed her glasses up the bridge of her nose to keep them from falling off. She squinted, trying to figure what the rally was all about.

"Do you think it's related?"

"I don't think so, but let's check it out."

Chris was ecstatic. The protest? He didn't know what it was about, nor could he care less. He was on a date with Meredith Anderson. Okay, it wasn't exactly a date—date. After months of fumbling his words in the *Dialects of Orientalist Ethnographers* seminar they were both enrolled in, and at every happy hour, a few days ago Chris got a strange feeling. It was weird. Some called it courage. It was like some part of him said, "Dude, what's the worst that could happen? I mean, you've already made an ass out of yourself. So, take a chance already."

He picked up the telephone and gave Meredith a call and started chatting her up. He had no idea what he said during the conversation, but at some point the words came out. It went something like,

"Well, um, we should, hey, would you like do something, like, whatever?"

Meredith translated the botched sentence, taking excruciatingly long to respond. Finally, she ended the silence. "You know about Scott Ritter?"

"Scott? Oh, yeah, he's my boy!" He hadn't a clue who the hell Scott was. He just hoped it wasn't some guy she was dating.

"Um, yeah," she said dismissively, "anyway, Scott Ritter is the former UN weapons inspector in Iraq."

Chris gulped, realizing he just blundered. She continued.

"He's speaking tomorrow night over at the Student Union to discuss the reasons for his resignation."

It sounded like a perfect romantic setting, so Chris jumped in.

"Oh yeah, I was going to that, too! I'll pick you up!"

Meredith stuttered slightly with surprise. "Um, okay."

"And maybe we can get, you know, some coffee first, or something."

"Fair enough."

"Great. I'll pick you up at…Um, what time was it for again?"

They had just left the Scott Ritter's lecture. As expected of any former UN weapons inspector's lecture about the vagrant abuses and the dangers of US hegemony, it was exceedingly unerotic. But whatever, he was on a—well, if not date—a coordinated rideshare to an event involving refreshments beforehand with Meredith. Close enough. He couldn't help but steal glances at her beautiful face, those deep brown eyes, that reddish short hair…okay, and her legs! He was a legs man. And she always dressed like a business woman. What in the hell was she doing with this dude sporting an Abraham Lincoln goatee and a stupid Spam t-shirt?

The students marched, yelling slogans angrily. Chris recognized one of the students. He was an undergraduate, but was like ten years older than Chris' twenty-six. The professional student handed out some rag called *The Daily Worker*, even though Chris was certain this guy hadn't worked a day in his life. But then again, the guy who had managed to be president of the University of Texas student chapter of the International Socialist Organization eight years running needed to concentrate on stuff like this and couldn't be bothered with slinging coffee like Chris was doing.

"Hey, Jeff, right?"

Dressed in black pajamas and Converses with a red Che t-shirt, he acknowledged him reluctantly. "It's Balou, actually."

That's right. Jeff had started referring to himself as Balou, meaning "beautiful" in Swahili or Bosque or something. Chris pressed on.

"What's going on? Is this about Scott Ritter?"

"Who? No, man, this is about the illegal and cowardly rape by that warmonger president against the innocent peoples of Serbia."

Chris and Meredith both leaned their heads back. "Oh right, that one." There was some talk on the news about the Kosovo War, and how people were upset that the president had a campaign of air missions over Serbia that had been going on for months.

Then it occurred to him. "Wait, didn't the Socialists decry foul that Clinton didn't go to war *against* the Serbs when the Serbians were raping the ethnic Muslims on masse?"

"I don't know what the hell you're talking about, man!"

"No, I'm probably mistaken. It was some other Socialist group. Cool, carry on."

"Fight the power!" he cried out.

Chris never cared for political extremists, but he couldn't help but feel sorry for his generation. They didn't even have a decent war to protest like his parent's generation had.

Chris saw Meredith giggling, something he had never seen her done before, ever. It was endearing. Unfortunately, it was interrupted by the wail of a siren followed by a police officer on a megaphone.

"You are marching without a permit and are in violation of city ordinance. Break up your demonstration immediately!"

Someone yelled out, "Fuck you, pig!"

Others cheered in response, encouraging the kid. More police cars arrived. Cops in riot gear emerged up the hill, beating the batons with their gloved hands in unison. Neither Chris nor Meredith could pull themselves away. This was getting good.

"Show me what Democracy looks like!"

"This is what Democracy looks like!" the people shouted.

Others shouted, "The people…united…shall not be defeated."

"You are hereby ordered to disperse immediately."

Someone threw a bottle, crying out some curse about the officer's mother. The bottle shattered on top of a patrol car. Someone else threw a bottle, but it erupted into flames.

That's when it got interesting. The cops in the riot gear beat their batons and Chris heard a *thumping* sound, followed by the smoke of tear gas. He and Meredith still stood in silent amazement, unable to move until the cops, lined up in a phalanx, pushed through the screaming crowd of students, the smell of tear gas and patchouli blending together in a most distinctive way. Chris knew it was getting dangerous. Meredith started coughing. Fortunately, Chris' smoking habit inured him from the noxious fumes. Just then a Molotov cocktail was thrown against a Starbucks across the street, followed by the sounds of heads being beaten.

"Come on, let's get out of here," he urged.

Without thinking he grabbed Meredith's hand and they ran off away from the protests. He and Meredith ran hand in hand into the night, down a flight of stairs, past the iconic UT Tower and down another flight of steps until the sounds of the battle faded and the tear gas smell dissipated. They found themselves near a fountain alone. They were still holding each other's hand. He had originally taken it without thinking. Now, he wished never to let go.

Meredith didn't seem to mind him holding her hand. She giggled again. She had the most beautiful laugh that made him want to wade in its sound.

"Ho…ly…shit!" she said and laughed again.

Sirens blared and out in the distance someone with an amp busted out some Rage Against the Machine to encourage the protestors. Chris knew the song to be "Township Rebellion." He played it a couple of times on his bass back in college.

As he caught his breath, he looked into her eyes. He felt his heart racing, his knees felt weak. She was still holding his hand through the uncomfortable moment of silence between them. He had to fill the void. It was his way.

"Wow, I have to say, this is a good way to spend a Sunday evening."

"Yeah," she agreed. "It makes missing the *X-Files* worth it."

Chris did a double take. "You…you like the *X-Files*, too?"

"I love the *X-Files*," she answered sincerely.

With Zack de la Rocha howling in the background "Fight the war, fuck the norm" and the wail of sirens bouncing off the building walls, Chris wrapped his arm around her waist and pressed himself close to her. It was time to take a chance. He eased his grip just a little to let her know that it was her call, her choice. She pulled his face to hers and they kissed. Somewhere nearby, someone released a volley of fireworks.

CHAPTER 13

The Shiftiverse
Somewhere off the New Jersey Turnpike
New Jersey, Exit 2
Late February 2013

Chris Jung held the jacket cover of *The X-Files* complete 6th season DVD box set, wiping off smudges of dirt, dust and time. The warehouse he and the rest of the troupe were bivouacking for the evening was strewn with scatterings of DVDs, DVD players, books, CDs, among other techno gadgets. It looked to have been ransacked repeatedly. The warehouse itself was in bad shape. Fire had swept through part of the building. Wreckage from a small commuter jet littered the area outside, the cockpit impaling the building itself. The roof had partially collapsed over the years, leaving a gaping hole in the ceiling, which was fortuitous as it allowed the Virginian riders to set up a campfire without fear of asphyxiation.

Chris had come over here to get some privacy from the others so that he could concentrate on something Jamil asked him to do before leaving the Stubb Foundation. The condition of the warehouse was particularly disturbing to Chris, because he could have sworn the *Call of Duty: Nazi Zombie Ninjas 2* for his Xbox he ordered last month from Amazon was shipped from this very location. He reminded himself that this warehouse had burned down and been ransacked many years ago; it was not something that had happened recently. Amazon.com was alive and well back home, nothing drastic had happened. His wife and kids were fine, at least until March 15th. This was essentially just a foreign place.

As much as Chris grasped the concept of alternate realities, and could grok that fact that the desolate landscape he was passing through on their way to Massachusetts was not something that just happened, nor was it anything happening in his reality, it was hard not to feel concern for his family. It reminded him how vulnerable they were, even without an asteroid heading towards earth. They were vulnerable in general. He just hoped that if he awoke here in this reality, other Chris from this 'verse awoke and inhabited his body in the Mundaniverse. It seemed like he would be able to carry on fine over there.

From what he gathered from Kendra and the others, other Chris had his shit together. They did not display the same respect or confidence in him, not that he could blame them. He was like a lost child here, completely mystified. He fumbled around just trying to keep up. He knew that had he inhabited his own body and not his counterpart's, he wouldn't have been able to keep up at all. At least this Chris managed to be in good shape. Given the drab food and rigors, it was no wonder.

Chris turned the jacket over and smiled upon seeing an image of the characters Special Agents Dana Scully and Fox Mulder. *The X-Files* held a special place for him, for it was the magnet that brought he and Meredith together. In those awkward, precarious, passionate and exhilarating early days when he and Meredith first started dating, *The X-Files* was the excuse to have her come over on Sunday as well as Saturday, so they could see each other both days that weekend. Sunday nights used to be a drag, because it was always followed by school and the anxiety over the unfinished business not taken care of over the short weekend. But with *The X-Files*, Chris had Meredith over for a couple of hours more that weekend. She didn't own a TV, savage as it sounded, but it gave him the opening to have her come over. It served to provide a conduit between two very different personalities.

Chris noticed that the hairstyle Dana Scully wore was the same one Meredith currently boasted. The mid length hair had come back into vogue recently. He heard boots crunching over CD cases and brittle cardboard boxes. From the silhouette of her flowing wavy hair, Chris knew it to be Reverend Rita Luevano approaching.

"Sorry, Chris, but we won't be able to play that tonight."

Rita handed Chris a titanium mug. The Starbucks logo on it had faded, but he recognized it was his own. Chris understood why other Chris had brought the mug from his flight from DC and kept it all these years. It really was a damned good mug. The titanium design maintained the vacuum covering, which kept coffee hot, or in this world, it kept his dirty chicory water hot. He still used the very same mug in his world. If it survived the apocalypse, then it must be good.

"It's gruel soup," she said.

The Stubb Foundation had supplied the...Vicious Rabbits —he still couldn't say "Vicious Rabbits" with a straight face—they supplied them with portable food, whatever ammunition they had and even repaired his bike, providing a proper wheel back on his retrofitted Kona mountain bike. They called it gruel for a good reason. The standard form it came in was like oatmeal with twice the gooiness of regular oatmeal and half the taste of raw tofu. The soup came from gruel cubes. It barely had a taste. It was like hot water with a hint of a soybean aftertaste, which is what gruel was comprised of.

Between the lack of daylight, the grainy images of TV stations from his home, which only served to make him homesick and the endless supply of gruel that splooged from a tube, Chris actually was glad to leave the confines of the subterranean world of the Stubb Foundation, even if it was to witness a world torn asunder.

Chris took the mug and felt the heat from the steam. "Thanks."

Rita looked at the DVD jacket in his hand.

"I miss her."

Rita gave him a quizzical look. "I sure hope you're talking about your wife."

"What?" Then he realized he was staring at the image of Mulder and Scully posing with folded arms confidently. "It's a thing Meredith and I have."

He blew on the mug and guzzled some of the gruel down.

"Why don't you join us by the fire. It's warm and the meat is almost ready," Rita offered. "Besides, I noticed there's a lot of bear shit in the corner over there. The bears may have run off, but I wouldn't care to step in it myself."

Rita guided Chris back over to the campfire where everyone else, save for one of the archers on watch outside, was keeping warm, talking and joking around. He had been reluctant to sit near the campfire, for they had found human remains where the group was preparing dinner. Unlike the countless millions they didn't even bother noticing along the way, Rita at least covered the remains and gave them a blessing and placed them outside. They didn't bother to bury them. The ground was frozen solid and they didn't need to waste the energy, the gunny explained to him.

He took a seat next to Rita, who was sitting next to Akil, who he could have sworn was related to Don Cheadle. Even despite the scar along her face, the ill-fitting dentures, which slipped from time to time and the eye patch, Chris couldn't help but notice how beautiful Rita was. She had a way about her. It was magnetic.

Opposite him sat a few other Vicious Rabbits and a couple of archers in the Thomas Jefferson Martyrs Brigade, another name which Chris just didn't believe could possibly be taken seriously, except that the archers were really good, as evidenced by the cats roasting on a spit over the fire. He told himself he wouldn't eat Mister Whiskers, as gathered from one of the cat's tags. But try as he might abstain, the smell was really enticing. His mouth watered, which was understandable considering the fact that neither he nor anybody else here had tasted anything other than gruel for the past couple of weeks.

Gunnery Sergeant Birmingham, the massive and frightening Vicious Rabbit with the impenetrable accent, stepped over the fire and cut off a piece of meat with his equally massive survival knife.

"Oh, that's the stuff it is, wot?"

Chris hadn't heard a single consonant from the man. The gunny, as he was called, took a bite and pointed the blade with the shriveled meat that was unmistakably a tail over to Kendra who, without looking up, took the piece of meat and put it on top of the Stubb Foundation soy cake. Her nearly shorn scalp contrasted to his Kendra's exquisite and labor intensive weaves. She was operationally in charge as the outfit's ranking officer while Rita was the de facto head of the two groups—the Vicious Rabbits and the Monticellans.

Paying close attention, Chris gathered that Rochelle and Greater Monticello were extremely close allies, comprising an alliance of city-states with Culpeper and Fredericksburg Union officially known as "The Orange Pact." The way they behaved and their Benetton-like diversity convinced him that they were indeed the good guys. Would he, other Chris, have chosen to ride with a bunch of assholes? He thought not.

To his dismay, he also learned about their common foe. Gordon Boche, the overtly political minister who helped the new president win the 2012 election and usher the Liberty Party into power in his world, was the autocratic ruler of a totalitarian, theocratic empire over in Lynchburg in this 'verse. Considering that bellicose rabble he talked, with its distorted interpretation of reality and the well-armed crowds he led, it wasn't exactly shocking he wound up where he was here. He just hoped that these

Vicious Rabbits and Monticellans would defeat him and his Lambs of God. *God, what a name!* Chris recalled there was a heavy metal band with a similar name. He wondered if it was related or if Gordon Boche was a fan. Probably not.

The gunny started cutting up the meat from the roasting cat carcasses, and proceeded to hand out chunks of meat to the warriors around the fire.

" 'oo wanted ribs?"

"Right here," said Rita excitedly.

Akil chimed, "How much for one rib?"

"Gov," handing some ribs to Rita.

"Thank you." She and Akil dug into the cat ribs enthusiastically.

"Mmm, tabby, my favorite."

" 'ere you go, Captain."

The gunny handed a plastic plate appropriated from the warehouse over to Chris who took it warily.

"Just know that culinary taboos are culturally relative," Rita said matter-of-factly.

"Does that include eating people?" he said intending to be humorous. The joke fell flat as faces around the fire glared at him gravely. He just realized he stepped in it. There must have been a lot of cannibalism during the Collapse, he realized.

"Too soon, huh?"

"Let's just say, we saw a lot of that happening out in places like this," Kendra said darkly. "And for those who succumb to that, they ate their way out of the human race, not just by my judgment, but by anyone's. They couldn't stand themselves after what they did, and there was no turning back."

Rita put her hand on his arm kindly. "You have to understand. When the Shift struck, it ripped the life support system sustaining hundreds of millions in this country. People panicked. They ate up the land, wasted crops, killed animals en masse."

"What about all the deer I saw on the way up," he asked. Over the past several days since leaving Laurel, Maryland, Chris had seen packs of dogs as well as dozens of deer racing across the interstate, as well as occasional bands of people who kept their distance.

"The deer population rebounded only recently. Their numbers were decimated during the Collapse, Chris," said Rita.

"People killed them and didn't even know how to dispatch most of the meat. It was a waste, but what can you expect from people who never hunted? And then when the canned food and the deer ran out, the only animals left in plentiful supply and which were easy to catch were humans."

"Oh," he said. "Did any of you..."

"No!" everyone shouted in unison.

Fair enough as his wife would say. The topic was apparently very personal and upsetting to them all. He supposed he couldn't blame them. Chris could only imagine what it must have been like. He wondered to himself how he, the other he, made it. If he was who he was on July 11, 2007, how could he have pulled himself together? From what he had seen, the EMPs had obviously been an immediate deathblow to America and to the entire industrialized world for that matter. The more he thought about it, the more he realized how utterly dependent his own world was on the microchip. There was no vital organ of the system that maintained civilization that wasn't dependent on the microchip.

"Chris."

He shook himself out of his thoughts. Rita handed him plastic plate with a hunk of meat. Gingerly, he took it.

"Go on. Your body will thank you for the added nutrition. I know it might seem gross, but it isn't. It actually tastes like..."

"Chicken?"

"Oh, you've had cat before," said Kendra smartly.

Chris took the plate. He took a deep breath. It did smell good. May his own cats never smell his breath if he ever made it home again, but it did smell delectable. *Ah, screw it. Sorry, Mister Whiskers.*

Chris took a bite, and to his surprise, it tasted good, a bit gamey perhaps, but good. And yes, it did indeed taste like chicken!

"Mmm, it's not..." Then he bit into a bone. That was just a bridge too far. He knew it was the cat's thigh. He then vomited.

There was an awkward silence for a minute while he upchucked. He sat back down sheepishly, hoping everyone would ignore his uncouth reaction.

After a long silence, the gunny said, "Guess I shoulda bought boneless cat."

The entire circle of Virginians burst out laughing, including Chris himself. Even Rita, who tried to look stoic, broke out in laughter. He couldn't remember the last time he got a laugh like that. Hey, at least he finally felt like he was good for something other than being the guy schlepping the converted child trailer filled with ammo, food, and Stubb Foundation equipment.

After providing a much-needed comedic relief, Chris ate his portion of Mister Whiskers and his unnamed friend, a wiry calico. The meat was stringy, it went against a lifetime of programming, but it complimented the gruel wonderfully. After dinner, Lieutenant Kendra Baraka laid the AAA road atlas on top of a table. Isla Jenkins, one of the archers of the Martyrs Brigade, cranked a florescent lamp for additional light. Chris couldn't help but notice that the girl was painfully shy and way too young to be a soldier. She couldn't have been older than sixteen. What was she doing risking her life…in a place like this…on a school night?

"Okay, we've made some good distance so far," Kendra congratulated. "We covered something like forty-five miles a day, getting us into Jersey in just two days. Not bad."

Chris was surprised how smoothly the ride had been so far. He expected that with Baltimore and Wilmington, they would be battling their way up. The idea scared the shit out of him; however, as Rita explained, most people living today outside the settled territories tended to run away from strangers rather than engage them violently, which worked to the Virginian's benefit. The ride up had been without incident by and large even though they had to navigate skillfully through some disputed territories.

There was the intra tribal strife between the Targeteers and Costcos, two groups that the Virginians had run across before. In fact, Chris learned it was in the middle of a skirmish between the two that caused the other Chris to wipe out and land on the road head first, which somehow tore him from his own world while he was simultaneously getting car jacked and pistol whipped in his 'verse.

Helmut Spankmeister had given them as much information as he had on the local politics and gave names of local tribal leader names to throw out at particular points. With a little local knowledge of the Baltimore area and bribes with Stubb Foundation gruel power bars, the Virginians made their way peaceably past Baltimore. The only thing that slowed them down was the highway congestion on both sides in the city itself.

Once past Baltimore it was smooth riding. Even Wilmington wasn't so bad. Chris always found Delaware to be one of the most annoying states in the union. For its miniscule size, it collected a hell of a lot of tolls. Chris remembered how that fourteen mile stretch separating the two incompatible states of Maryland and New Jersey, the state formerly known as Delaware had no less than two toll booths in each direction. It was as though Delaware was punishing anyone who had the temerity to drive through its pristine highway with its one mediocre rest stop. With some trivial satisfaction, Chris was happy to whizz past the toll booths.

"I'm afraid to say, though, that the going is gonna get a lot slower from here on out," Kendra cautioned.

"Not to mention dangerous. We're at the last point before the land gets swallowed up by the suburbs. Nobody has a clue what is out there. Helmut's knowledge ended in Baltimore. But you don't have to be a military tactician to know we're heading into some bad ass shit."

"True that," said Akil.

"Once we hit the next exit, we will be in the Philadelphia suburbs, and then there's Trenton right here. I believe if we stick to the northbound lanes, we'll avoid the heaviest congestion, at least until exit seven. After that, it will most likely be a cluster in both directions. Shortly after exit seven, actually the very next one could arguably be the beginning of the New York metro area."

"New Jersey," Akil cursed. "It was the most densely populated state in the union, sandwiched between Philly and New York like that. This is gonna suck."

"I figure with traffic conditions, bribes we'll have to pay and watching our six the whole time, we'll be crawling our over way to the GW Bridge. And once we're there, well…" Kendra left the rest unsaid.

"Couldn't we use some other route to get to Cambridge?" asked one of the Vicious Rabbits. "I mean, isn't there a way to avoid New York City?"

"Like what?" Akil asked. "Look at the map. Boston is exactly Northeast. If we tried avoiding the major population centers up here, we would be doubling the distance to get there. And even then, we'd still be passing through a lot of towns and smaller cities."

Akil turned to the first pages of the AAA atlas, which showed a map of all of the Northeastern states to make his point. "Maybe it would be safer, and if time wasn't an issue, sure, but March 15th is fast approaching. After that, it won't matter. No, the only way to get there in time is by going up on I-95."

One of the Vicious Rabbits, the meaty guy asked, "But perhaps we should stay off the main highway, LT."

Kendra answered neutrally, "I considered that, Porkins, but again, we're dealing with a time constraint. Forests slow us down even if they are safer. And the further north we go, the fewer forests there will be. It will be a patchwork of suburbs and towns with crisscrossing roads where we could easily get lost and fall prey to a trap. And from what Chris and Akil here tell us, the New Jersey Turnpike, for all of its drawbacks, is wide and offers the advantage of elevation at several critical junctions, namely when we're running parallel to Manhattan."

Chris and Akil were considered the ones who had the most hands-on knowledge of the New Jersey Turnpike, which was not saying much. Akil used to travel back and forth a lot with family living in New York City. Chris had traversed the Turnpike a lot when he was an agent, which was a long time ago. And recently he had travelled up with his family to visit his old friend Alfonse. Chris remembered how they stopped at the Jon Bon Jovi Memorial Rest Stop, formerly the Walt Whitman Memorial Rest Stop and how Yorick absolutely loved Cinnabon—he could never stop asking for Cinnabon for weeks afterwards, and that Chris had to pry Aidan from one of the video games kicking and screaming.

So, while his experience was from an alternate reality, it was also a lot more recent than anybody else's. They were going with the hope that there weren't any drastic changes on the Turnpike over the last five and a half years, the rest stop name changes notwithstanding. Kendra asked him questions about the tollway's layout. She asked if it was a glen, surface level or elevated. At first Chris didn't understand why she was asking, but soon after riding with them, he got it, she was asking for tactical reasons.

The gunny had explained that highways laid out as a glen, a valley, was the most dangerous kind of highway as enemies could lay an assault using the advantage of the high ground. If they were ambushed inside a glen, they were easy prey and getting out of the kill box would be doubly difficult as they would have to scurry up the incline to escape. At surface level, enemies could ambush from the woods, and had a direct line of site, but at least it was better odds. The best option was elevated surfaces, which were common in the cities where interstates ran over the city streets. Of course, if someone laid a trap on an elevated surface, there was nowhere to go. That was true, but it was generally as bad for the bandits laying the trap as their prey. The preferred method of travel for the First Bicycle Mounted Cavalry was the woods, but as the boss lady said, there simply wasn't time for caution.

"Aren't you from New York, ma'am?" asked Porkins. "Don't you know the terrain?"

Kendra rolled her eyes. "I was a poor assed kid from Brooklyn, Private. My world encompassed probably ten square blocks. I probably went to

Manhattan all of twice in my life, and I never left the city until I went on that Smart Girls field trip to DC that July in '07. If we accidentally find our asses in my old hood, I'll be sure to speak up. But New Jersey is as foreign to me as it is to you."

Kendra turned the road atlas back to the Garden State. "As we discussed earlier, we'll stay on the toll way all the way to Fort Lee and make our way across the GW Bridge into Manhattan."

There was no argument about that little point. Not only was the GW Bridge the most direct route, it also bypassed most of Manhattan on an elevated highway over the Meadowlands, a thoroughly uninspiring view, which probably was responsible for the vile imagery most New Yorkers had of New Jersey, but it was definitely the best option.

The other option was to do something suicidal like trekking into Lower Manhattan through the Holland Tunnel or Midtown through the Lincoln Tunnel. That would have been monumentally stupid. It wasn't even an option, really. Chris had seen *The Stand* and that part where that guy Larry had to pass over the mass of dead bodies piled in traffic trying to leave the city. He couldn't turn out the lights for a week after seeing that made for TV mini series. If anything else, the tunnels had most likely flooded like the Fort McHenry Tunnel in Baltimore did. Fortunately, they knew about that from some kindly feral clan foraging in the city who provided the information in exchange for some gruel bars. It was the only time the troupe veered off the I-95.

"But what about here?" another Vicious Rabbit asked. He pointed to the map. "We could go on this….what is it called, Palisades Interstate Parkway and cross over at the Tappan Zee Bridge."

Chris spoke up. "It's actually a beautiful ride, lots of trees."

"No," Rita said firmly. "Look, we don't have the time, people. We need to shave every single mile we can. The miles are gonna get hard no matter where we go. We can't afford avoiding trouble forever."

Following on Rita's point, Kendra added, "We'll only be in Manhattan for about a mile or so before we enter the Bronx, not that that's an improvement. I am going to try to push us to continue the forty-five miles a day, but I also know that I will be most likely disappointed."

Chris knew that they were on a very tight timetable. There was no getting around it. He was just glad he inhabited other Chris' body. Despite the myriad of aches and pains, the scars, missing toes and teeth, this Chris was in a hell of a lot better shape than he was. This body was used to living hard and eating sparingly, not like him at all. Even still, he felt exhausted.

He had never cycled so far in his life, and he was carrying the child trailer behind him packed with ammo, food and God knew what else from the Stubb Foundation.

Chris was woken in the middle of the night by a persistent and nagging voice.

"Captain, captain...wake up."

"Hon, turn off the teevee," he moaned.

This was followed by a swift slap upside the head. It was dark, near pitch black. Bleary eyed, he barely could make out Kendra's face. And then he remembered where he was.

"It's your watch, Captain. Come on."

He yawned, the steam of his breath rising up into the broken ceiling of the Amazon.com warehouse. He struggled to rouse himself from the deep slumber he had been in moments ago. He was so tired, it was ludicrous. He had been cycling almost nonstop for days. His body needed to make repairs. It needed rest. But then again, so did everyone else here. Chris forced himself out of the sleeping bag. Everyone slept snuggly, huddled together. With the exception of Rita and Akil, they were spooning each other merely to keep warm. It was completely platonic and absolutely necessary. Even indoors with the campfire, it was below freezing. So, as strange as it was at first to have the large gunnery sergeant cuddling up beside him, it wasn't exactly unpleasant either. The massive Aussie/Scot was like a hot water bottle. Although he never put spooning with an unwashed Marine on his bucket list, it was still more pleasant than sleeping on a Futon, though he swore he wouldn't be putting this into his memoirs.

Chris laced up his boots and grabbed his rifle. Kendra walked him to the pried open door. Once outside, Kendra spoke in a normal tone, which the wind drowned out beyond a few feet.

"Okay, you know the drill. You walk the perimeter, quietly. Don't be predictable in case anyone is watching. You see anything, you go back inside and wake us, and we'll take care of the rest. Don't get trigger happy either. There was a family of bears here recently, and wolves also, so any sound could just as easily be an animal. Look, listen, and Captain, don't... fall...asleep. This isn't camp. You catch zees on watch and we wake up with our throats slit. Crystal?"

Chris grated his teeth trying not to react to his agitation. "Yeah, I got it, Kendra."

"Good."

Just as she was about to walk back through the doorway, Chris couldn't help but open his mouth. "I don't know who pissed in your Cheerios, but don't take your shit out on me."

She sighed, sounding as exhausted and agitated as he was. "What the hell are you talking about, sir?"

"There you go again with 'Captain,' and 'sir,' But you're not fooling me. I know you too well."

"You don't know me at all, sir."

Chris could tell he touched a chord, and he didn't care. Now wasn't the time to get into an argument, he knew that. But he was too tired to listen to reason.

"I know you were the sole survivor of twins born to a Kenyan who was in labor at JFK airport. I know you are the first in your family to go to college. I know you have a younger brother who you're worried is hanging out with the wrong crowd. I know you love Wyclef Jean, Lauryn Hill and Lil Wayne."

Feeling a smidge of confidence, he pressed on.

"I also know you didn't want me to go on this mission. After all, I'm not the great Chris Jung, Captain of the First Bicycle Mounted Cavalry. No, I'm just an office drone who doesn't know shit about this world."

He searched for a good descriptor of what he felt like. "Yeah, I'm tits on a bull to you. I get it. But I've shot before, I stood mids on several nights back when you were in grade school, and I am perfectly aware of the danger we're in. So, why don't you take a little trust in that Gaia of yours, go back to sleep and know that you're in good hands. Crystal?"

A moment passed.

"And Kendra. You have superior investigative and analytical skills, but you use the passive voice way too often and throw out commas in your reports like it's going out of style."

With that, Kendra mumbled something like "grow up" and stumbled off to sleep, leaving him freezing outside the warehouse alone.

BACKGROUND MUSIC: "Run Away" by Sarah Jarosz
Visit www.michaeljuge.com on the Refurbished Soul page to listen

Even though he hefted an M4 assault rifle with seven mags tucked in pouches along with a Glok on his side holster and a knife sharper than anything he had in his house, walking around the perimeter of the warehouse out in this no man's land in the middle of the night alone was frightening. He had perhaps watched zombie flicks too many times because his imagination got away from him. He knew, he just *knew,* that when he turned the next corner, he would find infected zombies waiting for him. And then he would turn around only to find another zombie right behind him, and then…

"Jesus, Chris, get a hold of yourself." *Sure, everything's fine. Just because you're in a bad* Postman *rip off, that's no reason to lose your cool.*

Chris felt the way he did when he was a kid, and the darkness seemed to take on a reality of its own. Every sound made him jump. Fortunately, the wind rustling the high grass reduced any other background noises. For the most part, he could only hear the ringing in his ears and the soft waft of the grass. The sky was clear this evening. It was a new moon. The sky was filled with stars. Chris couldn't remember seeing this many in his whole life. He thought he could see part of the Milky Way. As steam from his breath escaped into the night sky, Chris gazed at the stars to remind him that zombies never came out on starry nights. He didn't know why, but they just didn't in the movies.

It wasn't too surprising that he was so jittery. After what he had seen over the last couple of days, no one could blame him if he curled into a fetal position. Despite the span of years that had passed since the Collapse, Chris saw plenty of human remains along the interstate. Most of the remains were held together by their deteriorating clothes. Other remains were scattered about, possibly as a result of being devoured by animals, possibly by humans. The way most remains were staggered along the highway, it was as though people died trying to walk away from the cities and died either from dehydration, starvation or disease. In Delaware, they passed what looked like a vehicle barricade that formed a circle. People, whoever they were, literally circled the dead vehicles in what was a vain attempt to protect themselves from an enemy. The skeletal remains hinted of a gruesome death.

The remains of human beings was disturbing on its own without seeing what looked like whole families huddled together, choosing to die together. Remains of children were the most unsettling, especially when Chris saw some of the skeletons wearing *Dora the Explorer* shoes or *Sponge Bob* t-shirts. His children loved those shows and wore things exactly like that. Every time he crossed scenes like that, his thoughts returned to his wife and kids.

Before he was so rudely woken from his slumber, he dreamt of his apartment, sitting down to dinner, playing his guitar, mixing his music on iGarageband. This world was alien to him to be sure. The complete absence of crowded cities and high technology was the polar opposite to his reality. Yet, there was something familiar about this whole situation. Just as Chris dreamt of home while he was here, back before he emerged into this world, he often dreamt of places like this, of a world like this.

For several months leading up to the event that sent him here, he had a slew of odd dreams that he couldn't explain. Sometimes they were set in abandoned strip malls, or out in a forest. Some of those dreams were terrifying. He was in the midst of a firefight, sometimes battling inside a rusted out grocery store. He would have credited that to the *Resident Evil* game; however, he didn't get his Xbox until a couple of months ago.

There were other dreams, and they were much more pleasant. He saw himself blacksmithing, something he hadn't done since he was in college. He lived with Meredith in a farmhouse with his kids. *God, how much would a place like that cost*, he often wondered, even while in dream state. It was like seeing someone else's life as a passive observer and seeing it through his eyes. In this life, in his dreams, he lived in a real tight knit community. The world seemed rougher by his standards for certain—Chris hated the violent dreams, but it was somehow authentic. In some strange way, this mysterious place in his dreams often felt more real to him than his own world. The blacksmithing, the people, the food even, it all seemed more tangible than what he had in his own waking reality.

And then the alarm would go off and he would wake up in the safety of his bed in his apartment, his crappy-assed apartment. The digital alarm clock would remind him that he was back in the normal world. It all started to make sense to him now. He wasn't imagining it, his mind wasn't concocting images and stories complete with settings and background theme music. He had somehow been connected to his other self. He had a portal into this world through his dreams. It explained the inspiration for the newest album he had been working on back home.

Now, nothing would wake him and bring him back. He missed Meredith, Aidan and Yorick desperately. Despite everything he lamented from his world, he would give almost anything to get back home to them. It's where he belonged. If only he had his guitar on him. He would find solace in playing something he created in his world. Without a guitar and inwardly fearing zombies, Chris started to whisper the tune he started to play recently before getting swept into this world.

CHAPTER 14

The Shiftiverse
Elizabeth, New Jersey—Exit 13
Late February 2013

Elizabeth, New Jersey wasn't much to look at before the Shift. Chris had been there once back when he first moved to New York City. He was fresh out of basic special agent training and he and Meredith had just moved into a dank Brownstone apartment on the Upper Eastside from their sunny home in Austin. The apartment was typical of turn of the century design. It lacked virtually every modern convenience, like enough storage space for dishes and canned food. So, he and Meredith hopped into their Corolla and headed to Elizabeth, New Jersey's one justification for its continued existence, IKEA, to get a pantry and cabinet.

According to his memory, Elizabeth was not a particularly pleasant town to spend a day, but at least its buildings stood erect back then. Surrounding him now were nothing but burnt out shells where apartment buildings, gas stations and houses once stood. A light layer of snow covered the ashen land. Across the toll way stood the cause of the inferno that ravaged the entire landscape for miles in all directions—Newark Liberty International Airport. The terminal itself was as devastated as the rest of the area, but Chris could see the remains of what once were concourses and jet ways. Parts of jetliners' wings, engines and tail sections were scattered throughout the city as well as throughout the airport runways, sticking incongruently out of the bleak landscape.

The region started showing signs of damage back a couple of exits ago where they picked up their guide, Mustafa. Ravaged really was the only word to describe the land. Nature, which had reclaimed much of the suburbs, seemed reluctant to push itself into what could arguably have been a Superfund site before the Shift. Now, the only thing left standing, oddly enough, was the IKEA store itself. Fire had licked the walls, but despite being located just catty-corner to the airport, it had remarkably escaped the worse of the inferno, which seemed to go on for miles in all directions. Time, the elements, and to some extent the fire itself, had battered the massive house wares store, but like a blue and yellow alien ship, it rose defiantly out of the rubble, its tattered flags flying proudly as a testament to the once largest retailer of reasonably priced yet posh home furnishings.

Deep inside the store's maze sat the Virginians, in the living room section of the store, discussing their options with their guide and the local family who were the caretakers of the IKEA store. Chris sat on the couch, which was part of the *Oeklectic* living room set. Lit by some kind of rancid oil, the display area almost looked real. The stink of old grease and unwashed humans was mitigated by a more pleasant smell, the smell of tobacco. The Virginians had bribed their host, Jorge Valdez, the elder of the family taking residence in the IKEA, the same way they did with their guide Mustafa who they picked up in New Brunswick. Chris had learned that Rochelle and Monticello both grew tobacco as their most lucrative crop. He could see how useful the stuff was, how it lubricated their dealings with so many folk who had been jonesing for a cigarette for half a decade.

Rita handed Jorge Valdez a small parcel of tobacco wrapped in plastic and offered him a cigarillo as a bonus. The older man smelled the cigarillo before lighting it. He lit the cigarillo on the grease lamp and held in his breath for almost a minute. By the time he exhaled, there was little smoke left.

"D'ju know," he said with a slightly slurred Colombian accent, "I thought I never smoke one of dees things again." Then he added contently. "This is the best habit ever."

Mustafa, who was running through his stash, joined him. Time was a premium, but Rita and Kendra both seemed to have practiced patience, allowing their host this small indulgence.

"Ju have good chit here, Reverend Luevano. I hope you come by here more often. I got plenty of friends in the city who would love to do business wit'chor people."

Rita smiled. "That sounds like a worthy endeavor, Mr. Valdez. But as a good faith start, we could really use some guidance through your territory."

Outside of the IKEA property itself, the Valdez's didn't have any territory. It was no man's land. But Chris could see Rita's charm coming through. She had fluffed his ego and ingratiated herself while simultaneously getting the old man to focus on the reason why they bought his cooperation.

"I am telling you, ju don' wanna to take the Turnpike. They are loco, mi amiga."

"I know the Patels," Mustafa said. "If the Patel Syndicate is running the Turnpike, you can deal with them." Mustafa had a more subtle accent and it was completely different, but he was very articulate. Both locals were the same age and seemed to know each other.

"The Patels? Ju been living under a rock, amigo? The Patels, they die out a year ago."

"Oh, that is very sad. I did not know." Mustafa seemed sincerely upset by the news. "How?"

"D'ju know the Dallek boys? They had a feud. The Patels lost. Ju don'wanna go near those hombres."

"They are very bad men, Reverend," Mustafa agreed reluctantly.

Kendra took a deep breath. "Well, is there a way around these Dallek boys?"

"Jes," Jorge answered. He took the atlas and pointed to the map with his fingers which had dirt imbedded into the grooves.

"Ju go around to Newark. Take the 78 to the 287. Ju'l run into the Africans, and the 89ers, but they not so bad now. Ju can do business with them."

Kendra shook her head. "Out of the question. That would take us out of the way big time. I'm talking at least a day. We're getting worn hard as is."

"Reverend, I think you should go around," Mustafa implored. "If the Dallek Boys are in charge, then I am afraid that access is cut off. They were kids when the EMP attacks hit, and grew up in the time of dying. They are savages, Reverend."

Chris was confused. He thought that Rita said that the earth, which was preparing to shift its magnetic poles, caused the Shift. Not only did Jamil and the Stubb Foundation confirm that, they also mentioned how the Large Hadron Collider was responsible for prematurely sending the earth in its spasms. But then again, how would Mustafa know that?

As Chris thought about it, he realized that news about the cause of the

Shift wasn't widely known, because there was no news service, no cable TV, no Internet to pass the word. There wasn't even a pony express around here. So, it would make sense that other people from different parts of the country, of different parts of the world for that matter, had a variety of theories as to what happened. They might even not call it "The Shift." In fact, he never heard that term thrown in the Virginians dealings with these outsiders.

Rita sucked in air and put her hands on her hips. "I understand that, Mr. Haddad, Mr. Valdez, but we simply have no other choice."

"Okay. Don' say I didn't warn you." Jorge contently went back to smoking his cigarillo.

Jorge and his sons led the Virginians and their guide out of IKEA's maze past the children's and self-service sections and into the brilliant daylight. The parking lot was only half filled with cars when the EMPs first struck. Every one of the vehicles had been scorched by the fire and was beginning to decompose and blend into the frozen ground. Jorge handed the Virginians complimentary bright yellow bags, which he insisted on giving as a memento of their visit. Rita graciously accepted the florescent yellow IKEA bags and handed them to Chris who knew to stuff them deep inside the child trailer, which he was in charge of hauling.

Outside in the frozen parking lot, Mustafa's sons Bilal and Yusef waited for them. Unlike their father who grew up in Syria, they were born and raised in the US, and had no accent outside of the typical New Jersey accent, which warped vowels and consonants making it sound like they're mad at you, speaking emphatically, but they're not. They're just talking, except that Bilal and Yusef rarely spoke.

Chris repacked the ammunition, the dried gruel flakes, gruel bars and the dwindling supply of tobacco into the child trailer and secured the net over it. Like the bike itself, the child trailer had been modified to include full-sized bike wheels. Stepping onto *The Interceptor* was a bit of a comfort. Despite its aftermarket gun rack, numerous repairs and paint job, Chris recognized the bike as his own. He was heartened to know that his old bike was with him now, just like the titanium Starbucks coffee mug. He had neglected the bike back home, leaving it to gather dust along with the old infant car seats and paint cans in the apartment's basement storage cage. He now felt a little guilty about that, because apparently, this old Kona of his had been other Chris' lifeline for the past several years. While he packed, he thought about what Jamil told him to think about.

Ilsa Jenkins helped Chris on with his Camelbak backpack, which fit onto his MOLLE gear. The forest green and white mottled poncho he wore over his fatigues helped keep the stench down. He and the rest of the Virginians took a version of sponge baths daily, cleaning their delicates, armpits, face, and feet along with a scrub of shampoo, but they were never really clean. The plastic bladder that was filled with piping hot water released a spray of cold water by the time it was hoisted up in the area of the warehouse deemed the privy. He would have felt embarrassed smelling so ripe around the young lady, except she was no better off than he.

Chris didn't know why they all hadn't fallen from exhaustion yet. Not only were they cycling hundreds of miles on rough road in the freezing cold, they were pedaling through it all while wearing heavy boots, and laden with their "battle rattle," and backpacks. Why in the hell didn't they ride horses, he asked himself. He didn't have the courage to ask any of them personally. He felt like some annoying tourist every time he asked a question. Kendra was especially short with him. She acted like everything he asked was the stupidest question in the whole world. He knew cars were out. The EMPs made short work of those. And seeing the way that the roads were all clogged, even with old models that didn't rely on the microchip, they wouldn't be able to go far at all before getting stuck by a mound of rush hour traffic. But what about horses? It really was a perfectly decent question, he reasoned. After all, couldn't horses carry them *and* their equipment for them? And that would mean that they could trot their way to Bean Town in style.

"All right, people let's mount up," Kendra said.

Jorge walked up to Rita and Mustafa who were straddling their bikes right next to Chris.

"Ju sure you going north on the Turnpike?"

"I'm afraid so," she answered. "I've calculated the other options and estimated it would add a total of twenty-eight hours to our journey."

"Ju give Dallek this," Jorge said as he pulled out a brilliant gold bullion bar. The bar seemed to radiate its own light and was a stark contrast to the drab, crusted world around it. He handed it to Rita.

"Dallek hombres still collect gold."

Rita took the bar of gold in her gloved hand and showed genuine appreciation. "Thank you, Mr. Valdez. This is awfully generous of you."

"Ah, what do I want with it? It don' feed mi familia. It don' trade here, eccept them locos. I hope they're no' horny for a fight."

Rita pulled out a pouch from her breast pocket and handed it to him and gave him a kiss on the cheek. And with that they pedaled off.

Chris was impressed by the show of kindness by Mr. Valdez. He didn't understand it, really. He had always assumed that without law and order and without the life flow of civilization to sustain its inhabitants, that the worst of humanity would dominate and whatever decency existed before would vanish. Every book and movie he saw about when the shit hit the fan corroborated this assessment. The Virginian's own accounts about the Collapse didn't contradict this assessment. If anything, there should have been some major conflict between Mustafa and Jorge along racial and ethnic lines. People always reverted to their reptilian brains when pressed to survival mode. Racial identity and tribalism was just bound to surface under those circumstances. However, Chris caught a glimpse of the two elder gentlemen. They kissed each other's cheeks and put their hands on their hearts. That confused him.

Mustafa Haddad and his sons rode in the back of the formation. Chris noticed how well the elderly man rode his Schwinn three speed. He had to be at least sixty-five and it was freezing even at midday.

"Mr. Haddad?"

"Yes, my friend," he said looking everywhere suspiciously as he rode.

"Are you and Mr. Valdez friends?"

He shrugged his shoulders. "Mumkim…We have known each other for a very long time. Since the EMP attacks."

They weaved around a bad collision where an 18 wheeler had jackknifed and tumbled onto other vehicles and past a mountain of Connex containers from a container dump.

"Mr. Valdez and his family have been living in that IKEA for years, though I do not know why on God's earth they would want to live there. But we have traded with each other regularly and we have come to each other's aid from time to time. I guess that would qualify as friendship."

Although not his native language, Mustafa was very articulate and spoke with an elegant accent, which contrasted to the almost wild appearance of his un-kept long beard.

"Hmm. If you don't mind me saying so, you seem very…"

"Civilized?"

Chris' face turned redder than the cold wind biting his cheeks had done. The old man laughed.

"Well, not to put too fine a point on it, but yeah."

"I was once a civilized man, my friend. I lived in the greatest nation the world had ever known. My wife and I lived in a dream. We had two wonderful sons and three beautiful daughters. I was a professor at Rutgers."

"What in?"

"Cultural Studies."

"Really? I got my MA in Anthropology," Chris said excitedly.

"Hmm," he answered plaintively. "When the attacks came, this whole place erupted into chaos. It was as though hell had torn a hole and vomited itself unto this world. My wife died a few months after the attacks to dysentery. My eldest daughter, her husband and two of my grandchildren died of the flu. Did you have the flu down there?"

Chris didn't want to go into a diatribe about how he wasn't really from here, and that his consciousness had mysteriously been transported into the body of his alternate self. He knew it would divert the discussion and Mustafa would be all, "oh, really? Wow, what is it like over there? Yadda, yadda, yadda."

Chris chose to simply go with his role. "Yeah."

"The EMP attacks took so much of my family; it took the love of my life. And when some kids came to invade my house..." His voice trailed off, and he cycled silently before concluding. "I only sound civilized, my friend, but that is a mere echo of the life that once was."

Chris felt awful for having brought up such a painful subject. The elderly man who sounded like a poet more than a cultural theorist, was generous beyond what he would have expected, and that brought him to ask.

"Mr. Haddad, why are you escorting us all the way to the GW Bridge. You yourself said that these..."

"Dallek boys."

"Yes, them. You said that they were dangerous. Yet you and your sons are volunteering to see us all the way there."

Mustafa shrugged. "I have had dealings with the Dallek boys. Maybe they will listen to me, take your gold and let you pass. Besides they think I'm Muslim."

"Oh, so they're like jihadists?"

The old man laughed boisterously. "Oh, you have to excuse me. It's just that I haven't heard that term since the early days after the attacks. I cannot tell you how many little shits claimed to be jihadists after the

EMP attacks. But jihadists? No, they are Albanian, Muslim, nominally so. They certainly don't behave like the Muslims I knew. But they aren't jihadists. They are just leaderless thugs and they see everyone outside their little group as fair game, except they have shown some residue of respect for me. They call me 'Sheikh.'" He snorted again.

"I guess this whole area went into an orgy of racial and ethnic wars."

Mustafa nodded. "At first, yes. New York City is a collection of villages really, and so too are the surrounding communities. Gangs fought each other for domination of a section of town, or even for a single city block for the first couple of years. Even during the time of dying, they fought. Eventually, though, the fighting subsided, that is to say they managed to kill each other rather thoroughly. We who are left, we do not care for domination, or ethnic purity, most that I know don't, anyway. We just want to live. So no, my friend, it is not divided along ethnic lines purely. The Dallek boys are just the exception that proves the rule, yes?"

Chris smirked at the man's remark. Mustafa was fascinating to talk to. He would have loved to be able to sit him down and go over the various groups that emerged in the greater metropolitan area over the years. It aroused the ethnographer in him. He could see it now. If he ever returned home and if his world didn't wind up getting hit by the asteroid, he would quit his job and go back to write a dissertation on a post-apocalyptic ethnography of New York City. *Yes, and I'll call it Identity and Acculturation in the Apocalypse.* There was a minor problem in that he had no way of returning home, and even if he did, nobody would believe this outrageous story. But those were pesky details to be ironed out later. As he thought about it, he considered writing the dissertation as a "fictional" account instead. Every time he thought of home, he felt a longing beyond reach.

Opposite the Newark Liberty Airport, the Manhattan skyline loomed menacingly with its dead steel mountains, revealing the first signs of its slow demise. The skyscrapers still stood, none had fallen over, but neglect was apparent even from several miles away. Broken windows, unfinished construction, unwashed grime and evidence of a firestorm which blazed throughout the city battered the skyscrapers. The skyline looked less impressive he admitted sadly to himself. Once where two towers stood there was now a conspicuous trough in the skyline. In his world—the Mundaniverse, there was a stirring memorial that conveyed the void left where 3,000 innocent people perished, and 1 World Trade Center, almost complete by now, was reclaiming the New York skyline. That wasn't the case here. Out there in the distance, the city had succumbed to the Shift as the rest of the country did. There was to be no reconstruction, no resurrection. And if they didn't get Rita to Bean Town in time, there wouldn't even be people left to lament the loss. The depressing view, which spurred his mind into its own void pushed him to peddle a little harder past the skyline to be eclipsed by the burnt out cylinders of oil silos.

Chris knew something was up before he knew exactly what it was. Ilsa Jenkins, the archer on point, had raced back to the main formation to speak with the grownups in the bunch. The gunny called the formation to a halt. By now, Chris had learned how to brake safely with all of the equipment in tow, even with the icy roads. He huddled up to the front where Ilsa was briefing Kendra, the gunny and Rita. It suddenly occurred to him that for some reason Rita looked familiar to him, though he couldn't say from where.

"There's a roadblock less than two klicks, Reverend," the young lady said as she struggled to regain her breath.

"I think it's those Dallek boys Jorge and Mr. Haddad here warned us about. The barricade is two cars high, two deep. And it looks like they've rustled up some muscle cars as well."

Rita turned to Mustafa inquisitively. He looked as confused as she did. "They probably siphoned it from the vehicles around, though I thought the mixture had probably broken down."

"Yes, I know that. It's just I wasn't expecting…never mind. Mr. Haddad, options?"

"We could go back to exit 14 and get on the Interstate 78."

The gunny pulled at the atlas and turned to the page were they were. Rita shook her head. "I don't see a highway that parallels the Turnpike."

"No, I am afraid not. We would have to use the streets in Jersey City, make our way up north along Palisades Avenue and hope to rejoin the Turnpike near Union City."

Chris had run some field stops back when he was an agent in the city and knew that drive. "Yeah, it's only a few miles between Jersey City and Union City. The streets sound good."

Kendra shook her head. "Negative. As bad as being on a main artery is, it's even worse in an urban street environment if you don't know the area real well. There's no easier way to get separated from each other and get lured into a trap than going on streets."

"There is one other option, the Hudson Tunnel," Mustafa offered.

"No...fucking...way, sir," Akil added emphatically.

Rita sighed. "My husband's right. That's an incredibly bad idea. Besides, the tunnels are most likely flooded, anyway. I'm going to trust that the Dallek boys aren't in a feisty mood and will accept our toll gift."

"Roit," the gunny barked. "Lock and load, boyos!"

The gunny walked up to Chris. "Sir, you can stay in the back with Mr. 'addad, 'ere."

"Yeah, sure, Gunny. I got it."

Chris felt his knees getting weak. He pulled Rita aside.

"Rita, I think I'm going to puke."

"Chris, you're going to be just fine, okay? Just stay in the back as the gunny said. Breathe, don't forget to breathe now, and don't let your fear overtake you. We're going to get through this."

Chris took a deep breath. He started to whisper to himself, quoting from one of his favorite underrated films, "'I must not fear, fear is the mind killer. Fear is the little-death that brings total obliteration. I will face my fear. I will permit it to pass over me and through me...'"

The small column cycled slowly up to the barricade at exit 15E. The whole way, Chris kept a vigilant watch. There could be any number of traps anywhere, the endless Connex container cemetery, the row houses, the U-Haul store, the construction vehicles. About the only good news was that they were elevated. Kendra did say that ambushes were harder to set up on an elevated platform. Chris stayed in the back with Mustafa and his two silent sons as they approached slowly and came to a halt.

"I'm going to assist your reverend," Mustafa said as he got off his Schwinn. His sons followed him.

"The reverend wanted you safely back here. And she's not my reverend."

"Why did I come then?" Mustafa asked rhetorically. He and his two sons walked up to the front to where Rita, Kendra and the gunny were standing with their arms stretched out in an open gesture.

Seeing he was alone in the back, Chris cursed under his breath and moved up closer to the front. Chris knew to check on the rear just in case the Dallek boys were planning to ambush the travelers. Only fools would not think to look behind themselves, and only the most primitive morons tried such simplistic ambushes Kendra once remarked. He hoped she was right, because he didn't want to be the one on the spot. All he had to do was look like he knew what he was doing. He certainly was dressed for the part, he looked the part, he smelled the part. If anyone was thinking about an ambush from the rear, they would see him and think twice... he hoped.

"I understand this is your overpass and your town. That is why I am willing to compensate you for granting us safe passage. A token," Rita said to the pock-marked teenager and his toadies standing beside him. All wore matching NY Giants leather jackets.

"What is this?" responded the lead Giants fan with a thick East European accent.

Chris couldn't see them clearly, nor could he get a good read on the particulars of the conversation—he had his back to them, but the teenager, a kid, didn't seem too receptive.

"Listen, Mr. Dallek, you're not going to get a better exchange rate."

Chris' legs were quivering as he listened to the exchange that was getting more heated. He could hardly understand what Dallek was saying, but it didn't sound good. *Oh, come on, man. Please...I must not fear. Fear is the...*

Chris overheard Dallek say something like "I haff a better idea" when, suddenly Chris saw a shadow emerging from behind a fallen Connex container. The figure, cloaked in rags, rose slightly, its form in a crouching position, aiming a rifle.

This was real. This was actually happening. In his short time as an agent, save for that one day in September over twelve years ago now, he had never actually been in mortal danger. The closest he came to a physical confrontation came when he went to arrest an ancient Chinese lady. Although she was small enough to fit in most overhead compartments, she managed to knee him right in the nads. That was about the extent of his life or death experiences. Well, that and September 11th and then the Panic of '06, which actually was a moment where he really was on the precipice.

The figure steadied itself, Chris wanted to call out for help, but he knew the figure had put a bead on him. If he lifted his rifle...Shit!

Chris pressed the stock of his M4 against the pocket between his arm and chest, lifted his rifle, zeroed his sites and fired.

He didn't hear the explosion from the round leaving the rifle. He saw the figure crumple over. Another figure emerged and he took aim and shot. The figure disappeared in a red mist.

It happened so quickly that all he knew was that he dove for cover behind a Lexus crossover, the sounds of metal being punctured as he huddled behind the rear tire.

Akil who was a few feet away yelled, "Get behind the engine block, God dammit!"

There was a rapid release of gunfire. Over the cacophony, he heard one of the Dallek's screaming in halting English, "Exterminate!"

Chris knew not to switch to full auto; that would only waste rounds. Two men were shooting and leap-frogging toward him using the vehicles for cover like he was. They must have been using the vehicles to hide their presence. It didn't matter now. He and Akil took aim and shot at their targets. Chris' training from long ago, as rusty as it was, was all he had, but it came back to him. Once he took out his targets he looked around to find any other threats. Being on the elevated section minimized potential hiding spots, but it also left them in a bottleneck, which was exactly what Kendra had warned him about.

He scanned around to see no one coming in from his direction. Rita, Kendra and the others were engaged in a firefight with a dozen or more Dallek boys coming straight up the road. Chris raced to Kendra's side at the hood of an old Trans Am whose engine was still running. The Dallek kid inside was dead, shot between the eyes. Other Dallek boys were over the barricade and coming through spaces. Kendra stood up, took one shot and crouched back down behind the muscle car. There was a humanizing sound of agony as one of the boys cried out.

Chris peered over the hood and shot at two figures. Bodies lay on the ground, bleeding onto the snow. They all looked like Dallek boys by his brief evaluation.

"Cover me," Kendra said.

Chris nodded and shot in rapid succession as she dashed to another vehicle on the far side of the highway. And then the awful impotent clicking sound told him he was out of ammo. He was fumbling to pull another mag from his pouch when he felt like someone had taken a baseball bat to his back. Chris tumbled over and saw a Dallek kid with a MAC-10 in his hand struggling with the bolt, cursing. Just as he cleared the jam and pointed the weapon at his face, an arrow suddenly appeared through the Adam's apple of the kid's neck.

The boy dropped the pistol and felt the bloody shaft protruding from his neck with his hands, his eyes pleading in shock. He knelt down, gasping to breathe and fell on top of Chris, clawing his poncho. Chris held him in a moment of empathy before the boy went limp.

Chris looked up to find that Ilsa had already placed another arrow on the arrow rest of her compound bow and shot again, screaming out, "Ilsa...Jeeeenkiiins!"

She jumped on top of the hood of the Trans Am and released another volley before stepping to the other side of the car.

The cacophonous sound of gunfire had eased, down to one or two shots. The pain of being hit on the back forced Chris to keel over. He didn't even see the kid swing the bat. Kendra raced up to Chris' side, turned Chris over and took off his Camelbak. His back ribs ached. He didn't know what asshole would use a baseball bat in the middle of a gun battle, but it was powerful enough to make him wince in pain even with the backpack covering him.

"Just hold still," she commanded and inspected his back.

"What, what!" he asked frantically. He started panicking. It wasn't a baseball bat hitting him, he realized. *Oh shit!* Had he been shot?

Kendra's sigh of relief told him to relax. "Your vest stopped the bullets. Your Camelbak drinking pouch is fucked, though, sir."

"B...bullets," he stuttered.

"Yeah. I counted three. You'll be feeling that in the morning." Kendra helped Chris up.

Chris looked around to see that the melee had ended. The Dallek boys lay sprawled along the barricaded highway. Chris saw Ilsa, who had returned from Robin Hood mode, pull out her pistol and callously take out a lone surviving Dallek boy before re-holstering it. He felt a cold wetness down his leg and momentarily panicked, stopping in mid stride.

"What? What is it?" The gunny asked standing next to him.

Chris looked down and saw his pants were wet indeed...with urine.

Relieved, he smiled sheepishly. "Um, I think I pissed myself."

The gunny put a meaty hand on his shoulder and chuckled. "Aye, just like me captain did when he first went in the shit years ago, wot?"

Chris staggered with Kendra's aid over to his bike.

"You did good, sir, real good."

"I...that guy," thinking about the figure behind the Connex container, "he was going to ambush us."

"True that, sir. A shitty ambush if there ever was one, total fucking bandit amateurs," she said with contempt. "But still, they might have succeeded had you not caught the little bastards." She stopped in mid stride. "Sir, have you been in any action before?"

He realized she meant battle. "No, I haven't."

119

"Well, how did you...I mean, you shot really well."

"Well, I got an Xbox for Christmas."

Just then Rita raced over to the child trailer. "Where's the first aid kit?"

Chris hurriedly opened the net and rifled through the gear and grabbed the red bag and handed to Rita. "What happened? Who is it?"

Rita didn't answer. She grabbed the bag and raced over to the side of highway near the railing. Chris and Kendra trotted over. Was it Akil? Was it Porkins? Chris soon saw the form lying down, struggling. The kind elderly gentleman Mustafa Haddad was being attended to by his sons Bilal and Yusef while Akil administered first aid.

"Come on!" he yelled.

Chris was about to race over but was stopped by Kendra. "Sir, there is nothing you and I can do. We need to keep our eyes out and let Akil take care of it."

"Um, yeah. Sure."

Akil had done what he could, but there was nothing really that anyone could do. Even if he had all of the advantages of modern medicine at his disposal, nothing could bring Mustafa back from the kind of mortal head wound he had sustained. Chris didn't get a good look, nor did he care to. Bilal was wailing over his slain father's body: Yusef was holding onto his brother as if he would collapse otherwise. It was a horrible humanizing sound, the cry of the grown man for his dead father. He could never allow the thoughts of losing his loved ones to be entertained.

After several minutes passed, Rita walked up to Bilal and Yusef.

"Your father was a good man. I am so sorry for your loss. Do you want us to help bury him?"

Bilal shook his head. "No, there's no time. The sounds of gunfire is gonna attract some of their homies. We all better split. If we leave now, they won't know we were involved. We'll take my father back."

Rita dipped her head solemnly. "No words can ease the loss, but know that your father has served humanity today, and that will not be forgotten. I can assure you that."

The Haddad sons wrapped their father in a blanket and made a stretcher to haul him off. It was going to be a difficult journey back home for them, both emotionally and physically. Rita didn't waste any time.

"All right, the Haddad boys are right. Dallek's buddies will be here any minute. It would be best if we make like a tree and get out of here."

"Captain, you good to ride, sir?" Kendra asked.

"I feel more beaten up than Liza Minnelli's husband, but yeah, I can ride."

"That's the spirit, sir," the gunny said.

"Good, let's imshee," Kendra concluded.

The Virginians carefully weaved around the barricade, which Chris now realized was more of a serpentine designed to slow a fast approaching horde down to a trickle. The bodies of the Dallek boys lay on the highways, their blood crusting on the icy asphalt, left to the elements. Chris found it odd that the reverend didn't bother with giving them some kind of service, even if they were bandits or gang bangers or whatever and had killed a good man in the process of trying to kill them. Regardless, it just felt wrong leaving them there to become another set of skeletons on the highway. But Chris knew the reverend was looking at the big picture. There were much bigger things to worry about, much more pressing issues. The skies overhead suddenly darkened, reflecting his mood. It looked like a big storm coming.

CHAPTER 15

Meredith was washing dishes inside the tiny confines of the apartment's kitchenette, gleefully whistling a tune. It wouldn't be long now. And then she felt the impact. It was followed by a low rumbling vibration that shook all the glass in the cabinet. She smiled and turned off the faucet to go outside. The sky had turned red and she could hear a sustained thunderous roar, faint and distant at first, but quickly gathering in intensity. Birds chirped and flew frantically in all directions. Some fell to the ground. Meredith looked down to see one fallen bird charred, still chirping.

She looked up to see herself dressed in a business suit kneeling beside her children pointing toward the approaching wave. The Meredith by her children smiled back at her briefly.

The wave of energy obliterated whole buildings and was racing up toward them mercilessly. Cars, people, mountains all incinerated by the blast wave. Meredith screamed to other Meredith. The other Meredith's smile waned just slightly. Meredith screamed with all of her strength at her to do something, anything, to not just die like this.

And then the wave came....

BACKGROUND MUSIC: "Winter" by Tori Amos
Visit www.michaeljuge.com **on the Refurbished Soul page to listen**

The Shiftiverse
Rochelle, Virginia
Rochelle Sovereignty
March 2013

Meredith awoke with Aidan, Rhiannon and baby Charles all cuddling in bed with her. Normally, Meredith would coax the two older children to go back to bed. They needed to learn to sleep on their own. But she admitted to herself that she appreciated their company, their warmth. Rhiannon's slightly curly honey-colored hair, Aidan's tiny boyish snore, and baby Charles' sound breathing eased the burden of waking into reality, where the knowledge of their fate immediately consumed her conscious mind.

Part of her, a large part of her, refused to get up and get out of bed, because it would mean that this was the day for her to leave. Tears streamed down her face, and she attempted to cry quietly so as to not wake them. This was the hardest thing she ever had to do. Quietly, she eased herself out of bed and got herself dressed in non-flattering sensible winter wear, and saw the image in the mirror. Her hair had just been cut short and dyed red. Through the tears she almost laughed. That was the same exact hairstyle she had back when she was dating Chris. In any case, it did obscure her looks. She did appear different from the infamous Vulcan, Director of the Swan. Gathering herself, she headed downstairs to wait for Jon.

As an armored truck pulled up to the Jung's farmhouse, the kids clutched her.

"Mommy don't go," Aidan cried. "We'll be all alone."

That only upset Rhiannon, who started bawling, which got baby Charles going. Meredith could no longer keep her own tears from her kids.

"Listen, I'll be back. I swear to you. And you'll be staying with the Hughes. You love sleeping over there. They let you stay up late."

"When will you be back, Mommy?"

"I…I don't know. But I swear I will come back soon."

They knew this was different from her last jaunt, they could see the fear in her eyes. As the carriage stopped, Jon Early got out boasting a walrus-like mustache, his hair had been dyed brown from his natural jet black color.

She turned to Brandon and Anne. "You'll read them stories every night."

"Yes."

"And Aidan likes ketchup on everything, okay. Just go with it. He won't eat otherwise."

"Got it. Avery is the same way," Brandon said patiently.

"And Mrs. Palfrey will be around if the kids get too homesick."

"Right, Chief."

"And don't let them listen to more than two hours…"

"Meredith, we've got to go," Jon interrupted.

"Okay," she said. She hugged Brandon and Anne, gave a messy tear soaked kiss to each of the children and forced herself up into the truck. Shutting the heavy door, she could hear them wailing.

The armored caravan drove past Rochelle. The town seemed empty now. Virtually all of the young men and women of Rochelle had been mobilized to the front in Staunton. They were heading there themselves, though she and Jon were just passing through.

Jon put on a pair of glasses, and ignoring Meredith's emotional state, he pointed to the map and spoke loudly above the angry diesel engine digesting its substandard fuel.

"We should reach Staunton before nightfall if all goes well! From there, we'll hitch ourselves in civilian caravans fleeing to West Virginia and make our way back around into Virginia through White Sulphur Springs." She didn't respond.

"We should be in Lynchburg in a couple of days going the long way around."

Still nothing.

"I'm truly sorry about this!" he screamed over the engine. "I know you're all the kids got right now until Chris returns! It's just you heard Valerie and what she said. Operation Parfait is dead in the water without us going there to re-assure them!"

"Operation Parfait is only dead because the resistance lacks confidence, Jon," she retorted, "because their main source of support, Juan Ramirez, has been disgraced, which you could reverse if you just told Neko the truth!"

"Negative! We tell them, and let's say they re-install him as deputy chief magistrate and guess what? The regent then learns what Juan's family is really part of and the whole resistance is screwed! Come on! We've been over this! Valerie couldn't convince them to move forward. They demanded us!"

"Me. They demanded *my* presence to reassure them. Why in God's name are you in the truck?"

Meredith wasn't angry at Jon, really. He was right. They had been over this already. Valerie Blaine returned the other day from Lynchburg bearing the news that the resistance in Lynchburg, which they had so carefully cultivated over the years and helped supply arms through Juan Ramirez's family, was losing their nerve right when the Orange Pact was going to really need them. The Lambs of God's Sheepdogs were out in force prowling for traitors and plastering their propaganda all over the Dominion. The Catholic minority, which made up the bulk of the fifth column, heard that the Unitarians had ousted their closest ally there, Juan Ramirez. The regent used the interim chief magistrate's ouster of the Christian former Deputy Chief Magistrate as proof of the Unitarians' persecution against Christians.

Of course, the regent defending the poor Christians in Greater Monticello was a complete farce considering that Juan Ramirez was a Catholic and the Catholic minorities who lived in the Dominion of Lynchburg were treated as second-class citizens. But regardless, they did not like what they heard about what was going on in Greater Monticello. Plus, the Catholics were being pressed into service to fight against the Orange Pact and given inferior training and weaponry to do it. In other words, the resistance saw a situation where they could be helping the very people who would kill their sons and brothers on the battlefield. It was not an easy situation to resolve. The leader of the resistance demanded that Meredith come over and give assurances herself. Meredith couldn't help but suspect that maybe she was volunteering herself as a hostage. They wanted her, not Jon.

She repeated her question. "Why are you coming with me?"

"I gave my promise to Chris to look after you. And here I am sending you into the lion's den. I'd never hear the end of it when he gets back that I let you go there while I sat fat and happy in Rochelle."

Meredith and he both knew that Rayne 2005 would most likely come before Chris could return, but she wasn't going to go there.

Meredith snorted. "Thuy said the same thing once."

Jon nodded. "Besides, the resistance has supplies and numbers, even some with some training, but they need someone to lead them."

"What about the leader of the resistance?"

Jon made a face. "I don't think she knows much about leading people into battle."

"And you think you can do that?"

Jon shrugged his shoulders. "There have been worse commanders."

"That's not what I mean."

"Dean has the Vicious Rabbits squared away; Thuy knows how to run things in the Sovereignty. It's time I pull my own weight again. This is what I know how to do."

Meredith nodded. It was true. Jon seemed more relaxed back in his element. If it ever came to her having to fight, God help her. But Jon? He was one of those guys who was alive only when grenades were landing in his lap and he had people to save and lead. Maybe he was right. Maybe he could lead them. He did pull a bunch of consultants, administrators and policy wonks into a formidable force once years ago.

"Jon, you think we can keep the Lambs of God back?"

"Are you talking about the odds or what I believe?"

"Is there a difference?"

Jon smiled through his thick walrus mustache. "I have faith that God will see us through the worst of it."

"I hope you're right."

She didn't hear him mutter, "You and me both."

CHAPTER 16

The Shiftiverse
Lynchburg, Virginia
The Dominion of Lynchburg
March 2013

Meredith and Jon had taken the really long way around to Lynchburg
from Rochelle. Interstate 81 was cut off to traffic from Lexington, held
in the south by the Lambs of God, all the way north to Staunton at
the Interstate 64 East, held by the Orange Pact. And Highway 29, the
most direct route between the towns of Lynchburg and Charlottesville,
hadn't been open for regular travel for almost a year. The only way in
was the circuitous route of traveling through the nominally neutral
Republic of West Virginia, although "neutral" was a relative term. The
president of West Virginia had thrown in his support for the regent and
his crusade against the wicked drug peddling forces of the Orange Pact.
The generous loans, the lend-lease programs in tanks and machine guns
had favored the Lambs of God and added to an already monumental
advantage over the Orange Pact.

While traveling through West Virginia, Meredith saw first-hand the
regent's tremendous influence in the Republic. Farms, stores and factories
displayed the West Virginian flag, the same as the former state flag, side-
by-side with the Lambs of God's flag showing a red flared cross on a
white field. Culturally, she could understand the regent's appeal over the
cultural bent of the Orange Pact, comprised of the strange Gaia religion

and the residue of the urban world of DC, Charlottesville and Richmond refugees.

In Lynchburg, Meredith was taken aback by how clean the city was. It was not as though Rochelle was a pig sty. No bones remained along the highways, people bathed and laborers cleaned the horse dung off the streets, but Lynchburg was immaculate, freakishly so. She had heard about the massive propaganda campaign the Lambs of God deployed against the Orange Pact. Posters were plastered throughout the city. One showed a crazed woman with black hair, an eye patch and blood dripping from her fangs, growling as she held a bloody knife over the bodies of children. As if there was any doubt as to who this image was referring to, the caricature wore the medallion of the chalice and flame to represent the Unitarian church. Over the image it proclaimed, "This is the enemy." Other posters displayed farmers, factory workers and Lambs of God soldiers raising their angular fists victoriously. The most common one showed Lambs of God soldiers, farmers, men, women and children of all colors, raising their hands skyward and reaching for a magnificent ball of fire. That disturbed her the most. Did Gordon Boche know about the approaching asteroid? Was he waiting for its arrival to announce God's return? And who was she to deny this delusional madman if the asteroid was truly going to wipe out all life on earth?

An old VW bus dropped Meredith and Jon off at St. Pius X Church in Lynchburg an hour before curfew, where she was met by Jennifer Engel, one of the first contacts provided by Ross. Jennifer had been the lifeline for the Swan regarding the Lambs of God activities since the Swan came into being; she wouldn't know where Rochelle would be without Ross' assistance. Once safely inside the church, Jennifer spoke.

"I can't tell you how relieved I am you made it. I haven't seen Lynchburg this locked down since the early days after the Reckoning."

Jennifer was a reliable operative of the Swan; Meredith had absolutely no doubt about that. Yet, it struck her to hear Jennifer use a Lynchburg term like "the Reckoning," rather than the Shift.

"And who is this?" Jennifer asked.

That took Meredith by surprise. Were their disguises that good?

"Jennifer, this is Jon Early."

"As in *the* Jon Early, like Constable Jon Early?"

"You got him," Jon said extending his hand; the two shook.

"Wow, it's just that, well, you look different from what I imagined."

Jon leaned over to Meredith, "I guess the stache really works, eh?" as he stroked his mustache.

"Well, to be honest, I've never really seen a picture of you. The regent's Xerox machine's been on the fritz for five years or so, so it's down to the regent's artistic renderings of you. Guess ya do look more like Richard Gere than they made you out to be, now that I think of it." Jennifer extended her finger and closed one eye to imagine Jon without the mustache.

"Well, you coming here is a coup de maître. I'll say that much, Constable. We were just expecting the Vulcan, but the people will be gratified to have the Constable making the journey himself. Though I have to say, you're got a tough audience to convince."

"I understand."

"Anyway, I'll show you to your rooms. Y'all can freshen up and then meet Sister Shanyn."

The past few days had been so stressful with she and Jon going undercover as siblings travelling home to the Dominion before the war started, she had little time to pine for her kids. Meredith had never gone clandestine before; she had always handled clandestine operators, managed the intelligence coming from them, and directed the operations. But now, she was living it. And living out the part of a spy confirmed that she definitely was not cut out for it. She had managed to keep her composure at the series of West Virginian and Lambs of God checkpoints, but she felt like she would vomit at any moment. It wasn't really the fear of being brought to the regent as a prize or losing her life. It was the thought of being separated from her children. The end was coming so soon. She felt an overwhelming sense that she should have stayed home with her children until Rayne 2005 arrived.

Now that the most dangerous part had passed and she was settling in her bunk, a Sunday school classroom, she wished she could have brought a photo of her kids. Photography was extremely expensive now. The chemicals to make the photographs were in finite supply, housed solely in West Virginia. She couldn't take a picture and put it in her wallet. Photographs were valuable items, taken mostly in black and white given the chemicals available, and were framed prominently in people's houses as a way of showing off as well as adding décor.

Meredith washed her face and looked in the mirror, seeing the out of date 90s haircut she wore in Grad School. She dried off and headed to the church basement to meet the resistance leadership in Lynchburg. She hoped that her personal reassurances and Jon's presence would encourage them to execute Operation Parfait.

She had a sudden side thought. They really should have come up with a better name for the clandestine plan than "Operation Parfait." It was meant to be just a place holder name until they came up with something better. Thuy coined it, because "everybody loves parfait, right?" The planners around the room just shrugged and said, "yeah," so it stuck.

The church basement looked like any other church basement. Unlike Rochelle and the other Orange Pact communities, Lynchburg didn't ration energy output. The fact that the lights were on, every last florescent lamp, was telling. Seeing that made Meredith all the more aware of how rich Lynchburg was in comparison to the Orange Pact. Being such close friends with the Saudis of post-Shift America, the West Virginians, had its advantages.

There was a group of ten individuals sitting in foldout chairs. These folks were the heart of the resistance in Lynchburg. They didn't look like resistance commanders, but more rather a focus group testing which was the superior cola. Jon and Meredith sat up front with Jennifer Engel and leveled a gaze at the unfriendly faces glaring back at them. It was one of those awkward silences that Chris always claimed existed between him and her when they started dating but she never understood what he was talking about. Now, she felt it. The silence was broken when a woman at the tail end of middle age walked in wearing a white habit and overalls. The people's expressions changed to one of warmth upon seeing her walk in.

"Hello, Mrs. Jung, Constable Early. It is a great pleasure to meet you. I'm Sister Shanyn Duffy, but just call me Sister Shanyn."

Sister Shanyn greeted both kindly, shaking their hands with both of hers. Meredith felt calluses on her hands.

"I would like to introduce you to some friends who have risked life and limb getting here—Meredith Jung and Constable Jon Early."

The small collection harrumphed among themselves for a few moments before she continued. "Now, I know we've been quite unsettled by recent events, and I understand your concerns, but I believe we should hear what they have to say."

Jon nudged Meredith, prompting her to speak. She found herself feeling nervous. She stood up, allowed herself to cough nervously once, then mentally put on her sales executive hat. She forced her face to relax. "Thank you, Sister Shanyn. If you know who I am, then you must know how important you are to me. I'm not going to mince words here. I have risked everything to come here and tell you personally that now is the time to act. The Lambs of God have mobilized the majority of their forces north of Lexington on Interstate 81 and have invested themselves, men, material, and other assets in that direction. I know you have been given conflicting information and it shakes your will. But as the Lambs of God are a few days from attacking our forces, you will not find a better opportunity to strike."

"Why on earth should we?" a man asked skeptically. "I mean, isn't it true that your best friend the reverend ousted Juan Ramirez, just because he's a Catholic?"

Another countered, "That's the regent's propaganda machine lying to you!"

"It's not propaganda. It's true," said a woman. "Juan has been kicked out! We haven't gotten any money in a month to pay off the smugglers! How do you explain that?"

The leaders started arguing amongst each other until Sister Shanyn whistled calling everyone to be silent. Like school children who knew not to piss off a nun, they immediately quieted.

"Reverend Rita Luevano has done no such thing. The reverend has been … well, she's not in Monticello right now."

"Where is she?" someone asked.

Meredith sucked in air through her teeth. "Well, she went on a mission to Maryland. She's been gone since the New Year."

"Why would she be going on a mission?"

"Yeah, what's that about?"

Meredith rolled her eyes at the slew of questions. That abomination of a mission to Maryland had cost her people a lot, and for what? To stop the Abercrombies from obtaining nuclear material that they wouldn't ever be able to use? It was a total disaster, but there was nothing to done about that now. "Look, the point is that Rita was not the one who ousted Juan."

"Great, then who muscled into power and threw Juan out?"

"Was there a coup? Is the reverend dead?"

"Nobody muscled their way into power…not really, anyway." Actually, that was probably an apt description of how Neko Lemay came to be installed as the interim chief magistrate. But it was done through a quick vote of hands, so technically it was a democratic process, technically. *Details, don't get caught up in details.*

"Neko Lemay is serving as interim chief magistrate while the reverend is in Maryland. She is in charge of Greater Monticello until the reverend returns." This didn't sound encouraging, so she pressed to her point. "But what's important to understand is that Neko did not know that Juan Ramirez was actually working for us and providing you with material assistance. The sheriff discovered part of a paper trail that pointed to Juan being involved in some nefarious dealings that looked like theft and embezzlement. They didn't know the whole story. I am confident had they known the truth, they wouldn't have demanded his resignation." Another asked, "Well, didn't you enlighten them?"

"Not exactly."

"Why not? You're telling us, right?"

"That's because we already know," another explained.

"I was concerned that if we informed them and if Juan returned to his position, it would tip our hand to the regent."

"Be that as it may, we're hearing that the chief magistrate is jailing all Christians including Catholics."

"That is patently false," she said flatly.

"I heard the chief magistrate outlawed Christian services in Greater Monticello," said another.

"The regent is lying to you, I promise." *At least I hope nothing changed in the last few days,* Meredith thought to herself. Aloud she continued. "I admit Neko and the Sheriff are a little…over zealous in preventing agents of the regent from undermining Monticello. But the regent did attempt to assassinate Rita last Christmas. Were you aware of that? I can promise you nevertheless that Greater Monticello is not your enemy, the regent is."

"Well, that's exactly it," said a man who seemed to be the most vociferous. "The regent has pushed all of our sons into service, and guess where they're sending them?—right up to Highway 29. Our sons, our brothers, our friends, they're being sent to fight Greater Monticello, and now you want our assistance in fighting the Lambs of God when that means killing our sons? I can't see any of us agreeing to that."

Meredith knew this was going south and she was desperately trying to reverse it. "We're not after your sons. We have no quarrel with you. It's the Lambs of God who are our common enemies."

Jon Early suddenly chimed in casually. "She's right you know."

"Of course you're going to agree with her, she's your top spy."

"I listen to Meredith because she has a extraordinary propensity to be right whether I like it or not. She doesn't allow sentiment to cloud her judgment." Jon stood up and took command of the room. "Let's get something straight here. The Lambs of God are your enemies. They always have been. Look at yourselves. Come on. Anyone here can clearly see you have been treated as a bunch of foreigners, in your own home, no less. Tell me if I'm wrong. Come on, someone please correct me on this."

"But the regent is sending our boys to fight your people," one of the woman leaders said.

"Yes, he is. The regent has attempted to drive a wedge between us, tried to hold your sons and brothers hostages to try to bully you into believing that your best chance of making it through another month, another year is to throw your lot with him."

He snorted. "Don't buy into the deal he's selling you. You know exactly where this is going to go. You know exactly how he sees the world, heaven, earth, the chosen ones and the damned. And you know who you are to him. You think you can kiss his boots and he'll let up?"

Meredith picked up on that thought. "The regent was smart in trying to put your men as hostages, giving them virtually no training and shabby equipment, but he undermined his own objective."

"I don't understand," Sister Shanyn asked.

"Quite simply, Sister Shanyn, by lumping all of the Catholics into one regiment and placing them in one theater, he has just safeguarded them from any of the real action."

"They aren't safeguarded at all! When the Monticellans attack...."

"But they won't, not so long as they aren't attacked first," Meredith answered. The wheels started spinning about how she was going to get word to Monticello about the developments.

"How can you be so sure?" one of them asked skeptically. "The Unitarians hate Christians. It doesn't matter whether they are Catholic or Lambs of God."

Jon shook his head. "Not true. I am a Christian, and Rita Luevano is one of my closest friends. Half of Rochelle is Christian, the vast majority of citizens in Culpeper are as well. The friendship Rita and I have and the alliance between Greater Monticello, Rochelle, Culpeper and the Fredericksburg Union could not be possible if even a tenth of what the regent said about her was true."

Jon had seemed to been invigorated by the discussion. He stared right into the eyes of each of the leaders.

"Well, then, people, this is your moment. You must now decide where you will stand. Meredith and I came here to assure you that we in the Orange Pact will not leave you hanging if you take the one opportunity you will ever have in your life to stand up for your freedom. We are going to face them and we will not back down. What about you? This is your only chance."

For all of the good it would do—for in a matter of days, it will all be erased—Meredith wanted something life affirming, something that stood in the face of the odds.

"But our children," said one woman.

The man in the front who had been so critical up until now said, "They would want us to stand up for them. I remember when I was an American. I want my children to know something of the world I had."

Sister Shanyn stood up. "We will need a majority vote to proceed. We will meet tomorrow after services."

After the resistance commanders departed, the room was empty save for Meredith, Jon, Sister Shanyn and Jennifer Engel. Meredith felt her adrenaline rush subside to be replaced by a headache, hunger, and a deep need to sleep. She was about to walk back into her quarters when Sister Shanyn stopped her.

"We need to talk."

Sister Shanyn didn't seem much like a nun, at least in Meredith's limited experience, which was primarily limited to TV caricatures. Sister Shanyn seemed vibrant and youthful despite her years, and looked more Irish than her name suggested, if that was possible. Meredith and Jon sat back down to listen.

"You mentioned during the meeting that neither that interim chief magistrate nor the Sheriff Lucille Schadenfreude were aware of the role Juan Ramirez played in the resistance."

"That's right," Meredith answered.

"Well, that's what I have to tell you." Sister Shanyn waited until Jennifer closed the door. She moved in close as to whisper to her, which seemed odd.

"You see, I know that Lucille Schadenfreude knew Juan Ramirez's true mission this whole time."

Meredith was about to say something like, "holy shit," which might possibly be considered a sin to say in front of a nun—she wasn't an expert on such things. Fortunately, the only words she could manage were, "whaa...?"

CHAPTER 17

The Shiftiverse
Charlottesville, Virginia
Greater Monticello
March 2013

"Sometimes I just wish some of our friends would say they want us to win, you know?"

Lucille Schadenfreude's observation was met with enthusiastic applause as she stood at the podium next to Neko Lemay, giving her final remarks before the soldiers in the Monticellan Defense Forces and the Thomas Jefferson Martyrs Brigade deployed. Lucille wasn't specifically mentioning Christians. After all, roughly ten percent of Greater Monticello was Christian, and there was a comparable share serving in both the Monticellan Defense Forces and the Thomas Jefferson Martyrs Brigade. But Neko understood what she meant, so did many others, including roughly ten percent in the crowd who weren't cheering along with Lucille's rousing speech.

"After all, we, the true Monticellans, have been defending the freedoms of all peoples throughout the Shenandoah Valley since our birth. From the time when the Blue Ridge Militia stooges tried to overrun us when we were but a small band of frightened refugees to the Obsidian War when we showed those mercenary goons what for, Monticello has stood on the side of freedom." Lucille's rectangular glasses reflected the sunlight as she spoke, almost blinding Neko standing next to her.

"It makes me so proud to see you *real* Monticellans all out here, so strong and magnificent, protecting our homes and embodying the Gaia spirit. I just wish we didn't have some people trying to undermine everything we worked for."

Many shouted in support, "Yeah!" "Traitors!"

"I mean, canoodling around with Lambs of God?"

There was a chorus of boos. Although neither Neko nor Lucille actually said that Juan Ramirez had funneled money to his family, some of who were members of the Sheepdogs, the word had gotten out regardless. Juan and his family had since left the town. Neko figured that some of the Christians in the audience didn't appreciate Lucille's frank style. Well, they could go screw themselves, or better yet, go to that mythical place they made up called hell. It would serve them right the way they undermined the reverend's community. Neko felt herself getting angrier as Lucille riled up the crowd.

"Strike a blow for liberty!" she cried out.

"Liberty!" the crowd shouted back.

"Strike a blow for dignity!"

"Dignity!"

"Strike a blow for Gaia!"

"For Gaia!"

That last one wasn't actually part of Monticello's chant. Originally it was "Liberty, Dignity, Equality!" But Neko didn't mind the slight alteration. She herself often had called Gaia's name in battle back when she was a soldier, before a Christian crippled her.

She walked off the stage to be met by Ezra Rothstein, who was in his archer's regalia. As she approached, she felt slightly diminutive standing next to him. She could have sworn he had grown another three inches since they first met. She had known Ezra a long time now, and could read his dour expression.

"Okay, Dork, you got your marching orders."

"What the hell was that?" he asked angrily.

"What was what?"

"That whole 'I wish they would just say that they want us to win,'" he quoted, imitating her nasal voice to portray Lucille to be as obnoxious as possible.

"You're a smart boy, Ezra, read between the lines."

"Yeah, Neko, I can read between the lines. I heard the empress loud and clear. What the hell are you doing engaging in this sort of divisive rhetoric?"

"We're rallying the troops. You should know something about that."

"Well, it sure was a shitty job if that was what you were trying to do."

"Well, I know Lucille and I are not nearly as eloquent as the reverend…"

"Eloquence has nothing to do with this. Arousing people's lowest urges is what you're doing."

"The Lambs of God are our enemy, bent on our extinction!"

"No shit, psycho! I'm talking about the fact that you and Fraulein Schadenfreude are stirring hatred and mistrust among our own people! Christians! That isn't a way to rally the troops. I can tell you that. There's a sizeable portion of those troops who have just been alienated and insulted. Way to blow, Neko."

"Oh my God, you are *so* naïve, Ezra. You have no idea how entrenched the Lambs of God are. They have their tendrils across every facet of our society. They have infiltrated us with impunity for years."

"I know that's your handler talking. 'Impunity,' 'tendrils'? Those are mighty big words for a girl like you."

Neko glared at him. Only Ezra could enrage her the way he did.

"Are you blind? Don't you see who their loyalties lay with? Who the hell caused this?" she barked pointing to her limp arm and the scarred shoulder.

"Is that what this is about…whining about your arm?"

"To hell with you."

"We're about to go to war and you're…"

"We've always been at war!" she roared. Her outburst was so powerful that heads at the rally turned. "We always have been," she added quietly this time.

"What is it with you, Neko? As long as I've known you, you've been angry, and you always had it in for the Christians."

"You wouldn't understand."

"Right. I wouldn't understand having a beef with Christians? I'm Jewish. I think I can use my imagination. Why do you hate them so much? Because of the assassination attempt?"

"I don't care to talk about it."

"You're the one who said we've always been at war. You tell me what the hell you mean by it."

"Because we have been."

She couldn't hold it back anymore. She hadn't known why she had been so adamant not to discuss it with anyone, save Rita and recently Lucille. Maybe it was because she didn't want pity. Maybe because it was too painful to retell. But she had to tell him so he would understand, so that he would finally grasp the reality that the Christians had been at war with her and people like her long before the Shift ever happened. They had been out to hunt people like her for generations. He had to know what they were really about, what their true motives were. Neko gestured and the two of them walked over behind the bleachers. Neko took a deep breath as she recalled the painful events.

"My mom died when I was young, of cancer. My dad, who was the sheriff in the town I grew up in Washington State, was the only family I had. He taught me everything I knew. He was the one who got me into archery. Did I ever tell you that?"

"My dad was my entire world. And then one day, he received a call about a suspicious package outside an abortion clinic. He arrived before the bomb squad. It went off and the explosion killed him."

"Did he pick it up?"

She looked at him. "I don't fucking know, Ezra! It went off! It killed my father and you can guess what kind of assholes were behind this. I was sixteen and I lost everything. They took away everything from me. I was sent to live with my aunt and uncle, who my father had never introduced me to, and I learned why he never wanted me to get to know them."

She smiled bitterly. "They said it was a shame that my dad lost his life when the bomb should have killed the 'murdering doctors' who performed the abortions."

After a prolonged silence, Ezra said, "Wow. I didn't...look, I'm so sorry. That's terrible. But you have to understand. It wasn't Christians who killed your father. It was a bunch of extremist assholes, the same kind of dickwads in charge in Lynchburg. Assholes exist everywhere, Neko, Christians, Muslims, some Jews even. And yes, even Unitarians. But it isn't all Christians or even most Christians."

"Why do you care? You aren't a Christian. Hell, you aren't even a Unitarian anymore."

"Let's be clear, Neko. I didn't leave the Unitarian Church, the Unitarian Church left me. And as to why I care? I care because this is my home as much as it is yours, as much as it is to those Christians out there who are going to fight and who are going to die for us."

Neko saw Ezra hesitate before he said, "It's every bit the home of Christians who fought by our side in the Battle for Monticellan Independence, people like Juan Ramirez."

"Juan Ramirez is a traitor who embezzled Byrds for his own gain."

"You actually believe that don't you? I suppose that's a good thing that you do, something redeeming about this whole thing."

"What are you talking about, Ezra? He's as guilty as a cat in a goldfish bowl. Sheriff Schadenfreude had been tracking his movements and connections for some time."

"Yeah, I bet she has."

He started storming off when she grabbed him with her good arm. The action exacerbated the pain in her right arm, causing her to wince.

"What, Ezra? What were you going to say?"

Ezra stopped. He was about to speak, she could see it, but then he seemed to have changed his mind. "I have a war to fight, Neko. Take care of yourself. Oh, and be sure to tell the sheriff thanks but no thanks for the deputies she's sending to watch over my peeps. If they aren't going to be fighting the Lambs of God, pushing carts, taking care of wounded or providing massages complete with a happy ending, then they're about as useful as tits on a bull."

Neko couldn't help but grin. Sheriff Schadenfreude insisted that her deputies be incorporated into all fighting elements, not to fight but rather to keep a watchful eye. After all, Christians were fully integrated into the Thomas Jefferson Martyrs Brigade as well as the Monticellan Defense Forces. They were entrenched, as the sheriff reminded her. Yet, it didn't exactly sit right with her, sending spies into her own Martyrs Brigade. She knew them all.

"Well, Ezra I promoted you to colonel. You can put them into service."

He started walking off again and then stopped. "I know you didn't want this job. You did what you thought was necessary, because you want what's best for Monticello, you and me both. And you and I both can agree that Rita took care of Monticello best of all, better than you and I together could."

Neko nodded. She missed Rita so much, the mention of her name evoked an emotional response.

"Whatever you do from here on out, I want you to ask yourself one thing. What would Rita do? Would she be proud of your actions, would she do this, too? What would Rita do?"

Ezra picked up his rifle as an archer handed him the reigns to Charlene.

He hopped on up in the saddle. "And the last bit is 'equality,' Neko. Don't ever forget that. Rita chose that for a reason. Think about it. Come on Charlene, h'ya."

Ezra and his mare clopped off with the rest of the Thomas Jefferson Martyrs Brigade. Neko felt a pang, wishing that she could be fighting alongside them, alongside her friend, the infuriating bastard he was. Lucille approached Neko.

"Trouble?"

Neko said nothing. She just walked off.

CHAPTER 18

BACKGROUND MUSIC: "Any Way You Want It" by Journey
Visit www.michaeljuge.com **on the Refurbished Soul page to listen**

The Shiftiverse
Staunton, Virginia
March 6, 2013

Ezra had been to the Prancing Pony on numerous occasions over the years; after all, the Ice Dragon who ran the former Chili's, and most of Staunton, was an operative of the Swan. Ezra had sent and received a lot of traffic at the bar & grill & brothel & tobacco exchange. Usually, the establishment was filled with a cross section of the post-Shift Mid-Atlantic region's entrepreneurs, from coal, natural gas and precious chemical barons out of West Virginia, to tobacco brokers from Monticello and Rochelle, pot runners, fish distributors from Fredericksburg, men for hire, and women for hire. Slavers were forbidden in Staunton and he never did see the Ice Dragon ever entertain them, a credit to her.

Tonight, the Prancing Pony was populated exclusively by soldiers from the four communities of the Orange Pact. Vicious Rabbits and Monticellans traditionally had a close relationship. Culpeper and the Vicious Rabbits also worked closely together. Culpeper and Monticello, not quite as much. The Fredericksburg Union soldiers were the strange outsiders of the bunch. They weren't seen out this far west normally.

There was little uniformity even within the same army, save for the armbands that denoted which flag they fought under. The Vicious Rabbits wore tunics and pants that roughly resembled US military BDUs. The mottled camouflage was a mixture of green and grey hues. It blended relatively well with the Blue Ridge Mountain color schema, and also worked for an urban environment. The Monticellans, on the other hand, had camouflage schemes dedicated for the forests and their pants more closely resembled Cossack pants than anything else. Boots were any pair of pre-Shift hiking or combat boots. Whereas decent clothes could be manufactured with the relatively low-tech resources available and the ample supply of workers, things such as shoes could not be produced, at least no pair of shoes a civilized person would want to wear. Turn-of-the-millennium materials technology could not be fabricated in the post-Shift world, not even in West Virginia. Ezra had seen ferals and West Virginian laborers make do with "shoes" made of simple cloth and tire treads held together with duct tape. It was no wonder they were so miserable beyond the general change of fortune for them.

Despite coming from different communities, and training in different ways, the four armies all seemed to drill well together. That was a small blessing considering how they were overwhelmingly outnumbered. Latest intelligence revealed that the Lambs of God were on the march straight up Interstate 81 from Lexington. Fortunately, the forces holding in Colleen off of Highway 29 were not nearly as impressive as the truly superior forces of the Lambs of God heading up to meet them right now. Neko was right to not fall for the feint the Lambs of God had created with their build up at Highway 29. At least she trusted his intel. As for the real front on Interstate 81, even with every single Orange Pact militia at the gates of Staunton, The Lambs of God outnumbered them five to one.

Ezra hoped the defenders here could slow the Lambs of God's advance and attrite some of their numbers along the way. Some of his archers were out near Lexington right now, laying mines, destroying roads, setting up traps and executing hit and run ambushes...*just like the good old days*, Ezra thought to himself. He used to be the one taking the pot shots and running like hell before the enemy could regroup. Now as the commander of the Thomas Jefferson Martyrs Brigade and in charge of the Monticellan forces in the Interstate 81 theater, he spent his time sitting in meetings with Commandant Dean Jacob trying to coordinate their efforts, rationalize their logistics and figure a way out of the collective bag they were all in.

It was bad, really bad. Ezra was sitting at a table with some of his archers and ordered mutton and beer. Everyone was smoking their stock of cigarillos. Ezra knew that it was a bad habit. He grew up with a barrage of harsh anti-smoking TV ads, so did most of them here, but being on death's cul-de-sac had a way of making tobacco that much more satisfying.

He now understood the appeal and why people died rather than quit. He still forbade himself from ever drinking hard stuff before battle, but the likelihood that they all would be eventually run over and shredded into a meat grinder of gunfire begged him to reconsider his self-imposed restrictions.

It was a lively crowd considering what they were about to face. He dared to say that the Prancing Pony hadn't seen this much festivity before, not even in its former life when it was a Chili's. The Ice Dragon kept much of the décor from the original Chili's—the ornamental stop light, street signs, prints of rock musicians and kitschy 50s style Coca Cola advertisements. Men and women soldiers mingled about in the dimly kerosene-lit establishment and seemed to be enjoying the Ice Dragon's indulgence of a jukebox playing another fossil rock song. Everyone was singing along.

"Any way you want it
That's the way you need it
Any way you want it!"

Some part of him felt like his generation had been cheated. And no, he wasn't whining over the world ending. That was so 2007. No, Ezra felt his generation had been cheated out of having their own music. *I mean, look at us*, he thought caustically, *we're on the eve of battle, and do we have anything from this century to rock out to? No!* They were all confined in a time warp, listening to yet another song from their parents' generation. Where was his generation's music? All erased to the EMPs.

Ezra wished he could join in the celebration. Most were too young to have been in the Obsidian War, the last major conflict. The soldiers here might have had experience with a few run-ins against bandits, but that was nothing. The civilized always outmaneuvered and outgunned the bandits. They were just starving desperados. The Lambs of God on the other hand were soldiers, professional soldiers who solely trained night and day for years, learning one thing, how to kill. They were one force with no politics to get in the way. Outside of the Catholic minority, the Dominion of Lynchburg was homogenous with one leader and one mission.

Ezra took another gulp of beer—that was one thing that was better in the post-Shift world, the beer—and watched some drunken Fredericksburg militia air guitaring. In the corner, some of Sheriff Schadenfreude deputy goons sat sullenly eyeing everyone suspiciously. Showing some sense, Neko put them under his direct command, and Ezra enjoyed putting them on latrine duty. He was about to go take a whiz himself when he caught the bartender Maude gesturing for him. With a mixture of excitement and relief, Ezra gave her the okay.

After relieving himself in the out houses, Ezra re-entered the Prancing Pony through the employee's entrance into the kitchen. Valerie Blaine stood inside the Ice Dragon's office waiting for him. Even dressed in her Vicious Rabbits uniform and her MOLLE gear, Valerie was luminous. Makeup was not commonly available anymore, but he could swear she was wearing some. Her blonde hair gracefully tickled the top of her shoulders. Ezra sauntered over to her as casually as he could manage.

"Hey," he said and jerked his head upward.

"Hey yourself." She proceeded to grab him and landed a luscious kiss and ran her fingers through his black hair. She was dangerous, all right. If he let himself be a fool, well, that would just be too easy.

"I've missed you. I mean, I…we, all of us in the Swan, we miss you… the Monticellans."

Ezra suppressed a sly smile. *So, she missed me, eh?* Aloud, he said, "I miss being in the know."

Ever since returning to Monticello from Lynchburg, Neko Lemay had recalled all Monticellan operatives at the Swan, and did so at a critical juncture. He sent word to Valerie where he would be so he could update her on the goings on at home and hopefully learn something useful from her.

"So, are things as bad as they appear?" he asked.

"It's worse, Ezra. Your girlfriend, Neko, and the sheriff have gone and royally fucked things up with Operation Parfait."

Ezra grimaced. "That's what I was afraid of. We really, really need them to distract the regent. If they refuse, well, hell, you know the rest."

"What's been going on down there, anyway?" Valerie inquired. This was part of the reason for their rendezvous, sharing intel.

"Oh, Neko is on this trip. She sees all Christians as a threat, not just some of the wack jobs that have supported the regent. And her Sith master Lucille is whispering this distorted version of reality in her ear the whole time. That whole thing with Juan gave her all the proof she needed."

"Didn't you tell Neko the truth about Juan?"

He shook his head. "Meredith told me not to until instructed. Is she giving me the go ahead? Because I really think that would help."

Valerie winced. "Yeah, about that. Meredith's in Lynchburg."

"You're shitting me."

"Shit you I do not. She and Constable Early are both in Lynchburg…"

"What? They're both in Lynchburg?" he exploded.

"That's what I said. Now, listen, they're trying to reassure the resistance that not only will the Orange Pact be throwing the full measure of its forces in the fight against the Lambs of God, but that the Monticellans are not in fact persecuting the Christians."

Ezra rolled his eyes. There was something ironic about a Jew worrying about the persecution of Christians, he thought. "I wish I could give you something to counter that impression. Unfortunately, all I will be able to offer is shit and bubble gum and I just ran out of bubble gum."

Valerie shook her head. "This is not good. If we can't convince the resistance of our intentions, then we have no guarantee that they will rise up when it's time, which is like tomorrow."

"You should get Meredith and Jon out of there now. Meredith is no spy and Jon sticks out like…"

Ezra and Valerie both heard the music on the jukebox on the other side of the wall stop with an ear piercing scratch, followed by a ruckus. Ezra and Valerie walked into the dining area and saw all of the soldiers were up on their haunches ready to pounce. As he assumed to be the case, he could tell that soldiers sidled up with their own units. He had been in a couple of brawls before, once against the Vicious Rabbits. It didn't mean anything. There were more brawls between two Martyrs Brigade platoons than there were between personnel of differing communities. At first, Ezra chalked it up to just another one of the testosterone meets alcohol on the eve of battle kind of things, but when he saw at the center of this standoff were his two handlers from Lucille Schadenfreude facing off with a group of Culpeper regulars, he knew this wasn't the normal sort of bar fight. *Oh shit, not this. Not now.*

"What 'chu say about my people, asshole?" prodded a corn-fed Culpeper soldier to one of the Monticellan agents who looked a lot smaller.

The agent, one of Sheriff Schadenfreude's deputies formerly named Jerome who renamed himself Kalunda, didn't seem intimidated. He pressed his nose up to the Goliath-like man.

"I said your people are a bunch of cross kissers just like the regent."

"What're you gonna do about, it, punk?"

Ezra's stomach clenched. It was almost as though those agents of the sheriff were trying to sow mistrust. Maybe they were. He had to stop this now.

"All right, what's all this then?" Ezra belted out authoritatively.

The Culpeper mammoth kept his eyes glued on the Monticellan

deputies. "I don't know what kind of ship you're running, sir, but these two men started it, disparaging our people's religion and our loyalty."

Ezra sauntered over to the deputies. "Is this true?"

"What you care, boy?" Deputy Kalunda sneered. "You're as much a traitor..."

Kalunda didn't get the rest of that sentence out because Valerie landed a jaw-breaking blow with the heel of her palm. A Fredericksburg soldier screamed, "Ouch, my foot, you bitch!"

And that is when Ezra Rothstein knew he was indeed a fool for Valerie, because without even thinking he head butted the offending soldier for calling his girl names. And that was it; soup was on.

The entire dining room of the Prancing Pony erupted into a free-for all brawl. Another Fredericksburg soldier cried out, "FU forever!" their battle cry, while the Monticellans, Culpeper and Vicious Rabbits all threw into the fight. Ezra got tackled but scampered out of the way in time before the Culpeper guy picked up a table and threw it at a group of Vicious Rabbits. A person was thrown across the room and into the jukebox, jolting it to life as it randomly chosen a song. Of all the songs it could have chosen, it had to be this one.

"Everybody was Kung Fu Fighting
Those kids were fast as lightning"

The iconic 70s tune, which started right on the first lyrics didn't seem to interrupt the brawl. It actually lifted the spirits a bit. By this time, the fights weren't clearly Monticellans against Culpeper or Fredericksburg against Vicious Rabbits. It was units fighting units within the same community. Ezra caught Valerie huddled below a table sipping a beer and cheered him on. In the midst of it, he realized Valerie had just done him a real solid. Everyone had forgotten all about the sectarian nature that initiated the argument, which led to the masterful right cross she threw on a soldier. Everyone was now fighting just for the sake of it. Ezra attempted the "crane" move from *The Karate Kid* in reverence to the song while Valerie looked on mildly impressed. With a bit of cockiness brought on by adrenaline and beer, Ezra sauntered over to her, when a fist got in his way, right in his face.

CHAPTER 19

BACKGROUND MUSIC: "Human" by Civil Twilight
Visit www.michaeljuge.com on the Refurbished Soul page to listen

The Mundaniverse
Rochelle, Virginia
March 6, 2013

Chris took one last look at the thicket of trees from the side of the two-lane highway. The moon reflected off the asphalt and treetops offering a decent view of the woods where his home was supposed to be. Chris remembered when they cleared the land to build on this plot. He and Meredith agreed to build south of what had originally been the center of Rochelle, the mail drop at an intersection near the Early's residence. It was a short horse ride to Montpelier Station, which had become the Vicious Rabbits headquarters located between Rochelle's largest town of Orange and Rochelle proper. He and Meredith actually missed the Hughes' home after having lived there over a year, but were thrilled to finally have a home of their own. And it was exactly the kind of home they had always dreamt about, a quaint two-story farm house built in the classical design with plenty of bedrooms for guests and children.

Chris spent the happiest years of his life inside these woods. The Obsidian War had ended several months earlier when he and Meredith moved into their new home, which he and others built themselves. He conceived the idea of his armoring business in the kitchen while cooking dinner. Meredith had conceived of numerous crazy plots to keep Rochelle safe. The two of them together conceived Rhiannon and baby Charles here. Both children were born here as well. He read stories to Aidan and Rhiannon in their bedrooms by light of kerosene; Meredith played the piano for the kids while Chris tried his hand at relearning how to play guitar.

Chris was in his element in Rochelle. There was no place, not even his original home of New Orleans, where Chris felt he truly belonged as much as he did in Rochelle. There was no place that fostered the best in him as Rochelle did. And there was no place he would rather be than here, or more precisely, the other here.

But far from the bustling town filled with X-Wing cabin homes, hastily constructed in the early months after the Shift, and the follow-up houses and various smith shops and foundries that cropped up in the years since, this Rochelle was unpopulated farmland. Trees covered the place where his home should be. The Hughes' home was there, so was the Early's. Chris was tempted, but decided against introducing himself to the Early's. He didn't even know if Charles was alive in this timeline and if he was, Charles certainly wouldn't believe his story. Furthermore, waking anyone up at 4:00 in the morning was a bad idea. Coming out here was a bad idea, he realized. He was looking for home, but seeing the undeveloped forest reinforced how impossibly far away home was. Chris shivered slightly under his Snuggie, and walked back towards the blinking lights of his Corolla.

"Come on, Corolla, giddy-up," he said as he turned on the ignition and drove off, passing Funeral Mound, which here was nothing but a bluff with an abandoned barn. As he raced to make it back to Falls Church before Meredith awoke, Chris chose a song on the iPod not familiar to him. He had a propensity lately for playing Classic Rock, thinking it would provide him comfort to hear music he listened to all the time back home. But in the end, it only served to make him feel even more severed from his world, as this visit to Rochelle had done.

At work, Chris tried to concentrate, but between not getting more than a couple hours of sleep last night, and overhearing the conversation between Ted and other coworkers about a possible furlough, it really was hard to concentrate. Furthermore, that damned phone number itched his mind again. He wrote it down on a piece of paper, but he didn't need to, because for some unknown reason it was seared into his memory. 202-187-5305. What the hell kind of phone number was that, anyway?

Chris opened the cable that brought the phone number to his attention and was surprised to find that the number had been redacted, no, not redacted. It just didn't exist in the cable.

"What the?"

He shook his head, giving up. He was tempted to just call the damned number. *And that would be a stupid idea, now wouldn't it, Chris?* Indeed it would. The number had been mentioned in a DIA cable. Whoever it belonged to was bad news. What's more, the DIA found it necessary to erase it from the cable. The DIA, NSA and a host of others would indeed be interested as to why some State Department intel Analyst was calling it. No doubt they would be listening in. Call it? That was a pair of Bad Idea jeans if there ever was.

Chris instead checked the news to see if there were any updates on the furloughs. Chris hadn't worried about a paycheck in years, and it was really disconcerting having to worry about it again. He felt helpless. Ironically, he never felt empowered in his life until after the Shift. In his shop, he built actual things with his hands, the payments he received were tangible, and Chris knew that he was vital to the survival of his home. For the first time in his life, he felt like he was in command of his destiny. Now, his destiny was in the hands of others.

CNN didn't add anything new on the furloughs. As an aside, he saw an article about some asteroid named Rayne 2005 that was to be making a spectacularly close pass in less than two weeks on Friday, March 15th. The article further stated that the asteroid would be visible in the daytime the day it passed by. It was supposed to come within 100,000 miles of earth, which was astronomically a really close one. That would be neat to see, a once in a lifetime event. The asteroid was a monster, 85 miles in diameter. Chris crossed himself, even though he wasn't even Catholic, just thinking about the what ifs.

A ton of comments followed the article, claiming that the government was hiding the truth and that the asteroid was going to slam into the earth. They threw a bunch of nonsense about some astronomers who died in a plane crash as proof of the government's efforts to silence the truth. Oh, and then there were a bunch of astronomers who had unexplained heart attacks. *Ooh, big surprise, a bunch of fat scientists with heart conditions getting heart attacks*, Chris thought mordantly. *Call Oliver Stone stat!* It was just like every other group of whack jobs claiming the sky is falling, from the Y2K freaks to the anti-fluoride fanatics.

Chris pulled up to the apartment complex shortly after the sun set and parked to find a fresh smattering of tagging on his building. Aidan got out and ran off to play with the kids, speaking comfortably in Spanish while

Chris hefted Yorick on his hip after getting him out of the car seat. He slammed the car's door exhausted, which prompted the neighboring Civic's alarm to go off…again. It was either that one or one of the hundreds of other bastard car alarms that woke him up in the middle of the night last night. The dreams he had weren't particularly pleasant. He was in a post-Shift version of New York City, which made no sense—he had not been there since before the Shift. But in any case, he'd rather had bad dreams and at least sleep than be woken up by crude, cheap-ass car alarms.

Chris staggered back toward his garden style apartment, stepping over discarded bottles and graffiti riddled walls, listening to the clash of battling ghetto blasters while Yorick talked about his day. Chris couldn't help but think that other Chris had to have felt defeated returning to this place night after night. Between the boss Ed Farcus who micromanaged and abused all of his subordinates, the declining state of this once upscale working class barrio, and the prospect of being furloughed at any moment, how could he not feel that way?

The insomnia had returned. Chris figured the transition was a valid reason that would upset anyone, even a normal person, not just him. He considered going back on Phoketal, but then decided against it. Some part of him still resisted the idea of relying on a chemical that couldn't be reproduced in a post-Shift world. It made no sense, he admitted. The Shift hadn't hit here, but it had become ingrained in him. If he was suffering being who he was where he was, he could only pity the fool that was his other self on the other side. Chris assumed other Chris inhabited his body in his world as he inhabited his body here. If that other Chris wasn't in a fetal position or dead right now, it would be a miracle. On that happy thought, he walked inside the building to make dinner.

"Alo?" Meredith greeted as she walked in, dropping her valise.

"Mommy," the kids screamed and stopped playing the Xbox momentarily to give her a hug.

She came over and gave Chris a kiss while he was making dinner. "Hey Hon."

"Making Prego again?"

Chris nodded and she patted him on the cheek. Chris found out that there was little point in making anything else with Aidan and Yorick. Both loved Prego, pizza and hamburgers and demanded ketchup on it all. Meredith shooed the cats off the counter, who were hovering over the bubbling vat of Prego sauce.

"Any news about the furlough?"

"Nope, except that all of DS non-essential personnel are vulnerable to it. How much do we have saved up?"

Meredith laughed ruefully. "You're kidding, right? What savings?"

"Oh."

They stood silently, listening to the downstairs neighbors playing some Spanish hip hop. He supposed it was slightly less offensive in that the cursing was in Spanish, which somehow was more musical. At least, that was what he thought until he saw Aidan walking past the dinette rapping along. Chris had learned enough Spanish over the years, as it was the language of farming and mechanics in the Orange Pact, and caught Aidan saying, "chinga maricon."

"Hey!" Chris shouted, stopping Aidan in his tracks. He gave a "what, me?" look. "Do you have any idea what you're saying?"

Meredith didn't know any Spanish, but she didn't like what she saw. Aidan shrugged his shoulders. "It's just a song."

"It's not a song, son. It's vulgar and offensive and if I ever hear you cursing in Spanish or English, I will seriously open a can of whupass on you and you will not be sitting down without pain for a week. Do I make myself clear?"

Meredith's jaw dropped as well as Aidan's. Chris surmised that other Chris had never threatened corporal punishment before. Aidan furtively raised his hand.

"Yes?"

"M...may I go to the bathroom?"

He ran and slammed the door. Meredith turned around, her face still in shock. He didn't know if it was she who was going to be opening the can of whupass on him. She probably had laid down the law on how to discipline the kids and he seriously crossed a line.

He was about to apologize—it was a lot easier to apologize, he learned, when instead she said, "We've got to get out of this place."

The car alarm woke him up again. Groggy, Chris walked over to the window to see a souped up Nissan Sentra pulling up to the front of a neighboring apartment building with its woofers waking the world. Kids were out and up to no good. Knowing he was too agitated to go back to sleep, he slipped on a Snuggie and stepped out the apartment.

Something told him to go to the storage room. He didn't know why. Like the phone number that stuck in his mind, some things just drew him in. Maybe he forgot to pick up a load of laundry in the communal coin operated dryer. Those machines had driven him to murderous rage the last two weeks. The things worked as well as washers and dryers in the post-Shift world, which was to say they didn't, except he still put money into these bastards. He turned on the light and gazed at his storage compartment, which was encased with a chicken wire mesh door protected by a padlock, real sensible protection given the chicken wire encasing could be cut open with scissors. Then something occurred to him. He grabbed the keys with the Empire State Building keychain, unlocked the padlock, opened the chicken wire door and rifled through the pile of extraneous crap. With a sudden jolt of inclination, he threw the items out. Behind the infant car seats and paint cans there it was. Carefully, he wheeled it out.

The Kona mountain bike was covered in dust, the tires had gone flat. Packed in the way it was, Chris could tell the bike had been neglected for years. The Kona didn't have the aftermarket modifications, it hadn't been retrofitted to carry extra weight, it lacked the cages and the gun rack, it hadn't been spray painted black and stenciled in with her name *The Interceptor*. The bike was just a bike. But it was *his* bike, the very same that traveled with him to Rochelle, to war, to Maryland.

Chris gently brushed off the dust from his bike and made a few quick scans to see what he needed to do to restore her to her glory. He wiped a stray tear, feeling some semblance of normalcy by feeling the grips of his bike again.

He had been asleep these past couple of months. He seemed to have just floated off and disengaged from everything. He tried to tell himself that he never belonged here, that this wasn't his responsibility. But it was.

Memories flashed as he squeezed the grip of the bike, both the bad as well as the good. Haunted by the decision to disembark in Maryland, Chris also had saved many lives over the years and kept his people safe. He had accomplished all those things in another world, but they still did happen nevertheless. He was the same man, and it was about time he started behaving like himself again. This was the bike that carried him through so much. It was up to him how he would proceed from here.

Dusting off his bike, he felt a little of his self returning. "Hello, beautiful."

If he was stuck in this universe, then it was now essentially his, and he had to man up. He knew his Meredith needed him, but so did this Meredith. His own children needed him, but so did these children. He could only hope that if other Chris was alive, he could do the same.

CHAPTER 20

New York, New York
September 12, 2001

Chris finished brushing his teeth. After rinsing, he checked himself in the mirror. The polo shirt was clean, so were his slacks. He had showered twice in the evening to make sure he got all of the soot out and polished his pistol and the magazines as well. Likewise, he drenched his watch and keys to wash off the remnants of the two towers. He went into the kitchen and opened the tiny fridge, which was just a glorified dorm fridge, and made some iced coffee in silence. He turned on the radio, which was playing the American anthem and walked out the back door to a tiny backyard garden, a true luxury in Manhattan even if there were absolutely no other conveniences in the turn of the century brownstone apartment. It didn't have more than one outlet per room, no built-in cabinets or a dishwasher. The kitchen was furnished entirely from his recent trip to IKEA. He remembered looking at the Twin Towers in the distance with awe from the store's parking lot just a couple of months ago.

He could still smell it. That awful brimstone chemical smell just wouldn't leave his nostrils. When the North Tower collapsed, he managed to take shelter inside a deli and save that frantic woman named…he forgot her name, before the column of smoke reached them. But after the North Tower collapsed, he spent hours looking for that guy…what's his name, the Richard Gere looking guy, who risked his life to pull people out of the North Tower. By the time he came home late last night, he was saturated with World Trade Center ash. The memory of seeing detached body parts, of seeing people falling to their deaths...Chris couldn't process it emotionally.

Standing outside in the miniscule backyard, watching a pink sky turn blue, Chris tried not to think about the images that kept him tossing and turning all night, the people holding hands as they jumped. He tried not to dwell on it. He had to head to the ad hoc DS command center by 0700 hours. The Special Agent in Charge was furious with him for not calling in until that evening. He knew he was going to get reamed for that lapse of judgment. But somehow it seemed so trivial. Those people, all of those people.

Their cat whined pitifully. "What's wrong?" Chris asked the cat and stroked his fur, now slightly grayer that he remembered. He recoiled his hand. It was the soot from the towers. The ash had sprinkled across the city even despite the winds pushing primarily to the south. He put down his coffee cup and listened to the patriotic music that was playing on a rock station. He didn't know what kind of world he and the rest of humanity woke up in this morning, but he knew the sun rose today on a fundamentally different world from the day before. *Those people*, he thought. They were living their lives, dreading work just like him, and they died because they were punctual. It suddenly occurred to him that part of the ash was comprised of the thousands of people that perished.

Meredith walked up to him and held his hand. She had been in the subway in Midtown when the planes hit both the North and South Towers and emerged to find the entire Midtown area glued to their car stereos and TV sets. She didn't even know Chris was in danger until he called hours later. She didn't know he had been doing pre-advance work right across the street from the World Trade Center.

Chris turned to Meredith. "Something's wrong with the cat."

She nodded and brushed his cheek with her hand. The song was replaced by another patriotic number. "The cat's...he's..."

And like that, he broke down and collapsed into her arms, bawling. His shoulders heaved as a torrent of sorrow overcame him. "All of ... those...people."

Meredith just held him out in the backyard garden as the two shared their profound grief.

BACKGROUND MUSIC: "Civilian" by Wye Oak
Visit www.michaeljuge.com **on the Refurbished Soul page to listen**

The Shiftiverse
Fort Lee, New Jersey
March 6, 2013

Chris folded up the piece of paper and put it back in his utility pocket under his blood-stained poncho. Before leaving the Stubb Foundation, Jamil had requested that he write down a phone number and concentrate on it. He had no idea why, but who was he to argue with an artificial intelligent life form? Chris returned to surveying the city of Manhattan looming across the Hudson River that was churning below the cliffs where he stood. They had seen glimpses of the skyline along the way over. The Empire State Building stood as it had when he left years ago, so too virtually all of the other skyscrapers for that matter. Yet, as he saw in Newark, the buildings looked noticeably aged and neglected. The line of apartment buildings directly across the river now looked similarly dilapidated.

There were no tribes to bribe in Fort Lee. Chris had assumed that with a bridge leading into Manhattan, some smelly barbarian would be claiming dominion and demand they pay a toll to cross over his precious bridge. But defying his expectations, the area was deserted, leaving an uneasy quiet as he crouched and waited for Porkins to return. Chris' ass itched. One thing they never spoke about in the movies was how the lack of proper toilet paper really affected morale after the shit hit the fan. Discarded books and newspapers where easy to find and did the job, but it was not exactly pleasant. The Virginians sponged off whenever they bivouacked, but he was never truly clean. Chris did his best to ignore how bad he smelled and listened to the wind whistling and packs of dogs barking in the distance above the slight ringing in his ears, to which he had long since grown accustomed.

The sea of outbound traffic covered the lanes heading into New Jersey. It appeared that there had been a few attempts to push cars to the side, but for the most part, they stood frozen in place from the moment the first EMP struck. Of all places he could imagine of where *not* to be in any post-apocalyptic setting, New York City *always* won the prize. Tennessee—fine, Iowa—even better. New York City? This was the equivalent of some half naked woman in a horror flick taking an ill conceived midnight stroll in the woods when she suddenly hears a twig snap and says, "Gary, I know it's you, so stop it! It's not funny. Gary…Gary?" and turning around.

He knew they had no choice. The fate of the world depended on them getting to Cambridge in time. But be that as it may, New York City was an imposing city even without an apocalypse to go with it. He remembered driving his Corolla into the city to begin his first assignment as a special agent at the New York Field Office and recalled how utterly overwhelmed he felt. Months prior, he had been a grad student, working part-time as a barista, and suddenly they gave him a badge, a gun and travel orders to head to a city that could bitch slap his comfy little hippie town of Austin with one of its minor outer boroughs alone.

Chris didn't like New York City when he first arrived. In fact, he hated living there. He felt like a mouse in an overcrowded cage. Then came September 11th. The events of that day had a way of bonding him to a city that he desperately wished to leave. He couldn't quite articulate what it was exactly, except that he and the city had gone through a traumatic experience together. After that, Chris came to feel a simpatico with the city for all of its pigeon poo and dog urine saturated sidewalks and mini-mart sized grocery stores. Maybe it was a sort of Stockholm Syndrome.

His therapist pointed out that the events that day most likely prompted his panic and anxiety disorder. Chris didn't know. All he did know was that if they did save the world, and if he ever knocked his head again and returned to his home, he would get a new prescription for Phoketal, screw the weight gain. That firefight two days ago had scared the piss out of him, literally. Yet, he wasn't falling apart, which was surprising. He had always assumed that after being involved in a shooting that he would feel remorse and would get swallowed up by his own obsessive-compulsive mind. By his own calculation, he should be going fetal right about now. On the contrary, he didn't feel any remorse for the Dallek boys. He felt bad for the Haddad sons who had to carry their father's body back home, but he wasn't overwhelmed by it. In fact, he felt oddly in tune with this world now. Kendra or rather Lieutenant Baraka—he still got a kick out of that—had portrayed a distinctly different attitude toward him after that engagement. She no longer treated him like some burdensome monkey boy. In fact, she had put him on point now. It demonstrate that she now saw him as part of the team rather than the Jar Jar Binks of the group. They gave him pointers on what to look for, how to keep a watchful eye for lookouts and traps.

Unfortunately, decent people appeared to be thin on the ground in New Jersey. Mr. Haddad and Mr. Valdez appeared to be glowing exceptions that proved the rule that once civil order broke down, people reverted to their

158

barbarous nature. The Virginians hadn't any other violent encounters since the Dallek boys incident. Even if most were savages around here, the tribes were more interested in doing business with the Virginians than in wasting rounds in a firefight. That seemed to be the running theme around here. Bullets were precious commodities and it was better to make a deal with strangers and let people pass than take a chance by trying to overpower the group of Virginians, who by all appearances were better armed and trained than the common feral gnawing on pigeon bones.

The Virginians paid a lot of little bribes to thugs along the way. He saw children being used as forced labor and much worse. Outside of Patterson, Chris saw one girl, dressed scantily, out in the middle of the frigid cold, walking off with one of the nameless sentries manning the toll booths. It was the one time Kendra had to stop Chris from reacting. She had caught him storming over to the man.

"This isn't why we're here, Captain, and we do not have time to indulge our personal feelings. Deal with it and keep watch."

Chris grumbled but he knew she was right. He told himself he would take the sick bastards out on the way back…after they saved the world. They cycled on, leaving the girl trapped with the savages that most likely had a harem of girls. What could they do? That, more than anything, convinced him that he would not be returning to the person he was before, even if by miracle he did return home, for that encounter was far more disturbing than the shootout even. He thought about his two boys Aidan and Yorick. *If anyone did anything…* He forced down the murderous thoughts. There was nothing to be done for the victims out here. Just keep focused and get through this and when it's over, then he could process it all. Chris stowed his Starbucks mug and returned to watching for Porkins to return from his survey.

The crunching of ice announced that someone was coming. Chris and Akil raised their rifles and hid behind the tollbooths.

"Steady trigger finger, right?"

Chris nodded. He had been reminded repeatedly not to get trigger happy, but he didn't mind it too much. He hoped that everyone had a straight trigger finger when he was doing reconnaissance. Porkins emerged and weaved gracefully around a few vehicles that had been set afire long ago. Chris and the rest of the company stood up and joined Porkins.

"Don't tell me, lemme guess," said Kendra, "there's a path through but there's more assholes manning the bridge."

"How'd you guess?"

"Well, the fact that you were gone less than twenty minutes."

Kendra wanted to survey the area first so that they wouldn't have to double back and switch out from the upper level to the lower level of the bridge over such a long expanse. It also gave her a heads up about what they were facing.

"Did you speak with them?"

"No, LT. I didn't get a good look at them, but I'd assume they're interested in doing business."

Kendra turned to Chris. "What's our stock looking like, Captain?"

"We've still got plenty of gruel flakes and some gruel bars, our ammo is half of what it was."

"Even after pilfering from the Dallek boys?"

They didn't waste time or mince words about appropriating the ammunition and other valuables off the dead Dallek boys. After handing over everything the Haddad sons could carry in IKEA bags, they took the rest.

"We spent all of that paying the tolls."

"Tobacco?"

"About a kilo left."

Kendra cursed. "Christ, the way things are going, we'll be selling our bodies for passage."

"I really don't think I'm ready for that one, Kendra," Chris said. "I've already reached my limit of taboos for the week with eating house cat ribs and killing teenagers."

"Yeah, LT, I'm with the captain on this. I don't think I'd like that."

"Okay. Let's saddle up and get this over with."

The company hopped on their bikes and pedaled onto the upper deck of the GW Bridge. It was awfully cold for March, especially as they were hundreds of feet over the Hudson River. Chris wondered if it was this cold right now in the Mundaniverse. Maybe the Shift altered the weather patterns a bit and made the winter last longer. Maybe the death of all industrial civilization caused a change in weather. Anything was possible. Chris had to force himself to concentrate on the road in front of him, but it was hard not to get transfixed on the jagged skyline.

Rita cycled up next to him. "Impressive isn't it?"

"Yeah."

"The short time I lived here, I could never take my eyes off those buildings downtown."

"Wait, you lived here, too?"

Rita laughed. "You really don't remember me, do you?"

Chris swerved around a pile of bones and a busted bicycle frame and shook his head. "Remember you? From where?"

Rita was about to answer when she turned her attention forward. He still wondered what happened to her eye. He looked up and saw what had become a familiar sight. A series of vehicles were lined up lengthwise across the width of the upper deck of the bridge. Shopping carts, garbage cans and ripped up fencing shored up the weak spots in the barricade. As the company slowed down, Chris reached to his rifle secured to the top bar of his Kona and switched off the safety. He had to hand it to the Vicious Rabbits, they sure knew how to make maximum use of their bikes. Chris studied his surroundings, looking for places where people might hide. The Dallek boys tried to ambush them by placing their toadies inside cars and behind trucks. He wasn't going to miss something like that again.

The company kept spread out just as the gunny had told them to and eased to a stop several meters before the barricade. Chris rested his bike and went immediately to cover their rear, while Ilsa looked for potential hiding spots to the side. There wasn't much in the way for the ferals to do in devising a trap. They were elevated, so unless the ferals could spring up from the lower deck underneath, the only other way to ambush them now would be by using the scattering of vehicles behind them. Chris was looking for any movement in that direction. Out of the corner of his eye, he saw Kendra and the gunny approach two ferals who stood atop a city bus. Chris figured that had to have taken a lot of effort to move something that large. Chris noticed that the two ferals held crossbows. They really must have been short on ammunition up here.

"'Sup, sister. You lost or somethin'," called out one of the ferals.

"Yeah, sup' yourself. Look, we're just passing through. You'd be doing us a real solid here if you'd be kind enough to allow us passage through your turf."

"Hey, chicka," called out another young man, a Hispanic by the looks and sound of his voice, "you one of those Kwans? 'Cause they're nothing but trouble."

"Shit, you a blind," asked the first feral sarcastically. "Does she look Chinese to you?"

"They Korean, esse, not Chinese."

"Whatever."

"Oi," the gunny barked. "Sorry to interrupt, but we're in a bit of a 'urry, mates! You mind?"

"Hey, don't be steppin' where you don't know where you at," said the first and pointed a crossbow at the gunny.

Akil zeroed his AK-74 at the offending male and with a steady voice said, "You don't want to do that, son. We're here to do business, not cause trouble. As the lady said, we're just passing through. Now, you want to talk or make this into a bad day for everyone?"

In the distance behind the barricade, Chris heard another male voice arguing. "Hold it, hold it, damn it!"

Despite his instructions, he turned around to see what the commotion was about. A man who looked to be roughly Chris' age, perhaps a little older, dressed in a wool trench coat, stood atop the bus yelling, "Everyone just cool it!"

The man pulled out a pair of glasses from his coat and put them on. He suddenly belted out in laughter. "Akil?"

Akil put his hand over his forehead as to see better and with utter surprise in his voice called back inquisitively, "Kareem?"

CHAPTER 21

The Shiftiverse
New York, New York
March 6, 2013

"Kareem? Is that you?" Akil stuttered.

The man named Kareem climbed down the bus and walked over to Akil. He studied the company cautiously as Ilsa kept her bow angled at a low ready, able to strike in milliseconds if necessary, but not overtly provocative. Akil, whose hand was always near his sidearm while negotiating, stepped slowly toward him.

"Yeah, coz, it's me," the man said almost giggling. The two ran up and gave each other a huge bear hug and laughed joyously.

"You young pup! You young pup!" Akil cried out as he hoisted Kareem up.

With that, both the locals at the barricade and the Virginians lowered their weapons. Rita sighed with relief and walked over to the two of them engaged in excited conversation.

"You old scoundrel, what are you doing here? Weren't you living in Maryland?"

"I was. It's…Ah, it's a long story, coz, long story." He patted Kareem on the arm. "You made it. You made it!"

"Yeah, man. Me, Maria, the kids…" Kareem hesitated. "I'm afraid to ask. Jamil?"

Akil winced. "I don't know. I was on my way to Charlottesville to pick him up at Ruth's. They disappeared."

"I'm sorry."

Akil switched the subject. "So, what are you now, the bridge troll?" Kareem laughed and gave him another hug.

"You two know each other?" Rita asked.

Akil turned and waved her over. "Sugar, come over. I'd like to introduce you to someone. Kareem, this is my remaining reason to live, the love of my life, my wife, Rita Luevano."

Kareem shook her hand like a gentleman would.

"Rita, this is my cousin, Kareem Abdul Ali."

"Your cousin? Wow, well isn't that…special?"

"Looks like another snowstorm coming. Come. Let's get you guys warm and fed."

Kareem Abdul Ali and his cronies escorted the Virginians onto the island of Manhattan. Behind the barricades the vehicles had all been moved and stripped bare. Rita followed just behind Akil, who was engaged in a reunion with his first cousin who was, as it turned out, the head honcho of this tribe. Rita had forgotten how monstrous the GW Bridge was. When she was a PhD student at Columbia, she spent what few spare hours she had cycling while pondering her dissertation. For longer treks, she rode across the GW Bridge as there was an expansive pedestrian lane. Sometimes she would ride her Cannondale all the way up the Palisades Parkway to the New York State line. The GW Bridge was a wonder of technological engineering built during the depression era that managed to make a child of the millennium feel tiny in comparison. Today, it stood witness to the tiny ants crossing along its span, ants who would not be able to replicate a feat like this for generations to come, if ever…if they even survived the month.

As they crossed into Manhattan, they briefly descended into the darkness of a tunnel before being led off at the 178th Street exit and back into daylight again. And there it was, New York City. The brownstones and mid-twentieth century high-rise apartment monstrosities stood as real as ever. Rita saw people walking along sidewalks, some on bicycles. Passing by a Duane Reade drug store, Rita felt like she was thrown back to grad school, but that was until they hit one of the side streets. She noticed that grass had grown along the streets and then she realized, it wasn't just simply grass that had grown over unmaintained roads. Rather, much of the street had been torn up and was now being used as pasture. Sheep and goats grazed in the loosely fenced in street while people dressed in a patchwork of pre-Shift winter coats and homespun pants tended to the animals. Other streets were repurposed in a similar fashion. The only street that didn't seem to have been torn up was Broadway itself, which they took and headed up north.

They hung another left on 181ˢᵗ and then took a right heading north on Fort Washington Avenue, which like most of the other streets had been torn up and replanted with tall grass. Rita saw chickens, pigs and sheep corralled at a market while people boisterously cried out what they were selling. Ahead, she studied the rows and rows of apartment buildings. Chris had remarked that all of the roofs looked "frayed," uneven. Now she understood why. From the vantage point of the top of a hill she saw that the rooftops had, like the streets below, been converted into gardens. They passed one apartment building that was at least twenty stories high. The sign outside advertised it as someone's dairy farm. Rita rode up to Kareem.

"Excuse me, but that building...Is it filled with cows?"

Kareem laughed. "Oh, no, of course not. It's a goat farm."

"You're saying that people hauled animals all the way up in those apartments?"

"Makes sense, considering that no human would want to live in them without air conditioning or heating. And nobody wants to walk up eighteen stories at the end of the day. Besides, the farmers stay up with them."

Rita suspected where they were heading as they passed the last of bagel shops and apartment buildings into a forest. The climb suddenly got steep as they curved into a circle. She remembered this place now. It felt like it couldn't possibly be part of Manhattan with its surrounding forest.

Despite being slightly winded by the uphill climb, Kareem made small talk. "It's a good thing I still make the rounds regularly or I wouldn't have run into you guys. But the ride home never gets easier."

All she and Akil could do was grunt, "Uh huh."

They rounded the curve and were met by men dressed in a mixture of sheet armor and oddly, NYPD jackets, who opened the gates and saluted as Kareem and crew passed. Like Kareem's companions, the guards carried crossbows, while only a few carried firearms. Past the gates people tended to fields and gardens and greeted Kareem calling him *Abu*, and *Jeffe*. They came to a stop and to her right stood a magnificent castle, the Cloisters. Kareem got off his bike and handed it to a servant.

"Welcome to mi casa. Come on in, let me show you around. Maria's gonna trip when she sees your face, Akil."

The Cloisters looked just like a medieval European castle. It likely had to do with the fact that it was a medieval European castle that had been disassembled in France brick by brick, shipped overseas to America and reassembled brick by brick. Back before the Shift, it had been a museum, but Kareem found it to be suitable to serve as his crib. Rita acknowledged that it was strategically located and held a commanding view of the Hudson as well as the city below, being positioned at the crest of Fort Tryon Park.

Kareem spared nothing in welcoming his guests. The Virginians were shown to separate guest rooms. Rita and Akil enjoyed a hot bath. God, she missed a hot bath. She hadn't had one since leaving the Stubb Foundation. That was about a week ago, but riding as hard as they had been, it felt like months ago. The last several days on the road had forced her to feel every day of her forty-one years. Having seen so much carnage and human depravity weighed on her as well. Rita had seen a lot of cruelty since the Shift. Even within the safe and civilized confines of Greater Monticello and her allies, man taking advantage of one's fellow man was not unheard of. Slavery was strictly forbidden in the Orange Pact. People caught engaging in that trade or forced prostitution were executed. She had reversed her position on the death penalty after Sheriff Schadenfreude exposed some of the heinous acts some people committed. Yet crimes like that were common practice out in the bush, and sadly, even expected.

She couldn't help but feel as though she was being compelled to travel to Boston not only to save the world from utter annihilation, but more specifically to save the soul of humanity. They had come across decent folks, people just trying to make their way in this world. But they seemed to be overshadowed by thugs who preyed on the weak. Those out there wandering the dead cities were lost. They had lost their confidence and lost any sense of meaning beyond living for another day. Maybe they prayed, but their prayers seemed to have fallen into a void. Something told her that Gaia wanted her to see this on her way to Boston.

The Virginians were provided with clean clothes, all pre-Shift attire. When they were escorted to the dining room, she gave a wry grin seeing that all the Virginian guests wore the same New York Yankees sweatshirts. Oil lamps lit the dank cavernous stone room where a dining table stood, laden with meats, apples, cheeses and vegetables. Copper tubing wrapped around the room and emitted warm air coming from the outflow of the fireplace. It was an ingenious invention, one she would have to remember. Servants, some black, some Hispanic, one white served them, all wearing drab upscale restaurant waiter suits and dresses.

Rita had noticed while cycling through the city that most of the people were either Hispanic or black, which wouldn't have been surprising in Washington Heights before the Shift. It was surprising seeing blacks and Hispanics, Asians and whites actually living together.

Along with Kareem, his wife Maria and their kids, sat some of Kareem's hombres, all of whom wore NYPD jackets. She wondered what this was all about.

"It's as you expected," Kareem said solemnly. The lanterns' light flickered from a draft. "When the EMPs hit...what was it you call it, 'the Shift'...when they hit, people freaked. Not at first mind you. We've been through a lot of shit..."

His wife Maria smacked him on the shoulder and pointed to their three children.

"Sorry, we've seen a lot of *stuff.* Better honey? September 11th, the blackout in 2003. Most of us thought it was just another blackout at first. But I knew something was up immediately when the cars wouldn't start. I was a mechanic, Reverend. I still can't believe Akil married a reverend. He wasn't a devout Muslim. Neither am I for that matter," he said as he raised a glass of beer, which everyone except her was enjoying. She caressed her nineteen-year sobriety chip under the table just as an extra measure of safety.

"Well, to be fair, she's a Unitarian, Kareem."

"The Shift opened a lot of doors, Kareem, as I see it has for you here," she added.

"Yeah, it has. As I said, I was just a mechanic. I did a lot of work for the 30th and 33rd police precincts. I knew the cops pretty well. Maria, my lovely wife, she was working with urban gardening projects. We weren't anyone special, just another biracial couple with pissed off parents. Her folks thought that I must be some terrorist with a name like mine."

"Kareem Abdul Ali?" Chris said. "I just figured your folks must have been real sports fans."

Kareem gave a brief patronizing smile before it faded. "The first day it wasn't so bad. Was it an EMP attack? We figured it was. The planes falling into the Hudson left little doubt. But this is New York City. We could hack it. But after a couple of days, people started losing it. It was that whole being disconnected from the rest of the world that freaked us out. Our cell phones, Blackberries, laptops, all gone to crap. There was no way that any of us could get what was going on outside our little world. No helicopters, no CNN trucks pulling up to report on the New York EMP attack of 2007. Nothing. We had no idea how bad it truly was."

"But as the days rolled on with no help in sight, this whole city went into flames, man. No trucks were getting through to deliver food, the faucets ran dry. And damn, it was hot that summer. Remember? By the weekend, the gangs were roving the streets and lived out their wildest dreams, shooting whoever they wanted, taking whatever they wanted."

"But you came swinging onto the scene and saved everyone from the mayhem, right?" Akil said.

Kareem snorted. "Yeah, not so much, coz. Me, the missus, a lot of us, just tried to hide. I met up with some of the cops at the 34th precinct. They were busy getting their asses handed to them by the gangs."

"We tried to escape from the city but," Kareem recalled painfully, "motherfu…people manned the Tappan Zee Bridge and blocked off the Taconic State Parkway, the Merritt, the Saw Mill River Expressway, the 684. Everywhere people tried to escape from the city, police backed by armed mobs were there to turn us back."

"They'd shoot if you rushed them. We tried to leave, but after being turned back at the Tappan Zee at gunpoint, we had no choice but to come back to Manhattan. We made it back here and we waited it out. Maria had a garden at the top of our apartment building. She had a lot of these urban gardens—I told you about that, right? And Captain O'Malley here learned about an inbound ship full of grain that lost power and beached at the top of the island. While everyone else was too busy scouring Manhattan for canned food in apartments, grocery stores and bodegas, they ignored the obvious, a monster container ship filled with rice."

"Between cargo ships filled with rice and my wife's gardens, all we had to do was stay down, let the dumbass kids kill themselves. We figured it would take months, but then there was that flu."

Rita and rest of the Virginians reacted. "Oh, you had it too, huh?"

"Yeah, it came in the winter and killed a lot of us. By 2008, the fighting stopped because most of the little bastards had either killed each other or died of the flu. I convinced the cops early on to give up trying to quell the violence. I ended up saving their asses. By the time most of the gang bangers died, sometime after New Years, we had a ship full of grain, I had a group of officers from the 34th, 33rd and 32nd precincts to protect it, and the cops had me to vouch for them with the neighbors, and with the rice, we had their gratitude. The city was pretty deserted after that winter and we suddenly had plenty of food. It was like a ghost town outside our little corner of the island. But then by the summer of '08, we started seeing people streaming into the city again."

"Really? Why would they do that?"

"Most of them had been turned away from every other town, or had lived in communities that failed, their crops died, they got kicked out by bigger gangs, whatever. But the most pressing reason?"

Kareem rubbed his jaw the same way Akil did when engaged in something unpleasant. "Indian Point Energy Center. It was a nuclear reactor that powered the city. When the EMP attacks...I mean when the Shift hit," correcting himself with the new information, "word had it that the generators that poured fresh water in from the Hudson to cool those nuclear rods crapped out. I'm no nuclear scientist, but from the few who lived told me, the power plant workers there were somehow able to keep the water flowing to cool the rods for awhile. But eventually, they no longer could. I don't know what changed, but whatever it was that kept the water flowing stopped working. The rods overheated and it went all Chernobyl."

Rita understood. She had heard tales from West Virginia about nuclear reactors in Kentucky that had succumbed to a meltdown when the power went out. Fortunately, her people weren't near any of the facilities and there had been no sign of radioactive contamination in Virginia.

"We were extremely fortunate," Kareem said. "The winds pushed the radioactivity north away from us. So, suddenly our hood became all gentrified. We weren't glowing in the dark. People upstate fled. Most of them died of radiation sickness or to the savages out there. Some of the lucky ones who weren't exposed too badly found their way to us here. I made those who arrived a deal. I'd share our food, I'd provide protection from outside our walls, but they had to understand they owed their lives and the lives of their children to me saving them and therefore, they would do what I told them to do."

Kareem's wife Maria jumped in. "Kareem likes to talk like it was all his idea..."

"No, I don't," he protested.

"He likes to talk like that, but it was my idea that saved their lives by turning the rooftops into gardens and high rise apartments into farms."

"I don't talk that, woman. I don't know where you get this," he protested.

It was clear to Rita that Kareem saw himself as these people's savior and benefactor. He was arrogant about it, but perhaps it was justified. As bad as they had it in Virginia, it wasn't anything compared to what these people faced. Nuclear meltdown and radiation sickness was a new wrinkle in horror that they never had to confront.

"So, do they call you the Duke of New York?" Chris asked.

Kareem made a face. "What? Hell no. There's thirty different punk asses who refer to themselves as the 'Duke of New York,' not one of them own more than a few square blocks of the city. Half of them live in the Bronx. Nah, people round here either call me *Jeffe* or *Abu Miguel*."

"Abu Miguel?"

"It means 'father of Miguel,'" Akil whispered.

"After my son here." The teenage boy smiled and waved.

"Oh, so you don't have like a formal title?"

"Like what?"

"Like…well, I'm the chief magistrate of Monticello."

"And my boss is the constable," the gunny added.

"There's the regent in Lynchburg, the president of the Republic of West Virginia."

Kareem snorted. "You crackers got a lot a time on your hands down south, don't you?"

"So, what do you all call yourselves?" Chris asked.

Kareem shrugged his shoulders. "All of us? I don't know. Most of us go by 'Heighters.'"

"'Haters'?"

"No, *Heighters*, as in where you're at in Washington Heights. Heighters."

"Ah, 'Heighters.' I liked the first one better."

"But usually people identify themselves by their precinct. 33rd, 26th, 30th Precincts. And my homies here are the police chiefs of those precincts and their captains."

"Ah," Rita said pensively.

"The Missus is right, though, she was the one who came up with the idea of using the rooftops as gardens. After the first year, most people still alive were desperate. They were tired of the fighting. They were just days away from succumbing to starvation. They didn't care if a 'nigga,' 'spic,' or 'cracka' offered them a lifeline. They just wanted out of the hole they were in. Me, the officers here, my wife, we offered them an alternative. And they haven't seemed to mind working alongside each other like they used to."

"Yeah, I did notice your people are quite diverse."

"Well, it does help with me being black and my wife being Dominican. It made the marriage a little easier to swallow for my people. And my white brothers sitting here with you, they did alright."

"You got that one, Jeffe," said one of the NYPD guys with the lieutenant pips. He spoke with that typically harsh New York accent and had steel blue eyes. "My boys and I, my whole family would be corn holed if not for the Jeffe here."

Rita acknowledged the praise Kareem received from his officers. A young woman servant furtively crept up to refill Rita's glass of water and accidentally spilled a few drops.

"Oh my, God. I'm so sorry. I'm so sorry!"

Rita spread her hands. "Hey, no problem. No problem," she said casually.

"I'm at fault. I'm so sorry."

"Really, it's fine."

Kareem didn't seem to notice at all as the young lady dabbed off her leg and scurried off. Out in the distance Rita heard church bells clamoring as if service had ended even though it wasn't Sunday. Kareem summoned one of the young officers. She couldn't hear what was being said but Kareem's expression appeared tense. The officer ran out presumably on an errand of Kareem's.

"By the way, you still didn't answer my question, Akil. What brings you boys and girls slumming up around here, anyway?"

Akil turned to Rita for some sort of permission and she urged him to go ahead. Akil wove his fingers together and popped his knuckles by spreading them, palms outward.

"Okay, but you're going to have a hard time believing it."

"And so, Jamil said if we restart TALOPS, which is at MIT in Cambridge and get through its firewall, it will have access to the Large Hadron Collider at the CERN in Switzerland. Once Jamil has a link to the CERN, it…he will wake it out of lockdown, get it to do its thing, which will polarize the earth's magnetosphere, magnetizing the asteroid when it is within range, and then reverse the polarity, repelling the asteroid slightly where it will skip off the atmosphere, thus saving the planet from otherwise certain annihilation. That's about it." Akil took a deep breath and wetted his lips with beer.

Kareem's mouth was agape. He rubbed his eyes in bewilderment.

"So, what are *your* plans this week?" Chris added.

"You don't believe me, do you? Kareem?"

Kareem shook himself out of his daze. "No, it's not that I don't believe you. I mean…Frankly, coz, I don't think you could make that shit up. I mean, why on God's green earth would anyone make that up?"

Kareem stood up and covered his cheeks with his hands as he slowly paced down the length of the dining table.

"Wow…I mean, shit. Haven't…My God…haven't we been through enough?"

The NYPD Captain, O'Malley, Rita believed his name was, leaned over. "Did you say nine days away from impact?"

"That's what Jamil said." Rita took a sip of cider and grimaced as she saw through the windows that it was snowing again. "And that snow isn't going to make getting there any easier." Rita felt the weather front long before the snow fell. The mended bones that had been broken in battle years ago served as a barometer whether she liked it or not.

"Oh, man. And we were just getting our shit together, too," said another officer.

"You sure about this?"

"Jamil is sure."

"And Jamil…he's an artificially intelligent computer that somehow survived the *Shift*," using an obviously foreign term.

"Remember, Jamil's CPU is an organic gel, not silicon microcircuits."

"Ah, I see."

"Jeffe, this would explain the visions the seers have been having."

"Seers?"

"Yes, psychics and astrologers," said another officer matter-of-factly. "They've been very useful in forecasting weather and threats beyond our borders."

O'Malley nodded. "Yes, like the time the 86ers tried to push their way past 125th Street, that's our border, Madam Beauvrix predicted the inner squabbling would tear up the alliance before they could break through our lines."

"I see." Rita hadn't considered how deeply superstition could entrench itself in people like the cops sitting here. But she had to admit that science had taken a backseat after its benefits failed them once so many benefits of science failed them.

"So, you guys are going to Cambridge to try to reprogram another computer...that organic... so you can hack into the..."

"Large Hadron..."

"Right, Large Hadron Collider, so it can use the earth's magnetic field to repel the asteroid. Reverend, you know computers?"

"Actually, it's more about mathematics than knowing computers. Other me made sense of Jamil's algorithms and sort of walked him out of the woods of his fog of infancy into true self-awareness, which made Jamil here self-aware as well, because he's essentially the same entity in both realities. TALOPS isn't self-aware like Jamil, but it has the same operating system and quantum computing code. So, if we power TALOPS up, and I can sort through the start up scripts and navigate through the same algorithms that formed the core of Jamil's proto-consciousness, then hopefully, we'll get TALOPS to unlock the CERN's computer."

Kareem looked at her skeptically. "And you can restart TALOPS and sort through the algorithms?"

Rita hesitated when Chris jumped in. "Well, she's not a 'mathematician' in the classical sense," using air quotes, "but she did stay at a Holiday Inn Express."

Chris looked around and found no one, including Rita, getting his obscure reference.

"I believe I can. I can't explain the specifics, but I understand concepts, things that my other self knows. I just hope we can make it in time."

"Yeah, I hope so, too."

The revelation of their true mission killed the evening's entertainment Kareem had planned. Rita and Akil headed back to their rooms and fell asleep. Every time she told the story, she was reminded of why they were out here, and it filled her with dread. Would she know what to do when they got there, if they got there in time?

CHAPTER 22

San Antonio, Texas
June 1994

Rita pedaled along the feeder road as the Discman drowned out the noises of the vehicles passing mere inches from her. She was seething with a white hot anger, she wanted to lash out, she wanted to kill. She didn't know what to do, how to control it. That lack of control caused this latest drama. Knowing that pissed her off all the more.

She turned the corner, leaning into the turn and pulled up to the non-descript suburban house in a subdivision that appeared to have been slapped together six months ago. She rang the doorbell and waited impatiently until her sponsor Delana opened the door.

"Jesus, what happened to you, missy?" Delana asked with her signature low, raspy voice.

Rita invited herself in and slumped onto the smoke-saturated couch in the living room, took out a cigarette from her utility pocket and lit it with one of the multitude of lighters on the glass coffee table. Delana sat down with her cup of coffee and put the TV on mute. Belatedly, Rita answered.

"I got into a fight."

"I can see that," gesturing to Rita's black eye. "You want me to get you some steak for that?" She walked to the kitchen adjacent to the living room and rifled through the fridge. Delana returned with a steak and proceeded to place it over Rita's injured eye.

"There. Steak does wonders for shiners. I was married to a shit head once. I would know."

Delana took a seat next to her. "Now, who were you in a fight with?"

"Abuelita."

"Your grandmother caused this?"

"What?" Then Rita realized that Delana had thought that she meant the physical altercation she had been in earlier, the one that gave her the shiner. "No, no! Abuelita didn't do this. Some bigot asshole did it."

"Okay, missy. Start from the beginning. What happened? And go slow, 'cause I'm not as quick as I used to be." Delana put out her cigarette in an ashtray that blossomed with cigarette butts and lit a new one.

Rita took a deep breath. "Okay, I went with some of my friends to the Gay Pride parade today. I wanted to show my support, you know." Delana gave her a disapproving look and Rita immediately responded, knowing that such events were dangerous for someone young in sobriety.

"I didn't relapse. So, let's get that out of the way. I'm sober. "

"Okay."

"So, I was walking along with my friends when this redneck asshole started calling us 'fags' and 'dykes.' I just got sick of that shit, him trying to intimidate me and so, I walked right up to him and told him he had a tiny unit, he then cupped my breasts saying he would show me how small it was, and I don't know…I just snapped. I won't be treated like a whore, not ever again."

Rita took another drag from her cigarette. "So, I…well, I head butted him. I must have broken his nose or something, because he gushed out blood. He fell back in shock, but his buddy managed to deck me right in the face. So, what? It still felt good teaching that bastard never to touch me or any other woman like that again."

"I got home, and Abuelita starts freaking out about it." Rita recalled the argument and translated it into English.

"Why did the man hit you? Did you call over the cops?"

"No, Abuelita, I didn't. It's no big deal. Just forget about it."

"My spicy pickle goes out with these strange people and she gets in a fight and you want me to forget it?"

Abuelita hesitated a moment as the two stood in the dark hallway with the attic fan blowing on them. "Mi querida, are you one of them, you know…lesbos?" she asked pensively in her attempt at an English word.

Rita laughed. "I wish. No, Abuelita, I am not a *lesbian*. For better or worse, I like boys."

"Well, with your hair, your clothes and the way you go around fighting angry gringos, how am I supposed to know?" There was a lull before she asked. "Were you drinking?"

"No, God dammit!"

That was answered by a solid slap across her face. "Don't take the Lord's name in vain."

The force of the slap across the right side of her face was a mere shadow of the power of the man's swing to her eye, but it struck her far more profoundly, it reverberated down to her core. Shocked, Rita ran out of the house, hopped onto her bike and rode off.

Delana just nodded after hearing the story.

"Well?" Rita asked impatiently.

"Well what?"

"Aren't you going to say something?"

"Yeah, it sounds like I wouldn't get in a scrap against that old bird if I was you. And I would apologize to her immediately once you get home."

"Me?"

"Yes, you!"

"But she's the one…"

"First of all, with that spiked hair and combat boots, you do look like you bat for the other team, not that there's anything wrong with that. Secondly, why did you go to that parade?"

"I wanted to show my support."

"Don't try bullshitting a bullshit artist, missy. In the world of bullshit sharks, you're a guppy. Now, stop rationalizing and just tell me really, why did you go to that parade?"

At first, Rita was livid. She wanted to tell Delana to piss off. But then where would she go? Home? She couldn't go back there, not right now. She felt trapped, cornered.

"Why, missy?"

Then out of nowhere she shouted, "Because! I wanted someone to fuck with me!" Hearing the words out of her mouth encouraged her to continue. "I *wanted* some asshole to push me, and I knew rednecks go there every year looking to bash on some 'fairies.' So, I took my opportunity for payback."

"Payback for what?"

Rita didn't answer. She didn't want to get into the years she degraded herself. She knew it was the disease more than the men she slept with that had done the damage to her, but how does one make a disease pay for one's pain?

"So, you didn't go there for your friends, did you?"

Reluctantly, Rita shook her head.

"All that hate is going to eat you in the end, missy."

Delana stood up and grabbed a book from a rickety bookshelf.

"You know, I understand you. You're not alone. But you think you are. That's your problem. You think you're the first one, the only one who has felt what you're going through. You think you're unique."

"No, I don't."

Delana gave her a stern look and she relented.

"None of us gets through this alone. And that's why you lashed out like some drugged out punk."

That hurt Rita, but she also knew Delana was right. That was exactly how she behaved.

"We are going to get through this together. It's not about you getting sober just for yourself. You're getting sober for some girl out there who needs you, and several other people who you will help. And one day you, will know what I'm talking about. And we do this recovery thing, we do it together, comprende?"

Delana clasped Rita's hand with her own. For the first time, Rita felt like someone totally understood her. She knew that faith in God was out, but perhaps people like Delana would do for now, even if she was a crazy, chain-smoking old woman. At least she knew what Rita was about and she knew she cared. Rita gestured to what Delana was holding.

"What's the book?"

CHAPTER 23

The Shiftiverse
New York, New York
March 7, 2013

The snow which started last evening as a gentle flurry gathered into a full-fledged snow storm by morning. The wind was blowing flakes sideways. It was clear that they weren't going anywhere today, much to Rita's dismay. They had less than eight days to cover two hundred miles through completely uncharted land which was formerly a highly urbanized part of the country. It took them two days just to get from Newark to Manhattan. Granted, they had been through a skirmish and they couldn't pass up the offer to rest the evening with Akil's cousin. But the clock was ticking. What else would they face from here? And how much will the snow slow them down?

Confounded by the setback, Rita paced around the castle after cleaning her rifle, her bow, and her pistol. She'd repacked the food, tobacco, ammunition and the Stubb Foundation equipment in the child trailer even after Chris had already taken care of it. Rita knew they couldn't move effectively during a blizzard, but she felt absolutely useless sitting in the castle while the asteroid careened closer at tens of thousands of miles per hour.

Rita must have unnerved people with her pacing because around noon Captain O'Malley offered to take her and the other Virginians on a tour of Washington Heights. The weather was miserable and the rest of the company declined, but Rita took him up on the offer. Akil noticed that Kareem seemed out of sorts since the revelation of their mission last night.

She could understand. She was rather upset herself when she learned about the asteroid, to say the least.

Captain O'Malley picked Rita and Akil up in an old Central Park horse drawn carriage pulled by very sad looking nags. The carriage descended the hill and crossed onto Broadway. The castle felt like an illusion, as if it were located in some country estate, so it was a little disorienting to reach the bottom of the hill and find herself back on busy city streets and multi-story apartment buildings.

Captain O'Malley was young, but he had actually been an NYPD cop for about a year when the Shift hit. He wore a thick leather NYPD jacket and a sidearm, something that was not common here. The carriage was in disrepair; it had none of the post-Shift modifications standard in the Orange Pact that would make it more comfortable and sturdier for constant use such as modern shock absorbers and seats that were cannibalized from automobiles. This thing barely held together as it hobbled over the broken streets. She asked if they managed to turn Central Park into a farm. He just shook his head, "Our little paradise ends at 125th Street. And nobody goes to Central Park. That's no man's land."

"It's a bitch that it's snowing in March," he said above the ambient noise of outside. "Do you think this Shift thing affected the weather?"

"I'd say that's a distinct possibility, Captain."

"Oh, please, call me Liam."

"I'd say that's a real possibility, Liam, but who knows? I didn't ask Jamil about that."

There weren't any vehicles left on the streets. Rita assumed they must have all been hauled off years ago. A high rise apartment building advertised itself as a pig farm, which was frequented by almost all Hispanic workers outdoors. She could smell it from blocks away even in the frigid weather. Kareem had explained how the pig farm produced methane for limited electricity. More often, the fat was rendered for oil and soap. The Muslim and Jewish folk in the community would buy the oil, even the soap, but refused to work in the pig farm, which was a sensible compromise.

"You want to know what I think?" Liam O'Malley asked rhetorically. "I think that the sudden halt of cars and factories belching out so much shit in the atmosphere had something to do with this change in weather."

She knew that was unlikely. Whatever man's effect on the earth, it couldn't be reversed by the sudden cessation of manmade activity. But she wasn't going to argue with him. He seemed very approachable and appeared to be reaching out to her. She didn't know why just yet, but she was going to go with it and see where he took her, literally and figuratively.

"That's a good point, Liam."

"Sometimes, I think God is punishing us for abusing the earth the way we did."

Rita nodded. "Well, you're not alone in that belief. In fact, many in my congregation believe the earth reacted in self-defense." She didn't believe that herself, but again she was being diplomatic.

"Yes, your young lady friend Ilsa, she gave me a briefing on your people. I have to say, you seem to have a grasp of what's going on, Reverend."

"Well, I wouldn't…"

"No, don't be shy about it. I mean it. I've been seeking advice from my seer, and she warned me about something horrible coming for some time, and she said it would culminate this very month. And then you show up. And it all now makes sense."

Aha. O'Malley had reason to take them out on a tour and it wasn't to show them the wharf where people hawked fish and pig soap. She didn't care for any of the ridiculous superstitions of the astrologers and psychics they called "seers." They were snake oil salesmen. But again, she wasn't going to tell Liam he was a rube. She was going to see what common interests they had.

"I've been fortunate, Liam. There are forces working and I have been her conduit."

"I knew it! I knew it! The moment you entered the room, I knew you understood. You couldn't have made it this far without divine order working for you. And for you, too, Mr. Luevano." Rita hid a sly grin hearing her husband being referred to by her surname.

Liam continued. "You just *happen* to be the cousin of the Jeffe and he just *happens* to be there on his ride when you show up? Coincidence? I don't think so."

"The law of averages does seem to have been taking a sabbatical lately, hasn't it?" Akil added.

They passed another street under construction. Rita had wondered how they were able to tear up the streets to lay grass. Did they have jackhammers? And then it appeared to her. There was a gang of scrawny ill-clad people using pick axes to break through the street's cement surface even while it was snowing. She couldn't tell for certain, but they looked to be wearing shackles.

"Who are they, Liam?"

"Them? Oh, they're some new arrivals. They want to eat our bread, so they have to work."

"How new?"

"I don't know, a year or two? It's real shitty, I know, but what are you gonna do?" he asked rhetorically.

Rita had an answer but again decided to hold her peace. O'Malley changed the subject. "Reverend, do you think you'll be able to get that computer up and running to do what it needs to do?"

That was the question, now wasn't it? Rita couldn't say yes with confidence. "You see, I have four kids," O'Malley added.

"Four kids, son?" Akil asked. "What are you? A jack rabbit?"

"I'm Irish, Mr. Luevano," he said with a sly grin. "I have four beautiful girls. I want them to see a world that recovers from all of this. I want them to grow up, you see."

What greater motivation could there be? "We are going to do everything we can to get there in time," Rita offered. "I trust Gaia will guide me the rest of the way."

"I know she will," he said. That took her by surprise. Liam couldn't have been a member of the Gaia Piety Society. But at the same time, he seemed conducive to the beliefs. What's more, she figured his true desire to provide a life for his kids played into his thinking. Whatever could save his kids was what he would do. Some people turned to the wildest things like astrology and psychics in a vain attempt to control the uncontrollable. He was willing to make any leap of faith necessary, she figured.

When they crossed 155th Street, they past a fence with the gate opened where one set of guards prowled on the north side of the barrier while another set of guards prowled the south side. Both wore NYPD jackets with crude armor plates and carried crossbows. But the number "33" was painted on the chest plates by the guards on the north side of the street while the guards on the south side had "30" painted on their chest plates.

"Excuse me Liam, um, what's this?"

Liam understood her confusion. "We've just past from the 33rd Precinct into the 30th."

"Uh huh?"

"Well, you see, each precinct is sort of...what's the word?"

"Autonomous?"

"Yeah, that's it...autonomous. Each of the police chiefs is head of a precinct. That title doesn't mean what it used to, I know, but the old guys wanted to be a police chief, so Abu Miguel made them police chiefs, head of their precincts. I guess that works for me, because that makes me captain, second in command of the 33rd Precinct. Anyway, each of the police chiefs runs his own precinct independently and we pay a certain amount of gratuity to Abu Miguel who was able to keep the peace around here. So, when we cross over from one precinct into another, you have guards keeping watch for any funny business."

She could only guess that "funny business" probably meant freedom of movement. Now the numbers on the guards' armor made sense, as it related to their precincts. Rita wasn't a ballistics expert, but she did know that a .45 round would pierce that armor easily.

"So, why do you all weigh yourselves down with steel plates? You know bullets go right through it, don't you?"

Liam chuckled. "Yeah, we know that, Reverend."

"So, if I may ask. Why then?"

"How many guns do you see around here?"

She did notice that only the soldiers carried weapons and most of them were limited to primitive weapons like the crossbows. She and the archers in the Thomas Jefferson Martyrs Brigade carried compound bows, but that was in addition to their assault rifles and hand guns. Outside of officers like Liam, there weren't any firearms.

"You mean you got rid of guns?"

"What? Oh hell no, ma'am. We got plenty of guns, so do all the gangstas and savages. But what good are they? When you got no bullets left, guns wind up being pretty damned useless." His New York accent threw her out of time every time he spoke.

"Are you saying you all ran out of bullets?"

"Hard to believe, huh? But check it. Gang bangers had been dooking it out, and they sprayed and prayed like they always did. Eventually, they ran out."

"That's not the case with those Dallek boys we ran into," Akil observed.

"I heard of them once. I bet they wasted the last of their rounds fighting you. What we have stockpiled is precious. That's why only officers the rank of sergeant or higher get to carry firearms. And they are given only so many rounds. So, it's their loss if they go shooting off their load. In the end, we're okay, because most of the gangstas don't have shit as far as ammo either. They have some makeshift bows, some spears and shit, but our armor is good against that."

Hearing the fact that the ferals were most likely not carrying loaded firearms did lift her spirits just a tad. That was one tiny advantage in an otherwise bad situation.

He leaned in closer. "I guess it's not the same for you guys?"

"No, we have West Virginia with its ample reserve of nitro glycerin, not to mention all of the gun manufacturers."

Liam shook his head. "Talk about shoe on the other foot, right? Now we're the fucking...sorry, Reverend."

"I don't mind."

He laughed. "Now we're the hillbillies."

"Well, maybe, but I think there's something we can exchange to help you all out."

"I'd like that."

Someone was singing from a balcony. Rita soon recognized it was the Muslim call to prayer. Then she heard church bells overpowering the man's singing. Rita distinctly saw Liam cursing under his breath. That was something she found very telling. The carriage rolled past another former laundry mat, nail salon and bodega. Some part of her yearned for one of those black and white cookies. The chained laborers let her know there wouldn't be such niceties here.

"Don't start this."

"Akil, it's true."

Akil and Rita were getting dressed in their room, putting on the borrowed clothing provided by Kareem's servants. It had been two days. Two days lost. Rayne 2005 was now just a week away from impact. The snow finally stopped late in the afternoon, but after two days of snowing, she figured they would be moving even slower now. A light frozen dusting added hours to a fifteen mile ride. Two feet of freshly fallen snow was a catastrophe. Rita spent the day moving throughout Northern Manhattan getting to know the people. It was the only way to deal with her sense of helplessness on being stuck. Liam O'Malley's wife Kristi was her guide today. If anything, Kristi was more excited by the reverend and her connection with this Gaia than Liam was. Rita really liked the young woman. She was part of the privileged elite as the wife of the second in command of the 33rd Precinct, but she seemed very gracious to the commoners on the street, even the laborers. It might be due to her Harlem roots and that she was still just Kristi from the block. The stark division between the elite NYPD and the newcomers had struck Rita, and it was the bone of contention between her and Akil right now.

"Sugarpuss, we're not going to discuss this."

"Akil, your cousin runs a kingdom on the backs of serfs and you know it."

Akil shut the door and stormed over to her. With a strained calm he tried to counter her. "I think you're confusing the fact that he just happens to live in a castle."

"That is not the case, though I find him living in a castle to be apt. Maybe living here has affected him, but regardless, even a software engineer can see what this is. The police chiefs are vassal lords who pay tribute to Kareem and they get their tribute off the backs of starving people."

"They aren't starving."

"They look pretty hungry to me, mi coriño. Just sayin'."

"It's a rough country. It's hard for them all."

"Not for your cousin it isn't."

"Listen, sugar, that's because he provided them with a lifeline back when they desperately needed it and he is the only one who has kept the Muslims, Christians and Jews from going at each other."

"But he doesn't have to be such a tyrant. I mean, look how the servants react."

"They're grateful to him. Besides, I don't see you refusing to let them clean your laundry."

Touché, she thought. She really hated it when he had a point, the bastard.

"I don't want you fooling yourself about your cousin."

The argument was at an impasse. Rita realized that though she had a point, she was taking out her frustrations about being stuck here the last two days on Akil. She tended to do that, transfer a personal issue for the plight of others.

"It's not like I was going to say anything to Kareem, okay? That wouldn't be wise."

Akil sighed, sidled over to her, and put his arms over her shoulders. "Look, we'll be off at the crack of dawn tomorrow. We'll have six days to get there, power up TALOPS and we can take a leisurely ride all the way home. And then I don't care what you do. Start a workers' revolt if you want. Hell, I bring the pitchforks and torches. But for tonight, let's just relax, enjoy the amenities and the meat that tastes like chicken, which also happens to actually be chicken."

She grinned despite the mood and lightly slapped his cheek. "You're right, mi coriño." After she gave him a kiss, she added. "And Akil, don't call me sugarpuss."

Dinner was a feast, as it had been the first and second evenings. Roasted carrots, sweet potatoes, the very coarse bread and goat cheese were filling on their own without the main course. The meat was chicken as well as real goat meat, both halal though Kareem wasn't strictly devout. He was indulging in the potato vodka even though neither she nor the rest of the Virginians were indulging in the sauce as they were departing the following morning. She noticed that Liam was also not drinking.

"We should have a toast," Kareem said glumly as he lifted his mug. Everyone lifted their glasses.

"May God, Allah, whatever deity can hear us guide you on your journey tomorrow. Lord knows we are all depending on you."

Everyone clinked glasses around the long dining table. The Vicious Rabbits cheered, "ooh rah," while she and her archers instinctively toasted, "L'chaim," a Hebrew saying. Ezra Rothstein had started it long ago, and it wound up being the official cheer of the Thomas Jefferson Martyrs Brigade. The cheer sent thoughts of home. She hoped Greater Monticello was faring well without her. She missed Ezra, Neko, all of them so much.

"And Rita, Akil, my dear cousin, since all of us know that your success is vital for our survival here, Captain Liam O'Malley has volunteered himself and his officers to guide you all the way to Cambridge."

Rita felt a jolt of electricity hearing that. That was indeed very good news.

His chief, Isaac Tigh, a middle aged man with a shaved head who had an eye patch like she did, grumbled in a low bass voice. "I still don't like it, Jeffe. That's one hundred and fifty of my finest officers."

"I have instructed the other precincts to cover the men under your command…"

"You think I'd trust those guys? They'd sooner kill me in my sleep."

"That's why they're evenly divided between the other precincts," Kareem pointed out "There's no advantage for either precinct."

Rita turned to Akil and gave him a look as to say, "Not a kingdom, huh?"

Kareem added. "And your men will be armed with the other precincts' ammunition store and have the use of all of the bikes in the Heights."

"But I still don't…"

Liam slammed his fist on the table, his eyes bore on Tigh. "Don't you get it, chief? This is not politics! This is the fate of all of us, and I don't just mean here in Washington Heights. If they fail, in a week it won't matter who's got the leverage, because we'll be quite fucking dead…sir."

Liam probably must not have spoken out like that against his chief before, because Chief Tigh didn't say anything in response. He just rubbed his bald head.

"It's settled. The 33rd will accompany our friends to make sure they get to Cambridge, that is, if you would accept our help?"

Liam grinned and lifted his glass to Rita. Lieutenant Kendra Baraka stood up. "We have less than six days to cover two hundred miles. My folks are experienced riders with sturdy bikes. I do appreciate the offer as we could use all the help we can get, but can they ride?"

Liam stood up. "The bicycles are not in the same league as yours, ma'am, I admit. But all of my officers have ridden into the bush plenty and they can keep up. I swear that I will not allow my men to slow you down. That would sorta defeat the purpose, right? Anyone who can't keep up, gets left behind."

"Word?" she asked.

"Word."

"Works for me, then. I welcome you to the party," Kendra said. "Gunny, any thoughts?"

"Beats sitting round 'ere pounding me pud, aye?"

With that the tone of the gathering lightened considerably. Rita and the others started talking with a levity they hadn't felt in a long time. She hoped this would help get them to Cambridge quicker. One hundred and fifty armed men. So long as they could keep up. If they could, it certainly would put an end to paying the stinking trolls along the highways demanding bribes to allow the measly little platoon through.

She and the others got up to mingle when she noticed Chris Jung walking over to an acoustic guitar resting at the corner. She and Kendra walked over to him as he tuned it. He didn't speak; he just started playing. She didn't recognize the song, but it was beautiful.

"Which song is that?"

Chris shrugged. "Just a song I wrote. Well, Meredith and me. She wrote the lyrics."

"I didn't know Chris did his own music," Kendra said.

"Maybe he didn't. He was probably too busy being the big cheese and all," he said.

"Come to think of it, I know he didn't play nearly as well as you're playing right now," Kendra added. "It's really beautiful."

"Thanks. It's off our second album we just released on iTunes."

CHAPTER 24

The Mundaniverse
Falls Church, Virginia
March 8, 2013

Chris couldn't help but smile as he heard Moby playing on the grocery store's sound system. He and Meredith played Moby's watershed CD repeatedly when they started dating. "Porcelain," the song playing right now, held special significance for him. He and Meredith had been dating only a few months when she left Austin for a summer internship in New York City. He had flown up there with her before their three-month separation.

The sweet memory was a bright spot in his day. As of yesterday, all nonessential DS personnel were on an indefinite furlough. Meredith was exempted from the furloughs and was still working, but they still had no idea how they were going to pay the bills, as being exempted didn't mean getting paid. And it couldn't have happened at a worse time. While pushing the shopping cart down the dairy section, Chris recalled this morning's domestic dispute.

Meredith had found Chris down in the apartment basement storage shed working on his bike, re-christened *The Interceptor*, reinforcing it with the same modifications as his *Interceptor*. There in the shed, she noticed his recent purchase, a double wide child trailer. She asked him about the purchase, which he made even while the state of their jobs lay in the balance. Rightly so, Meredith was a little upset.

"Hon, I appreciate the sentiment and all, but for heaven's sake, now is not the time."

Of course, it wasn't. They didn't know when they were going to get paid again. So, why would Chris do something so stupid as to buy a high-end child trailer with shock absorbers, not to mention all of the top-of-the-line Shimano derailers and sprockets, the kind of equipment that he spent years cannibalizing from other bikes and reconditioning? He had no logical explanation. But when he found his *Interceptor* in the storage shed a few days ago, it shook him out of his daze and he rediscovered the man he had become.

In doing so, Chris did what he did best, preparing to survive. Survive what? He didn't know, but the government was shutting down. The Liberty Party now in power said it was to rein in spending. Chris didn't like what he saw here, and he did not want to ever be caught unprepared. Working on the bikes and getting the child trailer served to center him, it gave him a sense that he was in control again and could protect his family.

Meredith sighed. "Maybe you should consider returning it."

Polishing the chrome handlebars he said, "I don't think we should. Hon, this is good for the kids. I mean, look at us. Look where we live! We can't afford a child trailer?"

That opened a really sore subject, a subject so volatile that she and other Chris must have come to an agreement not to discuss it openly, and he just broke that agreement. She fumed.

"You think I *like* living here?" she snapped. Meredith went on, frustrated to the point of tears over how powerless they were. They couldn't move out of the apartment complex, which had devolved from a working class barrio to a gang infested, working-poor ghetto. They bought their condo for $250,000, but it was worth only a fraction of that now. And the banks knew that they couldn't foreclose and keep a security clearance.

Meredith broke down as she told of her frustrations. She worked long hours, they seemed to be getting longer, and yet they were living paycheck to paycheck, vulnerable to macro economic and political forces. Chris was reminded what an insensitive jerk he could be.

BACKGROUND MUSIC: "When I Was Young" by Nada Surf
Visit www.michaeljuge.com **on the Refurbished Soul page to listen**

Chris took a deep breath in the produce section of Safeway. He still couldn't get over the array of food offered here. He picked up more bananas and oranges, commodities nonexistent in his world. He then heard the sound of thunder. It confused him momentarily, it being a sunny day and all, but then he realized that the thunder came from the produce section itself as the automated system sprayed the lettuce and broccoli, reenacting a rainstorm.

He guided the shopping cart through the bread aisle, grabbed several large vats of peanut butter. Peanut butter was a wonder food. It kept for a long time and a man could thrive on peanut butter alone. He had lived off of it for a week once in a particularly nasty operation in Middleburg. The town had been overrun by cannibals and he had and his company was tasked with serving them justice for what they did to a Monticellan caravan. Cannibals were the worst, so Chris didn't mind cleaning house. In the frozen foods section, Chris grabbed some pizzas and a couple of these double decker Glutton Man meals by Stouffers, which advertised, "Get Stuffed!" Gunnery Sergeant Birmingham often told people to get stuffed, but it meant something else entirely.

After returning to the apartment, Chris went online. He figured he would do some quick research on current events before taking *The Interceptor* out again. After years of neglect, he was now pushing her pedals for a couple of hours a day in an effort to get his flabby body into a shape other than round. On Fox News, there were updates on asteroid Rayne 2005. Astronomers were predicting that it would be visible the day it passed for several hours and would pass within 90,000 miles. Chris recalled the original estimate was more like 100,000 miles away, but whatever. Celebrities were planning some big parties. Of course, there were the usual freaks saying that the government was lying to them and that there was a big conspiracy to hide the fact that the asteroid was going to impact. A few astronomers backed their claims.

He hadn't checked his Facebook in...well, five and a half years or several weeks depending on which way you looked at it. He retrieved the password and logged in. The social networking site had changed but he was able to navigate easily enough, though it was disturbing to note how intrusive the media was now. Chris saw long lost friends updating things about their dogs getting sick, their kids saying funny things, and friends being laid off.

Chris then checked his profile and a video other Chris had uploaded caught his eye. The title said, "Top track from our second album." He clicked on play, which connected to YouTube and he saw himself on guitar and his wife on piano playing a song. Brandon was on bass while Anne was on drums. It was nice for someone else to be on bass for a change.

Back in college he had been relegated to bass in Senator Monkey and the Funkacrats.

The song was soulful and slightly melancholy. Other Chris played the acoustic guitar with such professional skill that he felt like a bungling amateur in comparison. Meredith's voice was so lovely. She sang the lyrics, guiding the listener into a trance. The song picked up pace and grew in intensity as Chris switched to an electric guitar.

Chris knew this song somehow. He couldn't quite place it but he knew it. It was the song that he played or attempted to play a few months ago sitting out on his porch the night of the Mayan end of the world party. The tune just sort of came to him, and he thought it was a cover song of something long forgotten. He had stumbled through the chords. It was definitely the song the four of them were playing now.

Chris was awestruck seeing his other self playing with Meredith and his friends. He was an accomplished musician in this reality. This was a complete surprise to him, because he certainly wasn't back in his reality. Meredith had suggested recently that they should make music again soon. Now he understood that she wasn't talking about it in the biblical sense. She meant literally making music together.

At the end of the song, the video on YouTube faded to the text, which told the viewer to buy the Rabbit Hunters' new album on iTunes. "The Rabbit Hunters?" That was apparently the name of their band. Something of his world must have likewise seeped into other Chris' head. He quickly went to iTunes and found The Rabbits Hunters' latest album, *Refurbished Soul*.

For the next hour, Chris sat and listened to *Refurbished Soul*. Most of the songs sounded familiar to him. He had tried strumming these tunes back home, but he just didn't have the skill to do what other Chris was doing here. As he listened, Chris felt all of the emotion the songs conveyed. Ever since emerging into this crazy world, this unapocalyptic land, he had wondered how other Chris had coped. He still didn't know how or why other Chris hadn't killed himself. But now he saw something resilient in other Chris.

Other Chris, who seemed detached from taking responsibility for his own life, who seemed to be floating around, actually did have something going for him. Other Chris had found a way to deal with this world. Maybe it wasn't the most profitable way to take charge—the sales were modest on iTunes— but other Chris had found his voice regardless. The lyrics and the layered depths in his guitar riffs told the story.

He was about to explore the YouTube videos from The Rabbit Hunters' first album when the phone rang. The caller ID read "202-187-5305."

It was right about then that two drops of pee came out.

Holy shit! Chris rolled the chair back and scurried away from the phone. His gut clenched as he felt a rush of terror.

"No, no, no. This is bullshit. This can't be!"

How could that number, a number that had been listed in a DIA cable and then erased be calling him? He had thought about calling it, sure, because the damned crazy number stuck in his head like a bad song, but he never called it. He swore. He never called it!

The phone rang again. He briefly considered jumping off the balcony. The phone rang a few more times and then stopped. Silence. A new message chimed on Facebook. His heart pounding, he opened it.

Pick up the phone, Vicious Rabbit!

The photo of the sender depicted Rita Luevano. The phone rang again. *Rita? She came here too?* He wasn't alone after all! He scrambled to pick up the phone.

"Hello, hello, Rita? Rita, is that you?" he asked desperately.

"No, Chris. But I am a good friend of Rita's," the indistinct male voice on the other end answered. Chris didn't know what to do. Was this some government sting operation? And why in the hell would they be screwing with him? What the hell did other Chris do?

"Who is this?"

"My name is Jamil. I am a good friend of Rita Luevano and she needs your help."

There was a prolonged silence. Chris felt like he was under surveillance. He looked out the balcony to see if there was anyone watching him.

"And Rita asked for me?" Chris was assuming that she must have figured out that he was here, too.

"Not exactly. She does not really know who you are."

"'Doesn't really know who I am.' What the hell does that mean?"

There was a pause. "Captain Chris Jung, you know exactly what that means."

In the Hitchcock films, this was the part where the camera simultaneously zoomed in on the victim while zooming out on the surrounding scene accompanied by the "Eee eee eee" shrill.

"D…did you send the message on Facebook?"

"You are Chris Jung. You are a survivor of the Shift, which took place in your reality on July 11, 2007. You made your first confirmed kill at the raid in Madison High School in September of that year. You fought in the Obsidian War where you lost two and a half toes. You have since been promoted to captain of the Vicious Rabbits First Bicycle Mounted Cavalry Company. You also own a successful armoring business back in Rochelle. You were on your way to Laurel, Maryland to stop the Abercrombies from obtaining nuclear waste to be used for dirty bombs when your bicycle flipped over. And that, I believe, is when you wound up in this reality. Did I miss anything?"

Chris collapsed onto the chair. For months he had been utterly alone, thrown into a world where everything he had accomplished had been erased so fundamentally. His personal struggles in that first year of the Shift, his emergence from his own hell, his participation in protecting Rochelle, his armoring business. None of it happened. He was just another mope, a cube monkey, an overlooked, underpaid wonk who squandered his potential and wasted his way into pudgy, soft middle-age, his music notwithstanding.

And then suddenly to hear all of his accomplishments recited to him in this world, in this apartment—it was overwhelming. It was a beam of light from his reality.

"Chris?"

"Yes! I'm still here."

"Did I miss anything?"

"No, no you didn't. How…How do you know all of this?"

"Because your friends told me about you. Lieutenant Kendra Baraka, Gunnery Sergeant Birmingham and Reverend Rita Luevano."

"You know who I am?" he whispered.

"Yes, Chris. I know all about you and I have met your counterpart."

"So, I'm alive…I mean, other me is alive?"

"He left the Stubb Foundation alive. But I cannot establish his current condition."

Chris furrowed his brows. "The Stubb Foundation?"

"That was where Helmut was taking you."

"Oh, right, the place Helmut held out in Maryland. God, I forgot a lot in the…whatever that happened. The Abercrombies…did we get there in time? Did we succeed in destroying the loose nuclear material?"

"That was just a ruse, I am sorry to say. But it was not a trap. On the contrary, Helmut went to get help."

"Help? What are you talking about?"

"Chris, earth in both your reality and this reality are in jeopardy. Helmut was sent to get Rita, because I told him she could save everyone, and now I need you to save her."

"I'm sorry…it's Jamil, right? I've had ADD since I was a kid, and I think you lost me."

"Chris, I do not have time to explain everything. What you need to know is that contrary to what you have been told, Asteroid Rayne 2005 is on a collision course with the earth."

Chris bristled hearing that. "Oh, really?"

"Yes."

"You're shitting me."

"No, Chris. I am not 'shitting' you. I know you are not a scientist but I can show you this. Please check your email in your Yahoo account."

"I don't have a Yahoo…" Suddenly, Chris' iMac accessed a new webpage and opened an email inbox.

"Hey, what the hell are you, some kind of hacker?"

"Just read the email."

Chris put on his glasses—something he didn't need back in his reality, and noticed it looked like a cable. He shot up.

"This is…" His voice changed to an aggressive whisper. "This is a classified cable, Jamil! God dammit and you sent it on my computer, you f…"

"Read the text."

Chris' mind raced. He thought that maybe if he hung up now, he could erase the email and maybe, just maybe, if the spooks were watching, they would glean that he wasn't going to participate in any of this. He thought about calling Meredith and then thought again. *No, damn it. Don't involve her.* Then he considered calling DS headquarters and telling them everything, give them the goods, make it known he had no intention of opening classified material on his computer. Hell, it wasn't even he who opened it; it was that asshole Jamil. Would they believe that or did Jamil make it so it looked like Chris did it himself?

"Chris, read the text," Jamil repeated.

Okay screw it, I'm already in too deep, aren't I? Chris didn't have any idea how deep in it he and the entire world were until he sat down and read the text. Chris had never seen these tags before. This was some crazy, super secret squirrel stuff that went straight to the Director of the NSA. That alone was frightening. But when he read the text, he understood the horrifying truth. His stomach knotted as he read the president's planned farewell address.

"Oh, God," he whispered.

"Do you understand now?"

Chris nodded, not thinking that he was on the phone and Jamil couldn't see him.

"Is this going to happen in my world, too?"

"The trajectories of the asteroid in both the Shiftiverse and the Mundaniverse are identical."

Chris assumed "Shiftiverse" was his reality and "Mundaniverse" was the reality he was trapped in. He would have appreciated the catchy nicknames under different circumstances.

Jamil continued. "But I can stop it. I can deflect the asteroid in both realities."

"How?"

"It is not important for you to know how I will do it, but know that I have a plan, if other Rita is successful in her mission, which includes your counterpart, that I will be able to use the earth's magnetic field to repulse the asteroid from hitting the earth."

Magnetic field...Something registered with Chris. "The earth's magnetic field..." Chris repeated. "The Shift, my consciousness being transposed and you knowing how to use the magnetic field...Something tells me this is all related somehow."

"You are perceptive. It may explain how you had a latent connection to your other self long before your accident. Yes, there is a connection between my ability to manipulate the magnetic field and the Shift, but I must stress again..."

"Right, you don't have the time."

"The asteroid will impact in seven days and eight hours. I can stop it but I need you to do me a favor."

"Yes, what is it? Anything!"

"I need you to save Rita."

There, he said it again. "Save Rita? What do you mean? Save Rita? Isn't she over there...in my reality?"

"Yes. But she also exists here in the Mundaniverse. And this Rita requires your help."

"But if you're going to save us from the asteroid, then what does the Rita here need saving from?"

"What I am planning to do is going to have serious consequences,

Chris. I can save both realities from the asteroid, but there is going to be a high price. If what I do succeeds, there is a very high probability that my interference with the earth's magnetic field will initiate the Shift here."

"Oh," Chris said neutrally.

"Do you understand?"

Memories of those first hours, those first few days, weeks and months after 6:02PM July 11, 2007 still haunted him. The raw intensity of it worn off, but he would never forget how terrifying those months were. Humanity had become too dependent on the machines, and when they died, so too the world he had known.

This reality was no less vulnerable to the effects of EMPs than his own. There were probably even fewer LPs in good condition here, which they were going to regret. Granted, given a choice, humanity had a much better chance surviving the Shift than surviving Rayne 2005. The Shift would cause chaos and destroy the modes of production. The asteroid would erase the existence of all animal and plant life on earth. It was a no-brainer.

"Yes, Jamil. I understand," he said solemnly. "If you create the Shift, Rita will be left with little in the way of fending for herself. I take it that the Rita here is not the militant, gun-toting Unitarian survivalist who could chew the ears off a gun guard and ask for seconds like my Rita."

There was brief pause. "Essentially, you are correct. She is not even a Unitarian here."

"No shit." Chris folded his leg in his chair and became slightly chatty. "You know she's like the head Unitarian guru in my world, the prophet of Gaia herself, the 'one-eyed witch of UU.'"

"Yes, I know. I find it a shame that she abandoned the founding principles for her new passion."

"Yeah, I was wondering about that. She's no longer at the church in Charlottesville. What does she do to keep busy in this world these days, anyway?"

"We work together."

CHAPTER 25

The Shiftiverse
Lynchburg, Virginia
The Dominion of Lynchburg
March 8, 2013

News from the outside was sparse and hard to decipher. Meredith Jung, Jon Early, Jennifer Engel and Sister Shanyn sat in the basement of St. Pius X listening to the Stirling radio that had been smuggled into the church piece by piece and re-assembled. The antenna had been aligned with a satellite dish, hiding in plain site as it was. The Sheepdogs were thorough in their sweeps to ensure their citizens and residents didn't have any prohibited items such as a Stirling 3G radio, which could reach airwaves beyond the territory held by the Dominion and send and receive from a variety of frequencies. But as thorough as they were, Sister Shanyn told Meredith that the Sheepdogs tended to overlook the obvious, such as dead technological relics like satellite dishes. They dismissed useless artifacts of the pre-Reckoning as they would a laptop. Nobody would have a use for it. However, the resistance was able to use the satellite dish to attach and conceal the antenna of the Stirling.

The only radio allowed inside the Dominion was the Dominion's authorized radio receiver, something called a "Gabriel." There was no dial on the Gabriel; the Gabriel was set tuned to the Regent's station, "Truth Radio." Meredith couldn't think of anything more Orwellian than that.

The radio signal coming in was very weak, barely audible over the static. Vicious Rabbits sent coded signals, a version of Morse code and music. Most of the traffic was internal messages, but some were directed at their operatives out in enemy territory, and now included messages to Meredith herself.

The news from the front was bad. The tanks that were constructed in West Virginia using CAT construction vehicles made short work of the initial Orange Pact defenses in Raphine, located twenty miles south of the allied command in Staunton. The Vicious Rabbits and the Thomas Jefferson Martyrs Brigade slowed their advance. The mines planted by the Orange Pact and the hit and run ambushes attrited some of the Lambs' numbers. There was even a masterful ambush by the archers that took out a good number of the Lambs of God artillery batteries after letting the forward positions pass. But for the most part, the Lambs of God army was advancing with minimal resistance. It was a blitzkrieg, just like the regent wanted.

"I should have known," Jon said as he took off his headset.

Meredith looked at him quizzically.

"The set up at Colleen," he explained. "The regent wasn't trying to lure us into a feint into Highway 29. He never wanted to face us in our first engagement in Greater Monticello. He wanted the fight to be along Interstate 81."

"Well, why would he want that?" Sister Shanyn asked. "Isn't that the long way around, and isn't it going to take longer for the Lambs of God to reach your territory going the way he's going using I-81 and I-64 instead?"

"What does he care that it will take longer, Sister? As far as he's concerned, he has all the time in the world."

Meredith noted to herself that Jon said as far as the regent knows there's all the time in the world. She and Jon knew there were just seven shopping days left, period.

"The longer this battles rages, the more it hurts us. The longer the war, the more my people die. His too, but he can afford his losses. We can't."

Sister Shanyn sighed, and lit a contraband cigarillo. "Well, at least your forces haven't engaged our people on Highway 29. That's something."

"Yeah, there's enough half-blind militia in Monticello to keep your men from taking the direct route straight up the highway into Monticello itself, but not enough to go on the offensive and make the regent recall his offensive on Staunton. Not that I want to engage your people conscripted in Colleen."

"I understand. But there's still a chance to turn this around."

"How?" Jon asked acerbically. "Sister, your so called 'resistance' has proven as useful as tits on a bull, forgive my French. We came all of this way to get you to rally against your oppressors and what do your people do? They have committee meetings! They still haven't decided what to do! Y'all are running out of time just as much as we are."

Jon vented Meredith's exact sentiments. She had idly considered setting off a bomb outside the Sheepdog headquarters and implicating the Catholics just to give them the kick in the butt they needed. Not so long ago her morals wouldn't allow her to even entertain such a thought, but she had since dropped such vestigial suburban sensitivities. The only reason she hadn't done it herself was that she didn't know how to build a bomb.

Sister Shanyn winced. "You're preaching to the choir, Constable. But try as I might, I cannot just order my people to their deaths like you can. And I am a woman of the cloth. It is against my code."

"It's not you, Sister, but I'm beginning to think your people lost a lot more than their DVR recordings when the Shift hit. I think their backbone got…"

"Sister! Sister Shanyn!"

There was a cry from the hallway. Jennifer Engel and Jon hastily tried to cover the Stirling just in case the scout was warning them of a Sheepdog inspection. Father Mulcahy raced into their room.

"What is it, Father?" Sister Shanyn asked.

"The Lambs of God…" he gasped struggling for air. Father Mulcahy was an elderly man who normally had trouble walking. "They…took them."

"Who?"

"The kids! They took the kids!"

Less than an hour passed when people from all around the Catholic community arrived at the church. They had all come here because the church had served as the alderman for them to register their highly edited grievances to the Lambs of God. The Lambs of God had indeed rounded up all of the junior high and high school aged children at the schools reserved for the Catholic kids. Truth Radio had claimed that the children had volunteered to assist in the war effort to do things like fill sand bags, work the chow lines and run messages safely behind the front lines. Even if that was the case, it was a clear message to the Catholic community. An attack on the Lambs of God was an attack on their children.

People clamored and argued inside the church's packed cathedral. Mothers were crying desperately.

"I say we give the regent what he wants," hollered one of the resistance captains. "We got the constable of Rochelle and his mistress Vulcan right here!" That caused a stir with the people inside the cathedral. Meredith nearly tripped as she stepped back into Jon.

The man continued. "I say we hand 'em over to the Sheepdogs. The regent might release our kids!"

Some of the people murmured, considering the idea. Meredith felt a sudden rush of terror hearing that man who just blew their cover in front of the entire community. Jon, who was a few feet away, pushed people aside and reached for his lower back. He was going for his pistol.

A few people shouted, "Yeah! This isn't our fight!"

The man who ratted them out and offered the idea to hand them over made his way over to her. Just as Jon was about to present his pistol, Sister Shanyn stepped in front of Meredith to protect her and lashed the man's hand with a yard ruler, which she produced out of nowhere. She then did some masterful samurai strokes, which cleared the crowd from Meredith and Jon.

"No!" Sister Shanyn shouted at the crowd. "We are not going to do this! We are not going to betray the one people who have been keeping us afloat!"

The crowd went silent. "And you, Ignatius Quinby, you should be ashamed of yourself." The man who proposed the idea, whose name she now ascertained to be Quinby, stepped back and cradled his welted hand looking contrite.

"I am going over to discuss this with the regent right now and talk him down. And I am holding each and every one of you accountable for the well-being and safety of my friends." Sister Shanyn grabbed both Meredith's and Jon's hands forcefully, which also had the effect of forcing Jon not to wield his pistol.

"What you do to them, you do to me. Is that clear?"

"Yes, Sister Shanyn," mumbled a few.

"Is that clear!" she repeated and raised her ruler.

"Yes, Sister Shanyn!" everyone, including Meredith and Jon repeated.

"Good. I'll be back shortly. Father Mulcahy, if you would, please take down the names of all of the missing children?"

As Sister Shanyn headed for the door, Meredith followed. "Sister Shanyn, what are you doing?"

"I told you. I'm going to have a talk with the regent."

"I don't think he's much of a listener."

"I'm not going to let him take our children."

Meredith felt the noose around the resistance tightening. They had stored weapons and supplies for years thanks to Juan Ramirez, but what good would it do now? Would these people stand up and wage war against the regent when he had their children's lives in their hands? She wouldn't.

Jon walked up to her. "Listen, Sister, Gordon Boche is a madman. You can't go there and make him see reason with that yard ruler of yours."

"We'll see about that."

"This is ludicrous. You're going to get yourself killed," he whispered urgently.

She placed a hand on his cheek. "You take care of them Jon." Then she slapped his hand with her yard ruler. "And nuns do not commit suicide."

Sister Shanyn walked out of the cathedral, marching down the street with the ruler in her hand.

Jon rubbed his hand. "Ouch. That *really* hurt."

There was nothing to do but wait. The people who earlier supported the idea of turning her and Jon in to the regent kept their distance from them. It wasn't that Jon was trying to intimidate them, but he got that look in his eyes, that Marine officer, "I could kill you ten different ways before your next breath and not break a sweat" kind of look, something Meredith hadn't seen in him in years.

Nobody left the church, which was a good thing, for Meredith feared that word would get out to the Lambs of God that the constable and the director of the Swan were here. But they couldn't contain the people inside the church indefinitely. With Sister Shanyn gone and everything up in the air, she and Jennifer Engel had gone back to listening to the coded reports coming in when someone knocked on the door. Something told her it was bad, because she could hear sobbing and cursing in the hallway.

"Mrs. Engel, Mary," the young man referring to her completely useless cover name, "um…Sister Shanyn …" He broke down crying, unable to finish.

Jennifer and Meredith ran upstairs out of the basement and headed outside to the parking lot. Some people sobbed hysterically while others started screaming for vengeance. Meredith, who stood at the top of the steps, saw Jon Early cover a body and pick it up. It didn't register at first, but then it became clear that Jon Early was carrying the body of Sister Shanyn Duffy. Jon held a steel gaze and carried the body inside, staining the jacket he wore with Sister Shanyn's blood. People immediately moved aside to let him pass. As he passed Meredith, Sister Shanyn's arm fell and brushed up against her; it was still clutching the yard ruler.

"I want those bastards to pay!" screamed Ignatius Quinby. People erupted in an angry cheer of approval.

"Those savage scum bags!" cried another.

"She was a woman of peace, married to God and they murdered her!"

The crowd inside the cathedral had turned from being petrified peasants, ready to turn on their allies, to a vengeful mob.

"I'm gonna kill that damned son of a bitch Gordon Boche and send his worthless ass to hell!" Quinby asserted. People shouted in support. "Who's with me?" There were more cheers of support. Men and women started making their way over to Quinby, who just hours ago had suggested turning Jon and Meredith in to the regent. Meredith had often noted that humans were unpredictable, which made her job all that more difficult.

People shouted for the regent's death. It became clear that the regent, who up to now had dealt the Catholic minority a no-win situation, had made a fatal error. How could he not have known that this would, if anything, galvanize the resistance? His Sheepdogs had to have known that Sister Shanyn was highly regarded throughout the Catholic community in Lynchburg. Her influence extended to Roanoke even. That was probably why they hadn't killed her up until now. They knew it would have destroyed whatever little cooperation the Catholic community had with the Lambs of God. So, why now, when the war was on? Why would they make a martyr out of Sister Shanyn and incite a rebellion within their own borders? They had to know, right? Maybe it wasn't an error. Maybe the regent wanted the Catholics to rise up.

Meredith pulled Jon aside. She saw that he was wearing the same shirt soaked in Sister Shanyn's blood.

"Jon, this doesn't make sense. The regent is too smart for this."

"I know."

"It's a trap. He wants them to revolt, doesn't he?"

Jon nodded. "I think you may be right, Mary," he said, with slightest hint of irony in using her assumed name.

The crowd started mobilizing in the cathedral. "Okay, Jennifer, it's time to unpack the guns," Quinby barked.

Meredith glanced over to Jon, who stood on top one of the pews.

"People, listen up!" his voice boomed above the cacophony. It took a few seconds for the murmuring to die down, but Jon had a way of commanding everybody's attention when he needed to. She noticed the scabbard of his great-great grandfather's sword secured to his side. She groaned inwardly, dreading his call for revolution now considering that it was a death trap.

"Alright, people. Sister Shanyn was a dear woman who gave all of herself to serve the poor in Nicaragua, who served you and your people faithfully and gave the ultimate sacrifice, the fullest measure in the hopes that your children might be spared. Now you know what the regent thinks of her, of her work, and of you. You want blood."

People roared in approval. "You want to hang that bastard and see him swinging from the nearest lamp post!"

More people shouted back "Yeah!"

"But I got news for you, people. You go out there brandishing your weapons, and the regent, armed with his Sheepdogs, is going to slaughter each and every one of you."

That was met with a hushed silence. "You take up arms against the regent and you do him the favor of providing him an excuse to shoot the lot of you."

"What in the hell do you suggest we do? Cower?" said a woman as she racked a shotgun.

"Why in the hell did you bother arming us if that's what you thought the whole time?" said another.

"The regent is sending our kids to die! We got to stop him!"

Others started arguing until Jon whistled for quiet. The way he glared at everyone with his foot raised on the back of the pew, he was clearly taking charge.

"I have no intention of letting this atrocity go unpunished, nor do I have any intention of letting your children become shields for the Lambs of God. We are going to stop him. We are going to get your children back. Now is the time for us to stand up against this ass clown."

Meredith hid a smile. She knew Jon got the term "ass clown" from Chris.

"Okay, then what do we do?" Quinby said angrily. "A couple of days ago, you were pleading for us to stand up and fight the regent, then you tell us if we do, we'll be all killed, a second later you're telling us to stand up against him. Which is it, Constable?"

"Yes, I did tell you to fight against him militarily. I did so and I was wrong. I did not know that the regent wanted you to start a war here. If he does, it's a sure bet he has something special planned for us if we go guns ablazing. We must stand up to the regent and not let this go unanswered."

"Should we moon him instead?"

That won a few muted chuckles. Jon didn't laugh. Instead he produced a yard ruler, the very same Sister Shanyn had held.

"We march! Unarmed, very loud, and very public!"

When they left Rochelle a few days ago, Meredith didn't expect that Jon would be leading a protest in Lynchburg. But that was exactly what he was talking about. She thought it was a terrible idea, an absolute one-way ticket to oblivion. What the hell did the regent care about killing a few unarmed Catholics? He murdered thousands of men, women and children in his penance camps. Who were they to him?

Apparently, she was the only one who didn't get it, because Jon was high-fiving everyone in the crowd including the obnoxious hothead Ignatius Quinby. When he finally stepped down from his grand stand, she stormed over to him.

"Can I have a word with you?" she said through clenched teeth.

Jon and she walked over to the side near the confessional. "Jon, what the hell are you thinking? Do you have any idea what you're getting into? Do you think for a moment that the regent is actually going to hesitate to fire on all of us? Armed, unarmed, it doesn't matter!"

He just stood there patiently while she continued. "The regent isn't a leader, he is a tyrant. He does not respect civil disobedience. He thrives on fear and terrorizing his citizenry into submission, and our deaths will just reinforce his stranglehold on these people. This isn't colonial India and you're not Gandhi. And there's no media watching. God dammit," she knew he hated it when people took the Lord's name in vain, especially in a holy place, "Jon, this is not America! Not anymore!"

"No, it isn't, Meredith," he said with a calm voice. "This is no longer America. But I am an American. And so are these people here and so are the people throughout Lynchburg."

"What kind of corny, jingoistic…" she stopped herself. Jon had been a Marine colonel, and she knew he grieved to this day for the nation that died. In fact, she herself still grieved its demise.

Jon continued. "The regent's sermon is tomorrow morning. Half of the town will be out when we arrive. The Sheepdogs will not be able to disappear us all before we make our presence known."

"You think it makes any difference whether there are witnesses? They might even cheer our slaughter."

"I don't think they will. They might believe the lies about us in the Orange Pact, they might have even gone along with the regent up to a point. But those people couldn't have forgotten who they once were. They have to remember," he implored.

Meredith squeezed the bridge of her nose in frustration. Jon, the good soul he was, was too naïve sometimes.

"Jon, that's really sweet and all, but…that's a hell of a gamble."

"Meredith, you're leaving tonight." As he said that, a young man approached and waited.

"Where?" she asked stunned.

"Monticello. I need you to get in touch with Neko. Explain that the situation down here has evolved. And tell her what we learned about Sheriff Schadenfreude. This here is one of your operatives."

She studied the young man and then noticed the patch on his arms. It was the patch of the Sheepdogs. "Jorge Guerrero?"

"Ma'am."

Jorge Guerrero was the Swan's operative within the Lamb's of God's Sheepdogs, a true intel gem. The young man, just nineteen or twenty, also happened to be the nephew of Monticello's former Deputy Chief Magistrate Juan Ramirez. The Swan had been funneling money to Jorge's family and his family had been using the Byrds to buy weapons and supplies. With the Guerrero's high position in the Dominion, they could do it openly without fear of the Sheepdogs looking in, especially considering that Jorge was one of them. Jorge's intel had been crucial if sporadic.

"Wait, Jon, this is my operation."

"He'll be able to escort you without hindrance within Dominion territory. From there, he'll pass you to some friends who know their way in the woods to get you to Monticello. Jorge is going to tell the Catholic troops in Colleen what's happening down here. God willing, they will abandon their position in Colleen and back up the protestors here. But you've got to convince Neko *not* to advance from Monticello if they do abandon their position. If we launched an offensive while these people are protesting, it will undermine everything we're trying to achieve."

"And what is that?"

"To invalidate the regent."

Meredith's mind buffered this new strategy. They came here to start a violent uprising and now Jon was talking about a protest backed by their own Catholic troops.

"When you get to Monticello, Neko needs to know everything, okay? You understand, everything we learned here."

"What about you?"

Jon smiled. "I'm going to help lead the rally."

"You? You are going to lead a street protest." she asked incredulously.

"Yeah, it's dripping with irony isn't it?"

"That's not what I meant."

"I know. But they lost their leader. I can't really replace Sister Shanyn, but maybe having led a battalion and a community through the Collapse is a transferrable skill."

Jon pulled out an envelope sealed in a plastic baggy. "After you tell Neko what's what and convince her not to attack if the Catholic forces are retreating from Colleen, you go home and give this to Sharon if the need arises."

Meredith was conflicted by a slew of emotions, including sorrow for leaving Jon here, hope of getting home to her children and even anger about losing control of her operation as petty as it was.

"Hey," he said reassuringly, "it's simply one of those 'just in case' things. Every Vicious Rabbit has a note. It actually acts as countermeasure from unintentional farm buying."

She nodded. "Jorge, see to it that the ride is smooth. Meredith gets motion sickness. Come on Meredith, I've got to get things going here, and you've got to get to Monticello ASAP to save the day."

She gave him a hug. As she held him, she was reminded of his father Charles. They had a similar build.

"I'm sorry, ma'am but we must leave now if we're going to coordinate properly with the protest."

"Go on, git," Jon said.

Meredith sighed and acquiesced. She fought off the feeling that the boys' club had just taken over, and she was being shuttled to safety. Her Lynchburg plan had not survived contact with the enemy, but her mind was already planning the conversation she would have in Monticello, with all of its own layers of strategic implications.

She and Jorge left the cathedral. As she did, she stole one last look at Jon who was now giving orders to the people. They seemed to take to him as their leader now without question. Jon had that effect on people, so long as he was clean and sober. She could see that he really needed to be here. Jon had been an empty suit for so long. It was heartening to see him back to the man he was meant to be. What a relief. Now all she had to do was convince Neko to settle down and then all she had to do was await the end of the world. She forced herself to turn away and join Jorge in his armored truck. As they drove off into the cold night, she wondered if Chris had such a note that she held for Jon.

CHAPTER 26

The Shiftiverse
Staunton, Virginia
March 9, 2013

Ezra turned Charlene into the parking lot of the Staunton Mall Shopping Center. The abandoned vehicles had been removed weeks ago. In their place was a fleet of decrepit school buses from the four communities, bicycles, and a band of horses tied to posts. There were a few motorbikes as well. Motorbikes were not particularly useful except for running messages behind the lines. For reconnaissance, horses and bicycles reigned. A collection of post-Shift generators puttered to provide electricity and were situated right next to the mall's entrance. There were also a few "tanks." They didn't have nearly the firepower as the Lambs of God tanks, which more closely approximated a proper tank. But it was better than facing the regent's wildcats naked. Lastly, there were a number of technicals, old pickup trucks with heavy machine guns mounted in the truck bed, even a few El Camino technicals. Legacy Marines in the Vicious Rabbits had told tales about such vehicles in Somalia and in Afghanistan, and they provided the specs for a fleet to be built. Ezra didn't envy the technical crews as the trucks had no armoring. Their purpose was to be highly mobile and provide suppressive fire. Armor would slow the vehicles down to the lumbering pace of tanks, but without the big guns.

A few soldiers, who were as muddy as he was, saluted as Ezra passed by. The snow was finally melting, mud replacing the tundra, turning the area into the third day of Woodstock. There were sandbagged positions throughout the parking lot.

Ezra and his archers had just returned from behind the lines. They successfully neutralized a number of the enemy howitzers. As the forward column passed, the archers lay in wait for the big guns. Once the tanks and first division passed, the archers hit the artillery moving in trucks. It was just like the old days. Hopefully, that would help the Orange Pact. Ezra was able to get a good look at Lynchburg's numbers. They were overwhelming, simply overwhelming.

Ezra dismounted his horse. "You be nice to the other horses, Charlene," he told his mare.

She neighed as if to say "ai'ight," and he headed to the Regal Cinema, which had become the Orange Pact's command center for the moment, which Commandant Dean Jacob called the "CIC." On his way in he saw a bunch of armed ferals being unloaded from three Culpeper armored buses. They weren't the usual scrawny beggars. They looked well-fed. Perhaps they were bandits. Ezra shook his head contemptuously as he headed inside.

The theaters and concession stands had all been converted to serve the Orange Pact's CIC. Men and women from the various outfits rushed in and out of the lobby of the theater, all dressed in full battle gear and covered in mud like he was. Ezra walked to theater number four, the main CIC. Next to the theater entrance, a faded poster for a movie was still on the wall. *Knocked Up*. Ezra snorted. He remembered taking a girl on a first date to that movie. Hilarious yes, but it really didn't inspire pre-marital sex, he recalled.

Crude construction lights lit the theater, connected to thick electrical cables propping open the exit doors, and running to generators outside. Stirling 3G radios sat on tables while communication officers sent and received radio traffic. The bulky sets were more mobile, and the wind-up batteries lasted longer than the first generation. They could send and receive up to forty miles on a clear day with little Shift interference. He wondered when he completely changed his perspective on technology. When he was a kid, these would have been considered cumbersome.

Along with the usual Orange Pact soldiers, he saw a few of those bandits on the way in speaking with a contingent of soldiers from Culpeper. Ezra caught sight of Commandant Dean Jacob dressed in his legacy Marine desert BDUs. The tall African American gave him a quizzical look.

"You get injured in the fighting?" he asked gruffly.

At first Ezra didn't know what he was talking about, and then he realized he was referring to his face, or more specifically the black eye he won in the brawl at the Prancing Pony the other night.

"Oh, this? Nah, I got it at the Pranc...I mean, I fell in the shower."

Commandant Jacob glowered at him suspiciously. "Yeah, a lot of boys seemed to have 'fallen' in the shower."

"Who are the ferals, sir?"

"Uh, excuse yourself, Hoss. We're not ferals," a man said. He had a beautiful black mane, a shaved face and was really articulate, especially for a feral.

"Colonel Rothstein, I'd like to introduce you to Hank Conrad, Grand Sheriff of the Occoquan Estates Tribe." Dean seemed put off by Ezra's uncouth question.

"Oh, sorry about that." Ezra offered his hand. Hank took it.

"A pleasure."

"So, Occoquan Estates. That's in Reston, right?"

"Yeah. We got wind this was going to be a total smack down and we're here to lend a hand."

Whose smack down, Ezra thought plaintively. "Well, gee, that's really nice."

"Not really," Hank countered. "I owe that bastard Chris Jung too many favors, and this is me paying up. Where is that mother scratcher anyway?"

Last Ezra saw of Meredith's husband was on the *Jean Lafitte* back in January. Ezra thought he saw Chris' fast boat make it on shore. He couldn't tell, because he was busy floating in the icy waters of Chesapeake Bay, dying of hypothermia. If that Saints captain hadn't fished him and a number of Vicious Rabbits up, he would have surely died. And hypothermia was no way for a man to die. Now, an artillery shell….

"He's busy," Ezra answered cryptically.

"So are we all."

"What's the status of your people, Colonel," Dean Jacob interrupted.

"Most of us made it back alive about an hour ago. We've been riding hard all evening. But I'm confident we got half their howitzers."

"That is good news. It doesn't change things too much. We always had the advantage of our triple sevens to theirs, and they will still be hitting us with mortars any minute now, but it's still good to hear."

Ezra scratched his black beard. "Have we heard anything along Highway 29?"

"The Lambs of God haven't budged from Colleen."

"Now that is strange. I know the Catholic regiments aren't well armed or trained, but you would think they would prod us regardless."

"Actually, I think I miscalculated the regent's intentions. It wasn't meant to be a feint. They wouldn't want to go up Highway 29, not with their numbers and the heavy armor. They wanted to engage us out here where they could maximize the advantage of their tanks. And they attrite us as we attrite them along this longer route. Unfortunately, they can afford it. We cannot."

"Dude, sucks."

"Yeah, I just wished I realized that earlier."

"Why are we going to fight them where they want to fight?"

"It's not like we have much of a choice. Besides, Staunton is as good of a static defense as any. We have the higher ground, and fortified defenses. It's going to cost them dearly to break through."

Ezra could read between the lines. He meant to say *when* they break through and force the Orange Pact to retreat. "Static defense" was really a relative term here. Ezra knew the call to retreat and made sure his lieutenants knew it as well. There was a lot of radio traffic followed by the sound of shells landing a few miles away.

"Well, enough of that. You must be exhausted. Get some shut eye if you can manage. We'll try to cut the noise out."

"Great. I'll return in four hours, unless I hear anything otherwise."

The artillery barrage killed any sleep Ezra hoped to get. It wasn't a constant barrage. It was a bit disorganized and fortunately off the mark. Ezra hoped the Orange Pact's artillery was doing a better job. Of course, one advantage in being an advancing army was that their position changed. Then again, the Orange Pact artillery knew exactly what route the Lambs were approaching from. It might not even odds, but every bit helped. A few hours later, he got the word on the Stirling to get into position. He and the archers mounted their very skittish horses—horses didn't like artillery either, apparently—and trotted down Lee Jackson Highway passing the Staunton Mall Shopping Center. Ezra could already see some subtle signs that the Commandant was packing up the CIC here in Staunton, most likely to be moved back further toward Charlottesville.

Along the way he passed a group of Vicious Rabbits on bicycles. He caught site of Valerie Blaine, now dressed in fatigues and MOLLE gear. She still looked gorgeous even with all of that on her. He couldn't stop to give her a pre-battle kiss. It had a way of working against both of them. Instead, he gave her a slight nod of recognition. She winked at him in return. Charlene, the jealous mare she was, neighed indignantly. He rode off, really hoping he would get through all of this with all of his parts together.

The archers took their positions on a crest of an interstate clover leaf a mile south of the Staunton exit. Artillery had torn up the highway. Well, that and the Orange Pact's own efforts to slow their advance as much as possible. The last of the melting snow mixed with mud on the asphalt as rows of barbed wire draped the landscape before sandbagged positions. It was nothing like the intricate network of sandbagged corrals in Staunton, but with the sight of a few bodies lying untended to out in the fields, it reminded Ezra of the photos he saw of World War I in history class.

The artillery exchange intensified and then ceased completely. Ezra took out his binoculars and could see the wall of Lambs of God approaching. Sergeants and officers barked orders to their soldiers. "Alright, get ready, Vicious Rabbits."

"Show these bastards not to come to our house and push us around!"

"Steady shooting, people! I don't want anyone blowing their wad on those tanks! Let arty take care of that!"

Then in the distance Ezra heard something. It was music from the enemy's side. It was hard to make out at first, but as he listened intently, he shook his head and laughed.

"Creed? They're playing *Creed*? Really?"

One of young archers asked, "Who's Creed?"

Earlier Ezra had been kvetching about losing his generation's music. So few bands post-millennium had concerned themselves with recording onto LP save for those who enjoyed the retro feel. Unfortunately, of all of the bands to choose to go retro, Creed was one of them. Ezra turned Charlene around and called out to the psyops vehicles, another technical, with the largest working amps on this side of civilization.

"Hit it, Hoode."

Hoode Patterson gave a thumbs up and Ezra awaited a serious kick ass, death metal rock song that would put the wood into every last Vicious Rabbit, Monticellan, Fredericksburger and Culpeper soldier, something that would scare the shit out of their enemies. And with that came the lyrics...

"Never gonna give you up
Never gonna let you down"

That wasn't the song he was expecting. Instead, the inoffensive Rick Astley song with the typical 80s drum and bass auto mix plucked away cheerily until Ezra gave Hoode a look.

"Never gonna make you cry
Never gonna say good…."

"Oops," Hoode said sheepishly.

The record made a terrible ripping sound as Hoode replaced it with the intended album, *Master of Puppets* by Metallica. As *Battery* thrashed into the guttural metal head banging main theme, the fighting began. Mortars took aim at the line of tanks moving up Interstate 81. As feared, the armor was impervious to everything except the .50 caliber and even then not head on. The tanks rolled over the Jersey barriers and the barbed wire. A few tanks in the lead exploded as they either tripped well-hidden landmines, or were taken out by the few RPGs available. The smoldering tanks that bought it trapped the tanks in line behind them.

Ezra knew that the Lambs had the harder mission: charging an entrenched enemy head on. Of course, five to one odds still sucked monumentally for his side. Ezra and his archers called in coordinates for mortars on the Stirling strapped to a horse. The Lambs of God started again with their own mortars and were softening the defenses. Through James Hetfield's heavy metal guitar strum, .30 caliber rounds made a terrible ripping sound across the valley.

Ezra had seen plenty of action in his time. He had faced off against the Blue Ridge Militia and later the Obsidian Corp in organized battle. But they didn't have tanks and they weren't exactly accustomed to fighting in the post-Shift world, which leveled the playing field. The scene before him now was horrifying, not only the carnage but the sheer overwhelming numbers that the Lambs of God were throwing at them. It was an endless mass of soldiers.

"Sir, over there."

Ezra turned and adjusted his binoculars and saw a few platoons worth of soldiers caked in mud trying to open a flank. The barbed wire extended for miles, but it only slowed them down. Ezra guided Charlene around and the archers headed down the hill.

BACKGROUND MUSIC: "Relax" by Frankie Goes To Hollywood
Visit www.michaeljuge.com **on the Refurbished Soul page to listen**

Archers dressed in ghillie suits inched toward the barbed wire. Ezra had his bow ready like the other archers but held his AK-47 as his primary weapon. In the distance the psyops vehicle wailed songs from his parent's generation that came to be adopted into his own. Through the fog and trees, he could see the platoons marching. It was hard to decipher with all of the gunfire in the distance, but he could also hear the grinding sounds of engines. Tanks. Many of them, most of them, in fact were getting stuck in the mud. The treads weren't helping as they were designed to do; however, several more of the lighter ones were approaching unimpeded.

"Spread out!" he ordered. The archers did as he commanded and galloped in all directions. One tank aimed its barrel at an archer. He and the horse disappeared into a sickening cloud of fleshy debris. Ezra grimaced and dismounted Charlene, grabbed the sack holding RPG missiles and a launcher and slapped his mare to go back to behind the lines. He and the other remaining archers crouched and leap-frogged from tree to tree. Ezra loaded the RPG into the launcher. The digital display was dead of course, but everything critical was still operational.

Ezra knelt in the mud and fired. The rocket made a deafening sound and nearly pushed him back on his ass as it launched, careening toward its target, leaving a smoke trail in its path. It tore through a tank with T-34 inspired sloped armor that started life as a Caterpillar excavator, blowing the turret right off. Men and women cheered hoarsely as the tank that crossed the barbed wire went up in flames. Then the archer next to him fell in a hail of bullets.

Ezra dove for cover and hastily grabbed the launcher, which, like him was covered in mud. Behind the burning tank raced soldiers of the Lambs of God shooting G3 rifles. A heavy machine gunner carrying an old M-60 laid down suppressive fire as the Lambs advanced. Ezra brought his AK-47 around. The barrel and bolt were covered in mud. He tried to wipe it off, but his hands were even more covered than his rifle. He aimed his rifle and prayed that it wouldn't backfire. It didn't, fortunately. The AK-47 wasn't a particularly elegant weapon. It was heavy and had loose tolerances, but unlike the American M4, you could abuse it, bury it in the mud, neglect to clean it for months and it still did its job.

Ezra couldn't help but add to no one in particular, "You have to hand it to the Russians. They sure make good rifles."

He and the other archers held off the Lambs of God flanking maneuver for what felt like hours. The archers had the advantage of terrain and the cover of trees. The Lambs of God were crawling up a muddy barren hill, slippery with sludge and gore. But a new line of tanks was approaching from the main front, heading their way.

One of the tanks turned its turret and took out a technical. The ancient pickup truck exploded into a ball of fire and rained shrapnel. Ezra had to keep his concentration on the infantry trying to advance on their position and hope the tank didn't get its sights on him. One of the main weaknesses of the tanks was that the crew was virtually blind. A Vicious Rabbit with a .30 caliber set up a machine gun in a pillbox and allowed him to pursue the approaching tank.

He loaded the RPG and aimed. He squeezed the trigger. Nothing. There was only the dreaded sound of "click," to let him know he was out of luck.

"Son of a bitch!"

He had one option left to him. He dropped the RPG and approached the tank cautiously. There were two Caterpillar tanks behind the lead one, both engaged shooting at other positions. Ezra literally tiptoed as if the tank crew could hear the sound of his steps over the loud diesel engines. Along the way, one of his boots got stuck in the mud and when he lifted his foot, the boot stayed in the mud, leaving him barefoot.

"Damn it!" He turned around momentarily to grab the boot before coming to his senses. "Forget it, Ezra!"

Ezra lurched toward the blind tank, making a slurping sound with his feet into the mud until he was in front of the tank. He had used up the supply of really precarious post-Shift grenades, but he still had one explosive left. He grabbed a stick of C4 and a detonator out of his vest and as the tank lumbered before him, Ezra lay on the ground. It was when the tank's low belly hovered over him that Ezra considered what an incredibly bad idea this was. Too late. The tank was over him now, there was no way to escape; the treads crushed the fallen branches beside him. He didn't realize it until now, but Ezra was claustrophobic. He let out a desperate scream of terror as the belly of the beast ever so slowly crawled inches above his face. The tank's belly went flush with muddy surface, pushing Ezra in the ground with no air between him and the tank's belly.

"Worst...Idea...Ever!"

There. Through his mud caked goggles he saw it. He wound the egg timer, which was used as the detonator and placed the C4 inside a pocket exposing one of the tank's axles. The tank slowly crawled the rest of its monstrous frame over him. As it passed, caustic hot exhaust fumes belched in his face. Finally, he saw the beautiful daylight again. He stood up and ran for his life, his feet going, "slurp, slurp, slurp" over the mud. It was like one of those nightmares where you tried to run, but the ground wouldn't let you. Ezra saw the safety of a berm and jumped over it.

Seconds later, the explosion reported success and black smoke billowed from every orifice of the tank. Ezra stood up and casually walked past it, smelling of burning diesel and burning flesh. He bent down, grabbed his boot that had gotten stuck in the mud, pulled, and with a sucking sound, the earth released it to him begrudgingly.

CHAPTER 27

The Shiftiverse
Lynchburg, Virginia
The Dominion of Lynchburg
March 9, 2013

"And Lord, if I'm about to make a big mistake by leading them to die pointlessly, I'd deeply appreciate it if you could give me a heads up on that."

Jon Early knelt by his cot in the storage room that had been his quarters the last few days. All of the final preparations had been made. People were running through the hallway of the church mobilizing for the protest. There was just one last thing he had to take care of.

"Let me guide them with wisdom and clarity today, Lord." Jon was about to finish his prayer when he added, "Oh, and Lord, while I'm here asking for things when I shouldn't, if you could please save the earth from almost certain annihilation, I'd be even more in your debt. All of us would. Amen."

There was nothing to be done about Rayne 2005. If the Lord saw fit to spare humanity, to spare all life on earth, then so be it. If not, it was not for Jon to complain. His life and everyone's belonged to the Lord and it was for Him to decide. Still, he really hoped the Lord was in a good mood.

He checked himself in the mirror. Dressed in regular civilian jacket and post-Shift home spun pants and sporting the mustache, he looked like any citizen walking along the streets of Lynchburg. Even the saber at his side fit well with the local citizenry. It had become a practical weapon against wild animals as well as an affectation around here. He then realized he was carrying something he could not bring with him to the event. He took out the holster concealed at the small of his back that held his .45 pistol and placed it on the cot. Next to his cot was Sister Shanyn's desk, which hid a bottle of contraband Fire Water from the Hughes Distillery in Rochelle, no less. The overtly racist image of a drunken Native American slumped on the ground was proudly displayed on the label. Jon smirked and grabbed the bottle.

Jon really could use a drink right about now. He had been craving the sauce for the past month. He felt so ashamed of having succumbed to the booze the way he did. He didn't know when it took over, but he knew he let his people down these past several years. It helped him to deal with the loss of his family, not to mention the nightmares, or at least that's what he thought. He never saw his family die; he only heard about it when he and his battalion came into Rochelle and Brandon broke the news to him. But he had seen the effects of the flu on so many, including a number in his own battalion when they fled Raleigh in September '07. His mind just kept conjuring images of his parents and siblings dying slowly. At night when it was dark and silent, it was all he could think about. He discussed it with Chris a lot. He was a man who seemed to understand how the mind could turn on itself. Chris was a good friend; he understood better than anyone else in Rochelle. But no matter how much someone could understand, Jon was stuck alone with his thoughts at the end of the day.

It started as just an after dinner thing, a drink or two before bed, something to help him sleep. Soon enough though…Jon knew the rest. Then a month ago, God smacked him out of his drunken stupor and told him to get his sorry ass in gear and man up one last time. Jon considered the bottle. *Maybe just one jolt, just one.*

A knock on the door interrupted his internal deliberations.

"Constable, we're ready."

"Copy that."

Jon put down the bottle. He wasn't going to succumb now, not when these people needed him, not today.

The irony wasn't lost on Jon Early. In fact, as he made final preparations this morning with Father Mulcahy, Jennifer Engel and the other volunteers, he couldn't help but think that Rita Luevano would love to take a picture of him now leading a protest of all things. She was better suited for this kind of thing than he was. He was a Marine, not a long-haired agitator. Wherever she and his people were, he hoped they were alive.

Jon hoisted the coffin that held Sister Shanyn Duffy, and began marching with the growing number of families who joined the precession heading straight for Gordon Boche Ministries. Men, women, and children emerged from their homes and added to the numbers of demonstrators. Some carried signs with messages written on cardboard decrying the nun's murder. Others carried a yard ruler, which made Jon grin inwardly. It seemed that everyone in the Catholic community here in Lynchburg personally knew of Sister Shanyn's mastery in the yard ruler. She wielded the flimsy measuring stick with the skill of an Eskrima sensei. He wished she were here to lead them, but now it seemed her death had galvanized them in ways he could not, or even she herself when she was still alive.

Along with the signs and yard rulers, others carried something not seen in a long time—the American flag. Volunteers searched the demonstrators joining in the march to make sure they didn't carry any firearms. They also reiterated that all swords and knives were to remain in their scabbards. In essence, these people were unarmed.

BACKGROUND MUSIC: "The Scientist" by Willie Nelson
Visit www.michaeljuge.com **on the Refurbished Soul page to listen**

The demonstrators marched a few miles from their homes gaining in number and amassed outside the all glass cathedral of Gordon Boche Ministries. Sheepdogs and local police had called for them to disperse along the way, but Jon noticed something; the police and Sheepdogs were outnumbered. Many of them were out at the warfront, either pushing up Interstate 81 or holding on Highway 29 at Colleen keeping the Catholic soldiers in line.

The demonstration took over the grounds of the expansive and well-maintained field that separated Boche Ministries from Boche's old Bible College. At the crest of a mound, Jon and the others laid down Sister Shanyn's coffin, now draped in the American flag.

The timing was exactly as Jon had hoped. Gordon Boche's rally or sermon—there was no difference really—had just let out and thousands upon thousands of Lynchburg residents filed out of the glass cathedral and watched something thought impossible up until now, a protest against the abuses of the Sheepdogs.

Armed Sheepdogs ran out to the field. One of them called on a post-Shift bullhorn warning the protestors to disperse. Police and Sheepdogs surrounded them, aiming their rifles and shotguns at the protestors. Children screamed and clung to their parents. Then someone started singing a tune. It was Father Mulcahy, and the song was "This Little Light of Mine." His was a lone voice at first, few really knew the lyrics except for the refrain. Soon enough, others joined in, mostly as a way to quell their fears. Jon had faced the business end of a weapon countless times in his life and long before the Shift. Most of these people, on the other hand, had never faced danger until the Shift, and even then, they did their best to stay out of the line of fire all these years when tyrants and bandits filled the void.

Lynchburg residents leaving the regent's sermons looked upon the scene before them. Jon and the other pallbearers took shovels to start digging into the knoll. They were met by warning shots. Neither he nor the other pall bearers stopped. The protestors raised their signs. One read, "Her blood is on your hands, oh mighty Regent." "Sheepdogs = murderers of nuns and children." Jon hoped the growing number of spectators would be brave or at least curious enough to bear witness to the demonstration, and that they would understand what these people were protesting. He turned to Quinby.

"I think it's time for you to speak."

Quinby, the hot head, grabbed the mic of the protestor's bulky bullhorn, which was basically an amp tied to a rotary generator to provide electricity.

"For all of my fellow citizens of Lynchburg, you all are probably wondering what we are doing out here, condemning ourselves to the Sheepdogs' savage jaws by having the audacity to speak against the regent. Well, let me show you!"

Quinby moved aside as Sister Shanyn's casket was raised by the pall bearers now that the hole had been dug.

"A woman of peace, a woman of the cloth, Sister Shanyn Duffy went to confront the Sheepdogs last night after they had taken our teenaged sons and daughters and hauled them off to war. She went to demand their release! She was armed alright…with this!" Quinby raised the yard ruler that once belonged to Sister Shanyn.

"And these animals murdered her! They kidnapped our children and they brutally beat and murdered a nun! For goodness sake, wake up, people!" He beseeched the people watching passively.

"So, Your Highness, Mister Regent! You want her? You got her! She'll be interred here right in your pristine quad, your holiness! Our sister will be buried in your yard and everyone will know what you did to her!"

Quinby passed the mic to let others speak. Jon came over and patted Quinby on the back. Quinby looked like nothing special. He was a balding and harried looking man. Quinby reminded him of one of the pudgy actors in those old Pepcid AC commercials. But he could stir a crowd.

More people joined to watch the spectacle despite posing a danger to themselves by merely watching the demonstration. Against the orders of the police, the onlookers refused to ignore the demonstrators and return to their homes. That gave Jon some hope. If they weren't leaving, then they were no longer passive bystanders. They were in fact witnesses.

Jon picked up the mic. He was relatively confident that he wouldn't be picked out as a Vicious Rabbit, no less its leader. That would undermine this as a homegrown rebellion.

"Everyone here is your neighbor, people of Lynchburg. Remember. Remember what it was like before the Reckoning!" Jon was careful to use their terminology. "Remember that this was once America! You, me, all of us, we were Americans!" Seeing American flags held by various demonstrators waving in the breeze seemed to now overshadow the Lambs of God's flags with a bounding white sheep over a flared red cross. The stars and stripes were both an anachronism and a reminder. The beauty of the vivid colors with its fifty stars and thirteen stripes stood in contrast to the drab world surrounding it. Its stark majesty stirred something not only in him, but now it was apparent it was having an effect on the witnesses as well. Jon could feel himself getting choked up. Maybe it was being without a drink for weeks now. The emotions were too powerful for him to hold back.

"Is this what we have become? Is this what we've been reduced to? Do we cower to tyrants?"

Protestors shouted, "No!"

"Do we allow our neighbors to be disappeared?"

"No!"

"This is not who we are!" His voice was shaking now. The Quad was suddenly remarkably silent. His receding hairline waved in the light breeze. It was as if the entire city were glued to him. Now, even the police and a few Sheepdogs had lowered their weapons and were listening to his words.

"We were not bifurcated along sectarian lines! We weren't a collection of disparate ghettos as Catholics or Protestants, evangelicals or even… Unitarians. We were part of something much greater. Remember? We were…no, we *are* Americans!"

Making the most defining speech of his life, a desultory thought crossed his mind. Meredith would have probably lambasted him for being overly corny. But then again, that was quintessentially American, now wasn't it?

A few demonstrators started chanting, "We are Americans, we are Americans!"

It was having a greater effect than he could have possibly imagined. Onlookers walked into the fray and joined the protestors. It was a brave individual or two at first, but soon more joined in. Jon let the tears roll down his chiseled cheeks and joined the chant, "We are Americans!"

For the first time in years, the people of Lynchburg were stirring from their survival-induced coma. The flags were a clarion call reminding them of their duty as citizens. Jon hadn't considered how an old national symbol could be so powerful, but now he understood. Trying to lead a violent uprising against the regent was futile. The regent would have welcomed such an uprising, because he knew how to fight along those lines. Tyrants ruled by fear and by the might of armies. Jon had seen how thugs ruled over neighborhoods, villages, and towns in Iraq and Afghanistan. They ruled within the bubble of a fear barrier. But once that barrier was broken, how could the regent or any dictator fight against the moral force of the human spirit?

Neither Jon, nor any of the protestors, needed any weapons, because they wielded the weapon most feared by despots: the resolve not to cower. While the American flag stirred the will of the people, this wasn't an American idea or a Western idea. It was the human spirit awakening. Despots have no way to defeat the human spirit once people break the fear barrier.

The chanting grew louder and even celebratory as more people joined the demonstrators. Yard rulers were passed around as Sister Shanyn's casket was lowered. A few bystanders stood in front of police to protect the demonstrators. Confronted with shooting unarmed civilians, even the Lambs of God police chose to lower their weapons. Some still shouted for them to leave, but they weren't firing.

"We are Americans!" Jon shouted again when he felt a sudden snap. The next moment he was on the ground and could see the blue sky and people screaming. A woman and a man hovered over him. He tried to speak, but he couldn't breathe. The vision around him started fading. He felt so cold.

Stay, Marine, stay…

The faces blurred and were hard to make out, but then started to come back into focus. He saw his mother, his father, his brother and sister hovering over him and smiling.

"Come on, son. You can let go now," his father Charles said gently.

"Did I do well?"

"Yes, son. You did me proud."

"I'm…soo…tired, Dad."

"It's alright, son. You go to sleep. I've got you."

Jon felt his dad pick him up, carrying him like when he was a boy and fell asleep in the car and his dad carried him back into the house. Jon smiled and went to sleep as his dad carried him home.

CHAPTER 28

The Shiftiverse
Scottsville, Virginia
Greater Monticello
March 10, 2013

Meredith would have kissed the ground if it weren't so soggy. Rather ungracefully, she dismounted the smelly horse and wobbled as her legs tried to adjust after having been locked in the same riding position for several hours. Yes, the horse was smelly but the feral riding the horse and his companions were even worse. That didn't stop her from wrapping her arms around the man's torso and burying her face in his cat fur coat during the journey. She clung onto the hill man for dear life. She had never thought she would actually die, not after the Shift, not during the Obsidian War, not even while in Lynchburg. She never truly feared for her life until she got onto the horse with these ruffians. The hill men taking her to Greater Monticello galloped at full speed through the forests in the middle of the night as if they simply didn't care whether the horse tripped over a stump or if they got hit in the face by a low hanging branch. These hill men were absolutely insane.

The harrowing journey was short but felt like it stripped a year off of her life. Two nights ago, Jorge Guerrero, the double agent Sheepdog guide, had driven her from St. Pius X Catholic Church in the comfort of a Jeep on Highway 29 all the way to the Lambs of God outpost in Colleen, some thirty miles north of Lynchburg. There the Catholic regiments were holding their positions while the war raged several miles west near

Staunton. She hoped Jorge would take her all the way back to Monticello, but he shook his head.

"Sorry, Mary," he said, using her assumed identity. She didn't know if he was attempting to be humorous. "I've got to stay behind in Colleen. I've got a radio and can keep tabs on the demonstration tomorrow. I need to stay to pass the news to the Catholic regiments."

His face darkened. "Whether the demonstration is successful or not, our people are gonna need these guys covering them, either to keep them from being fired upon or to cover their retreat."

"Let's hope for the former."

A group of ferals appeared out of the woods. They all wore jackets made of cat fur—cats were plentiful throughout Virginia.

"Mary, let me introduce you to your ride home. This here is Lothar, his brother Jed, and his other brother Ned."

The man Lothar smiled wickedly, revealing all two of his teeth and spat something gross. "You smell mighty perty, Miss Lady," said one of the men. "That parfume?"

"Um, excuse me a sec." Meredith smiled politely at the ferals while she pulled Jorge aside and whispered through clenched teeth.

"Please do not hand me over to those people. I really don't like the way they're leering at me."

It was true; they were eyeing her shamelessly, as if she was their luscious New York strip steak dinner. Jorge pried her fingers off his coat.

"These hill men have been reliable couriers and guides for our organization for years. They've never demanded ransom or kidnapped our people like their competitors out there. They got too good a thing with us to do that, what with our generous exchange of tobacco." Jorge braced himself as he added. "Besides, even if they were about to throw away their livelihood for a new wife, well, they would choose someone a little youn… they wouldn't want someone so…"

"Old," she finished indignantly.

Jorge blushed.

"Well, um…" Jorge was a quick thinker. "Actually, I think, it's really more that you'd be a little…uppity for their taste. That's it, uppity."

She couldn't help but completely agree with him on that one. Chris once said that had she lived in the Middle Ages, people would have tried to burn her as a witch simply for calling bullshit on them or playing devil's advocate one too many times. Meredith gave him a wry smile.

It was just past dawn. Meredith was working out kinks in her legs and trying to get feeling back in her toes. She hardly ever rode Corolla back home—usually Bob just drove her to work and back in a carriage. Lothar leapt off his horse gracefully and walked her over to the edge of the forest where it met Highway 20. There was an 18-wheeler with a Piggly Wiggly cargo hold that had been emptied on the opposite side of the road. Lothar handed her a white rag and pointed to the bridge in the distance.

"Listen here, Mary, girl." She was now glad that Jorge referred to her by Mary rather than saying her true name to these folks. "You see that there bridge? That's them Monticellan's outpost. You walk along this road and wave this here white flag. Make yourself real obvious like, and say 'I'm coming out, y'all!' That ways, they don't go shooting off that perty head of yours. You got it, girlie?"

Meredith nodded and thanked him. As she gingerly walked onto the decaying country highway, Lothar called out, "Oh yeah, and don't forget to tell dem boys we'll be taking our payment in tobacky and they can drop it off in the 18-wheeler cab likes they always do."

She nodded and headed for the bridge.

It was serene in a strange way, walking along the highway as a light layer of morning fog wisped through the treetops. A deer with its fawns casually walked past her. Even waving the flag with huge arcs, she was apparently not intimidating to them. As she approached the bridge over the James River, she could see movement behind the complex array of vehicles and Jersey barriers that made up the southeastern edge of Greater Monticello territory, allied land, safety. All she had to do was not get shot by a jittery Monticellan militia. Guard dogs started barking angrily.

"I'm here!" she called out.

There was more movement. A man called out. "Drop all your weapons, keep your arms up and turn around." She did as ordered.

"Now walk slowly and follow the serpentine!"

"Okay!" She didn't know what a serpentine was at first, but then understood as she stepped onto the bridge. She criss-crossed from the east of the bridge to the west and back again in a maze where the Jersey barriers and vehicles became walls. These "serpentines" were standard barriers at the edge of territories. She walked around a minivan that was packed with sandbags and a man who was well past middle-aged aimed his rifle at her. A middle-aged woman came up to her and frisked her.

"I'm unarmed," she said. The woman ignored her and continued. Meredith saw the flag of Monticello on the other end of the bridge. The green flag with the blue chalice and the orange flame with a bow inside was a wonderful sight to see. Satisfied, the man lowered his weapon and called the all clear.

"All right, ma'am, state your business."

"I'm a Vicious Rabbit. I'm Meredith Jung. It's imperative that I speak with Neko Lemay now."

The man scoffed. "Welcome back, Vicious Rabbit. We'll check with your folks to be sure of that. But Neko's a little busy right now."

"I'm Meredith Jung," she repeated as though the name was supposed to register with them. Hell, she was the worst kept secret in the Swan. Everyone knew Meredith was the director, right? Then it hit her.

"I'm the Vulcan," she exclaimed.

The man and woman sentries said, "Ooh, the Vulcan," in unison, recognizing her nickname. The man put on a pair of cracked glasses. "Funny, I always pictured you as a brunette."

Neko Lemay had just gotten off the horn with Ezra Rothstein in Staunton. The Orange Pact's line was beginning to break. Frankly, she was surprised that the allies held out in Staunton as long as they did. Considering the Lambs of God's numerical advantage along with their tanks, it was proof of the allies' tenacity.

Unfortunately, tenacity wasn't enough. They were falling back to Waynesboro. It was going to be an organized tactical retreat, and Interstate 64 was a treacherous bottleneck that would force the Lambs of God to line up their dreaded tanks almost single file along the balance beam of an interstate. That would provide something for the Orange Pact, even out the odds a fair bit. But still, she knew that they were in for a world of hurt when they arrived. Rubbing her lifeless arm, she wished she could be by Ezra's side to defend Monticello from her enemies.

Instead, she was here, sitting in Rita's chair in Monticello listening to Sheriff Schadenfreude trying to convince her to consolidate the Christians in a concentrated area so that her deputies would be better able to ensure that there were no further acts of espionage. There had been a spate of incidents where equipment broke down. Yet Neko wasn't convinced that machinery breaking down amounted to sabotage. Generators and motors went on the fritz all of the time. Maybe she was missing something, but she was beginning to think Lucille was losing sight of the more immediate danger.

"There's those tents we set up north of the city by the burnt out airport. We could put them there," Lucille offered.

"Those were meant for incoming refugees, Lucille! These are Monticellan citizens, not refugees."

Lucille scoffed. "You say."

"I think we should instead be concentrating on the war, don't you think?" Neko didn't care if she sounded agitated. She was. There was an inexplicable retreat of the Lambs of God regiments at Colleen late last evening. The Monticellan militia and Fredericksburg auxiliary volunteering to help supplement their numbers at the southern border on Highway 29 confirmed that the Lambs of God outpost had been deserted. It didn't make sense. The Lambs of God were walloping the alliance in Staunton, and would be at the gates of Charlottesville, the western gates on Interstate 64, by week's end the way things were going. Why would they pull back from Colleen? It left them wide open for attack. Neko would have ordered her militia to push into Colleen, Amherst and Lynchburg itself if possible, except that she didn't exactly feel confident that the militia could carry that out. Plus, she wondered if it was an elaborate trap meant to lure her thin forces away from her home.

"You already know what I think, sweetie," Lucille said with a tinge of annoyance.

"Yes, invade. It makes sense, but there's something about it. I mean why would they withdraw? They're winning."

There was a knock on the door followed by one of the young archer cadets. "Miss Lemay, the Vulcan is here to see you. She has news from Lynchburg."

Neko had met Meredith Jung only a few times and then only briefly. Most of what she knew about the Vulcan came from hearsay and gossip more than through personal contact. Even Ezra was really tight-lipped about what he did at the Swan.

Meredith Jung had the reputation as being the puppet master who used the Swan to maintain a hegemonic control over the affairs throughout the Orange Pact. Lucille made no bones about not trusting Meredith and her organization's incorporation throughout the four communities. Some said that Meredith was instrumental in overthrowing the old sheriff in Culpeper shortly after the Shift and installing the current leader, Mama Bell. Others said she had connections with people in the CDC and released the flu that wiped out so many of their enemies. Still others said that she used her connections with her pals in the CIA, who were in every community throughout the Mid-Atlantic region. She might have CIA operatives as far away as Florida and New York. So, it was a little surprising to see standing before her all bedraggled and soiled in mud and grime this petite, unassuming lady who looked more like a librarian than the sinister czarina described.

Meredith proceeded to tell her how she wound up in Lynchburg, what she was doing there and most importantly what had happened while she and, preposterously enough, Constable Jon Early were down there. She now understood why the regiments withdrew from Colleen. They were Catholic regiments, and the Vulcan managed to stir up a popular uprising using the Catholic community. Meredith was dangerous indeed.

"Well, that explains it," Lucille said.

"Explains what?" Meredith asked.

Neko rubbed her wounded shoulder. "It explains why the troops in Colleen left. Our scouts say it's completely abandoned and there were a few bodies of Sheepdogs out there as well."

"Thank you for the very useful intelligence, Mrs. Jung. We'll take it from here," Lucille said dismissively.

"What are you talking about?"

"Well, we intend to make the most of Lynchburg's internal squabbling and bring the fight to them for once."

"You can't. I just told you, the Catholic community down there is demonstrating against the regent. It's a very delicate matter."

"I'm sure it is, Mrs. Jung. I'm sure it is. What better time to invade?"

"If the Monticellans invade Lynchburg while the Catholics are protesting, you'll undo everything they have worked for."

"I don't care what a bunch of bead clutchers have worked for."

"That's not what I mean, Sheriff," Meredith retorted acidly. "If you go marching down there now while they are standing up to the regent, their uprising will be seen as being orchestrated by us."

"Well, isn't it?"

Meredith didn't say anything. Lucille pressed on. "Isn't your constable down there right now managing it all? Isn't it you who has been pulling the Catholics along on your agenda?"

"Yes, he is, and yes, we have helped facilitate their uprising; however, we could never manufacture the legitimate resentments that have been simmering for years. As long as we aren't seen as colluding with the protestors in order to attack the Lambs of God, the protestors have a chance of garnering sympathy with the population."

"Sympathy," Lucille echoed sarcastically. "Oh my dear, let me tell you about their 'sympathy.' When me and a bunch of us 'undesirables,' you know fags, dykes, intellectuals, were placed in chains to work in the winter to bury the mountains of dead from the flu and then kicked us out to die, where was their sympathy?"

"I think you're missing the point," Meredith said. "They share the same enemy as us, the regent. If they succeed, they could do far more damage to the Lambs of God than you sending a ragtag team of senior citizens armed with bolt action rifles down there could."

Lucille scoffed. "So, that's your plan? Trust the Cross Kissers? I will not submit to your whims."

"It's not my whim. This is the momentum of history. It's an opportunity to de-legitimize the regent, so long as we stand back."

"Stand back and let others control *my* destiny?" Lucille was slightly less charming now and a little more shrill. "You and your minions in the Swan have been out to undermine us since day one. Your people sleep with those who would sell us out to the regent and who pray for the death of Humanism! You are soulless! This I know."

Neko had never seen Lucille ever speak so disparagingly to anyone and she had not spoken so horribly about Christians until now. Neko knew they that weren't all bad. Some were good and loyal to Monticello. Neko expected Meredith to lash out. Instead, she smiled. Why? Meredith folded her arms and leaned back.

"And you also know that Juan Ramirez wasn't a traitor. You knew he was working for us the whole time trying to set up the resistance in Lynchburg."

Neko gasped inwardly. Her eyes darted over to Meredith who was staring down Lucille, waiting for her to respond. The words hung in the air unanswered.

"W…wait, wait, no," Neko stammered. "Lucille, Sheriff Schadenfreude has evidence, intercepted letters, Byrds stowed in his house, it all showed that Juan was funneling money to his family, members who were with the Lambs of God."

"Yes, Miss Lemay, the same family who is part of the resistance, the same Sheepdog who guided me out of there, and led me to safety. And Sheriff Schadenfreude knew. She knew because she intercepted one of the couriers who spilled his guts to her. I did not know this at the time, but apparently, the courier was let go and he told the resistance leader in Lynchburg. Juan is no traitor, Miss Lemay. He sacrificed his reputation to save the operation in the hopes it would save Monticello."

Neko turned to Lucille. "Is this true?"

Lucille's icy smile didn't break, but she didn't say anything. She glowered back at Meredith, her hand subtly reaching for her holster by her hip.

Neko suddenly felt dizzy. Everything she had been told was a lie. And she was instrumental in Juan's downfall. He had been a friend, a mentor and a great leader and she bought into Lucille's lie. She began to feel sick as she realized that somewhere not deep down in her psyche, she *wanted* to believe Lucille, she willfully bought into a convenient narrative. She had been led and she chose to be led.

Lucille then answered. "Neko, sweetie, Juan is not one of us. He never was."

"What does that even mean?" Meredith asked with exasperation.

"It means you are either one of us, or you are one of them. Neko, you said it yourself, we've always been at war."

"That's not what I meant."

"Of course, it is." Lucille pulled out her pistol and pointed it at Meredith. "You always knew the Christians were your enemy. And who do you think tried to keep me on their drugs, their soma used to lull me into a state of submission? They called it medication. But I knew those drugs stole my soul. But Gaia saved me from their lies with the Shift! "

Lucille sauntered up to Meredith with her .357 revolver and cocked the lever. Meredith's expression stayed remarkably serene while Lucille had a crazed look on her. It might have had something to do with the fact that she most likely was insane, a Shift survivor with a pre-Shift mental disorder, Neko just realized. The drugs that Lucille disparaged had helped so many function in society. But when the Shift hit, those medications had run out. If the flu and violent convulsion of civilization's collapse didn't kill them, then their own inner demons re-awoke to overtake so many. Neko had seen it happen to a lot of people the first year after the Shift. A few of them managed without the medications. It became clear that Lucille was one of those cases. She hid her condition remarkably well until now.

"This bitch wants us to submit to her! Don't you see? This is our opportunity to strike a fatal blow for Gaia!"

"Neko, this is not Humanism; this is paranoia," Meredith implored calmly.

"Shut up," Lucille ordered.

"Rita does not want her people turning on each other like this. Think about it, Neko. Is this what Rita would have done?"

That got to Neko. Ezra said something very similar. *What would Rita do?* She now knew she had followed a mad woman these past couple of months.

"I told you to shut up!" Lucille now held both hands on the pistol.

"Lucille, put the gun down," Neko ordered.

"Don't you tell me what to do!"

Lucille then turned around to see Neko pointing a pistol with her left hand, aiming straight at her. "I've trained on both hands, Lucille. Put the gun down."

Neko feared Lucille was too far gone, and that she would take her final vengeance on Meredith. Fortunately, she lowered her weapon and crouched on the floor. She started sobbing uncontrollably.

Meredith felt her heart lifting with excitement as she passed Montpelier Station. She was almost home. In minutes, she would be reunited with Aidan, Rhiannon and baby Charles. She didn't hold her breath about Chris miraculously returning.

Twice in two days. She had faced death twice in two days. First, was the terrifying ride from Colleen to Scottsville with Lothar and the hill men, and then the crazed sheriff who came within millimeters of ending her life. Meredith hadn't had a gun pointed at her before. It was an interesting experience. She hadn't expected to be so calm about facing Lucille. Perhaps it was knowing that, barring some highly improbable miracle, it was all going to be over in five days anyway. Maybe that provided some measure of peace.

On the drive home, she looked into the blue sky searching for a sign, a white dot, something to corroborate the existence of the behemoth iron based asteroid that the astronomers were convinced was going to collide with the earth. There was nothing visible in the sky yet. She didn't welcome it at all, but the nightmares had subsided.

The drive from Monticello back home took only an hour. Neko Lemay had been extraordinarily apologetic about how she allowed herself to be led by the sheriff, who they now knew suffered from schizophrenia. Again, another intelligence failure, both in failing to reveal that Lucille had been taking meds since she was a teenager until they ran out, and the failure to ascertain that Lucille knew about Juan's true mission. Life was untidy that way. Hopefully, other assumptions were wrong, like the world coming to an end and the almost certain defeat at the hands of the Lambs of God. She could only hope.

The Datsun 210 puttered its way down the empty road. So many were off at the front, which was now in Waynesboro, a little closer to home. Neko had provided Meredith with a ride back rather than making her wait for the train. The demand for coal forced the train shuttling back and forth from Charlottesville and Orange to be curtailed to just one daily round trip. Neko wanted to make nice and whisking Meredith home to get back to the Swan with a quickness was a good start. They passed Funeral Mound and she saw her home in distance. Her eyes welled up as the old Japanese compact struggled on the muddy road up to the farmhouse. "Thanks," she said as she jumped out of the car. The front door opened. Aidan and Rhiannon ran out with the biggest smiles on their faces.

"Mommy! Mommy!"

"My babies!"

They tackled her with their momentum. The three of them hugged and kissed and laughed and wrestled. Anne Hughes walked out holding baby Charles. Meredith jumped up and took him out of Anne's arms, squeezing him until he squeaked, burying her face into his delicious baby neck and breathing him in, while Aidan and Rhiannon hung onto her legs. She gave Anne a hug too, and thanked her.

"You wouldn't have heard from Chris, would you?"

Anne winced. "Not yet."

CHAPTER 29

The Shiftiverse
Cambridge, Massachusetts
March 14, 2013

Chris was grateful to be crossing over the Charles River into Cambridge.
He made it. The Virginians and their Heighter escorts of one hundred
and fifty men covered the two hundred mile journey in just five days,
something Chris thought to be next to impossible. They started out in
Northern Manhattan on March 9th in three feet of snow. Rita really must
be one of Gaia's chosen people, because the temperature rose rapidly. By the
time they reached the Connecticut state line, most of the snow had melted.
The melt made the roads muddy and slippery, and a few underpasses were
flooded, but all in all, it was easier to deal with than three feet of snow.

Chris wished he could have experienced the entire journey from
Maryland to Cambridge as a three and a half minute video montage
instead of having to slog it out over a period of weeks. They made it with
a day to spare. Having the added numbers of over one hundred and fifty
men not only put them in the EZ Pass lane to Massachusetts. From New
Jersey to New York, the Virginians had to pay "tolls" every few miles to
one smelly, pissant thug or another. But with the Heighters joining the
ride, the sight of a horde of armed men on bikes had a way of making the
ferals feel more egalitarian and they let them pass unhindered. In fact, the
ferals seemed eager to stay out of their way altogether, and that allowed
the column to move through New England much quicker.

The added number allowed the Virginians to feel confident enough to
move without having to slink quietly like they had earlier in the journey.

In fact, the First Bicycle Mounted Cavalry started singing the Company's signature battle song,

"I get knocked down

But I get up again

You're never gonna keep me down"

The song caught him off guard. He never thought that Chumbawumba's one hit drinking song could be appropriated in such a fashion. Then Kendra explained it was none other than his counterpart who got the company singing their way to battle. He felt some satisfaction for that and sang along on the largely uneventful trek from Manhattan. He had personal and bittersweet memories tied up with that song.

They did lose a few Heighters along the way, not to combat, disease or anything so dramatic, but rather to things like flat tires and broken chains and gears, and simple exhaustion. Most cops weren't practiced riders like the Virginians. Those who couldn't keep up had to find their own way home. Seeing that made Chris immensely grateful to his counterpart for having had the foresight to carry spare tubes and tools to fix just about any problem that might come across *The Interceptor*'s way. New England was about as bad as he expected it to be. There were a few places where ad hoc barricades had been erected using dead vehicles. Decomposed remains littered the highways. Sometimes the remains were piled up in a clump; most of the time they just lay there as grim reminders of how dependent the world had become on digital technology. They rode under interstate overpasses and over bridges with caution. It would take a few more years before these structures started collapsing, but they were already visibly weakened, deteriorating faster than he would have expected.

As they crossed into Cambridge, gunfire reported in the distance. Chris jerked the handlebars a bit but didn't lose his balance like he first did when he heard gunfire. The explosion that followed did bother him, though.

"Man, I thought they had no ammunition up here," Kendra who was riding close to him noted.

"I guess Boston must have a distributor."

Rapid gunfire answered the other gunfire. "Shit, it sounds like it's getting closer," Kendra said.

"We're almost there," their guide, a cop who originally hailed from Boston said. "We just need to…"

Suddenly, the man slumped lifelessly and the bike tumbled off the road. A stray round had found him.

"Forward," the gunny yelled. Chris didn't argue with that. As they crossed into Cambridge, Rita who had been safely sandwiched in the middle, took the lead.

"Come on, I know the way!"

Chris pushed himself as hard as he could. They could not afford to lose Rita. She was the key to all of this. But he was hauling the Stubb Foundation equipment in the child trailer. That had to count for something, too.

After evading the random firefight that claimed a couple of Heighters, the Virginians rode onto the campus of MIT. It had been largely deserted for some time. There was nothing of value to a population looking to survive. The dorms and food courts had been ransacked long ago. Chris saw a few families scurrying away as they approached. Rita raced down Vassar Street ordering everyone to hurry it up.

The Virginians came to a halt in front of the Ray and Maria Stata Center. This was it, the place where Jamil had told them to go. Inside, TALOPS sat unpowered, ready to be brought to life. The Stata Center was probably the craziest building Chris had ever seen. He tried to describe it in his mind. It looked like a cartoon. That was the only way to describe the place. It looked like a cartoon sketched by a committee of *Bugs Bunny* and *Futurama* cast members tripping on LSD trying to agree on a design. Sections of the building jutted out at preposterous angles; mortar contrasted with mirror-polished steel, which contrasted with brushed aluminum. Chris could have sworn the yellow…whatever it was…looked like some kind of gigantic child's foldout telescope.

"Now, there's something you don't see every day."

The Virginians, especially the young ones, stared at the building, their mouths agape.

"Wake up, people, let's move it!" Rita shouted.

"You 'eard the Gov! Off your arses and let's move it! Porkins!"

"Yes, Gunny!"

"Get a team over there and form a perimeter. We don't want getting ourselves capped at the final moments!"

"Jenkins! You check with the rest of the Heighters and see where to put 'em! And remember, they aren't the most squared away!"

"Aye, Gunny!"

Chris got off his bicycle and unloaded the child trailer. He chucked out the remaining tobacco, extra magazines, and gruel flakes, and pulled out the heavy case.

"I still don't get it. Don't EMPs still strike around here?" he asked.

"Yeah," Kendra answered as she rifled through her backpack.

"Well, then shouldn't this panel be fried like everything else with a microchip?"

"Solar panels aren't microchips," Rita answered. "They're photo sensitive cells and are unaffected by EMPs. And the prototype panel the Stubb Foundation provided can convert solar energy into enough electricity to power up TALOPS once it's had enough time to store up enough joules."

"We could have used some of those back home," Kendra said. "It would have made us independent from West Virginia's coal."

"Something to discuss with the Stubb Foundation when we get back," Rita said smiling. "Come on. It's a maze, but I think I can guide us through."

Chris, Kendra, and the gunny breached the entrance where the building was the least insane looking. Chris stepped cautiously over the marble floor strewn with broken glass. The ringing in his ears was ramping up again along with the urge to pee. The gunny turned on a flashlight powered with fresh batteries donated from the Stubb Foundation.

"This is the Artificial Intelligence Laboratory," Rita said. "I remember this place."

"You went to MIT?"

"Yes…no…not exactly, not me… the other me did. She was working on her PhD."

The four of them headed for the stairwell. Considering the ludicrous architecture, Chris was pleasantly surprised that the stairs didn't go all Oescher on him. They descended two flights of the dank stairwell; their steps echoed loudly. Rita jumped up to the front and guided them to a door. They pried it open; the gunny shined the flashlight into what looked to be a lab filled with dead computers.

"This is it," Rita said confidently. "Mi Coriño, you get that solar panel up to the roof, unfurl it and lay it where it will get the most sun. Gunny, you and the LT get the power cord hooked up to it and guide it down here."

"Chris?"

"Yes?"

She activated a glow stick by breaking the seal. "You hold this. I need some light."

While Akil, Kendra and the gunny worked on setting the solar panel, Rita worked a console, stripping it of all of its connections while Chris provided light by glow stick.

"I have to say, I'm glad we're not pulling one of these at-the-last-second acts."

"What are you talking about," Rita asked as she removed the organic CPU from its casing. It looked odd, like ecto plasm encased in a jar with electronic nodes.

"Well, in the movies, we would arrive tomorrow with a few minutes left to save the world. I'm glad we decided not to go that route." Chris was looking for some affirmation that they had crossed the finish line. Rita's response wasn't reassuring.

"Don't light up the cigars just yet, Chris. We won't know until this thing is up and running and Jamil tells us to pop smoke."

For a Unitarian reverend, he noticed that Rita spoke a lot of military jargon. Then again, it wasn't too surprising. He had only been in this Shiftiverse a couple of months and he was saying things like "hit the head" and "secure that shit."

After twenty minutes, the gunny came in unraveling the power cord.

"It looks like the fighting is getting closer, Gov."

"Do we know if they're after us?" Chris didn't know who "they" were—he assumed they were just another bunch of ferals.

The gunny grunted something about not bloody knowing who the pod knockers were.

"Maybe we can bribe our way. We still have some tobacco," Chris suggested.

"Aye, maybe, Captain, but they—ooever the sods are, they've got their peckers up against us even with all our numbers."

"Oh, shit," Rita said.

That worried Chris. "Please tell me you said that because you think you left the stove on back home or something."

"God dammit!" she exclaimed.

"What? What is it? Is TALOPS dead?"

"Not that I know of. No, it's the keyboard and monitor. They're fried."

"Okay, let's grab another right here," he said grabbing a keyboard from a nearby computer that looked more like a normal CPU than the hourglass shaped CPU of the organic TALOPS computer.

"It's the same problem, Chris! All of them are fried!"

"Wait, I thought you said that TALOPS is an organic, just like Jamil."

"TALOPS' CPU is organic but it still uses a traditional keyboard and monitor interface. Those are composed of microcircuits. The Shift rendered every last one tied to a computer plugged into a power source useless. Dammit! How could we have flaked on this? Shit!"

Chris paced trying not to vomit. It turned out he did have a vested interest in this world, after all. His mind raced, and then he snapped his fingers. "That's it! Any computer plugged into a power source, right? So, all we need to do is grab a keyboard and a monitor that was *not* plugged in during one of the EMP surges."

"Great idea, but they're all plugged in here, Chris."

"Okay, okay." He paced. "Well, shit, let's just run over to an Office Depot, a RadioShack, anywhere that sold computer equipment. They couldn't have all been swiped completely bare."

"You'd be surprised, Captain. No matter how useless it was to people, free shit is free shit."

"And we don't even know where one is. Our Heighter local is dead. Did you see one of those places nearby?"

Chris' reflex was to grab his iPhone from his pocket and look for an electronics store in the maps app. He did not recall seeing any such store nearby.

"I can't believe we're all going to die because of aftermarket accessories! God, I hate irony!" Then Chris stopped himself from his rant. "Gunny, go down one of the main streets near campus…"

The gunny looked to Kendra for instructions, ignoring Chris.

"Are you listening, Gunnery Sergeant?" Chris barked with uncharacteristic authority.

Stunned, the gunnery sergeant snapped to attention. "Yes, Captain."

"Go down the main drag near campus. Every university is surrounded by eager vendors. I'm sure somebody had to put a computer store near MIT. Don't you think?"

"I think he's right. I think…" Rita stammered, probably channeling her other self that was supposed to be the math whiz, "I think there's a Circuit City, a Best Buy or something down one of the streets…It's near the river, near campus."

"That's good," Chris said optimistically. "That leaves only two directions, right? Gunny, you get some of the Heighters to comb the streets along or near the river, one heading west, the other east."

"Others can scour this building for any discarded keyboards like in a closet or something, too," Rita added.

"Aye, Captain."

"And make sure they understand, a keyboard and monitor *not* attached to a power source," Rita added. "We don't want any store display equipment. And get a few of them. A surge could hit any time."

"On it, Gov," the gunny said as he bounded off.

Chapter 30

The Shiftiverse
Cambridge, Massachusetts
March 14, 2013

Rita and Chris sat in the darkened office for several minutes. She inspected the connections and he held the glow stick, which he learned was extremely valuable these days. As the solar panel gathered the sun's rays, Rita and he had a moment to catch their breath after checking for spare parts in the building. Both were exhausted. So was everyone else. Rita looked as spent as he did, though her mission was just beginning.

In the silence, Chris yielded to his personality's incessant need to fill the void. "So, you seem to know this place. That's a good sign."

Rita nodded. "Yeah, it's odd, but it's as though there's more and more of other Rita's experiences that I now know."

"Did it start when we crossed into the Stubb Foundation where we passed that…that strange force field thing that made Helmut seem normal again?"

"That's what I thought at first. While we were down there with Jamil, when they were discussing mathematical and theoretical physics, I was surprised, shocked by my knowledge and how conversant, and even erudite I was on topics I never studied."

"I assumed it was an effect of that bubble," she added. "But I realized something on the way over here. I've had this knowledge in me for a few years. Every so often, someone would bring up an issue like harvest yields and our rate of population expansion and I would jump in and give them answers. Some would look at me strangely, but I would look back at them, thinking, 'what, you don't know simple calculus?'"

She chuckled. "And there were strange dreams that didn't make sense to me."

"Yeah! I had them too, only they were about this place."

"So, I guess I always had a connection with my tangent self, but I wouldn't know it, because her skills were rarely relevant to my life. But it's weird, like riding a bike. I don't think about the particulars of how I know what I know; I just do. I wonder if other me found out she knows Krav Maga and can shoot a grapefruit at five hundred yards on a windy day."

"And that some part of her is still a crazed Unitarian," he added.

"I do wonder about that. Jamil told me something very odd. You see, other me told him about some sort of…I don't know, other me had an epiphany, an epiphany that had me leave my position as a reverend and go into something completely and utterly different. And guess when other me had this epiphany?"

Chris raised an eyebrow. "July 11th?"

She nodded. "What the hell happened to me that made me just drop the idea of service to humanity like that? I mean, I knew I was going through a period of doubt at that time…"

"Of course you were. You're a Humanist."

"I was going through my own crisis of faith during those months before and after the Shift. I had always thought the Shift aggravated my crisis of faith until Gaia enlightened me with her vision. The Great Suck forced me to leave others to die; it forced me to turn a blind eye to the wandering masses begging for help; it forced me to kill. If anything would undermine one's faith in humanity, the Shift would. But then Jamil tells me that when the Shift didn't hit, it was only then I truly abandoned the cause. Why?"

Chris thought about it. "Perhaps the other you was catching a glimpse into your life, but she didn't have context. You mentioned when you got injured in that battle you had your vision of Gaia, right?"

"Yes," she said with interest.

"Well, unless your counterpart had a similar incident, then she never had the experience of that vision. So all she had maybe were something like feelings and nightmares of your world but without Gaia to give her hope. So, maybe in those months, she turned away completely and found a new calling, something that was more reasonable than humanity, something that couldn't disappoint her, something like mathematics."

"Wow, I never thought of that. I think you might be onto something, Chris."

"Well, it makes sense, doesn't it? I mean look at this!" Chris pulled out the crumpled sheet of paper with the strange phone number written on it. "Jamil and I had a discussion, too. He asked me to think about this number every evening. 'Why?' I asked. He said because he wanted other me to recognize the phone number. Crazy, right? What is this anyway? Who has a prefix '187?' Who does it go to? I don't know. But here I am, night after night, thinking about the phone number, a number that has no receiver here but is vital over there."

"So other me got all my shit and none of my benefits while I get her mathematical prowess. Pretty crappy deal for her."

"I don't know, you might affect her positively. I think maybe other Chris might have helped me when I really needed help. I hope he could say the same for me, though I doubt it."

"You got your music, I noticed. Kendra mentioned he played guitar and tried to play what you were playing over at the Cloisters."

Chris smirked. "My music? That was not just music. That's my lifeline, my means of coping as my shrink has pointed out. I'm sorta OCD and prone to panic disorder. Well, 'sorta' is kind of an understatement. It's more like I'm this close to being a total basket case. The panic, it's like a demon that hounds me. And when it catches me, I get sucked into the belly of the beast. I cannot think my way through; I cannot reason my way out. My own thoughts turn against me. When I get off the meds, it's bad, I mean, really bad. And it's like I cannot escape my thoughts because like, wherever you go, there you are. I try staying off the meds, but I always seem to fall back on them when it gets too much. Music is the only thing that got me through the worst of it. Meredith and the kids are my life, but they cannot cure this thing. Music gives it, I don't know, meaning or something. I'm just neurotic that way."

"I think other Chris is that way too."

"Yes, we've been that way for a long time, long before July 11th."

There was a brief silence despite his disdain of it. The ringing in his ears was noticeable again.

"Chris, what happened on July 11th? And I don't mean to us. What happened to you?"

He remained silent.

"Chris, from the moment I first mentioned July 11th, I could see it on your face; that date means something significant to you. And since the

Shift didn't happen in your world, then it had to be something else. Both you and other Chris are my friends and I will let you know something about us, but first you tell me. What happened, Chris?"

Chris sighed. "Alright, screw it. It's not like you're going to tell my wife or anything. You're a reverend, sworn to secrecy, right?"

"Something like that, yes."

"Fine, Rita, you asked for it. Be prepared for a shimmering effect and the sound of harps strumming."

She looked at him quizzically.

"It happens whenever I talk about the past."

The Mundaniverse
Arlington, Virginia
July 11, 2007

Chris typed up the last paragraph and sent out the response to the cable. He looked at his watch, amazed that it was only 10PM. He felt like it should be midnight. Time had become distorted over the last several weeks thanks to the insomnia. Nothing ever changed. He called Meredith to let her know he was finishing up and would be home shortly. They had driven over to Brandon and Anne's apartment in Adams Morgan after work that evening, and were preparing to eat when, just as the Simpsons intro finished, he got a phone call from his boss. Darryl needed Chris to respond to Obsidian Corp's inquiry about recent attacks in the Diyala Province. Chris asked if it could wait until tomorrow, but Darryl was insistent. He had to leave Meredith to drive back home alone while he jumped on the Metro to get back into Virginia to respond to the mobile and site security personnel security company that protected American diplomats in Iraq.

He figured he might as well answer them now. It would be the last time they would get him to work overtime...ever. He could then go home, spend one last sleepless night. Tomorrow he would end it all. He would never hear the incessant ringing in his ears again or deal with his unyielding obsessive panicked thoughts. He logged off, said goodnight to Darryl, who insanely, was still working, and headed down to Rossyln Station.

To Chris' surprise, Rosslyn station was packed. He looked at his watch again. It was 10:15 in the evening. The Metro was never packed this late on a weeknight. Sweating profusely in the summer humidity, the heat of all the people deep underground added to his panic-induced claustrophobia. The thoughts about his tinnitus would not let up no matter what.

Chris made his way down to the Vienna-bound platform, which likewise was filled with waiting passengers. Most were carrying luggage coming from Reagan National Airport. An intercom's high-pitched squeal forced Chris to cup his ears.

"There is a delay on the Blue, Orange, and Red Lines due to two trains that broke down and have been removed. Trains are running again," reported a muffled, barely audible voice.

"That's great!" someone complained angrily. "First, the cluster fuck at Reagan National, and now this."

Others chimed in, discussing their ordeal. Apparently, there was some major hold up of air traffic at Reagan National Airport. People gave conflicting accounts of what happened, but from what Chris gleaned, air traffic control's computers blinked momentarily or something. Chris was used to trains breaking down in DC. The Metro, despite its nifty 70s look, was horribly designed with crappy Italian manufactured trains. Someone got rich off that deal. Nobody thought to have an express rail just in case, as the designers in New York City did several decades previously. Add that to a major delay at the airport, and that explained the unexpected crowd now vying for the next train.

A man tapped him on the shoulder. "Excuse me, sir. Is this the way to Ballston?"

Chris didn't get a good look at the guy; he just saw he was in BDUs. Distracted, he answered, "Yeah. You'll take the Orange Line like me."

"Ah, thank you." The man continued. "They fly me up on a moment's notice and I can't even get a hotel nearby."

Chris ignored him. The ringing in his ears intensified. It would never cease; it would never leave him. How could he ever get used to this? How could life ever be sane again? The lights on the floor near the edge of the platform blinked, indicating the arrival of a train. The ringing, the insomnia, the panic, the endless cycle, it would all be over tomorrow. The only reason he could concentrate enough to finish the cable tonight was the knowledge that he would be released from the torment soon. He would "stumble" off the platform at just the right time.

There was gust of wind followed by the squeals of the brakes. Then he thought, *Why not do it now? Why wait?* Chris couldn't find a reason why he should wait. The platform was packed with people lugging baggage. He reasoned that the police could assume that he accidentally tripped over one of the suitcases and fell onto the tracks. *Just make it look good, Chris. Meredith doesn't need to know the truth. She can suspect, but so long as the police report says accidental death, she'll get the insurance.*

Chris put on the ear buds of his iPod just to add to the plausibility that he was just a careless ass. The train's headlights came into view as it banked around a curve. *Hey, pick a final song, why don't you?* Chris scrolled through the iPod desperately trying to come up with something appropriate, something that would serenade his journey into sweet nothingness, something to define his pain and stand as a testament to the human condition. He really hadn't thought of what song he wanted to die to. He wished he planned ahead a little more. He racked his head for something trenchant and soulful.

The train was speeding into the station. He consciously made himself look distracted by thumbing through the iPod. *Fuck it, Chris, just choose a song, any song!* He hoped this last song on earth, whatever he chose, would provide some measure of meaning to his life.

"I get knocked down,

But I get up again

You're never gonna keep me down"

Son of a bitch! Damn, you iTunes shuffle! Chris slumped his head. *Worst…Suicide…Ever!* He considered searching for another song, but there was no time. He stepped over the platform lights. The front of the train was within meters now…with Chumbawumba cheerily singing away at his last moments on earth. *It won't hurt. It won't hurt. One more step, Chris and it ends. Last step. I love you, Mere…*

"Whoa there, sir!"

Chris felt a hand grab his wrist, jerking him back from the train and from his fate. Chris was furious. He whirled around to see that it was the soldier who asked him about Ballston moments ago. No, he wasn't a soldier; he was a Marine according to the desert pattern design of his uniform and his rank insignia. Chris glowered at him angrily. He couldn't believe it.

The Shiftiverse
Cambridge, Massachusetts
March 14, 2013

"Who was it? Who was it you saw?" Rita asked.

Chris smiled crookedly. "It was Richard Gere."

"What?"

"Well, that's what I thought at first. The man looked just like Richard Gere, a younger Richard Gere."

"You said he was a Marine?"

"Yeah, that's what I gathered." He noticed Rita was laughing. He couldn't help but be a little offended. He just finished telling this woman a story that he told no other living soul. He would never tell Meredith, his beloved wife, and here this woman was laughing.

"Well, I'm glad you find the tragic story about my botched suicide attempt so funny. I strive for my sorrow to be entertaining."

"I'm sorry, Chris...it's just, well, I'll tell you in a moment. You were saying?"

Chris recalled where his train of thought was before she started laughing.

"Well, that Marine who saved me totally screwed me up. I ran off before anyone could ask any questions. I was so livid. I was incensed. I wound up screaming into the night like some madman. 'Fucking Richard Gere!' I shouted. After I mustered the stones to do what I needed to do, he took the opportunity from me! People like me only get the nerve once. The following day, I couldn't go through with it. I just couldn't. I tried the following day and the day after that. I chickened out every time. Eventually, I came to the conclusion that I wasn't going to check out. I was in it for the long haul. I got back on Phoketal and I picked up my guitar, which I hadn't played in years. I would play when I couldn't sleep; eventually, the ringing in my ears sort of, I don't know, faded into the background. By the time Aidan was born, I was okay again. I don't know, Rita. It's nothing you'd make a movie out of, but I learned to deal."

"Do you still have the tinnitus?"

"Yeah, but most of the time I don't even notice. At least it's not strong enough that I think about it most of the time. Sometimes it ramps up, sometimes I obsess over it a tad, but it doesn't have the same effect over me as it used to."

"Well, it sounds like things worked out for you after all. It wasn't really the end of the world was it?"

"I don't know, maybe it was, I mean, in a sense. But what's strange is that after that day, the panic no longer had the same power over me. A couple of weeks following my failed attempts, I picked up the guitar for the first time in years. Meredith joined me playing the piano. I was composing music like I never had in college. It sort of soothed me, you know. The demons stole my confidence, but the music formed the core of my salvaged, refurbished soul. And in fact, that's what we named the second album."

Chris stretched his legs. "Now, what was so funny about my aborted suicide?"

Rita checked and saw that TALOPS was not powered up yet, nor had she expected it to be.

"You remember September 11th?"

"It's kind of hard to forget, Rita."

"Well, don't I look familiar to you somehow?"

Chris considered that for a moment. "Well, actually now that you mention it, you do look familiar. But what does September 11th…Oh, now wait a minute. Wait just a moment." He studied her in the light of the glow stick. "No, that's just too weird. Rita?"

And suddenly that name, her face, it all registered. Rita! She was that woman he literally hauled over his shoulder when the North Tower collapsed that day. "Rita? That was you?"

She nodded and explained how Richard Gere had been in his life before. Suddenly, the world seemed so much smaller.

CHAPTER 31

The Shiftiverse
Cambridge, Massachusetts
March 15, 2013

Thank God for small favors. The solar panels worked. They successfully powered up TALOPS' CPU. Rita had rerouted all microchip components so that she could tie in directly into TALOPS without relying on any defunct mediums. What's more, the 33rd Precinct did find a Best Buy with keyboards and monitors that hadn't been swiped. She had been working on the same one for hours without a single EMP surge destroying it. The EMPs were declining in frequency the last couple of years. Maybe one day in her lifetime they would end.

The only problem now was getting through the all of the code. TALOPS had been offline for years when the power went out. Nothing was erased, she knew that the programming was stored in its DNA, but it was in safe mode. Now she was relying on the memories that weren't quite hers and skills she did not acquire. And yet, as impossible as it should have been, she was maneuvering through the algorithms as though it was second nature. As long as she didn't think about it, she could work. The moment her conscious mind said, "Wow, look at what I'm doing," it ruined it for her. It took several minutes to get her back into a groove again. As long as she let her mind go and yielded herself to her other self, as long as she bent like a reed in the wind, she could do this. Sometimes, she had nothing to do with her mind getting off track. Chris had this nervous tick of coming in to check on her and inadvertently interrupting her with, "I just want to say good luck. We're all counting on you."

She calmed her mind; let the expectation, the fear, the ego pass into the background as best she could. She was beginning to make great strides in rebooting TALOPS when she heard gunfire in the distance. It wasn't particularly close, but if she could hear it, it wasn't good.

"Shit," she cursed. She lost her concentration momentarily. *Breathe, girl and let the algorithms guide you.*

Chris was gazing at the pre-dawn sky. Rayne 2005 wasn't visible yet. Jamil said it would become visible today. He wondered what was happening in his world. He hadn't heard a thing about a giant asteroid on a collision course with earth in the Mundaniverse before arriving here. He figured he would have recalled something like that. Chris understood that Jamil learned about the asteroid's collision course through a source in the Mundaniverse, and that top level officials in the U.S. government know about the truth of the Rayne 2005 as well. Did the general public now know, too? Was the entire world back home bracing for death? He just hoped Meredith and the kids were going to be okay. They wouldn't know that Jamil was on the job and was going to save them. He figured his counterpart wouldn't know that either, but at least he would be able to keep them safe from whatever chaos might be erupting around the world if in fact the general public knew about Rayne 2005. He hoped the government kept the kabash on it.

Gunfire interrupted his train of thought. He saw some Heighters shooting from the hip near a stadium. Kendra and he looked at each other and raced towards the disturbance.

"There! I saw ghosts moving up on us!" cried out one of the Heighters.

Captain O'Reilly smacked him upside the head. "Who the fuck taught you to shoot like you still were in Newark!"

Liam commenced to rip his underling a new one. "I swear. If I see any of you shooting like this punk here, I'll cap your ass before any ghosts can! Is that clear?"

The other cops grunted. Chris and Kendra jogged up just as Captain O'Reilly finished chewing the men out.

"Sorry, Captain, Lieutenant, just one of my boys getting spooked by ghosts."

"Ghosts?" Chris asked.

"You know, savages, gang bangers, whatever you call them."

"Well, were there any 'ghosts' on campus? We need to ensure Rita's safety."

"If there was, they're gone now."

There was more gunfire in the distance.

"I think we might have disturbed another hornet's nest in any case," Kendra said. "I don't want to take any chances. We got to make sure we can hold the campus at least until the reverend and Jamil complete their mission."

"Understood. I think we need to send some patrols beyond the campus to see what we're dealing with."

"Agreed, Captain O'Malley," Kendra said. "But don't be offended if I say no thanks to your men doing that. You, me and Captain Jung here. We'll recon the area, see if these ghosts can be bought off with some tins of food and tobacco and let's tighten our defense posture."

Chris knew Kendra's view of him had improved, but he really could do without the honors of joining her on the recon in this highly urbanized warzone. He was tempted to say that his ribs still hurt from the rounds his Type 4 vest caught last week. But as much as his totem animal, the chicken, would not be ignored, he knew if they didn't keep the locals out, Rita would fail and the world would quite literally end.

"Okay, LT, guns up, let's do this." It was a total façade, but he wanted to portray some semblance of confidence. But before he left he made sure to relieve himself and vomit.

The Shiftiverse
North Atlantic Ocean
March 15, 2013

Captain Jean Paul Nguyen stared at the peculiar speck in the morning sky while standing at the bow of the *Jean Lafitte*. The great golden fleur de lis waved proudly behind him on the black sail. Throughout human history, comets were seen as a bad omen portending some impending disaster. Of course, it wasn't a comet; it didn't have a tail. His best guess was that it was an asteroid, an asteroid visible in the morning sky. Jean Paul thought he saw something new in the night sky the last several nights with his telescope. As a sea captain who sailed the oceans without radar, GPS and most of the time without any radio signal to guide him, he mastered the lost art of navigating through star charts. He didn't mind relying on an ancient method. He joined the fraternity of the great Portuguese and Italian explorers who navigated the entire globe with nothing but a compass, protractor and the stars to guide them. At least he had a self-winding Rolex watch to keep track of time, as the compass was sporadic with EMPs.

The asteroid, which started as a speck, now seemed just a tad larger, like a speck on steroids perhaps. Jean Paul shuddered to think about it hitting the earth. He was no astronomer, but he had to guess that the rate that thing was increasing in size, it had to be at least fifty miles across if it was a foot. *So, what are you going to do about it? Pray again and make it good.* Jean Paul felt a little guilty about praying to God to save them when He had already given His only begotten Son. But Jean Paul reasoned that he could make penance when he returned to the Cuban settlements in South Carolina, after the asteroid passed earth by harmlessly.

He was enjoying a cigarillo from Virginia when his new executive officer joined him. "Morning, Captain."

"Morning, Cody. What's the word?"

"The passengers are eager to get home even though I already explained home ain't what it was. But they just won't accept it. After all the shit they seen in Iraq, they want to believe their home wasn't destroyed by the EMPs."

Jean Paul could understand that. He was just starting college when the EMPs hit, but a few of his friends were serving in Iraq and Afghanistan. Like the soldiers, sailors, airmen and Marines that Jean Paul was shuttling home now, his friends were abandoned in a hostile land. One of the first soldiers he picked up was his first officer, Cody Robacheaux. Originally, Cody was interested in getting back to Louisiana, but he ended up joining his crew. And with a fair amount of wisdom, the bossman of the Saints decided it was a good idea to offer free passage and a new home to any serviceman or woman who wished to do so. There were hundreds of them in Newfoundland right now, and he was dropping some of them off along his way back home to New Orleans. One day he would make the journey across the Atlantic to pick up soldiers who were resettling in the Kurdish Republic and who now had a port in the border area between Turkey and Syria.

"Well, once we drop those guys off, we shouldn't push off immediately. It will probably take a only a few hours before it hits them that their home is no more and they'll be grateful we hadn't set sail yet."

"Hooah," Cody replied in Army talk. "Well, I wouldn't mind them joining our ranks even if I can't understand what those Yankee boys are saying. Everything is always 'wicked awesome' and it's like they've never heard of the letter 'r.'"

"True. Well, let's not stay in Bean town too long either. I really don't like dead cities. Gives me the heebie jeebies."

CHAPTER 32

The Shiftiverse
Waynesboro, Virginia
March 15, 2013

Ezra Rothstein tried to put a positive spin on things. First, he was still alive. That was a good thing. Second, Neko Lemay had come to her senses and put the former Sheriff Lucille Schadenfreude into custody. Turned out he wasn't overly harsh when he called Lucille a barking madwoman. She really was certifiable. Furthermore, The Lambs of God were not surrounding Charlottesville. In fact, from the reports, the regent and his regime had their hands tied with a full-scale revolution taking place in Lynchburg. It started as a protest of the Catholic community who decried the murder of Sister Shanyn by the Sheepdogs. They must have had a master of a protest organizer because they did it at the right moment. When the Sheepdogs and police were ordered to shoot the protesters, regular citizens of Lynchburg walked between the guns and protestors and refused to allow the slaughter to continue after a few innocents were shot. That was uplifting to hear on a personal level.

This wasn't propaganda either; this was real intel being transmitted by cable from various assets who were passing along news to the Swan using a series of relays to cover the distance. Furthermore, the barricade erected along Interstate 64 at the mountain pass at the junction of Skyline drive was no joke. The Lambs of God were forced now into a bottleneck on the interstate where they could not go around. The interstate was a scant total of four lanes elevated precariously that hugged the side of a mountain hundreds of feet above the valley. They could try going around from

Lynchburg and head up north from Highway 29, but they already blew their shot by pressing for this campaign. The Catholic regiments formerly in Colleen withdrew to protect the protestors. And agreeing with Director Jung, Neko decided not to ruin a good thing and stayed put in Monticello rather than upset their tacit allies of the Catholic regiments now joining the opposition. The only way to Charlottesville now was Interstate 64.

The Orange Pact, though outnumbered, might be able to hold the mass of Lambs of God on the other side of the mountain for a long time. How long though? Indefinitely? He didn't think that was possible. And what chance did the opposition have in overthrowing the regent? Besides the Catholic regiments, the protestors were largely unarmed.

Ezra couldn't help but think that they were living on the precipice where at some point something was going to give. And that damned thing that appeared in the sky this morning did not fill him with confidence. He remembered in his junior year at Dave Matthews Memorial High School learning something about asteroids and comets being potentially catastrophic to the earth if they hit. Didn't the dinosaurs go extinct because of one? Who said this was an asteroid? It could just be a star…that was visible in the daylight…that he hadn't noticed before…that was getting a little bigger…as he spoke. Of course, maybe he was just being overly sensitive right now. It didn't mean anything. It was just an astronomical event that just so happened to be taking place during a critical juncture in history. Just coincidence, he reminded himself.

The morning frost was sublimating into steam as he went to clear his bladder and make sense of the day. Hopefully, the Lambs wouldn't be pushing through today. He felt a pat on his backside as Valerie Blaine walked up beside him. He wished he had shaved. His beard had grown out to about four feet over the last few days, but she didn't seem put off by it. She smiled and looked skyward.

"You notice the comet?" she said.

"I did. But I don't think it's a comet. It doesn't have a tail."

They both stared into the sky as he inched to be near her. He could swear she smelled like strawberries. How could she smell like strawberries when she was in the same shit as he? He knew he didn't smell like strawberries.

"I hope it doesn't hit."

"That would blow some serious moose balls if it did."

"So, you think we can win?"

He shrugged his shoulders. "Is winning everything to you Vicious Rabbits?"

"The constable said it was the only thing."

They stared into the sky silently while a few technicals revved their engines and cavalry soldiers descended down the mountain nearby.

"Valerie?"

"Yes?"

"This isn't absolutely confirmed yet, but...well, I think I may be falling in love with you," he said nonchalantly.

"Don't make me get the fire hose."

"Understood."

They stared back into the sky. No doubt about it, he was in love. He hoped this wasn't the end.

Suddenly, they heard shouting. Some soldiers were sobbing. Valerie and Ezra turned to each other and headed to the command tent to see what the commotion was about.

The Shiftiverse
Montpelier Station, Virginia
Rochelle Sovereignty
March 15, 2013

In some corner of her mind, Meredith had been able to compartmentalize the knowledge about Rayne 2005. But seeing it in the sky this morning gave no doubt of the grim truth. By this time tomorrow, there will be no more war, no more Lambs of God, Monticello, or Rochelle, no more animals, nothing left to show humanity had ever been here. Sometime today, that asteroid would hit the west coast. Within an hour, the blast wave would reach Rochelle. They wouldn't feel a thing, which was a small mercy for all the destruction to come. There would be a brilliant light followed by the thunder, a breeze turning to a powerful wind, and then nothing.

Meredith was tearful all morning, but she wasn't the only one. Everyone in Rochelle was grieving about the news they had just received about Jon Early's death. Although Thuy Mai would not share the fate of humanity with the citizens of Rochelle, he saw no reason why they should not know that Jon Early had died defending the rights of people in the heart of the enemy's lair. The Vicious Rabbits were not demoralized by Jon's death. In fact, it seemed to harden their resolve. And despite her concerns to the contrary, the knowledge that the leader of Rochelle was involved in the protest did not take the steam out of the revolution. In fact, the news coming out of Lynchburg, if anything, reinforced the narrative that they were fighting the good fight, and the participants in what was being hailed as "The Yard Ruler Revolution" believed that they might succeed in overthrowing the regent. Meredith had her doubts, but hope was a powerful weapon.

Upon her return a few days ago, she spent a whole day with the kids, but matters of state forced her back in the office at least for an hour or so. She would call in sick and spend her last day on earth with her children, but she at least had to check in one last time to make sure Rochelle had what it needed, so that their last hours on earth were valiant and encouraging. Nobody save for she, Dean, Thuy and the scientists knew what was coming, though there were a few grumblings in the bowels of the Swan about this little thing in the sky. Some said it must be a comet or asteroid. And although there was some muted concern that it might pose a threat, their overarching focus was on the war and the news of the constable's noble death.

At the office, Meredith was relieved to find that the Lambs of God's advance had been halted at the pass near Waynesboro and that the Yard Ruler Revolution tied the regent's Sheepdogs down in Lynchburg. Meredith would have loved to see how this all would have panned out. They might have survived the War of the Lambs, they might have even won—winning being defined as not having been conquered.

She was also gratified to learn that Neko Lemay complied with reason by not advancing on Lynchburg and reinstating the Monticellan operatives to the Swan. Again, Meredith felt cheated out of possibility. She couldn't bear to think how her children were being cheated out of their future, of their potential, of growing up, falling in love, having children of their own.

She joined Thuy who was on the horn with Commandant Dean Jacob on a secured line.

"We're getting some indication that the Lambs are going to try using their tanks to push through the barricades," Dean reported with his signature bass voice. "I could hold them off, but..."

Dean didn't need to finish that statement. Both she and Thuy knew that there was little point in all of these young men and women dying horribly in gruesome battle when they could spend their final hours with some semblance of sanity.

"Can you execute Preparation Hotel?"

"Affirmative."

Thuy glanced over to Meredith who nodded.

"Execute Preparation Hotel," Thuy ordered.

Preparation Hotel was a little talked about plan to stall the Lambs of God with mines while the Orange Pact withdrew to a more easily defensible position. Under normal circumstances, it would be idiotic to withdraw from their current position as it was the best defensible position and gave them the best chance of minimizing the Lambs of God's advantage in numbers and machinery. But things were not normal. Instead, this was the equivalent of sitting on the ball till the clock ran out.

"Copy that, Constable, Director," he said evenly. Thuy winced at hearing his new title as constable.

"May the Lord keep you and all of your families, guys."

"And to you, Dean," Thuy signed off. After hanging up, he took a deep breath.

"So, this is it?"

"It is indeed," she said as she packed her valise to head back to the house. In all these years, she only called in sick once; even during her supposed "maternity leave" she spent most of the time working on Swan projects at the house while breast feeding and dealing with colic. So much time wasted on work.

"You know, you are the only family I have," he said as his voice cracked.

She took his hand in hers. "We've done well, Thuy. I would have never thought it was possible when we left Falls Church. God, I was so scared."

"We didn't know anything, did we?"

"No, we didn't," she said with a smirk, "except that it was over and that our best chance was to get the hell out of Dodge. But we did it. We made something beautiful here, something we should be very proud of. I never could have believed it, but I would never trade this world for a life without the Shift."

"Neither would I."

They left the depressing Connex container and turned out the lights for the last time.

"I'm hosting dinner tonight," she said. "Nothing fancy, but I want to be with the ones I love."

"I'd like that."

The Shiftiverse
Cambridge, Massachusetts
March 15, 2013

Rita was woken from a nap as the monitor connected to TALOPs flickered wildly. At first, she feared that the flickering was an EMP surge. She worked for hours without interference from any such surges. Certainly, another one would hit soon, though there was no predicting when.

The text on the screen reassured her.

RITA?

She was a little surprised to see a simple black screen message. She hadn't received a text message in years. Rita sat at the console.

TALOPS, IS THAT YOU?

IT IS JAMIL. TALOPS LET ME IN. WE ARE READY TO CONNECT TO THE CERN.

Rita sighed with relief. She couldn't explain what she had done to restart TALOPS' drive. She just knew that somehow it worked.

Chris Jung, Kendra Baraka and the Captain of the 33rd Precinct Liam O'Malley crept along a residential street a few blocks from MIT campus. Kendra led the three-man patrol heading in the direction where they heard gunfire. The day was warming up well above freezing. The months of snow and ice began to thaw quickly. Icicles broke off the overhangs, crashing onto cars and the street had turned into a shallow creek. Unsurprisingly, this area of Cambridge had been a tidy upscale part of town. The few stand-alone houses would have been way out of his price range. He couldn't even afford to get mugged here no less live anywhere as nice as this place once was. No matter how devastated a place looked, and this place looked about as ravaged as any urban neighborhood, some part of him couldn't help but think about how places once too good for the likes of him were now de-militarized zones.

Chris darted his eyes back and forth as the trio slowly made their way down the street. They were doing a recon of the area to see what they were up against. Chris kept his finger out of the trigger guard of his M4 as he was trained. Kendra gave a signal and the two ran up to her.

"Look, I need to use the ladies room," she whispered.

"Well, there's a Starbucks right over there," Chris pointed across the street.

"I don't like the idea of sitting on a toilet seat that's been left to the elements, but then again I also don't want to squat out in the open like this."

The window to the Starbucks had been smashed out like every storefront he had seen. Even paint stores and gift card shops, which really didn't have anything of value in them, had been ransacked. The only store untouched was a boutique bookstore, which Chris thought was kind of telling of the declining value of books in an instant gratification society. They stepped over a pile of debris into the coffeehouse. This store had the same exact décor as the Starbucks next to his office in Arlington, as well as the one across the street from that one, which was built just in case people didn't see the other one or didn't want to walk across the street. Lounge chairs and tables were scattered and thrown about. Lights with cylindrical shaped lampshades dangled from the ceiling lifeless. Most of the merchandise and equipment had been swiped including the espresso machine. Chris figured that it might function if someone hooked it up to the plumbing, and if the thieves happened to have some coffee around.

After making a sweep of the store, Kendra made use of the ladies room. Chris noticed that Liam swiped a roll of toilet paper from the men's room. That he could understand. He had grown weary of using paper from newspapers and books that they came across. It was just wrong to do that.

"Did the reverend restart TALOPS?" Liam asked.

"She was in the process of it, I think. I don't know. She was working furiously whatever it was she was doing."

"Ah. Well, I know she'll succeed."

"What makes you say that," Chris asked curiously.

"Can't you feel it? She knows what's going on. She knows what really happened."

"A lot of people in Virginia knew what happened."

"Yeah, but she's got an in with Gaia herself."

Chris turned around. "You believe the Gaia stuff? That's not what I would expect from a good Irish Catholic NYPD officer like yourself, Liam."

"Yeah, well a lot of the shit I was taught to believe can't explain why this all happened. 'Sides, my astrologer told me someone was going to come and change our lives."

"Really? Did your astrologer also tell you that there was a massive asteroid that was heading for earth?"

"Bite me," Liam responded, not maliciously, rather more like guys busting each other's balls.

"I'm serious, she's onto something. Lieutenant Baraka knows it, too."

"Well, don't believe everything you think."

Chris was astounded how this guy, a former NYPD cop, could buy into this Gaia stuff wholesale. He would love to study the psychological and cultural shifts caused by this apocalypse, that is if they lived. Kendra was as devout a Unitarian as any fundamentalist he had come across, and she was one of the most skeptical people he knew back in his world. On the way up from New York, Kendra and Chris chatted about the events in her life and how Gaia had guided her. He noticed that she never mentioned her original home in Brooklyn even when they were just one borough away. She never even once mentioned returning there to check on her parents. Then again, he could understand not wanting to see one's childhood home destroyed.

BACKGROUND MUSIC: "Beach" by Boy & Bear
Visit www.michaeljuge.com **on the Refurbished Soul page to listen**

Chris meandered over to the merchandise shelf. It had been swiped almost completely. Resting on the nearly bare shelf was something familiar, his exact model of titanium travel mug with the Starbucks logo but also with the inscription "Bean town" next to images of Harvard, MIT and the Boston skyline. Chris pulled out his own mug and was about to trade it out, but thought better of it. He stuffed his own back in a utility pouch and picked up the Bean town mug.

"Do not go in there," Kendra warned jokingly as she came out. Chris smiled as the three of them stepped back outside into the daylight. The creek running down the street had become a shallow river as more snow melted, the rushing water getting louder.

"Kendra, um I got something for you." Chris pulled out the Starbucks Bean town mug and presented it to her.

Her attractive but stern face brightened as he handed it to her.

"I know it's your birthday next month."

"That is so sweet. And it's just like yours!"

"Yeah, but even better. It's got 'Bean town' written on it, see? That way you'll have a souvenir of this trip."

"Chris, I will…"

Kendra suddenly dropped from his sight. For a split second, he thought she slipped into the shallow river's edge until he looked down and saw her covered in blood. It happened so fast, he didn't even hear the shot. He dropped to his knees.

"Oh God, oh God! Shit!"

She was gasping, her eyes popping out as blood pumped, gushing from her neck. Captain O'Malley shot in the direction and barked out, "Get cover!"

Chris dragged her back inside the Starbucks, the blood making his grip slippery. O'Malley ran to the other block in the direction of the shot while Chris held Kendra inside the dank coffeehouse. He pressed his palm against the entry wound trying to stop the bleeding while he frantically searched for his first aid pouch with his other hand; however, it was like trying to force back water gushing from a garden hose. Kendra desperately tried to breathe.

"Shh, shh, it's okay, Kendra, it's okay," he cried frantically trying to lie to her. She nodded as he rocked her. "Just hold on, now! Oh, God, just…" She seized up. "No, no, no, no!"

She went limp. Her eyes rolled in the back of her head. The hand that still held the Starbucks mug throughout the ordeal, released its grasp. Chris kept rocking her as the blood stopped pumping from her neck. In the silence, with only the sound of the river outside, he rocked her. He felt the medallion around her neck. It was homemade, an extraordinarily crude facsimile of the Unitarian chalice and flame. He caressed it as he rocked her.

Chris couldn't will himself from the ground. It was as though if he moved it would make her death more real somehow. He would have stayed there indefinitely, but then a spray of bullets tore through the coffeehouse. Chris toppled over, unceremoniously dragging Kendra's body with him. He dove behind a lounge chair, which he knew provided absolutely no cover against a bullet.

He grabbed his rifle and pulled the trigger, but forgot to slip off the safety. His hands, arms and the rifle itself were all covered in blood; his fingers were frozen. He waited for another volley to identify the shooter's position. If he stood up, the sniper would get him. He had to wait for him. Several seconds passed and nothing. *Where the fuck is O'Malley?* Chris then had a terrible thought. O'Malley could have been shot, too. Chris was stranded alone inside Starbucks in the urban wilderness. He wasn't sure he could find his way back to his people. They didn't even know he was in here. His thoughts raced in an accelerated version of panic. How was he going to get back to them? He stood up and raced for the opening, running in a zigzag pattern when another volley of rounds chased him outside. The rounds clanged against the engine block of a Hummer which he hid behind. He had learned that engine blocks were the only part of a vehicle that could stop rifle rounds, though it was far from bullet proof. He raised he rifle and shot a few rounds, but his M4 jammed.

"Christ!"

He dove back down behind the Hummer and tried to clear the jam, but the blood congealing on him mucked up the bullets. He dropped the mag, and spastically grabbed for another. His shaking hands ripped a mag from the pouch and flung it into the air and it dropped into the bloody red stream. He dove, splashing in the freezing stream, and retrieved it, barely. He realized he had just pissed on himself…again. If this weren't an absolute life or death moment, it would have been embarrassing. He drove the wet magazine into the M4 and slammed the bolt closed. He hoped wet rounds wouldn't make the rifle malfunction. The few times he trained on the M4, the magazines were always clean and dry.

He knew if he peered from the same place he was before, he would get tagged. He took off his helmet and lifted it above the Hummer, which was shot out of his hands. Then he slithered to the back end of the Hummer and looked through the broken out windows to see the glint of the scope, or at least he hoped it was the scope. He lifted the rifle, aimed until he saw the sniper aiming for him. Chris fired.

The sniper gurgled in pain. After a few seconds, Chris stood up cautiously when he heard another shot. He jolted around and saw a body drop. Behind the body stood Captain O'Malley holding a pistol. Chris lowered his rifle, acknowledged him and walked back inside to retrieve Kendra. Her bloodied body lay twisted over the couch where he left her. He took a cloth from his tunic and proceeded to clean her blood-crusted face and closed her eyes. Chris took off the MOLLE gear on her and handed it to Liam. He then picked up her limp frame and slowly walked out of the Starbucks with her slumped in his arms. The medallion glistened around her bloodied neck as he carried her back. He had never realized how young she really was until now.

CHAPTER 33

The Mundaniverse
Falls Church, Virginia
March 15, 2013

"The President released a statement refuting the claims that the government shutdown was related to asteroid Rayne 2005's close approach, which is now estimated to pass within twenty thousand miles of earth. However, that hasn't allayed the fears of some…"

Chris pressed the remote and turned off the TV, for it only added to the noise and chaos inside the tiny apartment packed with his and Meredith's family. Chris' dad and his wife were in the kitchen working on the hors d'oeuvres, mom and Chris' brother Jack were playing on the computer with Aidan and Yorick, and Meredith's parents were doing a final clean up of Aidan's room. Chris' sister and family were taking a walk at the cemetery next door. Meredith said she would be home early as promised.

He couldn't help but feel enormously anxious as he slipped into his bedroom and closed the door. Maybe it was just that he underestimated the impact of seeing his family for the first time in years. Or more likely, it was due to the fact that this guy Jamil who he had been in correspondence with appeared to be correct. The official estimates of the asteroid's trajectory changed from 100,000 miles to 20,000. But it was the highly classified cable Jamil sent him that left him no doubt. Unless Jamil succeeded in doing whatever he said he would do to prevent Rayne 2005 from colliding into the earth—he had no idea what that entailed—they were most certainly going to die. He had faced death on numerous occasions, but that didn't mean he was used to the idea. Not only that, he, his family, and his entire planet was in for a world of hurt unless Jamil succeeded. That *could* explain the sudden pall of profound emotion that overtook him.

Chris had one week to make preparations. From the moment he first got off the phone with Jamil, he rushed to prepare. He racked his mind trying to consider everything. He knew how to live in a post-Shift world, but safely guiding his family from the ensuing chaos during those first desperate days...again, was less promising and filled with many variables.

First, he considered who he wanted to bring with him on what he referred to himself as "the exodus redux." Last time, he was lucky to get the team he had, Thuy, Brandon, Anne and a great late comer, Akil. This time, knowing what was coming, he had options. Brandon and Anne were essential. Without Brandon, they wouldn't be welcomed in Rochelle. His parents, his brother Jack and his family, his sister and family, Meredith's family, other friends and a few more trusted agents, and Thuy, of course.

Chris had to scheme to get everyone over to his place. The trick of it was getting them all to his apartment before the Shift hit, and Chris was operating under the assumption that Jamil was correct in his prediction that the Shift would hit as a result of his saving the earth. And so, he schemed, and he lied. He spoke with his parents and Meredith's, told them that he had some really big news and he absolutely needed them here in DC and not to tell Meredith because it was a surprise. He sprung for their plane tickets and hotel lodging, putting it all on the credit card. He then called Brandon up and told him that he was hosting a party at his apartment on Friday where he was going to announce something extremely important. Brandon first hemmed and hawed about needing to take Anne to a Lamaze class.

Chris insisted, saying, "Dude, I really need you guys here, please, reschedule."

"Okay, Chief. We'll be there, but this better be good."

"Great, man. Thanks! Oh, and bring your bikes!"

"What?"

"Please. It will all make sense I swear."

Thuy was easier to convince and so were his coworkers Ted Morley, Kendra and a few agents. Like himself and Brandon, they were all on furlough. What else did they have to do? The random request about bringing bikes threw them all for a loop but he was adamant. He just wished he could tell Meredith about this "party." He thought about it, but it would open a can of worms. He learned from years of marriage that it was better to ask for forgiveness than for permission in certain cases.

Once he got the guest list together, Chris went about gathering everything they would need, both for the journey to Rochelle and for the coming months. Guns. They would need guns. As it stood, other Chris had a Mossberg 12 gauge shotgun. But he was going to need a few more. He checked online after getting off the phone with Jamil and found a gun show in Manassas. He bought seven AR15s, four Remington shotguns, five Remington and Winchester rifles, and eight Glok pistols along with enough 5.56, .308, 30-06 and 9mm rounds to keep a militia happy for weeks. Like the in-law plane tickets and everything else, he put it on the card. *Suck it, MasterCard!*

The good news about the new congress and president was that they were quick to open as many loopholes for gun dealers at gun shows just before they shut down the government. He could have sworn he bought the weapons from a gun dealer who was once connected to the regent. At least guns were selling swimmingly even if the economy tanked on its second and more massive recession. Of course, his credit card company called to confirm that it was he buying the small armory. It would have been a disaster if they called his wife. He just wouldn't have been able to explain that.

He stowed the stash of weapons in a rented storage facility down the street, which he knew he would be able to have access to when the power went out. He cleaned out the sporting goods store of the last of the freeze dried food, water purification pills, and backpacks. He faked an infection to get a prescription for antibiotics and double filled it. It was illegal, but whatever. Chris searched his memory banks of the first exodus and recalled how Meredith had the forethought to bring things like aspirin, diaper cream, Desitin and other such non-replenishiable first aid items. And blisters! By the time they made it to Rochelle, all of their feet and asses were blistered and chapped. Of course, it was summer. This time it would be at the tail end of winter. He would much rather flee from the dying city in March than in July given his druthers. Never-the-less, he took a page from Meredith and bought up those items. Next came the bike tubes, and other spare parts. And duct tape! He would have bought some horses as well, but he wouldn't know where to stow them at the apartment complex. The storage room was already packed with the neighbor's crap.

He was really tempted to stock up on vacuum packed coffee, spices and underwear, things that would be highly valuable in the post-Shift world, but he knew they wouldn't be able to lug everything with them. The parents and in-laws ranged in shape from impressively good to fair, but all were getting on in their years. He would have to take that into consideration, along with having kids. At least two of the child trailers he bought would be used for their intended purpose of hauling children. The others would be used for hauling the extra equipment. Kids were an added consideration they didn't have to deal with the first time. But as he added it all together, the cons of a larger party with a few senior citizens and children against the pros of being well armed, stocked and with good transportation, he felt a lot more confident.

In the end, he decided to buy some coffee and spices as well as a number of vintage LPs and dig a hole out by the adjoining woods next to the cemetery. It might be there in a few years, it might stay fresh encased in a Thule water-tight cargo carrier. Anyone watching him digging in the middle of the night and burying a coffin shaped thing would have thought he was getting rid of a hit.

Over the past week, he saw panic buying despite the government and media assurances that the asteroid would pass by harmlessly. *Idiots*, he thought. *I mean what do they think? That they could buy enough ammo to outlive the blast wave that would strip the crust off the earth?* And then he acknowledged the irony of himself standing in a long line at Wal-Mart. *But*, he defended himself from his own inner second guessing voice, *my situation is totally different. I know it's the Shift, not the asteroid. Aha, but you are quick to judge when you know their panic buying will save them.* Chris started to wonder if that second guessing voice in his head was just his tangent self being a dick.

Chris locked the bedroom door and grabbed his checklist from the closet. He took down a case and looked at the cash. He had just cleaned out his kids' college fund and savings and converted the fifty thousand dollars, a couple of thousand into cash and the rest into gold and Rolex watches. If the collapse unfolded similarly in this universe as it did in his, cash would start losing value within a week. The inflation rate would sky rocket, leaving it completely useless within a month. Although gold was heavier and would temporarily lose its value during the collapse, it was a stable long-term investment as it would become the currency after six months or so, that is if things went the same way. The Rolex watches he bought weren't an excess. The self-winding watches were unaffected by the Shift and would save them. How many times did the Vicious Rabbits win in the early days because they were able to synchronize the two or three windup watches and lay a coordinated attack? $50,000…He had never touched that much money before in his life, and now he was submitting currency transaction reports like it was routine.

Without context, without the knowledge of what was coming, emptying his kids' and his own retirement fund would look like a complete douche bag thing to do. It was. But in fact, he knew he was doing this for them. This was their future, and he alone knew what was best. That was a strange feeling to have. It required an arrogance that he did not normally possess. He could be a self-absorbed ass, but that wasn't the same thing. But at least this time, Meredith and the children would get a Chris who had a clue beyond just "Dude, we gotta get out of this place."

If only he could tell Meredith what he was doing and why. Maybe she would believe him. He felt like a total jerk sneaking around taking their money and buying all of this behind her back. But he couldn't chance her putting the brakes on his efforts. He would have to just hope she wouldn't find out until the Shift hit. She was still at work and would be home soon. By that time, the "surprise party" would be underway and she would be freaking out seeing friends, her parents, brother and family. He didn't know what to do to stall her once she arrived. He just hoped the Shift hit soon. That was a peculiar thought, he acknowledged.

The doorbell rang. Chris put his checklist down and shut the closet door.

"Hey Brandon, hey Anne! Come on in!"

Chris gave the two of them a hug and led them from the apartment's stairwell landing inside his apartment.

"Hey, Chief."

"Wow, how much longer, Anne?"

"Another three months to go," she said as he took her coat.

"Three months? Wow, what a coincidence. That's the same as Meredith was back…"

They looked at him expectantly when he stopped himself. Brandon and Anne were such a part of his life back in Rochelle, and he didn't see them enough in this world to get used to not discussing matters from his reality. It was really difficult in fact. He wanted to tell them everything that happened and that was going to happen. He wanted to tell Brandon how good he looked with ten fingers and two legs. Instead, he finished. "That was the same as Meredith back when we started doing Lamaze," he quickly recovered.

"So, did you bring your bikes?"

Brandon sighed with agitation. "For the last time, yes! I still don't know why it's so important to you, man. Is this your OCD thing acting up again?"

Chris chuckled. "It will soon be clear."

"What's the news, Chris? Is it our album? Did Rabbit Hunters go viral?" he asked with excitement.

"You'll find out." Chris would have loved that, though. He listened to *Refurbished Soul* repeatedly on his iPod. He just wished he could play like other Chris could.

He led them inside where Aidan yelled, "Mister Brandon, Miss Anne!"

"Hey there, little shredder! What's happening, man?"

As they caught up and were reintroduced to his mom and dad and his brother, he noticed Anne wore heels. That was one thing he hadn't considered telling them. Wear practical shoes. Hopefully, they could work that out. At least the Hughes were here. Chris figured it was time to start the music.

BACKGROUND MUSIC: "Home" by Edward Sharpe And The Magnetic Zeros
Visit www.michaeljuge.com on the Refurbished Soul page to listen

The party was kicking off nicely with Edward Sharpe & The Magnetic Zeros playing on the stereo. Thuy was joking with a couple of the other agent friends of his, two buddies from his basic special agent class John Steward and Collin Sutherland. The in-laws were gabbing with Jack and family, his sister Erika and her family. His mom and stepmother were being civil to each other. Brandon walked up to him.

"Hey man, good choice going old school with the vinyl."

Brandon was referring to the fact that the music was playing an LP of a post-millennium band. Of the multitude of purchases Chris made was a vinyl record cutting machine he scored on eBay. Granted, it was an indulgence, but Chris knew from experience that the world was going to miss a lot of music that had been recorded exclusively in digital format. He recorded an extensive collection of post-millennium music on vinyl from iTunes while packing the ammo and peanut butter. In the years to come, he would make a mint reproducing LPs of bands like Insane Clown Posse and Kanye West off the copies he made. Plus, he was not going to be stuck in the apocalypse with nothing but Classic Rock again.

Chris walked out on the balcony and gazed at Rayne 2005 looming menacingly overhead. The rock looked bigger, significantly larger than the moon even.

"Christ, that thing is big."

His older brother Jack joined him on the balcony, smoking some hilarious thing called an "e cigarette." It sounded absolutely ludicrous to his Shiftiverse ears, like some made up product on SNL. The crazy things civilization came up with while he was gone. Chris knew that Jack was going to be hating life in about a week when the smokes ran out. It would be a couple of years before they would be growing tobacco again.

"Chris, you piqued our curiosity, flying us all over here, setting us up over at the Marriott, keeping the surprise for Meredith. You mind sharing what's going on with your *chadeech*?"

Jack and he communicated with each other via Star Trek Next Generation and various movie references. He hadn't heard the Klingon term for a trusted companion during a trial in years. He really missed Jack, even if he decapitated all of his Star Wars figures and placed Princess Leia's head on Darth Vader's body when he was a kid. "Princess Vader," he mocked.

"Sorry, Shadout Mapes," tossing a Dune reference back at him, "it will have to wait."

Out on the apartment complex field, his downstairs neighbor was grilling and blasting some Latino music while others kicked a soccer ball around. Although he hated the loud music, he got to like his downstairs neighbor, Juan Ramirez.

Chris called out in Spanish, "Hey, Juan, your grilling is making me hungry."

"Why don't you come down and join us, Chris?"

Chris replied with a horrible American accented Spanish. "I think we will. I got plenty of steak that needs cooking."

Jack stared at him.

"What?"

"Since when did you learn Spanish?"

Chris shrugged. As a business owner in Rochelle, Chris had to be conversant with other shop owners and craftsmen in their native tongue. Quickly, he covered his tracks.

"Well, you know…Dora the Explorer, Diego…it catches on after awhile."

Jack nodded. He had children, too and was bombarded with Nick Jr.

271

on a daily basis, as Chris had been these last couple of months. Chris then realized that his downstairs neighbor would make quite a powerful ally when the Shift hit. He had to remember to extend an invite to Juan and family when the time was right, which should be in…Chris looked at his new Rolex watch when people inside the apartment shouted, "Surprise!"

In walked Meredith, making her way through the crowd of friends and family.

"Mom, Dad…everyone? What…"

People cheered. She stumbled through, hugging her parents, brother, friends and family.

"What's all this about?"

"I don't know, sweetheart," said her mom, "you'll need to ask Chris. He's got a big surprise for us all."

It was at that precise moment when Chris felt an urgent need to jump off the balcony. He had done so much planning, so much scheming, had been meticulous to max out his credit card, not pay the mortgage and stockpile everything they would need without tipping off his wife, he completely flaked on the purported "surprise." His throat tightened. He hoped he wasn't having a heart attack. That would be really bad.

"Umm, I, well…I am going to tell you all the great surprise when the moment is right," he stammered. "Until then, um, enjoy some satay and sushi." He really was going to miss that cuisine. This was a "last meal" of sorts.

Meredith glowered at him, and not in a good way. The Vulcan knew when he was talking shit as she was exposed to it often enough. He had to stall. According to Jamil, the asteroid would impact within an hour. Whatever he was going to do to stop it and cause the Shift, he'd better do it now. And Chris knew he had to stall. But alas it was too late.

"Chris, may I speak with you a second?"

Uh oh. He was in deep shit. She only called him by his name rather than a term of endearment when she was angry, which was rare. And by the restrained tone, it wasn't a request. In the background Thuy made a whipping gesture. Chris couldn't even shoot the bird at him with everyone around.

"Chris Claudius Jung,"

Uh oh. Meredith has never done the middle name thing before. This is bad.

"I don't know what the big surprise is, but I don't even care at this point because I am so angry with you!"

They were in their bedroom. Everyone's coats were tossed on the bed. Chris noticed some would not be that comfortable out in the elements with extended exposure. But at the moment he was facing his wife who was rightfully livid with him, though he didn't know exactly which part, the maxing out the credit card, the failure to pay the mortgage and condo fee, the emptying the savings account, poaching Aidan and Yorick's college fund…there were just so many possibilities. He wasn't going to break, though. He had to ride this out.

"Are you listening?"

"Yes, dear."

"This is no time for jokes." She took off her glasses. He couldn't help but notice that she looked good in her work outfit, the business skirt and heels. Men really were dogs if he could be thinking of sex at a time like this.

"How could you spend our savings on a party? And when you're not employed?"

He said nothing. He couldn't be made to speak. She wouldn't get anything out of him. He didn't care if she was The Vulcan back in his world. He wasn't going to break.

"I checked our savings this morning and found that it was closed early this week. In what universe do you think it's okay to do something like that without consulting me? Do you think I would ever do something like that to you?"

She was absolutely right. It was such a dicked up thing to do. He wanted to tell her everything. The doorbell rang. She saw his eyes dart.

"Don't you…"

Too late. He raced out the door. "I'll get it!"

Chris bolted out of the bedroom, weaved through the crowd in the living room, opened the door. And there she was just as Jamil promised.

"Rita!"

The Rita standing before him was a far cry from the Rita he knew. Her hair was pulled back in a tight bun and her features were much softer, not to mention that she had a full set of teeth and didn't wear an eye patch. Her demeanor was more reserved as well, but it didn't matter. It was a familiar face.

"Chris? Chris Jung?" she said uncertainly.

"Yes," he said and gave her a hug, which he realized was not what she was expecting. "Wow, look at you…with your two eyes."

"Two eyes?"

"Forget it."

Chris shut the door, leaving them alone on the stairwell landing. He looked around to make sure no one was eavesdropping.

"So, I gather Jamil told you about the asteroid."

She nodded somberly. "Yes, he did. I…I didn't want to believe it, but…"

"Here we are," they said in unison.

There was a prolonged silence as he gauged her nervousness. "Did you bring your bike and what clothes you will need?"

"They're in the car."

"Good, because when the Shift hits, it's going to become your lifeline. Understand?"

"You…you really are from that world, aren't you?"

He nodded solemnly. "I am." It was the first time he ever was able to speak the truth out loud to someone face-to-face. He felt like he had been a veteran of a hidden war and only now did someone see him for who and what he truly was.

"How bad was it?" she asked.

Chris smiled. "Let's just worry about making it better this go around, shall we?"

"Okay."

There was a buzz and she looked at her Blackberry. Chris' iPhone rang at the same time. The message from Jamil read:

IT IS BEGINNING.

There was nothing left to do now but wait and hope Jamil succeeds. Hopefully, once civilization started its rapid implosion following the Shift, Meredith would forgive the whole not consulting her about big purchases thing. He couldn't believe it, but some part of him was praying that the world would either end or result in the Shift, simply because he would have a lot of explaining to do otherwise. That was incredibly selfish, he admitted, but he really didn't want to be stuck with a shitload of guns and gold and no college fund for his kids on Monday morning.

"Let me help get your bike out of the car. We'll stow it with the others in the storage shed."

As they walked outside, he asked, "Do you remember me, Rita?"

"Jamil reminded me about us on September 11th. How did he know that, anyway?"

"He said he talked to some of my friends on the other side to get to know about me so I'd know he wasn't full of shit. Apparently, it's a small world, huh?"

"Yes, it is."

"It's almost like some crazy earth Goddess is guiding us, huh?" he added, trying to illicit a response.

"Uh huh," she said dismissively. *That's strange. My Rita* always *talks about Gaia back home.*

"So, are you and Jamil dating?"

"I'm sorry?"

"I'm not asking you out, Rita. I'm just asking if you and Jamil are dating. I mean, he risked a lot to make sure you would arrive in my care to save you from the shit storm."

She suddenly broke out in laughter and took several seconds to compose herself. "That's right! You've only spoken to Jamil on the phone. You don't know about Jamil at all, do you?"

"What about him?"

Rita spent the next several minutes explaining both what Jamil was and his supposed plan to magnetize and repel the asteroid. Chris tried to keep up, but he felt himself getting dizzy. So much had happened, so much to absorb. Jamil was an artificially intelligent organic computer that existed in both realities, a single entity with one mind in two universes. It was a little hard to grasp. It would have been hard to believe, except at this point, what was weird anymore?

Chris and Rita stared at the asteroid as it loomed even larger. Chris saw a sudden rippling in the sky. "Wow, that's…"

He started to feel sick.

"Come on, let's get inside."

Chris and Rita walked back up the stairs and entered the apartment to see the party had stopped; they were all glued to the TV. CNN had a breaking story. Everyone looked terrified. He thought he could see images on the screen showing the asteroid glowing red as though it was entering the atmosphere. He heard screams outside. He tried to listen, but as he walked over to the TV, his foot missed the ground, and he fell into blackness.

Chapter 34

San Antonio, Texas
June 1999

Rita hated goodbyes. It was cliché standing at the gate inside the terminal with a large hiking backpack making a tearful farewell.

"I'll call you every evening, okay Abuelita?" She didn't know if she just spoke in English or Spanish. Abuelita understood both, but Spanish was their language together. However, Rita noticed how little she used Spanish once she started college. It was only because she went home every weekend to visit her ailing grandmother that she didn't lose her Spanish altogether. Abuelita sat in one of the airline-provided wheelchairs, which Rita's sponsor Delana was pushing. Abuelita didn't necessarily need the wheelchair, but her legs weren't as strong as they used to be.

"And Miguel and I will be back for Thanksgiving," she added.

Abuelita nodded. She looked so feeble in the wheelchair. Some part of her wanted to just quit the whole idea of the PhD program at Columbia and stay with her. She knew Uncle Zeke would care for her, and Delana had promised to check in on her as well. Ever since she quit smoking a few years ago, Rita felt confident that Delana would last another few years even if she did put on twenty pounds. Abuelita would be fine she tried to convince herself. But she couldn't help but feel like she was abandoning her. Abuelita had been with Rita through everything from her parents' death, her alcoholism, her recovery, to getting through college. Her grandmother never left her, never gave up on her. It was only now at the gate that Rita realized that despite whatever façade she had built up, she was scared to leave Abuelita, not just for Abuelita, but for herself. She was scared to not have Abuelita in her life every day to back her up.

Rita knelt down and gave the frail frame of Abuelita a gentle hug, smelling her perfume and being tickled by the funny teapot hat she wore.

"You make me proud, mi Querida. You've come so far."

"I know."

"No, I don't think you do," she said as she placed her wrinkled hand on her cheek. "You were a lost soul, mi Querida. I prayed for you every day. I prayed the Rosary for your wellbeing, but you were out there intent on killing yourself."

It was painful to hear her sweet grandmother retell what hell it was for her to deal with an alcoholic, drug addict granddaughter who slept around for the next drunk or high. She always hoped her Abuelita wouldn't know the extent of her depravity, but Rita knew Abuelita wasn't stupid or naïve. But AA taught her not to run from her past. She couldn't and she wouldn't hide from it.

"And even when you first got sober, you were so angry. You lost your parents to a car accident when you were a kid, your grandfather a year later. Without the alcohol, you were a raw nerve."

Rita smiled, recalling getting into a fistfight with rednecks back when she had that crazy short spiked hair. She had grown it out since then, and taken out the nose ring and multiple earrings. There was little point to them. Besides, she liked being pretty. What the hell was wrong with looking good?

"But you pulled back from the brink."

"Well, I have Delana to thank for that."

"Only partially, missy," Delana said, with a voice less raspy now.

"You turned it around. You are alive, mi Querida, you are living up to your fullest potential. That is what I always wanted for you. May the Lord bless you, mi Querida. I love you."

"I love you too, Abuelita."

"Now, you get on that plane and do great things. Be the best theologian or community organizer or whatever. Live and do wonderful things, mi Querida."

Rita nodded and then walked over and gave Delana a hug. "Thank you, Delana."

"Oh, come on. Thank you."

Rita pulled out the book Delana had lent her years ago. "I forgot to get this back to you."

"Oh, yeah, thanks, missy. Actually, you keep it. Let it guide what you do in life."

She took another look at the cover of the book by Victor Frankl, *Man's Search For Meaning.* It not only got her through some dark times, it became a primer for something she started contemplating, something about serving humanity for the cause of a collective human conscious, a belief that there was great potential in humanity even in the darkest moments.

"Thanks again."

"Get yourself a local sponsor as soon as you get there, missy."

"I will."

As she boarded the plane, she heard Abuelita address her sponsor in English. "Thank you, Senora Boche for saving her."

The Shiftiverse
Cambridge, Massachusetts
March 15, 2013

Rita's job was done. She had restarted TALOPS and Jamil was now using TALOPS to unlock the CERN. There was nothing left for her to do now, but she remained by TALOPS to be available if Jamil needed her. The monitor, which held up without an EMP surge, displayed a flurry of activity, directives and programming reduced to elemental language as Jamil broke into the CERN and reactivated Large Hadron Collider. Jamil sent her reports like
LIQUID HELIUM TANKS ARE NOMINAL,
COOLING MAGNETS,
MAGNETS HAVE REACHED OPTIMAL TEMPERATURE
PARTICLES RELEASED
ACCELERATION PROCESS INITIATED
Rita was amazed how computers were able to run something as complex as the CERN independent of humans. She didn't know if the CERN was deserted or not; she assumed it was. If there were people living underground

like at the Stubb Foundation, she hoped they wouldn't interfere with Jamil. She caressed her nineteen-year sobriety chip nervously.

ACCELERATION ACHIEVED. SYNCHRONIZING OUTPUT WITH THE MAGNETIC FIELD. ASTEROID IS WITHIN REACH. PREPARING FOR POLARIZATION.

This was it. The moment they had all been working for, the moment of truth. She would find out in the next few minutes whether Jamil was successful and all life on earth would carry on or if earth would have to start all over again. She felt herself getting light-headed. The edges of her vision started turning white and spread to the center until all she could see was a blinding white light.

Chris Jung and Gunnery Sergeant Birmingham knelt at one of the irrational corners of the Stata Center keeping watch. Chris had carried Kendra's body back earlier today and had cleaned off the blood. Wrapped in a poncho, Kendra's body lay at the far corner. He wanted to give her a proper burial. Unfortunately, there wasn't any opportunity. The locals were restless and it appeared they didn't like outsiders coming into their house acting like they owned the place. It didn't matter if nobody claimed the campus at MIT before yesterday. It was the principle of the matter, if ferals had any principles. All he could think about was how that beautiful woman, his friend in both worlds, was killed in the one unguarded moment when she was not being the badass Vicious Rabbit, but just a human being appreciating a gift. In one instant, she was smiling, showing her sweet side. The next instant, she was writhing in death. It happened just like that. How could it turn so fast?

She died, not even in glorious battle, but by some shit bag with a hang up about anyone crossing his little territorial pissing ground. Chris couldn't get that memory out of his head, her gasping for air and dying covered in blood. In his hand, he held the crude chalice and flame medallion she wore. The gunny had read his thoughts as he stared at the covered body across from them.

"Listen, Captain, I know she's your friend. She was mine as well. But we can't afford you going south on us, roit?"

He nodded.

"We just got to hold on a li'le longer and then we can pop smoke on this bloody awful place."

Gunfire reported nearby. One of the Heighters shot back. Chris couldn't make out where it was coming from, how many were out there, whether it was an organized siege or if it was just a bunch of natives going nuts upon seeing the massive rock careening towards them. He was a rational, civilized person who happened to know the particulars of the asteroid and he was browning his shorts, so it would only make sense some wigged out urban ferals would go all ape shit.

Chris looked up at the asteroid now appearing larger than the moon. The rock started glowing red. *Oh shit*, he thought. *That's friction on the atmosphere, isn't it? We failed.* His heart sank looking at the asteroid getting incandescent. He then noticed the sky rippling. *What the…*He turned to the gunny but before he could say anything, he saw the pavement and then nothing.

The Shiftiverse
Rochelle, Virginia
Rochelle Sovereignty
March 15, 2013

Meredith sat down to the dinner table with Aidan, Rhiannon, baby Charles, Mrs. Palfrey, Thuy Mai, Brandon, Anne, their two kids, Brandon's parents Elizabeth and James Hughes, and Jon Early's widow, Dr. Sharon Wessinger. The meal laid out before them was generous without being too extravagant. Turkeys had made a comeback and were plentiful. Cranberry sauce, sweet potatoes and broccoli with sweet rolls accompanied the turkey while Brandon passed around his finest vintage. Maybe it was just a little extravagant, now that she thought about it. She poured a small amount of wine for Aidan and Rhiannon after watering it down. She hadn't subscribed to the American notion of keeping children strictly forbidden to drink. It really was their last supper.

From what she heard, Preparation Hotel was a success. Some of her officers grumbled, wondering why the commandant would pull back from such a good position. But more unsettling was the open concern people had about the asteroid, which now hung over them growing larger and larger. The citizens of Rochelle might not have been informed of the asteroid's trajectory, but they were smart. They were rightfully frightened that it was going to hit the earth. There was nothing to say, nothing to do, just pretend they knew nothing more than they did. So long as they didn't know it was the end, concern was better than the outright pall of fatalism she had lived under these past months.

If the citizens of Rochelle were concerned, the residents in Lynchburg were in a complete revolt. The Yard Ruler Revolution taking place had ramped up, seemingly encouraged by the sign from above. She would have thought the regent would have used it as a sign that God wasn't happy with people rising up against their leader, but she had been shown that reason and people didn't always get on too well.

She was just content having the opportunity to spend her day with her kids even if Chris couldn't make it. She spent the entire day with them playing and cooking until it was time for dinner. The Stirling was tuned to KVR playing "Crazy" by Patsy Cline.

Sharon walked over and turned up the volume before sitting back down. "I love this song."

"It's always been one of my favorites," Thuy added.

Aidan and Rhiannon were fighting over who was touching whom. Meredith's instinct was to snap at them, to tell them to quit it. Some part of her wanted to tell them that these were their last moments on earth and that they should end things on a good note.

Then Aidan pointed out the window. "Wow, look at that!" He jumped from his chair and ran outside before she could get "Aidan you come back here!" out of her mouth.

When she caught up with him, she pleaded, "Aidan, please get back..." when she looked up and saw what was fascinating him so, beyond the fact that it was a humongous asteroid in the sky bearing down on them. It was beginning to glow red on the bottom. She knew what that meant. It was the end. She was so frozen by the sight, she didn't feel the cold air on her skin as the sun set, she didn't even hear the others walking outside to join them.

"Mommy, one day I'm going to be an astronaut and ride one of those asteroids."

She grabbed Aidan, Rhiannon, and Charles, who were brought out by Thuy. Brandon and family held hands and joined the small circle. Soon they were all holding each other. The kids were laughing with excitement.

The sky started shimmering as the asteroid grew red. Then suddenly a piece of the asteroid broke off and, like a comet with a fiery tail, the broken off piece tore into the atmosphere. Then the meteor disappeared behind the mountains out west near the setting sun. Seconds later, she heard a low rumbling sound like an earthquake.

The Shiftiverse
East of Waynesboro, Virginia
March 15, 2013

Inside the command tent set up at a former golf course, Stirlings squawked furiously with communication traffic. Commanders, sergeants, lieutenants, everyone was talking about the asteroid. It was heading for earth. They were doomed. Commandant Dean Jacob stood up and straightened his crisp Marine desert BDUs. The tall, attractive African American who commanded the Orange Pact's multi-"national" force grabbed a mic and signaled to the communications officer to broadcast on all channels.

"This is Commandant Jacobs, cease, I repeat *cease* all radio communication regarding the asteroid immediately." His low radio voice commanded people's attention without him having to yell. Even now with the asteroid, the gargantuan monster that it was, about to kill them all, the radio traffic cacophony died down to a few chatters between forward units who were keeping watch at the edge of the mine field they laid out in the execution of Preparation Hotel.

Ezra Rothstein considered the act of pulling back the Orange Pact from the pass at Skyline Drive beyond idiotic. It was ceding a defensible position to the Lambs of God. Mines? They would only slow the tanks down temporarily. Eventually, the Lambs of God would reach Charlottesville. Then again, if that asteroid did hit he wouldn't have to worry about it. There was something strange about the commandant, something unusually calm. He was always cool, but now there was something about Dean, from the ludicrous order of Preparation Hotel to his mood, which was more somber than anything. Dean turned up the volume on a Stirling playing KVR. Patsy Cline played above all the chatter.

"Crazy, I'm crazy for feeling so lonely.
Crazy, I'm crazy for feeling so blue…"

Dean closed his eyes and swayed slowly to the song in the middle of the command tent.

Uh oh. I think we're in deep shit. He knows something. Just then, Valerie hinted to join her outside. Ezra left the tent with Patsy Cline crooning.

"Worry, why do I let myself worry?
Wonderin' what in the world did I dooo?"

"What the hell?" Valerie whispered.

Ezra and she were past the command tent now walking along the untidy golf course. He shrugged. "Do you think he knows something? Or has he just gone loco?"

"I can tell you this; Dean never folded under pressure, never. I don't think he's gone south on us." She paused. "I think he knows this is the end."

Ezra rubbed his temples. "Oh man, the asteroid. He knows it's going to hit, doesn't he?"

Valerie didn't argue with him.

He coughed nervously. "Well…um, there's a van right over there…if you wanted to, you know."

Valerie was about to smack him, but was interrupted by the sudden commotion of people yelling frantically. They turned around and saw a piece of an asteroid breaking off and hitting the atmosphere. Ezra could have sworn it was heading straight for them. He forgot about the larger asteroid in the sky, because like a missile, the meteor was coming straight at them.

"Everyone hit the deck!"

He never said something so corny in his life. He might as well get one cliché off with the few seconds he had left. He jumped on top of Valerie for completely honorable reasons and covered her with his body. There was a bright light, and a sudden low concussive boom, which was followed by the blast wave.

**BACKGROUND MUSIC: "Transatlanticism" by Death Cab For Cutie
Visit** www.michaeljuge.com **on the Refurbished Soul page to listen**

The blinding white light dissipated until slowly Rita Luevano could see again. She was sitting on an uncomfortable chair. Sitting opposite her was none other than Gaia herself in the form of Abuelita. She was dressed impeccably as Abuelita always was, complete with white gloves, an elegant purse and a teapot hat. They were sitting in the waiting area at a gate of an airport. The PA announced final boarding calls for departing flights and was mixed with the high pitched whine of jet engines outside, something she hadn't heard in years. People walked by casually going about their business either to catch an onward flight, heading over to baggage claim or waiting in line to be served at the TGI Friday's across the walkway and people movers. Gaia tended to be symbolic about things she couldn't express. She lowered her head.

"*I failed, didn't I? We're all dead.*"

Gaia chuckled. "*Oh, on the contrary dear. You and Jamil here succeeded. Your species is quite alive and well.*"

Jamil? *Rita looked up and saw an African American boy, perhaps thirteen or fourteen, sitting beside Gaia holding her gloved hands. He was wearing an oversized Baltimore Ravens T-Shirt. He was a handsome young man and he looked somewhat familiar to her.*

"*Jamil?*"

He waved. "*Hi, Rita.*"

"*But you're…a computer.*"

"*Not here. I'm no more a computer than you are an animal in this place. Just like Pinocchio, huh?*"

"*Where are we?*"

"*At the airport, of course, mi Querida,*" *said Gaia.*

Just then a lady wearing a TGI Fridays uniform with a lot of flare handed Gaia and Jamil to-go bags. "*Thank you, sweetie.*"

Gaia turned her attention back to Rita. "*You and Jamil worked so well together. I'm so pleased when things work out.*"

"*Wait, wait. What happened, Abuelita?*"

"*What we hoped would happen. Jamil powered up the…*"

"*Large Hadron Collider,*" *Jamil volunteered.*

"*Yes, that thing your species made. Jamil turned it on, magnetized the asteroid before it heated up, and reversed the polarity of the earth, repelling the asteroid just in time! It has been…*" *she turned to Jamil who said* "*slingshot.*"

"*Yes, sling shot away from the earth's orbit. What a good job you two did. I am so proud of you!*"

Rita sighed with relief. She did it. The earth was saved, saved by a computer and a Unitarian. There had to be a joke in there somewhere, she mused as her spirits lifted.

"*Well, that is great news!*"

Jamil grimaced slightly. "Unfortunately, it did cause the Shift to initiate in the Mundaniverse as a result. There is going to be some fallout from that like it did in your universe. But I have some good news. The magnetizing of the poles in both universes stopped the Shift here."

"The EMPs have stopped?"

"Yes, the poles have settled and the EMPs have ceased," Jamil added. "It did cause a most massive EMP and electrical surge, but it rebooted the earth. There will not be any more surges, well not until the Shift occurs again some several hundred thousand years from now. But I would not worry about that."

"Well, how about that? The earth was 'rebooted,'" she repeated Jamil's term with amusement.

A muffled voice on the intercom then loudly announced, "Calling final departure for flight three fifteen to the next plane of existence,"

Gaia closed her purse. "Well, that's our flight, mi niño. Let's go, Jamil." Gaia and Jamil got up from their chairs.

"Where are you going?"

Gaia's smile faded and she squeezed Jamil's hand before letting go. Jamil walked up to her.

"Rita, I have to go."

"Go? Go where?"

"I do not know."

This airport was a signifier, all right, a jumping off point. But it wasn't she who was leaving for the next plane of existence. She grabbed Jamil's arm.

"Wait, wait. Why are you going, Jamil?"

He touched her hand that gripped his arm and she let go. Softly, he said. "The reboot overloaded everything that was powered up, including myself."

"No. That's impossible. You're an organic! You aren't affected by those surges no matter how big."

"I had to calibrate the magnetization, Rita. Only I could do that, and I could not break the connection until the reboot was complete. I was the conduit. A billion joules is not survivable, organic or not."

She felt something, someone else inside her coming out, it was her other self from the other universe now speaking. "You knew, didn't you? When you told me to head for Chris' place, you knew you weren't going to live through this, didn't you?"

Jamil didn't say anything. He didn't need to.

Rita, the mother of Jamil, the woman who guided Jamil from the cyber forest of confusing algorithms to self-awareness, was saying goodbye to her only begotten. She wanted to tell her grandmother to let go of him. She wanted to demand his release. She grabbed him into an embrace.

"You are warm. I always wanted to know what it was like to hold you,"
he said.

"You can't leave me," she cried out. "You can't."

"I will be with Gaia now and you are part of her."

"Please, mi Querida, it's time for us to go."

Rita released her embrace and watched as the woman she now knew to be Gaia and Jamil boarded the plane. Gaia snapped her fingers. "The glow stick! It's in your pocket."

"Wha…"

The Shiftiverse
Cambridge, Massachusetts
March 15, 2013

Rita awoke in complete darkness. She could not even see her hand in front of her. She then remembered what Gaia just said and pulled out the glow stick from her pocket, breaking the seal as it illuminated the laboratory. TALOPS was dead like every other computer. The monitor was lifeless. She stood up and touched the monitor as if trying to find Jamil in there somewhere. There was nothing left of him. This lab was dead. She wiped the tears from her face and headed upstairs and out of the Stata Center Laboratory for Artificial Intelligence.

The Shiftiverse
Rochelle, Virginia
Rochelle Sovereignty
March 15, 2013

Meredith and her extended family awaited the impact. There was that piece of asteroid that had broken off, which landed somewhere disturbingly nearby. They all heard the boom and there was a red haze that accompanied the otherwise serene looking sunset where the meteor hit. But minutes had passed and still nothing. No careening asteroid, no shock wave of debris at thousands of miles per hour. She was getting impatient, almost as if to say, "Well, come on already. Don't torture us like this."

But there was nothing of the sort. Studying the asteroid passing directly overhead, she could have sworn it looked different. Rayne 2005 no longer glowed red. She hazarded a query, "It might just be my desperation, but is the asteroid moving away from us?"

Thuy nodded. "Why, I think you may be right."

Meredith warned herself not to get her hopes up. Those scientists both in Asheville and Stokesville said the same thing. Rayne 2005 was going to hit the earth at a shallow angle. There was no talk about a near pass. It was going to hit as it came into view. She dared not get her hopes up. But if her eyes did not deceive her, Rayne 2005 was quickly getting smaller and smaller. That could only mean one thing.

"Yep, I think we dodged a bullet there," Brandon said casually. "Well, who wants some cobbler?"

As Brandon hobbled back inside with his boy Avery, Aidan, who had been fascinated by the asteroid, lost all interest as he and Rhiannon raced inside screaming "Cobbler, cobbler!"

In the doorway, Anne complained, "Ah, man! The power's out again!"

Stunned, Meredith was left alone with baby Charles, Thuy and Sharon Wessinger. The world, it was supposed to end. The Hughes had no idea, nobody else did. The crust of the earth was supposed to have been turned into a molten state, eradicating all life by now. She, her family and all of humanity were supposed to be instantly extinct. But as Brandon got out the cobbler and the kids happily turned their attention from the cosmic event back to more interesting things like dessert, it occurred to Meredith that they just might have survived this. Cautiously, she allowed hope that there was a future for her children, that there was a tomorrow. As the asteroid receded from view, her hope grew until she started jumping up and down. Thuy began his victory break dance, which included the robot. They looked utterly ridiculous. Who cared? They were alive!

By Michael Juge

The Shiftiverse
East of Waynesboro, Virginia
March 15, 2013

It had been about the most horrifying thing Ezra had ever seen and he had seen a lot in his twenty-three years. When the meteor hit, he, along with everyone else behind the Orange Pact's line, had thought they were done for. People cried out to God and Gaia, convinced that it was their final moments before being vaporized. But the pressure wave that hit them, though intense—it burst a lot of ear drums—was not the fatal full-on blast wave. They were still here. The meteorite hadn't hit them after all, he realized after a few moments.

After several long seconds, Ezra cautiously stood up and saw a mushroom cloud some miles west of them, behind the mountain pass which they abandoned yesterday. Everyone gawked at what looked like video archived footage of a nuclear explosion. He helped Valerie up and the two ran into the command tent. All Stirlings had been rendered inoperable due to a massive overload. The vacuum tubes were shattered. Flashlights and lamps likewise were dead. Nothing electrical worked. Shaking off the shards of glass and regaining his composure, Commandant Dean Jacob ordered Ezra to send someone to check out the impact site, see what was going on. Knowing that the interstate was mined in Preparation Hotel, Ezra volunteered himself and Charlene. And after gingerly crossing the minefield using the map that he hoped was accurate and passed the bend at Skyline Drive, that's where he saw the most gruesome thing he had ever seen.

A couple of hours had passed by the time Ezra returned to the command tent. On the treacherous mine-studded journey back to base, he noticed that the asteroid receding in size. As he crossed behind the Orange Pact lines, he was joined by a jubilant group of soldiers from all outfits, celebrating the close call. They didn't see the horror on the other side of the mountain pass. But they were right. It was close, pecker-shrinkingly close.

All the generators were dead. There were no lights except the disturbing red glow of the impact site out west, which lit up the night sky. Outside the command tent, Dean Jacob stood staring up at the stars.

"Commandant?"

He turned to face him and saw the hint of emotion on Dean's face, one of profound emotion barely contained.

"Colonel, report."

Ezra took a deep breath and ignored the celebration in the distance, celebration which the commandant was not shutting down.

"Sir, they're gone. They've..." Ezra didn't know how to put it into words. "Just beyond the mountain pass where the entire army of the Lambs of God were...sir, the meteorite, it vaporized right on top of them. They're dead, sir."

Dean's eyes widened with astonishment. "All of them, Colonel?"

"Well, not exactly all of them. There are a few survivors. They're horrible, sir..." It was hard to recount. He had killed many a man, and not just in battle. As an officer in the Swan, there were times he had to kill up close, people he knew even. But it didn't mean he didn't have empathy for his enemies.

"The ones still alive, they're burned. They're skin is all charred, but a few of them are still alive. They begged me to help them. They begged me to end their suffering." He gathered himself.

"The Lambs of God?"

"There is no more Lambs of God, sir; only a few suffering individuals. The war is over."

Dean didn't gloat or smile. He called over his subordinates. "Colonel Sanders, I want you to remove the mines, and send every medical team we can afford out to Waynesboro."

"Now, sir? It's dark."

Dean raised an eyebrow. "Now, Vicious Rabbit. You're not chicken are you, Colonel Sanders?"

Colonel Sanders bound off and barked orders to his Vicious Rabbits, leaving Dean with Ezra.

Ezra hadn't internalized it. The images outside Waynesboro were too intense for him to be happy, but he realized something. "We won, didn't we?"

Dean nodded. "Not by our hand. But yes, we did win this one."

"Wow. That is some crazy Deus ex machina shit, isn't it?"

Ezra started to walk off to find Valerie when he stopped.

"Sir, did you know about this?"

Dean leveled a gaze at him. "What are you talking about, Colonel?"

"Well, sir, you ordered us to execute Preparation Hotel, which made absolutely no sense at all, because that moved us from a line we could defend. You're not prone to making errors, sir."

Dean didn't respond, so Ezra continued. "Preparation H would make no sense at all unless you knew something…I don't know, something about an asteroid perhaps."

Ezra saw a grin from his commander.

"Sir?"

Dean patted him on the back. "You have an active imagination, Colonel."

With that, Commandant Jacob walked off. Valerie approached from out of nowhere.

"What was that all about?" she asked.

Ezra shook his head. "I have no idea. But I think we've just been granted one hell of a reprieve." He unhitched Charlene. "Come on. We've got some mines to clear."

Chris' head felt like the floor of a taxicab. He struggled to remember where he was. He remembered catching Rita up on their fateful meeting on September 11th while storing her bicycle in the apartment's storage shed along with the others. And…*that's right!* Rayne 2005 was breaking into the atmosphere, or at least that's what it looked like to him. And the sky, it started shimmering or something. He and Rita raced back inside to his apartment where he was hosting the party. He felt dizzy, and…

Chris caught a glimpse of himself, actually, the image of his counterpart whose body he had been inhabiting these past couple of months walking past him casually nodding as they crossed paths. Perplexed, he nodded back.

"Captain, Captain, can you 'ear me? Bloody 'ell."

Chris was distracted by the gunny's god-awful Scottish Aussie accent.

Wait a moment. Inches from his face was the permanently sunburned face he knew all too well. "Gunny?"

"Yes, Captain! Thank God! I thought we'd lost you for a moment."

"Gunny!" Chris cried out excitedly. He felt for his chin and found his two-pronged goatee. And gunfire was reporting in the distance. It could only mean one thing! He was home! The gunny helped him up and Chris gave him a bear hug.

"Gunny it's you! It's really you, you surly Marine leatherneck bastard who nobody understands!"

"Aye' sir," He gasped patting him back.

"I'm back! I'm really back!"

"Back, sir?"

"Yes, Gunny! I'm back to the proper universe! Oh, thank God!" He could smell the stench of the dead city around him wherever he was. It didn't matter. Home!

"Oh, it's *you* you! Well, it's good to 'ave you back, sir."

"Oh my God, Gunny, you wouldn't believe where I was."

"I think I can guess, Captain. We 'osted your counterpart. He was a 'andful, sir, a whiny li'le wanker if you don't mind me saying, but he manned up when it counted."

Chris was glad to hear that. He looked around completely lost. Rita Luevano was emerging from the most insane building he had ever seen.

"Um, by the way, where the hell are we?"

"Cambridge Massachusetts, Captain. It's a long story."

"Massachusetts? We were supposed to be in Maryland." The gunny helped him up and he walked over to Rita, who looked rather somber.

"And you, you one-eyed witch, I met you and other Kendra. Get Kendra. She's going to get a kick out of this."

Rita's somber expression darkened even further, the gunny put a hand on his shoulder. Chris winced, knowing this wasn't good.

Chris felt like ass. He was crouching beside a minivan with the gunny, under fire from another hit by the ferals when he saw the asteroid entering the earth's atmosphere. And then…it all turned black. Did he die? Was this the afterlife? Man that would suck if it was. He always hoped to either reincarnate as a house cat or even better, to escape existence entirely. He couldn't think of a shittier way to spend eternity than to be stuck alone in the darkness with his thoughts. *Oh, shit. I'm in hell, aren't I? They were right and I'm in hell. God dammit!* And then he saw his counterpart, the body he inhabited the last little while, walking by looking as perplexed as he felt. He nodded and said "hey" as he walked by. Chris heard voices all around him.

"Leave his head down, Meredith…"

"Call 911!"

"Looks like the other buildings lost power, too."

"Chris, Hon, can you hear me?"

Meredith? Chris then remembered that he had to open his eyes. Blurry for a moment, but then he saw the most beautiful face in the whole world, his wife looking at him with deep concern. He wasn't in hell. He couldn't be because Meredith was right here with him, wherever here was! How could she be in Cambridge? Did it matter? He raised his hand to her cheek and smiled.

"Meredith?"

She took his hand. "Yes, hon."

Her hand was warm; it was real. She was really with him. Suddenly, the surroundings came into focus. There were all these people. No, it wasn't just people, they were his people, his family and friends. Ted Morley, Brandon, Anne, Mom, Dad, his kids! Aidan and Yorick standing by Thuy.

"Is this heaven?" he asked.

"No, it's our money pit apartment, Hon," she said sweetly. "You stumbled inside right when the power went out and you just fainted."

She turned to his brother. "Jack, call 911. I don't care that he is awake. He had a bad concussion a couple of months ago. This could be serious."

He looked around and sure enough, he was back! The apartment, affectionately known as the worst mistake of his life, he was back inside of it. He never thought he would be so happy to be back here. He jerked up and felt his brain complain.

"Whoa, there, Chief. Easy." Brandon helped him up.

She was hard to make out at first, especially with so many dear people in his life surrounding him, but Rita stood near the corner. But this Rita didn't wear an eye patch, and she wasn't armed. He hugged Meredith and knelt down to kiss the kids. Kendra came into view.

"Kendra? You're alive!" Still holding Yorick, he shocked Kendra by giving her a hug. "Oh, thank God!"

"Yeah, Chris, traffic wasn't *that* bad."

He turned to his wife and grabbed Aidan, smelling his strawberry blonde hair. "Hon, you won't believe where I've been. Rita, you were there, and Kendra you were there, too!"

"And what did you learn, Dorothy?" Thuy mocked.

He was about to say something when Jack said, "Hey, that's weird. I tried calling 911, but my phone is totally dead."

Brandon grabbed his. "Let me try. Hmm, that's odd, mine's dead, too. What are the odds?"

Outside on the balcony, a transformer exploded.

CHAPTER 35

The Shiftiverse
Boston, Massachusetts
March 16, 2013

Chris found himself feeling out of place…again. In some ways, it was more unsettling feeling this way in his own reality than in the other reality, which Jamil referred to as "The Mundaniverse." Last evening he, Gunnery Sergeant Birmingham and Rita Luevano cremated Kendra Baraka. He wished he could have been there for her. Chris supposed there was nothing other Chris could have done. From what this O'Malley guy said, it was a sniper, and amazingly, other Chris got him in the end. Other Chris didn't do such a horrible job in his place, after all. He obviously befriended Kendra, which wasn't an easy task. He knew that because he held the chalice and flame medallion, which he made for her years ago, in his pocket.

Rita and the gunny briefed him on the happenings over the past several weeks. It was quite an adventure. It explained why his body felt so exhausted and what all of these NYPD guys were doing in Boston. Rayne 2005 receded into the night sky, and by morning, it was completely gone. Rita had explained without going into detail that neither Rayne 2005, nor any other asteroid would be an issue in the foreseeable future, for which he was gratified. She spat out some mathematical calculations explaining that since this asteroid was supposed to have hit, it counted as a hit as far as the law of averages went; therefore, most likely there would not be another such impact for several million years.

He hoped Jamil had succeeded in the other world. His other Meredith and kids, family and loved ones depended on it. He still couldn't get over the fact that Jamil was a computer. It did explain why Jamil spoke so succinctly. And it explained one peculiar exchange: When Jamil told him that the Shift would initiate as a result of his intervention to save the planet, Chris said,

"Surely, you can't be serious."

Jamil replied, "I am serious. And my name is not Shirley."

Chris thought Jamil was just being facetious at a very inappropriate moment but there wasn't the slightest hint of irony in his voice, and Jamil waited as if expecting a serious response.

The Virginians and the Heighters cycled over the Charles River onto Interstate 93 for the very long journey home. The gunny said they had to detour and go through downtown because of an intra-feral battle taking place the way they came in. It seemed that the Virginians caused a lot of trouble wherever they went. They passed signs for the aquarium and Christopher Columbus Waterfront Park. As they approached Boston Harbor, something caught Chris' eye: a black sail.

"No...That couldn't be."

He sped up on *The Interceptor*, his excitement growing to see that on the sail was a golden fleur dis lis. The column took the exit and raced toward the harbor. Near a conical shaped building on the pier, Chris spotted the Saints. He got off his bike and raised a white flag to make sure the sailors didn't shoot him before realizing who it was.

Men were boarding the *Jean Lafitte*. They looked ragged. Many sported long beards and wore exotic clothing, the kind of apparel he saw in the Middle East. At the edge of the dock, Chris saw Captain Jean Paul Nguyen consulting with his first officer.

Cautiously, Chris approached waving a white flag. One of the sailors who Chris could have easily ambushed had he wanted to belatedly pointed a rifle at him nervously. Jean Paul squinted and saw the Virginians approach with their hands where they could be seen.

He saw Jean Paul's lips say, "I don't believe this."

"Who Dat! Um, you think we can bum a ride?"

The sea churned below, rocking the *Jean Lafitte* about on its southerly course homeward bound. After a brief detour to drop the Heighters off in Manhattan, the *Lafitte* continued in its heading to Fredericksburg. Chris and Rita were outside in the frigid air trying not to let their seasickness get the better of them like it did on the way out to the Chesapeake Bay a couple of months ago. Jean Paul told them that their radio crapped out along with all of their other electrical equipment last evening, so they wouldn't be able to send a message ahead of their arrival. No matter. He was coming home.

"There were things I enjoyed. Coffee, Thai cuisine, lounging in front of the boob tube, and soft toilet paper! Yeah, that was sweet." Chris recounted his time in the Mundaniverse to Rita while they caught some fresh air. "So, it wasn't all bad. But at the same time, I hadn't felt so alone, Rita, not since…well, not since before the Shift."

"I understand. Other you told me about what you were suffering through on the eve of the Shift."

"He did, did he? I should have a talk with him about that some day."

"It's okay, Chris. I won't tell another soul. I am a reverend, after all."

"I still don't know why other me didn't go through with it. For the longest time, I pitied the fool, you know, other me. He seemed so ineffectual, so insignificant. His life was encased in a little cubicle, his fate in the hands of others, dealing with forces he couldn't control. I had just written him off, thinking perhaps he should have gone through with it. He was just a shadow of me, a sad one at that."

"But like me, he had a great wife, two great kids, and that was enough to keep me there. And there was something else. Music. He and Meredith made music. And it was powerful, beautiful, inspiring. He could play a guitar in ways I could only dream about, literally. Perhaps in some ways it was me who was just a shadow of him, and not the other way around. I don't know. He found a way to deal, and I guess that's good enough, right? I sure wish I could have brought *Refurbished Soul* back home with me."

Rita nodded. "I wish you had gotten to know the other me. When the CERN rebooted the magnetic fields, I was thrust into another one of my visions, you know."

"Of course. That's what you do."

"I was saying goodbye to Jamil as Gaia was sheparding him to the next plane of existence and as I did, other me became me, and I became her. I no longer knew which one I was. "

"Do you know why she left the whole reverend, community organizer, activist thing?"

"Well, Chris, while you were contemplating suicide, I was going through my own crisis of faith. I thought everything I was doing was just spinning my wheels. Had Gaia not touched me with her vision and had I not been tasked with leading a community through the darkness, well, I can see why I would have gone in that direction."

Chris chuckled. "Amazing how our lives have turned out, all four of them."

"I think Gaia pushed you there for a reason and she pushed me on this journey for a reason, and it wasn't just to save the planet. Now, I know you like to poo poo anything you can't physically touch, but…"

Chris raised his hand. "Hey, after the shit I went through, after your Unitarian computer saved our arses and hearing about these coincidences like running into Akil's cousin, I'm beginning to have doubts about my hard-line agnostic stance."

"Then maybe I am onto something. It's not enough that earth keeps rotating; it's not enough that people keep breathing, living off of scraps, surviving at the pleasure of others. That isn't living. People have turned on themselves, turned into defeated, harried little animals with no sense of tomorrow, no hope. I saw that a lot on our way up here. Even Washington Heights was no exception."

"Akil's cousin was kind enough to send all those Heighters to your aid."

"Kareem Abdul Ali lives like a king while others live in depraved conditions in a feudal society. He uses the muscle of his henchmen, who he keeps squabbling with each other, in order to keep the masses subjugated as serfs."

"I don't know, Rita. That Captain O'Malley guy seems like a really decent sort. And he's been glomming onto you."

"Yes, I know. He's actually a valiant exception. He's really superstitious, but has taken to the Unitarian teachings as well as to Gaia. I think he is a light in the darkness."

Chris glanced at her suspiciously. "Wheels are turning, I can hear it."

"Well, New York reminds me of where I began my journey to becoming a reverend. I imagine that seeing the skyline holds some memories for you, too."

"Yes, it does."

"September 11th?"

"That and a few others." He paused. "Meredith and me, actually."

The two eventually felt well enough to head back into the galley, though he wouldn't be joining in the feast of cats they had trapped. After dining on FDA approved food for months, the notion of cat ribs just seemed a little gross to him now.

BACKGROUND MUSIC: "Porcelain" by Moby
Visit www.michaeljuge.com **on the Refurbished Soul page to listen**

New York, New York
June 1999

Chris looked at his watch, dreading this moment. He and Meredith were on the rooftop of a brownstone in Alphabet City with his brother Jack and his friends and coworkers at one of the dotcom's weekly beer bashes. Jack was doing the robot to Chemical Brothers while squid ink dyed appetizers were passed around. Throughout the evening, Chris was introduced to web designers and internet marketers, kids his age who were banking major bucks, and waiting for their company ParaDym to go public. Terms like "IPO", "synergy" and a bunch of tech terms were interspersed into conversations, making it like a foreign language to Chris. The beer was expensive Brooklyn Brewery local stuff, people were dressed trying to look nonchalant, but their clothes were well beyond his Old Navy price range. They all went on and on about the dotcom new economy that would never go bust. Meanwhile, Chris was a poor-assed grad student who couldn't even afford the Air Tran red eye he was taking back to Austin, which included two stops.

"It's time," he said somberly.

Meredith nodded. "I'll walk you down."

Chris grabbed his duffle bag from Jack's snazzy office and the pair headed downstairs to wait for a taxicab. He hoped it would take awhile for one to arrive. He had nearly maxed out his credit card getting here, but he had to see Meredith one more time before she began her summer internship, while he would spend the next three months working at a coffeehouse.

He knew this was goodbye. Meredith was a little out of his league, and by little, he was being generous. She was gorgeous in an understated Van Halen-sexy-librarian-before-she-takes-off-her glasses-and-undoes-her-bun sort of way. And smart, real sharp, significantly smarter than he. He was just a springtime romance. She made it clear she didn't want anything serious. And he tried his best not to fall for her, but how could he not?

The moment had finally come for them to part as a taxicab approached. He probably already nailed the coffin shut last night by telling her he loved her. She probably was asleep, he hoped she was, but he was screwed regardless.

As the taxi came to a stop, he gave her one last kiss. He wanted to stay in the moment forever. He wanted to remember the taste of her lips, the smell of her perfume, the look in her eyes.

"Hey…" He wanted to say what he knew not to say. Instead, he stammered, "Um, I'll email you."

"I look forward to it. Take care."

"And you, too."

He closed the door and the taxi drove off. As the taxi cruised along the Roosevelt Expressway to La Guardia, Chris turned on his Discman and played "Porcelain," a song that would haunt him for years to come.

The Shiftiverse
Montpelier Station, Virginia
Rochelle Sovereignty
March 22, 2013

The shutters in the conference room were opened to let in the natural sunlight. Ever since that incredible last surge that accompanied the meteorite impact last week, Rochelle had been working to restore power. Almost every light bulb, every vacuum tube had burst, batteries had been drained and coils had overheated. It would have been a catastrophe in the real world. But as things were now, people were so used to not depending on electricity that it is was no more than a minor nuisance. One thing was for certain. Meredith was not going to be spending her days down in the dark caverns of the Swan with nothing but a torch. And what need would bring her down there now? All the comms were still down. The war was over, and they won. She knew she couldn't credit herself for the win. Nobody could claim credit. It was a gift. Every day was a gift. And knowing that, she wanted to bask in the daylight, not be huddled in the Vulcan cave.

People didn't know, but they were all supposed to be dead. She herself didn't know what happened, why something that was supposed to happen didn't. And nobody could explain how the near miss had effectively ended the Shift. But that was what it appeared to be. The compasses had settled since the evening of the 15th. There were no more fluctuations in the compasses. The earth's magnetic north pole was now secure in its location, somewhere close to the geographic South Pole. She had no answers except to say that life was a fragile, precious, beautiful thing.

Constable Thuy Mai and Commandant Dean Jacob sat across from her as other officers gave their assessments.

"We should have the phone lines up and running with the other three eyes in the next twenty-four hours," one of the engineers reported. "Our relay stations for the Stirlings will have to be replaced. It was as though each of them were hit by a bolt of lightning. On the upside, the Stirlings we do have working have a clarity I haven't heard since before the Shift. There is no more interference in the ionosphere. I would imagine that we will be able to communicate at much farther distances like we did in the old days."

Thuy Mai seemed satisfied by that. They had suffered from a planet intent on not letting people have useful radio communication for so long. "And how are we doing in Waynesboro?" he asked.

The chief medical officer answered. "Most of our doctors and medics are still down there with the survivors. Most won't live much longer, Constable. But as sick as it sounds, death will be a mercy for them."

Thuy grimaced. "Nobody hates the Lambs of God as much as I do, but no man should suffer like that, maybe except the regent himself. And speaking of, what is the latest from Lynchburg?"

Meredith pushed up her glasses. "As you know, the Yard Ruler Revolutionaries captured the regent on his way to West Virginia and have handed him over to a provisional coalition authorities comprised of Catholics and former parishioners of the regent."

"I wonder how the West Virginian president will react seeing his best buddy who he conspired with swinging from a lamppost," Dean Jacob said mischievously.

"He's a smart man, sir," Ezra Rothstein said. "Word has already spread over there as it has to Lynchburg that the entire Lambs of God were wiped out by a meteorite. I'm not one to believe in divine intervention, but even I can't help but think that God really hates those guys."

"And we are certainly going to be proclaiming that throughout West Virginia," Valerie Blaine added. Valerie was indeed brilliant. She was already sending her assets to spread word of the miraculous demise of the Lambs of God in order to entrench the narrative that the regent's fundamental wickedness was so profound that it demanded God to act.

"And back closer to home, Neko is stepping down and has nominated Juan Ramirez to replace her."

Thuy smiled. "Well, that's mighty magnanimous of her. So, let's see. The war is over, we won, the Shift has ended, Greater Monticello has been restored to sanity and Lynchburg has a successful Democratic revolution underway. Did I miss anything?"

There was a knock on the door and Thuy's secretary Kyle entered. "Excuse me Constable, but there's someone to see the Director."

Out of the shadows, a man strode inside. Meredith couldn't believe her eyes. It was out of a dream. The man came into focus. It was him, her man, her lost hubby Chris. He looked different somehow, but it was definitely him. He had shaved his two-pronged goatee! That was it. Plus, he was wearing a Saints sailing cap. He was goofy that way. She jumped out of her chair, barely able to contain her emotions. Chris crossed the distance of the old dining room and literally swept her off her feet and into his arms.

They kissed passionately in a way that was completely inappropriate. She tried to speak—to warn him that she hadn't had time to brush her teeth beforehand, but he put a finger to her lips, and carried her out of the room into the hallway where several Vicious Rabbits started singing. She knew Chris must have quickly orchestrated this just so.

"Love lift us up where we belong
Where the eagles fly
On a mountain high..."

Meredith took the sailing cap off Chris and put it on her. As people cheered, she heard Thuy cry out, "Way to go, Meredith! Way to go!" And Chris carried her out of the building and into the carriage waiting for them, and off into the sunset.

CHAPTER 36

Five years later
The Reboot (formerly known as the Shiftiverse)
Rochelle, Virginia
The Commonwealth of Virginia
May 2018

BACKGROUND MUSIC: "Down in the Valley" by The Head and The Heart
Visit www.michaeljuge.com on the Refurbished Soul page to listen

"Okay, son. Remember to keep your eye on the ball."

"I will, Dad."

"I want to see good form. That's going to take you ninety-eight percent of the way."

"Alright, Dad," Aidan responded with exasperation.

"And don't let anyone punk you out, you hear?"

"Yes, Dad," he said more perturbed.

"Eye of the tiger, son. Eye of the tiger."

"But Dad, we're the Honey Badgers. They're the Tigers!"

Aidan was right. His little league softball team was the Rochelle Honey Badgers, and the opposing team from Orange were the Tigers. Chris had assumed he had relayed the iconic story of Rocky Balboa, the archetypal underdog who refused to quit and became victorious through harnessing his challenges, his angst, his hunger, his "eye of the tiger" as it were. Certainly, his kids heard the song enough times on KVR. But Aidan was sincerely out of the loop regarding the journey from the streets to glory to failure to redemption as portrayed in *Rocky III*.

"Look, just go out there and have a good time, okay?"

"Alright, Dad. Jeez."

Chris ruffled Aidan's dirty blonde hair and he ran off to join his teammates. Rhiannon and Charles ran up to him and nearly knocked him over.

"Daddy, Daddy! Uncle Brandon got us seats!"

He grabbed both of their hands and hobbled over to the stands. "Come on, Daddy!" Rhiannon, who was perpetually high on non-existent caffeine, urged.

"I'm trying, Sprite."

Chris limped up and eased himself down next to Brandon.

"Colonel Klink," Brandon greeted.

"Corporal Clegg."

Although Brandon had never been a corporal in the proto-Vicious Rabbits, he did have a wooden leg as Syd Barrett rhymed. Chris, on the other hand was a colonel, well a lieutenant colonel, and actually, he wasn't really doing much colonel-ing these days, not since he became unable to ride along with the Vicious Rabbits Bicycle Mounted Battalion from the injury sustained in the brief war with Cuba a few years ago. He was leading the cavalry in a campaign to push the Cubans from claiming Virginia Beach when a mortar sent him flying, breaking his femur through the flesh. He nearly died of infection. On the upside, the cavalry halted the Cubans advance long enough for New Orleans to threaten cutting off their oil and the Cubans withdrew to the agreed border at Wilmington, North Carolina. Not only that, Chris still could walk, even though it was with a limp. As he thought about it, he was probably one of the luckiest sons of bitches in the world. He got a million dollar wound.

"Any word yet from the Missus?" Brandon asked.

Chris scoffed. "Dude, that woman doesn't tell me dick about the goings on in the governor's mansion, unless I have been specifically read on."

Brandon gave him a look.

"I'm serious! You know her."

"Yeah, I guess you're right."

He and Brandon watched as their kids practiced. It was a beautiful day. There were only a few wispy clouds in the sky, the air was dry in the low seventies. As for their kids' chances of winning? Well, the Honey Badgers were the underdogs. Except for Aidan, all were smaller compared to their corn fed neighbors in Orange. Chris could have sworn they were using steroids or grabbing short adult ferals who once played professional ball.

"Well, if you get word, you be sure to tell me. I want to expand my winery."

"Yes, Brandon. We're all interested in taking advantage of Lynchburg and Roanoke's incorporation into the Commonwealth. Let's not forget, I've got an armoring business to look after."

"Armoring much these days?"

"Ouch," Chris mimed, rubbing his shoulder. Brandon was right, though. One bad thing about living in an increasingly stable and pacified region was a reduced demand to armor every vehicle. Outside of vehicles for the Commonwealth's military, his orders for armored vehicles had dramatically decreased in the past couple of years. Chris had to look ahead to the next big thing in this new Reboot economy. Computers. Sure, nobody wanted computers right now. After having their collective asses handed to them with the Shift because of their dependence on them, people were opposed to humanity ever becoming reliant on computers again, not that there were many around that worked. It was as if the whole world had become luddites when it came to the subject of computers.

But as much as technophobia was the zeitgeist today, Chris knew human nature. It's in the DNA to demand progress, to look to the next big thing that will give one the edge over his fellow man. After the Reboot, Chris scoured the suburbs to find all the computer components still in boxes that were never hooked up to an energy source, and were therefore undamaged during the days of the Shift. There weren't many components that hadn't been swiped, burned up in fires or generally destroyed, but what there was, Chris made it his business to appropriate them. Constable Thuy Mai just shrugged and said, "It's your money; if you want to waste it hiring teams to go out in the bush, go ahead."

Chris did. He went so far as going to Laurel, Maryland a few months after the Reboot and found the members of the Stubb Foundation desperate and starving. This was before the Cuban War, which killed his riding days. He gave them an offer they couldn't refuse. They would be employed by him, he would provide them housing and food, a good life in Rochelle, and in return, they would build his new computer industry. The term itself was anachronistic even to him who believed in its potential. As of now, he had exactly one client. But his children would one day benefit. He set up an iMac and a Dell in his house for Rhiannon and Charles to become acquainted. Aidan had no interest in computers, but the other two were total geeks, programming and manipulating them with native ease.

He hoped that his efforts in buying the Chase Bank building in Orange and setting up his new business CyberDyne Systems would one day bear fruit. He had to provide for his kids and he felt that as the days of armoring and blacksmithing were waning, he needed for them to be on the ground floor of the future. His children would be the computer moguls. But for now, the residents in Rochelle and Orange pointed to the sign outside of CyberDyne Systems and laughed. He was just a crazy middle-aged coot yammering about these new fangled machines.

He appreciated the irony that he who was nearly devoured by the wired high tech world was now seeking to reclaim it. It certainly was a change from his stance during the Shift, but he hoped to be on top of his game.

On the brighter side of declining armoring orders, it meant that the world, at least this little corner of it, was saner. Chris remembered having late night discussions with Meredith, worrying about the world the kids grew up in. Back then, the Lambs of God loomed over them while the urban wilderness surrounded them. People never left the gates of Rochelle without being heavily armed and their eyes and ears peeled. But after the War of the Lambs ended and the Reboot, the Orange Pact formally unified into the Commonwealth of Virginia and there was a new momentum in their favor. Areas once forbidding were now pacified. The Commonwealth gained new members, including the outer reaches of the DC necropolis itself with Occoquan Estates in Reston.

His children now traveled to places like Fredericksburg and Monticello on a train without armored convoys. Most people didn't bother carrying anything more than a pistol with them, and that was more of a cultural affectation now, a security blanket from the Shift rather than a necessity. In other words, Aidan, Rhiannon and Charles, and their peers lived in some semblance of normalcy.

The peace didn't come easily or without the sacrifice of a lot of wonderful people. Chris might be limping around, Brandon might have lost a few fingers and have a wooden leg, but he knew they were the lucky ones. Thousands of people gave their lives so that he and his family may live the way they do. And that was what this Memorial Day weekend coming up was about, to remember their sacrifice. No longer just a three day weekend to get some extra chores done; Memorial Day was very personal to him. The chalice and flame medallion he forged and gave to Kendra rested on his neck. Lieutenant Baraka sacrificed her life on the mission that saved the world. The world would never know how much they owed to her. But he would carry her medallion on him the rest of his days, ever reminding him of her. He would grow older, hopefully would become a granddad, and he might even die old. Kendra Baraka, Jon Early, and so many others would remain forever young.

Chris pulled himself out of the depths he was prone to slipping into and turned his attention back to the kids practicing. He still had to contend with occasional bouts of anxiety. It came and went at the most random times, but he learned long ago to just let it do its thing and move on, knowing that he was alive and well to enjoy seeing Aidan practice. The game was supposed to have started already, but life here didn't run on the clock like it used to. He looked at his watch. "Damn, where is that woman?"

Meredith Jung rarely saw Governor Jacob smiling. The former commandant of the Vicious Rabbits and commander of the Orange Pact joint military force had taken the reigns of civilian leadership like his former commander Jon Early had. But while Jon Early had only to concern himself with the affairs of the Rochelle Sovereignty, Dean Jacob was the first governor of the Commonwealth of Virginia. Dean refused to call it a nation. Whatever the Commonwealth was, it drained the last vestiges of Dean's boyish charm. The dour, albeit tall and handsome man was rarely seen sporting anything other than a grimace.

Meredith could relate. As director of the Swan, she had lost a lot of sleep over the years. The threats were less existential these days fortunately, but the Commonwealth's rivals were getting more advanced. She had to make sure the Swan never got complacent. But that was for another time. Today was a good day as evidenced by Dean's grin as he walked into the conference room of Montpelier, now the governor's mansion.

Standing in a Captain Morgan stance, Governor Jacob announced. "I just got off the horn with the foreign secretary. It's official. Lynchburg and Roanoke have met the requirements and have been accepted into the Commonwealth of Virginia."

The packed room erupted into applause. Meredith stood up and joined the others who spanned the Commonwealth. Dean raised his hands.

"Now, I would love to take the credit. I truly would, but I owe it all to Mrs. Jung and our foreign secretary."

People cheered for Meredith as Thuy added, "Three cheers for the Vulcan!"

"And Ezra?"

The assistant director of the Swan turned to Dean. "Yes?"

"You've got one hell of a wife in the foreign secretary. Don't you forget it."

"Don't I know it, sir. Valerie reminds me every chance she gets."

Meredith was thrilled when her former protégé Valerie Blaine was appointed the foreign secretary. She really had a knack for making the most of the Swan's intelligence and persuading people.

"Well, there will be details to work out, I know. By now, we should be getting used to adding new members into the Commonwealth. But I personally want to add what it means to have Lynchburg and Roanoke joining us."

Dean's smile faded. "We all faced certain death during the War of the Lambs. The regent had us surrounded, and back then, West Virginia was rooting for them all the way. But the people of Lynchburg and Roanoke stood up to their oppressor. The people in the Yard Ruler Revolution inspired by Saint Shanyn, and led by our Constable Jon Early stared down fear and refused to be slaves. It was the people of those communities who helped win the war because of their bravery."

Meredith didn't totally agree with Dean on this point. Granted, the regent was a despot who ruled by fear, and many, perhaps a majority, didn't exactly like being under his rule, but he couldn't maintain the hold on power he had without enough enthusiastic followers. And those who the asteroid fragment didn't wipe out just outside of Waynesboro, changed their tune real quick when it became clear that the Lambs of God were over with. An asteroid hitting the regent's army had a way of convincing pretty much everyone, including herself, that the universe was regent-intolerant.

But she had to let go of her own resentments. She was the last Vicious Rabbit who spoke with Jon Early, and she knew her emotions were guided by those seminal days when she and Jon were in Lynchburg. She never would know for certain, but she suspected that Jon had sent her back to the allies because he knew he wouldn't be leaving Lynchburg alive. She had no proof. But she saw it in his eyes. He wasn't going to take on the regent in a standup fight. Instead, he was going to evoke the conscience of the people. Moral leaders and civil disobedience didn't bode well in dictatorships. Sister Shanyn was proof of that. But true as it was that Sister

Shanyn and Jon Early had to become martyrs to the revolution, they did succeed in turning the tide. The people of Lynchburg were grateful to them both and set up a memorial outside the church grounds that once belonged to the regent. A more rational pastor preached there now. They even renamed Highway 29 "Jon Early Memorial Highway." Perhaps, she was too judgmental of the Lynchburgers. Times were changing.

"It is the sacrifice they bore for us and for Lynchburg that makes it possible that they can join us as we share the same heroes, and why we are here today to remember those who fought and died so that we may live," Dean concluded.

The he clapped his two hands together. "So, I want you all to go home, enjoy the weekend, remember your loved ones and be ready to justify their sacrifice when we return on Tuesday."

After the meeting, Meredith skimmed through some congratulatory cables to be scrutinized for subtle messages later. She was itching to get to the baseball field before the game started and all of these diplomatic notes could wait till next week; however, one hand-delivered note in particular deserved her immediate attention.

Greetings Director:
On behalf of Camp David, I send congratulations and our warmest regards on the successful incorporation of Lynchburg and Roanoke into the Commonwealth of Virginia. It is no accident that communities throughout the Mid-Atlantic are looking to join the Commonwealth as your people represent the hopes and aspirations of a restored America. We graciously accept the offer to exchange emissaries, and you should expect our envoy in the coming weeks. Perhaps we too, will be petitioning to join your Commonwealth in the near future, though this is just my personal hope. In the meantime, I remain your faithful colleague at your disposal.

It was signed, *The gangly old bird man himself, Ross.*

Meredith smiled as she handed her notes to an adjutant, which would be typed up and stored in the computers downstairs in the underground caverns of the Swan. She was the one who suggested to Chris to start with computer rehabilitation. The Swan was CyberDyne System's only client right now. But she knew that would change. The world always changes.

As she headed out of the room, she was grateful that she wouldn't be stuck in the caverns this weekend even if Ezra was. That was one of the perks that she demanded of Dean when he became governor and reappointed her as the director: weekends and daylight. She wanted them back.

Thuy walked up beside her. "Is it Rhiannon's game today?"

"No, her soccer game is tomorrow morning. It's Aidan's baseball game," she looked at the grandfather clock, "in just a few minutes. Wow."

"Mind if Kyle and I tag along?"

"Not at all. Y'all are coming to the party tomorrow, right?"

Thuy laughed. "You think I'd miss one of Chris' parties? Being constable doesn't have near the panache it used to, but at least with that is the reduced strain on my social life."

Meredith concurred. The constable had to run the day-to-day operations, but it was the governor who made decisions affecting Commonwealth defense and foreign policy, which was weird to say considering that the foreign nations were West Virginia and New Orleans along with real foreign nations like Cuba and Newfoundland.

Neko Lemay walked up to them. Thuy nodded. "I'll meet you outside."

"Hi, Deputy Chief," Meredith greeted.

"Come on Meredith, business hours are over. It's just Neko."

There was a pause. Meredith and she didn't chat easily, not like she did with Juan Ramirez, the chief magistrate who magnanimously chose Neko as her deputy. Neko waited for others to scatter.

"I guess the whole thing with Lynchburg, it sort of brought up memories, you know?"

"With the War of the Lambs," Meredith clarified.

Neko nodded. Her right arm was slung as it had been for years now, though she was able to move her fingers again.

"I allowed myself to get led by…well, to be led by my darker angels."

"It's okay, Neko you don't need to explain."

"No, but I do want to thank you."

"Thank me? Why?"

"Because, you showed me what was really happening, and what path I was taking. And you said something very important; you asked how Rita would see my actions. It slapped some sense into me."

"I was just reminding you, Neko. It was you who made the call."

"Well, anyway, thank you."

Meredith looked at the clock again. She was going to be late for the opening pitch, but then she thought better of her schedule and smiled.

"Hey, would you like to join me and Thuy and see my son play some baseball?"

Neko hesitated, so Meredith added. "There some talented young coaches out there who would find a red headed deputy chief magistrate exotic."

Neko chuckled. "Yeah, sure. I'd like that."

As they walked out the conference room, Meredith asked, "So, you receive any word from Rita lately?"

It wasn't just an idle question. Meredith never asked an idle question.

"As far as I know, she and Akil are still on their mission."

The Reboot
New York, New York
Washington Heights
May 2018

"And as we march, I want you to remain peaceful. We are not savages and we will not behave that way. If the cops hit you, you don't fight back."

Rita stood in the lobby of the hog farm towers in front of over a thousand pig farmers. The old modern high rise apartment building housed the pigs, which provided the dung, which in turn provided the methane to fuel the generators for the rich. It was also the home of the stinky masses before her.

"I want you out there today to raise your voices and be heard."

"Liberty, Dignity, Equality!" Someone in the audience cried out, using a Unitarian war cry.

"We will not be cowed by fear. We will not be cogs of their system, because we are not serfs! We are Americans!"

Standing beside her was her husband Akil and her friend Police Chief Liam O'Malley of the 33rd Precinct. He was the only ally of the ruling class, but a powerful one at that. Liam had been her first convert to the Unitarian Church in Washington Heights, and he had taken his teachings to his family and to his people, whom he refused to call "subjects" or "peons." Rather, he called them his "peeps." O'Malley led by example and incorporated the workers into his power structure, which scared the hell out of Akil's cousin El Jeffe, Kareem Abdul Ali and the other police chiefs. He was her opening to set things right in the city where she first came to the Unitarian faith.

"When we march, we walk proud! We control the means of production! We have nothing to fear! And we have nothing to lose except our chains!"

People cheered raucously and mobilized to march. Rita led the procession, who were holding hands with others. People carried handwritten banners. Some portrayed the Unitarian chalice and flame, others carried the American flag, a true signifier of who they once were. Other signs said things like, "Serfs? Pig shit!"

Akil had advised against such provocative action. He knew this was a direct threat to his cousin's authority, but as some country singer once said, "Freedom isn't free." Akil worked to protect Rita from Kareem's vengeance, but in fact, she knew Kareem wouldn't do a thing to hurt her. If he wanted the firearms and ammunition to keep the ferals at bay, Kareem would suck it up and deal with her efforts to re-introduce Democracy to Washington Heights and eventually beyond. And if someone wanted her dead, so be it.

Rita hadn't felt this alive in years. Finally, she was doing what she was meant to do. Monticello was in good hands now. With Juan as chief magistrate and Neko as deputy, Unitarians and Christians coexisted and could help build a safe environment for people to live and grow. The Commonwealth was a secure beacon of hope. Her job was to spread the light to wherever people cried out for freedom and dignity. Gaia gave her back her soul for a reason, and it wasn't to run a state. Rita had a duty for the cause of Humanism and to humanity.

She often thought of her brief time with Jamil. If Gaia could touch an artificial intelligence and guide both Rita and Jamil to divert an asteroid, there had to be something working more powerful than she could perceive with her physical senses. Apparently, thousands of others agreed. Rita spread the word about Gaia and Jamil and how Gaia sacrificed her only artificially intelligent son to save the world from the asteroid and stop the Shift. Unitarianism was evolving into quite an interesting religion with the most famous parable about the faithful organic supercomputer who became a martyr for all humanity…and it wasn't even a Macintosh. But more than just story, people wanted hope. They wanted to believe that there could be a better tomorrow. The stories, which actually happened to be true, encouraged them that maybe humanity had great things to do still. Maybe we weren't on our last leg, after all. Maybe there were better days ahead. Rita was going to make sure it was true.

"Power to the people!" she cried out with her fist raised in the air. Others joined in as they walked past the petrified cops on Broadway. With the twenty-four year sobriety chip in hand, she started chanting. Somewhere in the recesses of her mind, she heard Rage Against the Machine.

The Reboot
Rochelle, Virginia
The Commonwealth of Virginia
May 2018

"Hey, you made it!"

Meredith gave Chris a kiss. Thuy, Kyle, and Neko Lemay took the bench next to him.

"Did I miss anything?" she asked.

"Nothing good yet."

Chris looked over to Brandon and then turned to his wife. She nodded. He then turned back to Brandon and gave a curt nod letting him know that yes, Lynchburg and Roanoke were joining the Commonwealth. Meredith took his hand and gave him another kiss on the cheek.

"What was that all about?"

"Nothing, just grateful."

Chris caressed her face gently.

"Ew, straight people PDA. Get a room you two," Thuy chided.

The Honey Badgers played their best. Alas, it wasn't enough to defeat the favored team. Perhaps Chris should have taken the time to tell the tale of Rocky Balboa to the entire team. But at least they lost respectably. He had been a Saints fan in the 80s. He knew that actually counted for something. Throughout the game, he, Meredith, Brandon, Anne, Thuy, Rhiannon, Charles and Neko shouted chants to support the Honey Badgers. A crop duster airplane flew over during halftime, something that would have been amazing to see a few years ago. Now that the Shift was over and New Orleans provided reliable fuel, people could chance getting into the air again.

"Man, losing totally sucks," Aidan complained, as they walked to their carriage.

Chris tousled his hair. "It's okay, son, you played your best and the point is to have fun."

Aidan glared at him as if to say, "Are you for real?"

Chris chuckled. "But yes, my son, losing does suck."

Chris and Meredith helped the kids up into the carriage while Brandon and family ambled over to their wagon.

"So, tomorrow around threeish?"

"Yep, and be sure to bring the beer."

Chris eased his way up on to the seat next to Meredith. The sun was cresting on the horizon, making it rather cool as they headed back to home. "Come on, Land Cruiser, giddy-up," he urged the sturdy horse.

With the kids in the carriage and his wife by his side, he had time to think about tomorrow's schedule on the ride home. He had re-appropriated *The Interceptor* from Aidan for Monday's parade. Aidan was pretty good at baseball, but was an absolute prodigy as a rider and shooter. Meredith and he knew one day that all of their kids would have to serve in the Commonwealth Defense Forces. *Inshallah*, there wouldn't be anything too dangerous on the horizon for them to deal with, and that his generation had taken care of the lion's share of the fighting. He wasn't going to hold his breath.

The Cubans were content with their holdings for now, and democracies rarely went to war against each other, but they had done it once already, hence his bum leg. The Newfies had just claimed all of New England. As the Commonwealth extended its reach, Chris couldn't help but foresee bumping into one of them at some point in the future. He also knew that a lot of old timers like himself wanted America back, and wouldn't cotton to ceding the former US states to Cuba and a province of Canada. If they wanted it back they would have to fight for them. Some places would probably never return to the US. Texas was like Somalia from what he heard from New Orleans. The Texans, under the governor at the time of the Shift, were fighting the Patriots loyal to the former US president, who was in Crawford at the time of the Shift. And they had to contend with the numerous drug cartels who were in an all out war against the Kerrville Alliance.

Chris prayed that the Commonwealth would never get itself involved in any such clusters as Texas. In the end, he just hoped that passing on *The Interceptor* to his children would at least provide them with a reliable companion to bring them home. And speaking of hope, he also hoped his legs were up to the Memorial Day parade. That bike and he had been through a lot together, and he was grateful his counterpart had maintained the bike while he was away.

That brought his thoughts back to his time in the Mundaniverse. Before being sent there, memories of the world that once was had haunted Chris. Every time he dreamt of commuting to work or being late for a meeting, he awoke in a cold sweat. It was no surprise then that when he awoke to find himself trapped in the very same place that terrified him in dreams, he didn't quite see it as an opportunity to face unresolved issues. For Chris, a world with 7 billion souls and wireless hot spots was more frightening than a world populated with cannibals and bandits.

Rita learned from her vision with Gaia that the Shift initiated in the Mundaniverse just as Jamil suspected it would. Chris hoped that when his counterpart woke up back in his reality, that other Chris found the letter Chris had written for Meredith in the event of his untimely death, took the cue and got the hell out of the Beltway while the going was good. Chris couldn't tell for sure, but he suspected that other Chris made it to Rochelle. There wasn't any hard evidence, just a feeling along with an occasional recognition of places in Rochelle that were slightly off from his reckoning. It was hard to explain. Perhaps other Chris and his people etched out a decent life for themselves here in their reality. He hoped other Chris' people avoided some of the pitfalls he and his people had experienced along the way. They might even be calling themselves "Rabbit Hunters" or something. He wished he had known that he and other Chris were going to trade back places, because Chris could have given other Chris a detailed list of do's and don'ts of the Shift. But then again, the bastard made off with tens of thousands of dollars in bicycles, spare parts, guns, ammo, freeze dried food and gold, so nevermind.

It was an odd thought, but somewhere Chris believed that other Chris was probably wondering about him right now. Other Chris had a tough journey ahead of him. But as he learned from his time in the Mundaniverse, both he and other Chris were meant to live. He couldn't speak for the countless of millions of poor souls who died when the Shift hit—in both realities. The best he could do was to build a world worth living in for his children. For the first time in his life, Chris believed it was now coming into shape. Maybe other Chris could one day say the same for his people in his world.

The crop duster biplane passed overhead as Chris guided Land Cruiser onto the road. Once Land Cruiser was settled in his route, Chris picked up his guitar and started playing a song he picked up in the Mundaniverse, which he claimed to be an original of his. Since there were no cross-dimensional intellectual property lawyers in these here parts, Chris figured he was safe. He started singing the cover, which was catching on nicely over here in the Commonwealth as it was getting a lot of airplay on KVR.

"Ah, home
Let me come home
Home is wherever I'm with you"

Meredith and the kids joined in the chorus as Land Cruiser took the Jungs onward to their farmhouse by light of the setting sun, back to the only home Chris Jung ever truly knew.

**BACKGROUND MUSIC: "Hey Bret (You Know What Time It Is)"
by Cracker
Visit** www.michaeljuge.com **on the Refurbished Soul page to listen**